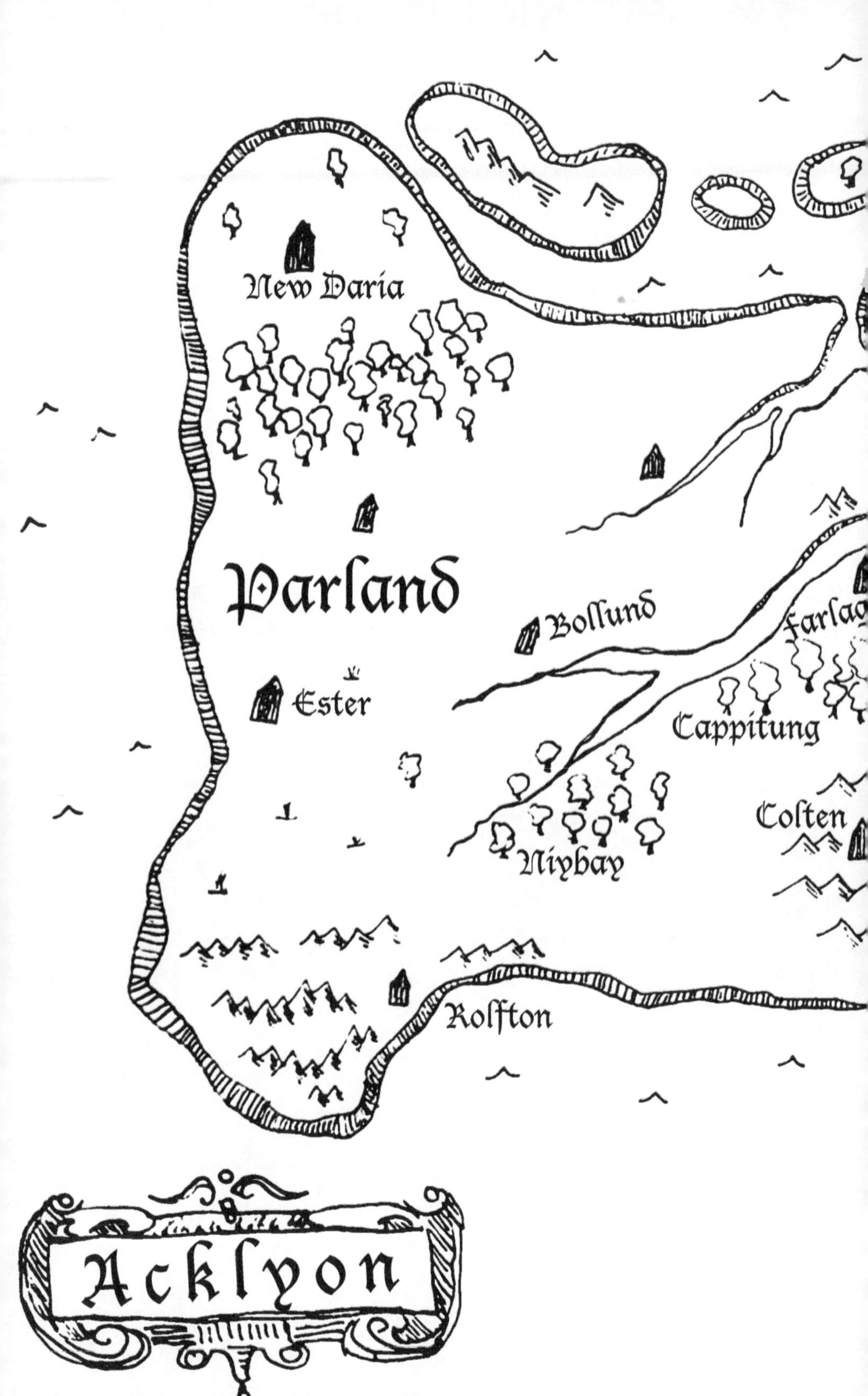
New Daria
Parland
Bollund
Farla
Ester
Cappitung
Colten
Niybay
Rolfton
Acklyon

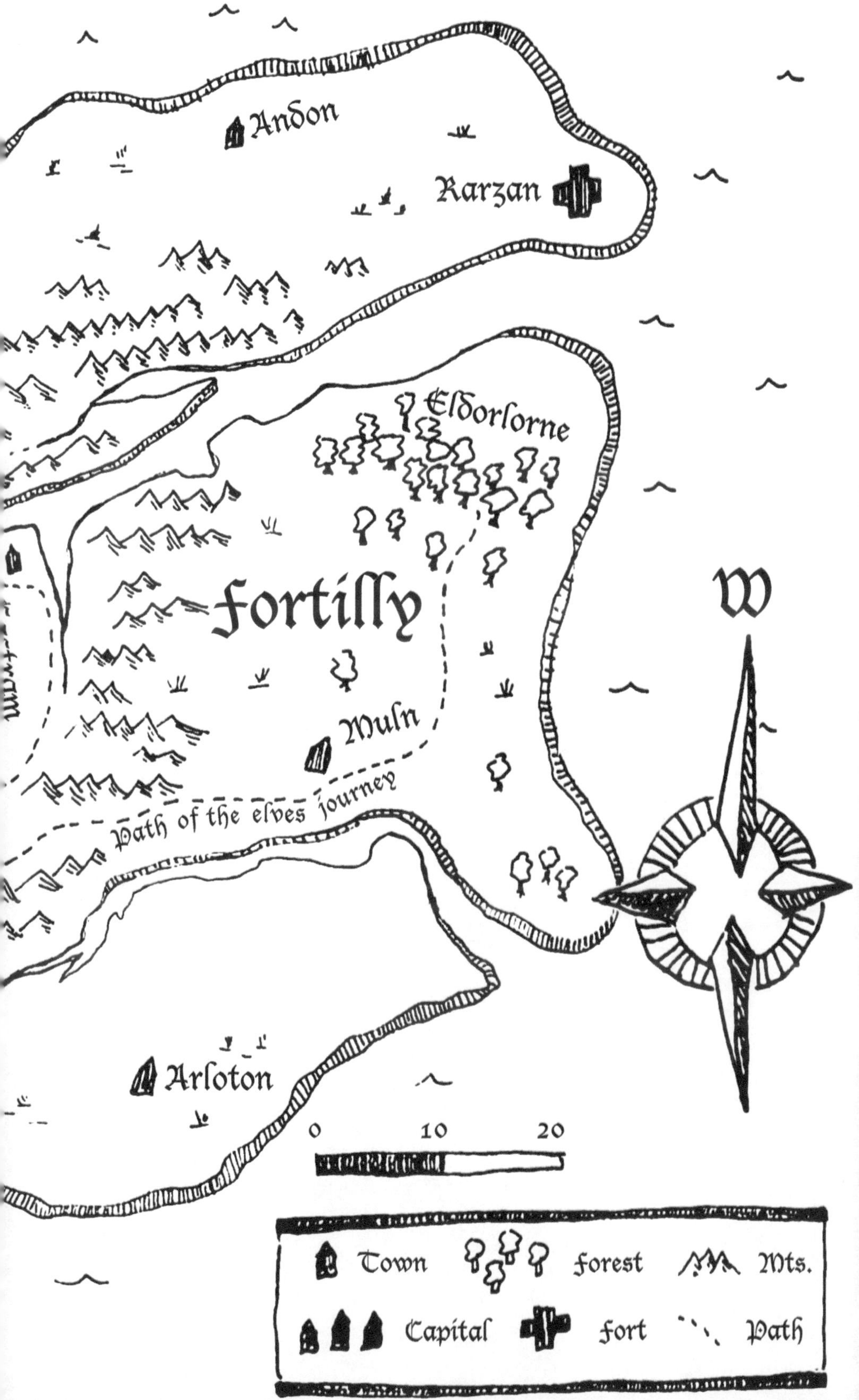
Andon
Rarzan
Eldorlorne
Fortilly
Muln
Path of the elves journey
Arloton
W
0
10
20
Town
Forest
Mts.
Capital
Fort
Path

the kingdom of dreams and shadows

PART I OF THE KINGDOM CHRONICLES TRILOGY

ADAM LAPALLO

Publisher's Note
This is a work of fiction. Names, characters, places, and incidents either are the product of the author's imagination or are used fictitiously, and any resemblance to actual persons, living or dead, business establishments, events, or locales is entirely coincidental.

ISBN 978-0-9833982-7-1
Library of Congress Control Number: 2013956187

Set in Book Antiqua
Designed by Inkwell Book Co.
www.inkwellbookcompany.com

Acknowledgements

First and foremost, I would like to thank my parents, Connie and Chris Lapallo, for their never-ceasing love and encouragement, without which *The Kingdom of Dreams and Shadows* could never have come to pass. I would also like to thank my three siblings—Sarah, Mike, and Kerry—for their help so long ago in constructing the world and characters that would one day become *The Kingdom Chronicles*. Specifically, I would like to thank Sarah for the hard work and creative genius that went into forming the fantastic cover design, Kerry for her literary critique and encouragement, and my brother Mike and soon-to-be brother-in-law Dale Beck for their web design skills.

In addition, huge thanks are owed to Jake Williams, Bell Germain, Julia Fraser, and Kieran Fraser, whose love and friendship inspired the characters of Aaron's four best friends. Though many of us have lost touch over the years, I owe each of you a huge debt of gratitude.

I would also like to thank the Deschner family and my beloved piano teacher Delane Floyd for their support and encouragement. You all believed in me even when I didn't.

Thanks also to my first two test readers, Stefani Deschner and

Alyssa Stimpson, for your enthusiasm in the project and for your critiques.

To those who taught me the practical knowledge I needed to know in order to write *The Kingdom of Dreams and Shadows*: Coach Bobby Robinson and Jenna Gauthier for being my fencing instructors, teaching me about real-life sword combat and the complications involved and Mary Bestafka for teaching me the basic skills of equestrianism in order to fully understand horseback riding.

To my friends Luke Hemphill, Kimberly Miller, and Bell Germain for the good times we've shared which made this project worthwhile, in particular to Luke for his help in digitally creating a visual representation of Acklyon in Minecraft.

Finally, to Marie Prys, the agent who first showed interest in The Kingdom of Dreams and Shadows when I was fourteen, whose professional enthusiasm served as a major jumpstart to my confidence as a writer and has influenced my professional career.

And so I am become a knight
of the Kingdom of Dreams and Shadows!

—Mark Twain

PROLOGUE

"People of Acklyon, I give you good tidings!"

Mutters punctured the silence as the crowd, gathered beneath the high tower, murmured in surprise.

"What could have happened?" A woman named Narra turned to her husband, Brotchurd. "What good tidings could come with Kane Malvadore as our ruler?"

"Perhaps the Kane is dead?" suggested Brotchurd hopefully. But the herald had cleared his throat for silence, cutting their conversation short.

"Adinyrom Forahn has returned!" said the herald dressed in red and black robes. Gasps and cheers erupted from the crowd.

"Perhaps the Kane *is* dead!" said Narra in delight.

And there stood Adinyrom—tall, handsome, long haired, and wearing a sweeping, blood-red cape. He waved lazily at the crowd, and their applause increased. But Brotchurd thought vaguely that something seemed wrong. The Forahns (and their cousins, the Parnors) were the legendary kings of the twin countries, Fortilly and Parland, that comprised the continent of Acklyon. The people were happy while the Forahns and Parnors reigned—until Malvadore had stolen the throne.

Adinyrom Forahn, the last in the long line of Forahns, along with his cousin, Jahkon Parnor, had vanished at the same time Kane Malvadore took over. The two had been mere boys when they left, and these boys had been the symbol of hope for the Acklyonians, for legend said they would return.

And yet—if Acklyon had been happy during Adinyrom's father's reign, why were Adinyrom's eyes not light and kind, but as cold and hard as steel? Why were the fingernails clutching the rampart of the balcony long and black? Adinyrom was very pale and thin, the bones of his hands visible through the white skin.

But then the applause died. All uncovered their heads and went slowly to their knees, for a very tall man had entered the balcony with Adinyrom and the herald. He was clad in spiked black armor; a long, red cloak hung from his shoulders; and a cruel, black helm rested upon his head. His skin was waxy and yellow, and his eyes burned a deep, inhuman crimson. Kane Malvadore's armored hand rested upon his sword hilt.

"People of Acklyon," said Adinyrom in a ringing, vibrant voice. "I have returned."

"My dear friend here," said Malvadore in a deep voice, "has come from beyond time to assist me in governing the Twin Countries."

Narra and Brotchurd exchanged worried looks.

"He shall be your new king, and I, his advisor."

"Oh no..." murmured Brotchurd.

"And I," said Adinyrom, "intend to raise the standards of Acklyon, as such, due to suspicious movements by our enemies."

What enemies? Narra wondered.

"We require each able-bodied man between the ages of sixteen and fifty to sign up for enlistment in his town's garrison. We shall excuse only the farmers, blacksmiths, crippled, and others who either cannot fight or whose businesses are essential to the social system."

Brotchurd gripped his wife's hand. Kane Malvadore had never been this fanatic about his army. And to think that almost every able-bodied man in Acklyon was forced into service... That was brutal.

"However," Adinyrom said as he continued this travesty, "we will expect those whose businesses are indispensable to do what they can for the cause. The blacksmiths will take it upon themselves to forge the weapons necessary for the army, and the farmers, butchers, and grocers must donate seventy percent of their produce to the welfare of the soldiers."

"Seventy percent?" demanded one bold farmer amidst the cries. "That's only thirty percent for us. We can't keep a farm going like that!"

"Then you should lay down your plow and join your brothers in service," snapped Adinyrom.

Stunned silence followed Adinyrom's words as every man reflected on what this would do to his business.

"As of tomorrow," said Adinyrom, "we will take a census of the land. You must present yourself to whatever city you were born of and be counted. We have banned foreigners, and you should report any you sight immediately. It would be wise of you to stay indoors as much as possible. Rumors are starting that Elves are on the move again. You should use caution at all times.

"These measures"—he raised his voice slightly over the complaints of the crowd—"are for the good of the country. Go now."

The people filed away in varying states of disbelief and doubt.

"What are we to do?" Narra asked Brotchurd. Brotchurd was eligible to be a guard.

"I'm not joining," said Brotchurd stubbornly. "Narra, we

should catch the first ship that leaves Acklyon. If Prince Adinyrom has indeed betrayed us to Malvadore and now requires me to fight for him—curse his filthy red eyes—then we mustn't stay here."

"But where shall we go?" Narra asked.

"Anywhere," said Brotchurd.

"What about the lumberyard?" asked Narra. "Should we sell it or—?"

"No," said Brotchurd firmly. "No time. Selling could take a month. We should just go. Adinyrom's return was our only hope..."

"Excuse me." Narra and Brotchurd whirled around as the captain of Malvadore's guards stepped up to them. "Did I hear right?" asked the guard sneeringly. Without waiting for a response, he clicked his fingers, and two more guards hurried forward.

"Seize him." The guards grabbed Brotchurd above the elbows. "You shall join," said the captain quietly to the struggling Brotchurd, and the guards walked off with their captive.

"No!" cried Narra, but one of the guards punched her with the butt end of his spear. She fell to the ground with a cry and watched them drag her husband away.

Within the tower, where none could hear them, Adinyrom Forahn and Kane Malvadore allowed themselves a satisfied chuckle. "Did you see their faces?" laughed Forahn.

"Aye," said Malvadore with a smirk.

"They were convinced, then?" asked Forahn.

"Definitely," said Malvadore quietly. "I could see it in their eyes. The eyes are their soft spot. All emotion comes out in mortal eyes. They thought you were he, all right."

"Doesn't it seem risky, though?" asked Forahn. "'Giving' the Throne to me? When he might not be coming after all?"

"Oh, he will come," said Malvadore even more quietly. "I know. I always know. He will come."

1
Aaron Tackers

"Aaron?"

Aaron jumped. He'd been gazing blankly into his cereal bowl for the past five minutes, but now he looked up at his mom.

"Are you all right?" his mother asked him.

"Yeah," he said, shaking his head to clear it. "Yeah, I'm fine."

"You look pale," said his mother. "Did you sleep okay?"

"Yeah," said Aaron again. "Yeah, I'm just...uh...nervous."

"About how you did on the test?"

"Uh, yeah."

She kissed him on the cheek. "I'm sure you did fine."

"Thanks," he murmured.

"Oh, look at the time!" said Mrs. Tackers, glancing at her wristwatch. "It's a few minutes to eight. You'd better get going!"

"Oh, right!" said Aaron, getting up and grabbing his backpack.

"And I've fixed your lunch. Here." She gave him his lunchbox.

"What kind is it?" Aaron asked.

"Baloney and cheese," said Mrs. Tackers.

"No spinach?"

She laughed. "No spinach."

"Good," Aaron said, relieved. "Bye, Mom!"

"Bye, Aaron!" said his mother as he hurried out the door.

"Have fun!"

Aaron jogged down the driveway and off toward the curb, not slowing down until he reached it. There, a few other kids were waiting, shivering in the chilly morning air.

"Hey, Ellie," he said to a girl with long brown hair and freckles who had been talking to her friend, Bonnie Evans.

"Hi, Aaron," she replied, smiling.

"The bus hasn't arrived yet?" he asked.

"No, it came, but we all thought it would be more fun to stay out here and freeze instead of going to school," said Bonnie sarcastically.

"Fair enough," Aaron laughed, but then his eyes hardened as his gaze fell upon a boy with reddish-blonde hair and heavy freckles. Due to a series of misunderstandings that had occurred since kindergarten—including a ruined watercolor picture, a dropped egg and cheese sandwich, and a carton of spilled milk—Jack Oswald had been Aaron's nemesis. Nobody could really recall when their rivalry had started, but everybody knew it was not likely to end any time soon. Fortunately, the bus arrived at that moment so that in the bustle of everyone getting in, Aaron lost sight of Jack.

"So anyway," said Aaron a minute later, turning back to Ellie as though nothing had happened. "How was your…evening?"

"Oh, it was very interesting," she said. "I said hello to my mom, I did my homework, I ate dinner, and I texted Bonnie!"

"Sounds *fascinating*," said Aaron, and they both laughed.

"Hey, Aaron!" said a voice.

"Hi, Roger!" Aaron replied, looking up at his best friend, Roger Killie.

"Hey, Aaron," said Roger again, sitting down next to Aaron. "Have you heard? *Three Days to Live* is on TV tonight!"

"Really?" said Aaron. "I gotta see it..."

"Ooh," said Ellie with a shudder. "I hated that movie. It was so *violent*."

Aaron and Roger stared at her as though she had sprouted a third nostril.

"It was!" Ellie protested.

"*I* thought it was great!" said Roger.

"Me, too," said Aaron happily. "I loved the part where George killed Eliot. That was epic!"

"Oh, definitely," Roger concurred. "And that part at the beginning when the terrorists attacked!"

Ellie shook her head and muttered, "Boys," then turned back to her conversation with Bonnie.

Aaron and Roger spent the rest of the bus ride discussing *Three Days to Live*. When they arrived at Avondale Middle School, Aaron glimpsed Jack leaving with Bonnie's younger brother, Gallagher.

"Haven't I told that nincompoop of a brother not to be seen with Jack?" whispered Bonnie venomously. "I've gotta talk to him."

As Aaron, Roger, Ellie, and Bonnie proceeded to their first class, Aaron saw Jack again, walking ahead of them. Jack had left Gallagher and was hanging his head, looking lonely. "Speed up," Aaron whispered to Roger.

"Why—"

Then Roger saw Jack and nudged Bonnie, who grinned. The four walked faster, closing the gap between Jack and themselves. As they neared him, Aaron put on a burst of speed and rammed Jack in the shoulder so that he staggered sideways. "Out of the way, buster." said Aaron sneeringly.

"Keep your hairy paws off me," snapped Jack, glaring at him. Aaron glared back with much enthusiasm.

Jack stood and scowled after the foursome, not moving a muscle until they had passed from sight, anger etched in every line of his face.

"Idiot," muttered Roger.

"So are you going to movie night on Saturday?" said Aaron to Bonnie, reaching into his pocket and pulling out a neon-green yoyo.

"Can't," said Bonnie. "Gallagher and I are going to a fencing tournament on Saturday."

"How's that going?" asked Roger.

"It's fun," said Bonnie. "You really ought to try it."

Aaron shrugged. "That would drive me nuts," he said. "I mean, there's so much calculating and strategizing."

"You're just saying that because I beat you that time I invited you," Bonnie gloated.

"That doesn't count," said Aaron delicately. "I let you win—and the judge wasn't all that good, in my opinion, and my equipment kept messing up."

"Not true," Bonnie retorted. "You were fencing as hard as you could, I could tell. The judge was perfectly fair, by the way, and your equipment worked fine."

"No it didn't," said Aaron. "It said that I was off-target every time I hit you in the arm or leg!"

Bonnie rolled her eyes. "That's how fencing *works*, Aaron; you have to hit your opponent on the silver jacket."

"Oh," said Aaron, rolling his yoyo down and then pulling it back up. "Let's sit near the front today. I want to see how I did on the test."

Ellie and Roger nodded, but Bonnie said, "How come *you're*

always the one who gives the orders in this group? Why not *me?*"

"Because I'm older than you," said Aaron simply.

"So? I'm still taller than you!" Bonnie pointed out. It was true.

Aaron, Bonnie, Ellie, and Roger found seats together close to the front.

"Good morning, class," said Mr. Lewis, their eighth grade teacher. The class gave its usual indistinctive murmur in return, and Mr. Lewis began the roll call. "Franklin Allen?"

"Present,"

"Ellie Birch?"

"Present," said Ellie, lifting her head from a conversation with Aaron.

"Damon Cross?"

"Present."

"Veronica Evans?"

Bonnie glowered. Her given name was actually Veronica, a name she dearly hated. When she was born, her Scottish mother had declared her a "bonnie lass." So as soon as she could, Veronica had nicknamed herself "Bonnie." Just calling her "Veronica" in her presence could arouse anger. "Present," Bonnie snarled.

"Roger Killie?"

"Present," chimed Roger.

"Jack Oswald?"

There was a long pause, then, "Present," growled Jack from the back row, his teeth gritted.

The roll call continued until finally they were done.

As Patrick Warren called that he was present, Mr. Lewis put away the sheet of paper and began scribbling on the blackboard.

"Right," Mr. Lewis said. "I've graded your tests and must say I'm impressed. Mandy, could you please pass them out—the stack's here on my desk. Thank you. Today, we'll be studying diagramming. Diagramming is splitting a sentence into…"

Aaron looked at the test Mandy had given him. An *A+* was scrawled on the top right corner. He had never gotten an *A+* before. He had never even gotten an *A*. He considered studying to be a waste of his time. Ellie was peering over his shoulder at his paper. He heard her mutter, "Wow! And I thought I had it good with a *B*."

Aaron happened to glance back just then, and his eyes landed on Jack, whose previous irritation had vanished – replaced by a surprised smile. Jack, too, had received an *A+*.

Aaron looked back at his paper, and something strange happened. As his eyes fixed on the *A+* on his page, an odd feeling swept through him, as though his heart were being swollen like a balloon. He could have climbed a mountain at a run or battled an elephant with ease. His left hand fell to his side – and he was surprised to find his sword wasn't there.

Wait a minute – he didn't have a sword. Did he? No. He didn't even own a cheap plastic toy sword. As Aaron thought about a sword, something inside him seemed to melt. It was as if a part of his soul had vanished, leaving an uncomfortable black hole in its place. An image swam to the front of his mind: a sword – a long, narrow sword. The pommel was a golden ring with a ruby engraved in its center. The crossbar was gold and in the exact shape of an *M*. But the blade…the blade was the color of honey, and the edge was clear and crystalline and made of diamond. And then he saw the name on it: *Forvalad*. Was that his sword? Yes. He felt a great longing for the sword and knew he would never fully rest until he obtained it. He gazed at the sword in awe, and he knew, somehow, that it *was* his, and that none could wield it but him and he must use it to free Acklyon.

What was Acklyon? He didn't know, and he didn't know

how he knew—but he knew. And then he heard a voice in his head. It was silvery and mystical and sweet. "*Adinyrom,*" it said. "*Adinyrom. Come back.* " The call was for help and directed at him. He knew that much. As with the sword, no one else could answer the call. He didn't know how he knew any of this, but he knew it as surely as he knew his own name… What was his name again? He couldn't seem to remember, somehow, nor did it seem all that important. He'd forgotten that he was in school, that he had received an *A+* in English, that his name was Aaron P. Tackers, and that he lived on Earth.

But then he saw in his mind's eye a boy that looked very much like himself, standing tall and noble, dressed in rich flowing garments, royal as a king—but the crown he wore was merely one half. Aaron felt a combination of wonder and bewilderment until his thoughts were interrupted by a nudge from Ellie.

"Huh?" he said blankly, looking around. Everyone was staring at him, and Mr. Lewis was standing over him.

"I was saying," said Mr. Lewis, "how much I liked your essay, Aaron. You used very good punctuation and your spelling and handwriting were flawless…"

Aaron was only half listening. Only one word had caught his attention: *Aaron.* That was his name? That couldn't be his name, no! His name was—was—he didn't know for sure, but it wasn't Aaron.

And then it passed. Aaron blinked and looked around. His classmates were gathering up their things and walking toward the door. The bell must have rung. Aaron slowly gathered up his books and pencil case and stuffed them into his backpack, then hurried from the room, his mind racing.

2
JACK OSWALD

Jack left the classroom with a troubled mind. What had that vision been about? He had a feeling that something peculiar had happened to Aaron, too. Did he have the same vision? It couldn't be. But the look on his face…

"Hey, Jack!" said a voice.

Jack turned. Gallagher was running toward him. "Hi," Jack said, forcing a smile.

"Hi," said Gallagher breathlessly. "How was English?"

Jack hesitated. "Fine," he said, deciding to keep his vision to himself.

"Math wasn't bad," said Gallagher, oblivious to Jack's discomfort. "I got a *B+* on the test. Highest grade in the class the teacher said…"

Jack listened without really hearing, thinking again about what he had seen.

As the bus stopped at the curb later that day, several kids hopped out and began walking home.

Jack didn't walk—he ran. He associated being at home with being safe and whole, and right now he wanted to be as safe and as normal as possible. He sprinted down the street, around the corner, and to the cul-de-sac where he lived. He jogged down the driveway and through the front door. "Mom, I'm home!" he called.

"Hello, Jack," said his smiling mother. "How was school?"

"School?" said Jack, for he'd completely forgotten he'd been there all day. "Uh, not bad."

"How did you do on the test?"

"Test?" said Jack blankly. "Oh! The test! Yeah, yeah, I didn't do too bad."

"Really?" said his mother. "What did you score?"

Jack had completely forgotten. "Oh, well, let me see, uh..." He shifted through his backpack until he pulled out the paper. "Here." He handed it to her, wondering what she would find.

There was a long pause in which his mother stared at the paper in disbelief. Then she laughed with delight. "*An* A+*?*" she squealed. "Darling, that's *wonderful*!" She ran over and hugged him.

"Yeah," he gibbered. "Yeah, I got an *A*+ alright, yep, I got a *K*. I mean, *A*."

She paused in her crusade to kiss every square inch of his face and frowned down at him. "Are you feeling alright?" She asked him, squinting into his eyes. "You seem funny."

"No," he said, almost before she'd finished. "No, I'm just fine!"

"Are you sure?"

"Yes, positive. I'm just...uh...hungry," he finished lamely.

"Well," she said, "dinner will be ready in about half an hour, so see if you can finish your homework before then."

"Oh, don't worry!" he said. "Yeah, I'll finish up that homework before supper, or my name isn't Jahkon Parnor! Jack Oswald, I mean."

Jack spread his homework on the desk up in his room and fished a pencil out of his drawer.

As he began researching Cortés's assault on the Aztecs in 1518, Jack's mind returned to dwell, ever more confusedly, on his vision. He'd seen himself wearing half a crown on his head and had heard a magical voice calling him *Jahkon*. And he'd seen a sword—a bright, shining silver sword with a sapphire engraved in the pommel, a long, winglike crossguard, and an edge of pure diamond with the name *Parvelad*. Jack gazed for a moment into space, remembering the magnificence of the sword. It belonged to him. He couldn't say how, but he knew that it did. He couldn't explain exactly *how* he even knew any of this, but somehow he did. He mentally shook himself. He couldn't answer any of his questions about the vision, so he might as well forget it.

But he couldn't.

The next half hour was spent, not in studying, but in struggling to keep focus while images of half-crowns and silver swords swam around in his mind. At last, his mother's voice rang through the silence, "Jack? Jack! It's time for dinner!"

Jack leapt to his feet and rushed downstairs.

He went bounding into the dining room where his parents were waiting for him.

"Hey, sport," said his father genially.

"Hi, Dad," said Jack.

"How was school?"

"He got an *A+* on his grammar test," said his mother, swelling with pride.

"*A+?*" asked his dad in delight. "I thought grammar was your worst subject!"

"It was." said Jack, forcing a smile, but inside he was

wondering how the heck he'd done it without doing much proper studying.

"Did you finish up that homework?" his mother asked.

"Homework?" said Jack blankly.

"Homework," said his mother, looking suddenly stern. "You did finish it?"

"Yeah!" said Jack, as an ice cube slid down his throat and into his stomach.

His mother gave him a searching look and then turned to the bowl of spaghetti and meatballs. "Well," she said, "let's eat." She ladled spaghetti onto everyone's plates.

Jack entwined some spaghetti around his fork and lifted it to his lips, but then had to keep himself from spitting it out. It was completely tasteless. His mother and father, however, were savoring it!

Jack excused himself from the table early, skipping dessert, and sprinted upstairs to his room. He threw himself onto the bed, his mind racing. He couldn't taste his food, he couldn't be excited about getting a perfect score on his test, he couldn't concentrate on his studies—what was wrong with him?

Out loud he gave a whimper, and then saw once again in his mind's eye the silver sword and himself wearing half a crown. And he felt that same feeling of courage and nobility as he heard a magical voice calling, "*Jahkon...Jahkon...*"

He rolled over in bed and tried to block it all out, but to no avail.

3
The Mysterious Pool

Aaron passed a restless night. His dreams were obscured by golden swords, far away countries, and that same mystical voice calling *Adinyrom*. Once again he saw himself dressed in royal clothes and wearing half a crown. When he woke, he was sweating and shaking so badly, he could hardly get dressed.

The rest of his morning was the same—he couldn't taste his omelet, his backpack seemed so heavy he could barely lift it, and he scarcely felt it when he cut himself slicing his bread.

"Aaron, are you feeling alright?" his mother asked, as Aaron spread jelly on his plate, a good six inches from his toast.

"Huh?" he said, looking up so fast he cricked his neck. "Yeah…yeah, I'm fine…" He didn't know why he couldn't tell her, but it seemed like the vision was his and only his. No one else could know. No—there was one other person who could. And it wasn't his mother, or Roger or Ellie, but it was someone. He must find whoever it was.

"Hey, Aaron!" said a voice.

Aaron looked up. "Oh, hi, Roger!"

"Did you see *Three Days to Live?"* asked Roger.

"*Three Days to Live*?" asked Aaron in confusion. He'd

completely forgotten about it. "Uh, no, I missed it."

Roger gaped at him. "Are you serious?" he asked incredulously.

"Uh, yeah. I had, you know, homework and dinner, and uh, piano practice."

"Piano practice?" asked Roger. "I didn't know you played piano."

"Uh, yeah...I just started a few weeks ago."

Roger shook his head.

All that day, Aaron barely concentrated on his studies. He didn't understand any of this. It made no sense. Something was disturbing his mind. He felt as if he didn't belong here. He couldn't describe it, not even in his head, but he felt that everything in his life had gone completely wrong in ways he didn't comprehend. It was a relief when the bell rang, signaling break time.

As the kids streamed onto the playground, laughing and shouting, Aaron sat alone on a bench and stared unseeingly at the gravel as he rolled his green yoyo between his hands. Nothing made sense. What was wrong with him? Why was this happening to him? He couldn't answer any of these questions, the questions whose answers he yearned for.

"Adinyrom."

He looked up. There was that voice again! He stood up, straining his ears to hear the musical tones once more.

"Adinyrom."

There it was again! He looked around. Nobody else had noticed it. They were all laughing and playing with no burden on their conscience.

"Adinyrom. Come back." The voice only he could hear, and it was coming from the forest around the school. He stared into the

trees for a moment, then got up, tucked the yoyo into his pocket, and headed towards the woods.

"*Jahkon.*" Jack looked up. The voice was calling him, too.

"*Jahkon,*" it said again. It was coming from the woods.

"*Come back, Jahkon.*"

Jack turned and followed Aaron into the trees.

Aaron and Jack walked purposefully toward the forest, side by side, each hardly aware of the other—their whole attention focused on the forest.

As they fought their way through the underbrush, both felt a growing sense of unease. The unease increased as they progressed deeper into the forest and slowly morphed into fear. As the strange, primal sense of terror heightened, the boys reached a clearing where a quiet little pool of water lay, reflecting sunlight.

Upon laying eyes on the pool, it became clear to them that this completely uninteresting puddle of water was the source of everything that was happening to them. The boys moved toward it, compelled by curiosity. However, they hadn't gotten more than a couple steps when the mounting fright that plagued them turned to all-consuming terror. The trees around them seemed to bend and twist as a howling scream tore at their minds. Aaron thought he saw black shapes moving just outside the range of his vision.

For a moment they stood, rooted with fear, staring down into the depths of the pool where they saw reflected back a scene of the two of them dressed in elegant robes, and each wearing half a crown, holding two swords—one pure gold, the other brightest silver.

Then feeling returned to the boys, and they turned and

ran—sprinting through the trees and bushes, leaping over stumps, their clothes ripping as they caught in wreaths of thorns.

They galloped until they reached the playground, panting for breath and clutching stitches in their sides.

"What *was* that?" gasped Jack.

"I don't know." Aaron panted.

For the moment, the boys had forgotten their mutual enmity.

"I wonder if that was connected to—" Jack started, but then broke off, knowing how odd it would sound to Aaron.

Aaron, however, was intrigued. "You wonder if that was connected to—what?"

"Nothing," said Jack, not wanting Aaron to laugh at him, but Aaron looked sincere.

"Was it, by any chance, a dream? Where you saw yourself wearing half a crown and a sweet sword and a voice calling you, but calling you something other than 'Jack'?"

Jack stared at him in amazement. "How did you know?"

"I had the same dream!"

"You what?"

"This is crazy!" said Aaron. "It's like you and I are—I don't know, fortune tellers or something."

"I don't think it's that," said Jack. "I feel more like—like something's *calling* us, using these visions, you know."

At that moment, a voice, soft and sweet, called to Aaron, "*Adinyrom*" and to Jack, "*Jahkon.*"

"Did you say something?" asked Aaron.

"No," said Jack.

"Yes, you did!" said Aaron. "You said, 'Adinyrom.'"

"No," said Jack. "*You* said 'Jahkon!'"

"I did not!" said Aaron indignantly.

"But if it wasn't you..." Jack whirled around, looking for

someone pulling a prank, though he now felt quite sure that he had heard the voice inside his head.

Aaron shivered, thinking of spirits swooping around them or of invisible people close by.

"This is insane!" Jack cried out. "This is totally demented!"

"I know," said Aaron, a wave of despair crashing over him. "What does all of this mean?"

"Do you think…" said Jack quietly, "that this is all…well…" He went pink. "Magic?"

In another life, Aaron would have burst out laughing and said that Jack was crazy, but now nothing was further from his mind.

In fact, as Jack uttered the word "Magic," a whole new world of possibilities came to Aaron. He saw Wizards with long staffs. He saw Elves prancing through the trees. He saw Unicorns trotting through the fields. It was an amazing possibility that Magic was the cause of all this, that Magic really existed. He looked at Jack and said, "It's possible."

As they stared at each other, something clicked between them. Aaron felt more warmly towards Jack than he'd ever felt in his life, and Jack inwardly forgave Aaron for all the mean things he'd done to him.

But then a voice—Bonnie's voice—rang out. "Aaron? Aaron! Come on! The bus is almost here!"

The moment passed. Aaron and Jack blinked, looking around, and then each hurried off in opposite directions.

4
Acklyon Uncovered

Once again, Aaron and Jack both had sleepless nights, their few dreams full of mystical voices and magical pools of water and magnificent swords and halves of crowns. That morning, their mothers each told them they were pale and thin, which was true. At breakfast and lunchtime, they ate very little, and the food they did eat had as much taste as sawdust.

Roger and Gallagher had both caught the flu and weren't present at school, which left Aaron and Jack without friends. Bonnie was refusing to talk to Aaron because she'd seen him with Jack the other day. Ellie was tired of bridging the distance between them and so was hanging out with only Bonnie.

Both boys sat alone during classes, deep in thought and not registering what the teacher was saying.

Come recess, Aaron was tired of this mystery, and so he confronted Jack.

"Look," he said uncomfortably, twirling his yoyo around in his hands. "We don't like each other much, right? But we seem to be the only ones who can see all this odd stuff happening, right? So, why don't we team up. Temporarily, of course. Once we solve this mystery, we can go back to hating each other in peace." He didn't know why he was saying this, but he was.

Jack considered that, and then said, "Why?"

"What d'you mean?" asked Aaron.

"Why are you offering to work with me? I thought you didn't like me."

"I don't," said Aaron, "but, as I say, it seems that this is just between us, and, well, two heads are better than one."

"Not if one of them is Aaron Tackers's." mumbled Jack.

"I'm sorry?"

"I said, uh, 'Sure.'"

"Well, then," said Aaron pompously, "let's go investigate that pool."

Jack nodded.

At first, they thought they might not be able to find the pool again in the thick woods, but after a bit of searching they did find it, sitting in its clearing, sparkling innocently.

"Well," said Aaron, taking a deep breath, "let's get this over with." And they walked forward.

A tidal wave of fear struck them as they approached the pool, almost knocking them backwards. Aaron shook his head in an attempt to rid his mind of the foggy tendrils of unexplainable terror, but the fear came on even stronger. "Don't look back," he murmured to Jack. "It'll be worse if you do." He had hardly finished speaking when he wanted to leave. But he mustn't. He must be brave.

They headed on, feeling as if they were moving underwater. Their hearts were booming in their ears like bass drums, but they kept on. And sooner than they expected, they were at the pool's edge, staring down into its depths. To their surprise and relief, their fear was minimized to a faint prickle at the very edge of the pool.

"Now what?" asked Jack.

Aaron didn't answer. His eyes were unfocused, his head sagging so that his chin touched his chest, and his arms hung lifelessly at his sides.

Jack turned slowly to look at him and felt fog fill his mind and heard the gentle voice calling, "*Jahkon…*" inside his head, louder and clearer than ever before. And then Aaron started to fall forwards.

"Aaron!" said Jack, grabbing Aaron by the arms and fighting against his own grogginess. Aaron's eyes were fixed unblinkingly on the pool as he went limp in Jack's arms.

And then weariness overcame Jack, and he fell with Aaron into the water.

The first shock of cold water went through Jack like a knife. But then, to his complete bewilderment, it became perfectly lovely; warm and dry, though he was still underwater. The boys seemed to be floating very fast through a river of water—filled with golden light—that did not wet them at all.

Jack closed his eyes, enjoying the sensation and not caring what was happening until the water changed again; cold, brackish water that filled his lungs and chilled his skin. The golden light shining through his eyelids turned greenish-black once more, and he gagged. But Aaron's hand tightened on his arm, and a moment later they were breaking the surface of the cold water, choking and gasping for air. They clutched at each other as they went under again and began swimming together toward the shore.

At first they didn't realize that they were now in a river, not a pool. But as they hauled themselves onto the bank, Aaron realized that they were no longer in the same small forest, but in a much larger and more luscious jungle. Though utterly bewildered, he had to get to safety before asking questions.

They crawled onto the warm sand and collapsed, exhausted and soaked to the bone. In another time, they would have panicked after being transported mysteriously out of Avondale—and the whole world—but they were tired, and their heads fell back against the sand and they went to sleep.

Aaron opened his eyes and lifted his head. He was dry and warm, baked under the hot sun, Jack lying beside him, fast asleep. His first thought was, *where are we?*

Acklyon…Acklyon… The name floated through his mind like a log on the river.

What was Acklyon? He was now sick of having information he didn't understand.

Jack woke up. "Where are we?" he, too, asked.

"Couldn't tell you," said Aaron wearily.

Jack got up. "This isn't Avondale," he said pointlessly.

"No, it isn't," said Aaron, looking around. But wherever this was, it was a beautiful country. They hadn't noticed the details hours before when they'd pulled themselves out of the river, but now they saw tall green trees, lovely flowers, woods filled with fresh golden sunlight dappled from the trees. Everything around them seemed somehow more complex than at home, as if there were more dimensions than three.

Slowly the boys began walking around, admiring the beauty of the land. "It's so peaceful here," whispered Aaron, gazing around with awe.

"I know," said Jack. "You feel like nothing could happen to you here…"

At that moment an arrow whizzed past, an inch from the end of Jack's nose, and slammed into a tree behind them.

5
KELLAOTH

Aaron and Jack both whirled around. The pretty landscape was ruined by a horrifying creature standing before them. It looked something like a man, but clearly was not. Broad, hunched over, and sinister, its head was long, it had shark-like teeth, and its eyes were hollow and deadened. It was wearing plated armor, a huge sword hung at its waist, and it held an enormous crossbow in its hands.

Aaron and Jack looked at each other and dived behind the tree as a second arrow slammed into it. Then another monster stepped out of the bushes, this one carrying a spear and a huge shield. It spoke in an unfamiliar language, which seemed to be made up of a horrible string of grunts and screeches.

Aaron picked up a stone and lobbed it at the monster. The creature blocked it with its shield and began creeping forward, dropping its spear and drawing the sword at its waist.

"What'll we do?" whispered Jack.

"I don't know," Aaron whispered back.

The monster's head appeared around the tree and he glared at the boys with an evil grin on his face. It raised its sword, prepared to strike, but then its expression changed from evil delight to horror, as it stared over the boys' heads.

Both boys turned as one and saw a huge white blur streaking toward them. It landed in front of them, silvery-white and terrible. Then it leaped over Aaron and Jack and tackled the first monster, rolling off it and galloping toward the other one. The second monster shrieked and began shooting with its crossbow, but to no avail; the arrows merely glanced off the beast's hide. Then a great claw descended upon the monster, and it fell.

The beast whirled around, and a jet of flame shot from the horn on its forehead. The flame blasted through the trees, burning nothing, but a scream from within the trees suggested another monster had met a fiery doom. Then there were hoots and screams and howls and rustling from the trees, as yet more monsters ran for their lives. The beast gave a contemptuous snarl. Falling trees and screams followed the retreating monsters.

Aaron and Jack stood rooted, terrified the great white beast would see them, but when it turned its head, it suddenly became so much less terrible and so much more beautiful. She was shaped like a very large horse, only with huge, feathery, angelic wings, front feet armed with sharp talons, and a long, spiraling silver horn on her forehead. She was snowy white with a silver mane and long ears. Her eyes were round as coins, very bright green, and looked as kind and gentle as a lamb.

"Hello," she said in a mystical and kind voice. "I am Kellaoth."

Both boys gasped, for they recognized her voice as the one they had heard calling them to Acklyon.

Once he found his own voice, Aaron spoke. "Hello, Kellith. I mean, Kellioth, uh—Kella—Kelo…"

"Kellaoth," she said. "Kell-ai-oth."

"Okay, *Kellaoth*. Who are you?"

"I am a Unicorn," said Kellaoth.

"Where are we?" asked Jack.

"In North Fortilly of Acklyon."

"*Acklyon?*" both boys cried in amazement.

"How did we get—" Aaron began, but was cut off by another arrow, which hissed past his left ear and slammed into the tree with its fellows, quivering.

"This place is not safe!" said Kellaoth as she whirled around and roared at the trees. The boys heard hooting and shouting as yet more monsters fled from her.

"Get on," she said, crouching down as though nothing had happened.

Aaron and Jack glanced at each other before scrambling onto her back. Their reasons for trusting Kellaoth they did not know, but there was something about her that suggested warmth and comfort—unless you were an enemy.

Kellaoth flapped her beautiful wings and lifted off the ground, soaring away to the east.

"Kellaoth," said Aaron, over the roar of the wind in his ears. "Can I ask you something?"

Kellaoth slowed and landed on a cliff nearby, so they could talk without shouting. Aaron and Jack dismounted.

"Yes?" she said to Aaron.

"What were those—those creepy armored thingies back there?" Aaron asked.

"Gertulk," replied Kellaoth, a dark expression forming on her beautiful face. "Ordinary men at their worst. They are undead horrors who stalk this land and spread Evil to the four corners of the world. Kane Malvadore has mutated an army of them for his vicious purposes."

"Who's Kane Malvadore?" asked Jack.

The dark lines on Kellaoth's face increased so that for a moment she looked as fierce and terrible as when she'd been fighting the Gertulk. "He is the warlord who took control of Acklyon many years ago. He himself is a mutant, transformed from a powerful man into the very worst kind of Evil."

"Is he one of those zombies?" Aaron asked.

"No." Kellaoth lowered her voice, a look of great pain in her eyes. "He is something far worse. He is what you would find if you took a powerfully magical and strong, hot-headed, arrogant man, and you fed off his worst emotions, his fears, his weaknesses—turning them all against him." She looked up. The dark lines and the pain in her eyes were even more apparent. "He is a Kane."

Aaron and Jack shivered, though they'd never even heard of a Kane. "He is at the core of any evil that goes on in Acklyon. Of course," Kellaoth added sourly, "there have been a great number of evils in this land—once so beautiful—since Malvadore seized control."

"It's still beautiful," said Aaron, staring around at the glittering trees and the strange roots around and below them.

"This is Elf country," said Kellaoth.

"*Elf country*?" said Jack excitedly and rushed to the cliff edge and peered down at trees below, as though expecting to see an Elf stroll out of his house.

"The Elves are the last remainder of the former land of Acklyon," said Kellaoth, her face easing. "After Malvadore stole the Throne, the thousands of Elves in Acklyon scattered and started forming underground societies in the larger forests. The Elf colony where I live, and where you two shall live, is one of the biggest in the area. The Elves are smart, merry, light-footed, and have exceptional abilities in woodcraft, which is unusual for mortals. Men say that they have Magical powers."

"Did you say Magical?" Aaron blurted out.

"Yes, I did," said Kellaoth, smiling at him.

"As in, as in 'hocus pocus'? Poof? Three wishes?" Now his voice was rising slightly, and his eyebrows were as high as they could go. "Visions? *Magical teleporting pools*?"

Kellaoth burst out laughing. "You are a sharp boy, Adinyrom."

"Aaron."

"I am sorry?"

"My name's Aaron, not 'Adinyrom.' Is that like Adinyrom Judson?" Aaron was thinking of the missionary he'd learned of in Sunday school.

"Adoniram," said Jack, coming back from the cliff edge, having not found any Elves.

"What?" said Aaron.

"It's Adoniram Judson, not Adinyrom. A-D-O-N-I-R-A-M, not A-D-I-N-Y-R-O-M," Jack continued.

"How do you know how it's spelt?"

Jack looked stumped by this question. "I just do," he said finally.

"You just do?" repeated Aaron skeptically.

"Yeah!" said Jack defensively.

"Wait a minute," Aaron said sharply. "Did you just say 'Adinyrom?'"

"I did," Kellaoth responded with a small smile.

Aaron sank to the ground as he recognized the name that had called him to Acklyon. Everything had gone topsy-turvy: in half an hour he had been spirited away from his home in Avondale to a completely different dimension, almost drowned, befriended Jack Oswald, been attacked by zombies, and now a Unicorn was calling him 'Adinyrom.' Somehow, he liked the name.

Kellaoth broke Aaron's spell of thought with the comment, "For the time being, you shall stay with my good friend Laza the Elf."

"We're staying with an Elf?" asked both boys in astonishment.

"Aye," said Kellaoth.

"Aye?" said Aaron.

"Old English term," muttered Jack.

"I knew that!"

"Oh, yeah?"

"Shut up."

"Come," said Kellaoth. "Daylight is waning, and we must be hidden before dark. Acklyon is a dangerous place at night."

Aaron and Jack scrambled onto Kellaoth's back again, and she took flight once more. The Unicorn swept over the trees of the forest until at last, she landed in front of a huge oak tree.

"We are now entering the heart of Eldorlorne where most of the Elves live," she said quietly.

"Eldorlorne?" said Aaron.

"This forest," said Kellaoth impatiently. "Now, be warned. Laza does not speak your language, and you do not speak his, but try not to hold it against him. He is a good Elf and will give you the best of treatment while you stay with him." She turned back to the tree, paused, and spun around. "Oh, and try not to laugh."

"What does she mean, try not to laugh?" Jack whispered to Aaron behind his hand. Aaron shrugged. Kellaoth returned to the perfectly ordinary tree and whispered something that the boys couldn't hear.

Then a door in the bark swung open, and there stood an Elf.

6
ELFISH

Aaron peered through the door, but couldn't see anyone. Kellaoth, however, said, "Bingbongwhoowekkawooloo."

Aaron looked down. He now understood that the reason he hadn't seen anyone was that he was looking too high. The Elf who greeted them was about three feet tall with several inches of curly red hair surrounding his perfectly round head. He wore a green tunic under a brown cloak, and at his belt hung a short sword. His signature pointed ears had no lobes, and were large and flat, rather like a monkey's. The full effect made him look so comical, that indeed, it was hard not to laugh. The Elf gave them an electric-blue quizzical stare and said in a high-pitched squeaky little voice, "WookaweekoLazawookaweeoowoo?"

Aaron gave a cough that sounded like a concealed snigger. Laza narrowed his eyes suspiciously.

Aaron and Jack began sneezing hard, trying to hide their laughter.

"Wookabingabong?" asked Laza to Kellaoth.

"Boungbut," said Kellaoth.

Aaron and Jack couldn't contain themselves anymore. They burst out laughing, slapping their knees and howling at the sheer ludicrousness of the situation.

Laza shrugged at Kellaoth.

At last, Aaron managed to contain himself long enough to say, "That's an Elf, is it?"

"Eh?" said Laza, raising an eyebrow.

Aaron collapsed again, giggling insanely.

It was half an hour before Aaron and Jack could restrain their laughter and come into Laza's tree, though they sneezed and coughed quite a lot. As they explored the two levels, they soon discovered that Laza's house in a tree appeared much larger on the inside than from the outside. The two boys did fit through the tiny doors, but only barely, and Aaron was glad he was short for his age.

Though the first floor was only one room, it was very cozy. Aaron saw a toddler-sized table and chairs, a wood-burning stove, a water pump, cartoons on the walls, a couch, and an armchair—all of miniature size. A wooden staircase in the corner led to the upstairs, which consisted of two bedrooms, one Elf sized, the other a double bedroom with Man-sized beds. This puzzled Aaron greatly.

Laza, for his part, thought that the boys were strange, too, with their slow, melancholy speech and dull laughter, and he felt they always took things far too seriously—which goes to show what an Elf's perspective of cheeriness is. Elves are as chipper and as fast as squirrels and are very skilled in martial arts, archery, and woodcraft, for forests are their natural habitats. Laza also didn't understand why the boys kept sneezing.

After the boys had gone to bed in the spare bedroom, Laza himself approached Kellaoth.

"So is we sure they're it?" the Elf asked the Unicorn in his native tongue.

"I am sure of it," said Kellaoth, also in Elfish. "They are young and foolhardy, but they shall grow older."

Laza erupted in squeaky laughs that were so merry that even a grouchy old man would have cracked a smile. "Foolhardy?" he chuckled, slapping his knee. "Hee hee hee! I don't reckon I've ever met two of their kind who was more solemn and silent!"

"You have never met any of their kind," Kellaoth pointed out.

"Oh," said Laza.

"And also," said Kellaoth, smiling, "many of their folk are even more solemn then they are."

Laza spat out the water he'd been swigging. "*More solemn*?" he repeated, coughing over his water. "How is that *possible*?"

"You've never met a Man from their dimension," said Kellaoth simply, "but try to keep an open mind."

"Yeah, I guess I should," said Laza. "I worked hard on those oversized beds, you know. But one more question: why were they laughing when we met?"

Now it was Kellaoth's turn to laugh. "Laza, Laza." She chortled. "I don't think it is possible for anyone to see an Elf without laughing!"

"Eh?" said Laza confusedly.

Aaron lay awake that night. The bed Laza had crafted was very comfortable, but still he couldn't sleep. Though meeting Elves and Unicorns was fascinating, he couldn't stop wondering what his parents must be thinking right now. Perhaps, even now, they were scouring Avondale in search of him. Twice he considered getting up and sneaking off to find a way home, but the thought of those Gertulk and Kane Malvadore kept him firmly in his bed. Besides, he still hadn't ruled out the possibility that this was all a colorful dream and that any second he would wake up back in his room with his mother shouting at him to get up.

He rolled over on his side and felt a lump in his pocket. He reached in and pulled out his yoyo. For a moment, he stared at it. Neon green with a red stripe running around the diameter, and his initials, *A.T.* carved into the side. He had quite forgotten that he had it in his pocket when he fell through the pool.

He heard the door creak open and instinctively lay flat against his pillow, pretending to be asleep. Squinting at the ray of light falling through door, he saw the shape of the Elf, Laza. Even in the poor lighting, he recognized those huge ears. Laza was carrying something, too.

Aaron watched as the creature walked over to Aaron's bedside. The Elf sat on a stool nearby, placing what Aaron saw to be a plate of cookies on the table and studying Aaron as though he had never seen anything like him.

Abandoning his feigned sleep, Aaron sat up and stared back. "Well, what do you want?" he asked in a somewhat unfriendly voice.

The Elf did not reply, but merely stared at him. Then Laza took a cookie from the plate and offered it to Aaron. Aaron hesitated, then took the cookie and bit into it. He chewed several times and swallowed, savoring the sweet, nutty taste. When Aaron had finished the cookie, the Elf began to speak in his absurd language, but slower this time and with a soothing quality. Aaron lay back in his bed enjoying the rhythm of the Elf's speech. Soon, the Elf's words formed into a song, slow and relaxing. Aaron began to nod as the Elf crooned his lullaby, and before he knew it, he was fast asleep.

Aaron and Jack tried their best to restrain themselves the next morning, but it was hard when they saw Laza wearing an apron and frying eggs, singing his cooking song to himself. It went something like this in English:

Doo-doo-doo-do –
Doo-doo-doo-doo-doo-doo- YEAH!
Rubba-dubb-dub, Rubba-dubb-dub.
Fryin' eggs, cookin' bacon, toastin' bread, makin' breakfast grub.
Rubba-dubb-dub, Rubba-dubb-dub. Makin' breakfast grub.
Pass the honey, and the butter, gimme salt on yummy omelets.
Rubba-dubb-dub, Rubba-dubb-dub. Shame we don't have chocolates.
Well, Kellaoth's with us, and so are Aaron and Jack,
Peanut butter, crunchy bacon, makes an amazing snack.
Rubba-dubb-dub, Rubba-dubb-dub. Makes an amazing snack.
So gimme all you got, and I'll make a scrumptious feast,
Rye bread, waffles, buttered toast, hope we don't run outta yeast.
Rubba-dubb-dub, Rubba-dubb-dub. Hope we don't run outta yeast.
Oooh, yeah, yeah, this stuff's good! Makin' breakfast is good,
I hope we don't all bust.
Rubba-dubb-dub, Rubba-dubb-dub. Hope we don't all bust.
Yeah, I hope we don't all bust.
Hope we don't all bust – YEAH!
Doo-doo-doo-do –
Doo-doo-doo-doo-doo-doo- YEAH!

Laza looked up from his work and saw Jack, who was waving his hands in time to the song, and Aaron, who was miming playing a guitar. The Elf chuckled. "Maybe they're not so solemn after all," he murmured.

Aaron and Jack were living peacefully enough in Acklyon since they had no choice, but they hadn't forgotten their old habits. Indeed, they sat on opposite sides of Laza's round table – Laza and Kellaoth between them.

Laza passed Aaron and Jack a plate of little cakes, set a platter of bacon on the table, tipped a fried egg onto each plate, and they began their meal.

"How are we going to get home, Kellaoth?" asked Jack, who had not touched his plate.

Aaron looked up.

Kellaoth thought carefully before answering. "That is rather a sensitive subject," she said at last. "And I am afraid that it must wait. No," she added as Aaron opened his mouth, "you must trust me on this. I assure you, you shall know soon enough."

"But what about our families?" said Aaron. "They'll miss us!"

"Do not worry yourselves," said Kellaoth. "We can return you to the exact point in time that you left. For now, I suggest you study the language and customs of the Elves. I don't want to be an interpreter for the rest of your stay."

And so they began. Kellaoth would teach Aaron and Jack different phrases in Elfish, and the boys would repeat them to Laza to see if they were comprehensible. Then Kellaoth would teach different English words to Laza and have him repeat them to Aaron or Jack. Aaron had appreciated how complicated the English language was when he took a class in Italian because phrases like "I am" and "it is" are often one word in Italian. However, Elfish was even harder. Aaron had to speak very fast, using no spaces and without the gibberish-like sounds being slurred, which in itself was an extraordinary feat. Oftentimes, when he spoke to Laza, all Aaron would get back would be another, "Eh?"

Laza, too, had difficulties with English. Aaron and Jack had thought that it would be a cinch for him, but Laza complained that it was too slow and mournful. He added that he didn't know how they could stand to say such boring things all the time—not to mention saying only what they'd intended to say and never throwing in random and pointless things to liven up the conversation as Elves often do. Often Laza's English sentences would sound like, "Hylloeemee-meeLazaandMee-meespeakingEnglishlikeya, uh, butter."

"The term is 'Man,'" said Kellaoth for the tenth time, "not 'butter,' and you must speak slower and stop combining words." Laza groaned and tried again.

But after several weeks, there was a definite improvement in the speech of Laza and the boys. Laza's sentences often sounded like, "Hello...Imee—Wo, *I am.* SpeakingEngl—*speaking English* like a...pumpkin? Wra, *like a, a,* Man!"

"Good job, Laza!" said Aaron.

"Eh?"

"I mean...*Wookapingyporramoroofrut.*"

"Pingywingy!" said Laza happily.

Though Aaron and Jack missed their home dearly, it was hard not to enjoy spending time with Kellaoth and Laza in the amazing forest. Before long, Aaron realized he'd been there an entire month.

Soon all three could speak to each other. At that point, Laza began telling the boys tales such as "The Song of Ivan the Young" about a boy who learned to fight, and "The Elf and His Baboon."

In return, Aaron and Jack told him of things such as cars, microwaves, televisions, and airplanes. Laza was fascinated. "So with this television thingy," he said, "youee can press a button and see things that aren't there?"

"Right," said Aaron. "And you can watch movies and stuff on them or see the news."

"It soundses like a very boring life," said Laza idly. "What is you doing for funnies?"

"Sometimes we use things like this," said Aaron, pulling the yoyo, which he kept with him at all times, out of his pocket.

Laza took the yoyo in his hands and studied it, sniffed it, and licked it several times. "Very easily entertained, you folks are…"

"Here," said Aaron, taking the yoyo. "You put your finger through this loop here, like this, and you let it go, and then you can pull it back up like this!" He demonstrated.

Laza stared at it. "Is that it?"

"It's all about the timing," Aaron told him, handing him the yoyo. "Here, you try."

Laza slipped his finger through the loop as Aaron had done and released the yoyo. It hit the floor and rolled. Laza looked up. "Idn't it supposed to come back uppy?"

Aaron laughed and shook his head wearily.

"Tell me about yo metheeds of flying again," said Laza.

"We have this thing called an airplane, and if you get inside it, it can fly you to wherever you want!"

"Youee doesn't need to call a bird and talks him into flying youee?"

"Right," said Jack. "Men can't speak to animals."

"Youee *what?*" said Laza, shocked.

A few days later, Laza took Aaron and Jack into his kitchen and stood beside his broom closet. "Nowee," he said in a combination of English and Elfish, "when Malvy-dor first took thee Throne, and Elveses went into hidey-holing, we builded undooground tunnels, to speaky, in case Malvy-dor sent Gertulk to burn us, and we needed to get messeeges to each other fast. Me-me wants youee to meeet my friends and to not being seen.

We'llee use the tunnels."

The elf then opened the closet door, stepped inside, and motioned the boys to come in. Aaron and Jack shared a quizzical look before also stepping inside. Laza closed the door, and the three were plunged into darkness for a moment before Laza pulled a trigger and a trap door opened beneath them, sending them tumbling into an underground tunnel.

They landed in a brightly lit, cheery passage with torches hanging on the walls and cartoons and comics painted all around.

Laza, having clearly used the passages many times, led them down the winding tunnel. The only break in the monotonous patterns was a huge, round, metal hatch engraved in the side of the tunnel halfway down. It was covered in large, triangular, black scales.

"What's that?" asked Aaron.

Laza glanced at the hatch. "Da shelter," he explained. "We-we builded dat a looong time ago, in case da Gertulk ever find us. You is seeing the scales on it? Dragon scales. Those things will keep out all forms of fire!"

After a short walk, they found a fork in the road. Over the two passages hung two signs, the one on the left featuring an arrow pointing towards the left-hand passage reading (in Elfish runes, which resemble spider webs) "Buky's Tree," and the one on the right said, "Deecal's Tree."

"We'llee go see Buky first," said Laza, taking the left-hand passage.

After several minutes of walking, they found a trap door in the roof and a rope ladder leading from it.

"Upee we go!" said Laza and started climbing the ladder.

A minute later, Laza, Aaron, and Jack were crammed inside another closet, and Laza was opening the door.

He stuck his head outside the closet, peered around, and said in full Elfish, "Hi, Buky!"

A cute little female Elf with curly brown hair and a wide mouth was in there, sipping what looked like a cocktail while she lounged in a chair. She looked up and saw Laza, and a grin spread across her face. "Lazee!" she said in a shrill voice. "How good to see you! Can I get you a drink? Mountain dew? Strawberry Slurp-slurp? Lime Oola?"

"Mountain dew, thanks!" said Laza, beaming.

"On the double!" squeaked Buky, and then—spotting Aaron and Jack—added, "And how about your friends?"

"Ooh, you should get the Lime Oola, Aaron," whispered Laza. "It's great!"

"Uh, the Lime Oola, please," said Aaron to Buky.

"One Lime Oola! And you?" Buky turned to Jack.

"Get the Strawberry Slurp-slurp," Laza whispered to Jack.

"One Strawberry Slurp-slurp!" said Buky, who had been eavesdropping and bustled off to make the drinks.

"What did you order again, Laza?" asked Aaron as Buky left.

"Mountain dew," Laza replied.

"You ordered soda?"

"Eh? Oh, soda! I remember you telling me about it. No, this ain't soda, it's mountain dew."

"You mean—" Jack said.

"A few months ago," said Laza, "Buky went on a vacation to the mountains and came back with five dozen barrels of dew she collected from the grass in the mountains. It's great!"

At that moment, Buky returned. She was hopping on one foot, holding a glass of lime green ooze in one hand, a glass of thick, pinkish-red liquid in the other, balancing a cup of clear water on her head, and carrying a glass of orange stuff on her other foot for herself.

"One Lime Oola," she said, dishing out the drinks. "One Strawberry Slurp-slurp and one mountain dew. Oh, and a Pumpkin Slushee for me!"

Aaron sipped his Lime Oola. It had a strong, colorful taste that was both sweet and sour.

Jack took a sip from the trough-like straw poking out of his drink. It made a very loud slurping noise which made Aaron snigger.

"Try your mountain dew, Laza," said Buky. "I added a special ingredient."

Laza peered into his cup and then threw back his head and drained the sweet-smelling water. For a moment he stood there, smacking his lips and beaming, but then he gasped. His eyes bugged out, his tongue shot out, he made an odd squawking noise, lifted his head, and a great spurt of flame shot out of his mouth and dissipate. Laza jumped off his stool and began running in circles, his hands over his throat. He then ran out of the door, and judging by the loud splash, stuck his head in the creek that ran through Eldorlorne.

He returned a minute later, water dripping from his hair and mouth. "What was that?" he asked brightly, as though Buky had just shown him a picture of the Grand Canyon.

Buky could hardly speak for laughter, rolling around on the ground and slapping her knees. "It was... It was..." She struggled to contain herself. "It was..." She held up a bright red-and-orange thing. "Extra-strong-undetectable-flaming-red-hot-pepper-juice!"

Laza squinted at the pepper and then roared (if any Elf can roar) with laughter.

Elves sure know how to pull a prank! Aaron thought, as he and Jack howled in laughter as well.

"So, tell me," said Buky as the laughter died down, "who are your friends, Laza?" (This is common among Elves; welcome them inside, get them a drink, pull a prank, and ask questions later.)

"These are Aaron and Jack," said Laza.

"And what are they doing in Eldorlorne?" asked Buky, squinting at the boys. "They don't look like anyone I've ever seen."

"They're from another world," said Laza bluntly—another Elfish tactic.

Buky's eyes widened with surprise, and the light of comprehension seemed to dawn on her face. "What are they doing here?" she asked slowly and with less of a grin.

Laza opened his mouth as if to reply, but then stopped with a glance at Aaron and Jack.

Aaron stepped in. "To be frank," he said, "we have no idea why we're here. Back home, we had these weird visions of us wearing half a crown each, and we kept seeing these cool swords. Then we found a pool of water in the woods, and we fell in—and next thing we know, we're here in Acklyon. And Kellaoth won't tell us why we're here, or how we'll get home, or anything!" He'd been longing to vent his feelings on the subject for quite a while.

Buky looked astounded now. She seemed to be about to say something when Laza gave her a "don't-say-one-word-about-you-know-what" kind of look.

In response, Buky gave Laza an "are-they-who-I-think-they-are?" look, to which Laza gave her a "yup-that-would-be-a-safe--guess" kind of look. (No kidding, Elves can do that.) "Laza," Buky now said out loud in an unusually serious tone. "Could I have a private word?"

Laza nodded and got up.

As the door closed behind them, Aaron turned to Jack. "What was that all about?"

Jack shrugged. "Who knows?" he said. "Elves can be a little weird sometimes, can't they?"

"A little?" Aaron gave a laugh.

7
Adinyrom Forahn

Aaron, Jack, and Laza paid visits to many more of Laza's friends—his drinking buddy Deecal; his second cousin Piki; the singing triplets Wrinky, Dinky, and Stinky; as well as Jolly, who played the banjo in Laza's band; Buky's two sisters Blippy and Binky; Meemee the watchman; Pokey the guitarist; old Grandma Bonkey and old Grandpa Ponkerd, whose feet were so big he couldn't wear shoes; Piki's twin brother Packa; Lilay, who ran a bed and breakfast; and Ploppy. Ploppy was somewhat of an outsider in the tribe. He was eccentric, carefree, and more than a little strange. But Aaron found that he liked Ploppy perhaps more than any of the other Elves. Ploppy understood how Aaron and Jack felt about being ripped away from their homes without explanation and treated them to lots of sympathy, as well as to a large lunch.

However, in the course of their visits to all of Laza's friends and business partners, they noticed a somewhat alarming factor. Just like with Buky, when Laza told each Elf where Aaron and Jack had come from, every Elf seemed as shocked as Buky had been and maybe hopeful, too. Wrinky, Dinky, and Stinky all yelped so loud they shattered china. Meemee swallowed his teakettle. Grandma Bonkey fell backwards over her rocking chair while Grandpa Ponkerd spat out the ginger beer he'd been drinking. Deecal leapt onto the floor at Aaron's feet as though he wanted to bow to the boy—but seemed to think better of it. Packa fainted from shock.

All but Ploppy. He was intrigued, but asked no questions. While the other Elves began treating Aaron and Jack with great respect without trying to appear conspicuous, Ploppy discussed the weather and asked Laza about movement from the Gertulk.

"So hows's you'd like it here in Eldeelorne?" Ploppy had asked cheerfully as he poured them all a cup of tea.

"Fine," said Aaron, not entirely truthfully.

Aaron remembered the understanding nod Ploppy had given him, but also the odd, calculating look.

After much debating, Aaron and Jack finally decided to ask Kellaoth. They had a feeling that she would decline to answer, as she had done the many times they had asked how they would get home—for though Acklyon had many inspiring wonders, it was simply not as good as the homey comforts back in Avondale.

The only important question they'd gotten an answer to was when Aaron asked where Acklyon was.

"Do you know the dimensions?" Kellaoth had asked in reply.

"Sure," Aaron had said. "A line (the ability to move up and down), a square (the ability to move side to side), and a cube (the ability to move back and forth)."

"And?" said Kellaoth expectantly.

Aaron gave her a blank stare. "There aren't any more," he'd said, but with less certainty. The truth was, Acklyon was so full of the unexpected, he wouldn't have been surprised if Acklyon had a fourth dimension.

He was half right.

"The fourth dimension, as few in the third dimension know, is *Time*."

"It's a theory," Aaron had pointed out.

The Unicorn continued. "But not a confirmed fact, which it is in Acklyon. The fifth—"

"There's a fifth?" Aaron blurted in surprise.

"There are many dimensions," said Kellaoth simply. "Do not interrupt. As I say, the fifth is *Magic* or the ability to tap into the deeper aspects of life as we know it."

This intrigued Aaron greatly. He'd known that Magic existed, for he'd seen Kellaoth use it fighting the Gertulk so long ago. But he'd never assumed that it was what held the world together!

"Wait," he said. "Are you saying that Magic works inside everyone?"

"Yes, I am," said Kellaoth casually.

"What *is* Magic, precisely?"

"Well," said Kellaoth, "that is a rather tricky question. I suppose Magic is...everything."

"As in—"

"What makes you think and feel? How does your brain work? What makes oak trees grow from acorns? How do you answer all the mysteries in your world? What causes humans to fall in love?"

"Are you saying that—"

"Magic is at the core of every world; it holds everything together and makes it be."

"I thought the power of God did that," said Aaron.

"Exactly!" said Kellaoth. "That is what Magic is, really, the Power of the Holy One. The fifth dimension is the ability to bend a small amount of that Power to your will as long as you do it for good alone. However, very few people have the mental discipline to control even that small a portion. The strongest king in the world could only levitate a stone. Unicorns, like myself, and Wizards are the only known beings to command the full extent of Magic. Acklyon is located in what is called the Fifth World. Where you are from is the Third World."

"As in...?"

"You are still on planet earth. At least, technically. Think of the Fifth World as... You might think of it as the 'new and improved' world. If I am correct, the land we call "Acklyon" is known as "Europe" in the Third World and is one of the Seven Lands."

"Wow," Aaron said. "If there's a Fifth World, does that mean there's a Sixth?"

At this, Kellaoth's face had darkened. "Yes," she'd said quietly. "There is a Sixth World and Dimension. Where the Fifth Dimension gives the power to build and protect, the Sixth makes that power complete. It is too much for any mortal to handle. It corrupts. If you were to pass through it, you would be mutated—torn from all the hope and goodness in your body—

and that kills your heart and soul. You are resurrected a horrible phantom of your old self with one purpose and one purpose alone—to conquer Good and to continue the spread of Evil. A Gertulk is a Man from there. Malvadore has sent man after man into the Sixth Dimension, and returned them as undead monsters whom he has tamed to be his servants. Every man he recruits is mutated, so they cannot desert. They are bound to him like a fly in a spider's web."

"So when you told us about turning a powerful man against himself to make a Kane, you were talking about the Sixth," Aaron had said quietly, unable to imagine a worse fate—to be undead, so twisted and evil that even your friends fled from you.

It was of this conversation that Aaron thought as he debated with Jack. It seemed even a simple question could result with his finding out something so horrible he wished he had never asked. Acklyon was, he thought, truly a kingdom of dreams and shadows; on the one hand, beautiful and exciting, on the other, dark and frightening. But in the end, the boys had no choice but to ask. They could not go on blindly in Acklyon, for there was obviously some secret about themselves that they did not know.

The next day, together, they confronted Kellaoth over breakfast.

"Erm, Kellaoth?" said Aaron cautiously. "Could I ask you a question?"

"You just did," said Kellaoth, smiling. "But you may ask another."

"Ha," said Laza sarcastically. "Ha."

"Well," said Jack, ignoring Laza, "Aaron and I noticed when we met Buky and Deecal and the other Elves they were acting weird when Laza said who we were. And—we want to know why."

Kellaoth and Laza exchanged uneasy looks which increased Aaron's sense of foreboding.

"Well," said Kellaoth heavily, "I suppose I have no choice. This question rather interlocks with your previous query, the one about how and when you shall get home as well as why you are here."

"Really?" asked both boys together.

"Yes," said Kellaoth. "You see, there is far more to either of you than even you know. There is rather a long story behind this statement, but I shall do my best to summarize it. Malvadore, before becoming a Kane, was a boy whose mother was Princess Halinda, sister to King Adinyrom the First of Acklyon."

"Adinyrom?" said Aaron in sudden horror.

"And Malvadore's father," said Kellaoth a little louder, completely ignoring Aaron and with a pained look on her face, "was one of the Neanderthal, a race of men far stronger and more foolish than the others. Malvadore, at the time called Bretulk, wanted dearly to learn the fair art of Magic. Many a time he pleaded for my good friend, Lord Cygon the Wizard, to take him in as an apprentice. But Cygon turned him down, for Bretulk—Malvadore—lacked the discipline required.

"Bretulk's parents were killed when the Neanderthal, lusting after their precious gold and power, attempted war on Acklyon. Bretulk, a grown man by then, went mad with grief and fled to the Sixth World, returning years later as the most feared and deadly Kane ever seen—Kane Malvadore.

"Malvadore, believing his parents to have been murdered by King Adinyrom of Fortilly or by King Rorard of Parland—the two countries that comprise the continent of Acklyon—assaulted Castram, the Castle of the Kings. In so doing, Malvadore killed both kings, their wives, their lords and ladies, their relatives, everyone who could take the throne except the two kings' sons. Each king had a thirteen year old son—Adinyrom II and Jahkon, named after his grandfather."

"Jahkon?" said Jack.

"You don't mean—" said Aaron.

"Lord Cygon, whom I named, assisted me in rescuing the boys from the clutches of Malvadore and sent them to the Third World where Malvadore would never find them. We fused them into two women's wombs and prepared them for rebirth. It is fabled that when the boys became as old as they were when they left Acklyon, they would return—prepared to take on the task of defeating Malvadore, who seized the thrones of both Fortilly and Parland."

"Are you saying—?" began Aaron.

"And, while in the Third World, the boys' names were changed from Adinyrom Forahn and Jahkon Parnor, to Aaron Tackers and Jack Oswald."

8
Training

"No!" shouted Aaron.

"Certainly not!" cried Jack.

"I *refuse* to be King of Acklyon!" Aaron's face flushed red with anger.

"Fortilly, actually," said Laza calmly.

"*I don't care what I'm king of, I'm not*!" Aaron bellowed.

"That didn't make very much sense," remarked Laza.

"Would you just shut up?" asked Jack.

"You see," said Kellaoth, "Lord Cygon and I placed a spell on the two of you so that once you reached the age you were when you left, you would return. One thing we did not take into account was that, having jumped between the Fourth Dimension, time passed differently than in Acklyon. It has been over a hundred years since Malvadore took over. "

"When did we leave?" asked Aaron before he could stop himself.

"On the…seventh day in October, I believe."

Aaron and Jack gaped at her. That had been the day they left the Third Dimension. "But what does this have to do with getting home?" asked Jack.

Sorrow filled Kellaoth's eyes. "You shall never see home

again. Acklyon is your world now."

"WHAT?"

"You—you mean I'll never see Mom, or Dad, or Roger, or Ellie or anyone?"

Kellaoth nodded.

"I won't ever go to college?" asked Jack.

Kellaoth nodded again.

"I'm never going to see my first R-rated movie?"

Kellaoth gave Aaron a curious stare. "What is an R-rated movie?"

Aaron ignored her question. "But won't everyone miss us?"

"No," said Kellaoth. "You see, Adinyrom, you are no longer who you think you are; Aaron Tackers lives on, but you are not him."

"What is that supposed to mean?" cried Aaron.

"You are a mixed person; half Aaron Tackers, and half Adinyrom Forahn. Over time, Aaron Tackers shall fall away, and the world shall see you as the King of Fortilly. The same is true for you, Jahkon."

"I still say—" Jack fumbled.

"You have both been dreaming of a sword, I believe?" asked Kellaoth.

Aaron and Jack stared at her, stunned, for they had, in fact, been dreaming of the two swords, Forvalad and Parvelad, every night now.

"Forvalad was the sword of your ancestors, Adinyrom, and has been passed down generation to generation from king to king of Acklyon. In fact, there is a legend that the rightful king cannot take the throne until the sword of Fortilly has chosen him.

"But there is more; Malvadore is aware of your coming and has prepared for you."

"What do you mean?" asked Jack.

"He has made a clone, a False Adinyrom Forahn, and is now ruling Acklyon through him. His plan is that when the people see you claiming to be the kings, they will think you imposters. A clever plan, to say the least."

"But," said Aaron, "I'm not who you think I am! I'm no hero. Neither is Jack! We know nothing about overthrowing warlords, or ruling countries, or any of that! We can't—"

"Which is why you shall learn," said Kellaoth patiently. "We know you are not heroes, you could not be at this stage! But you can learn, Adinyrom. Nothing is impossible, remember that."

She abruptly changed topics. "Now that you have mastered Elfish, I suggest that you learn the ways of an Elf. That particular skill has never let anyone of your size down."

Aaron sat down, fuming. He did not appreciate the way Kellaoth had ended the conversation so suddenly when he wasn't finished contradicting her. A part of him felt, deep down, that maybe she was right. Aaron Tackers was no hero, but Adinyrom Forahn was. But Aaron's stubbornness prevailed, and he wasn't entirely convinced that Acklyon was real anyway, that this wasn't just a colorful dream. No, he would not let this discussion end this way.

That night, Aaron lay awake in his bed once more, staring up at the wooden ceiling. So this was the reason. Kellaoth had yanked him away from his home, his friends, his life, because she believed him to be some prodigy destined to conquer Acklyon and free its people. But she had made a mistake. She had abducted the wrong boys. Aaron wasn't a leader. He had never led anything more than a schoolyard gang. This wasn't what he was meant to do. And Jack… *He's just some loser!* Aaron thought savagely, punching his pillow in frustration.

The door creaked, and Aaron looked up to see Laza's small silhouette entering the room. Aaron rolled over, pretending to be asleep. Laza pulled up a stool next to the bed and sat on it, watching Aaron closely. For a long time they stayed like that, Laza studying Aaron as though he had never seen anything like him and Aaron wishing Laza would leave.

Then Laza spoke, and there was no humor in his voice. "So now you know…" he said quietly.

Aaron ignored him, still feigning sleep. Not fooled, Laza continued.

"You're the one we've been waiting for all these years. The other Elves think you're some kind of demigod with power above all else, but you and I know the truth."

In spite of himself, Aaron rolled over and looked at Laza. "What truth?"

"That you're just a boy in a strange new world. That you want to go home above all else, but you know you never can."

Aaron looked at Laza, and as their eyes connected, they ceased to be Man and Elf, Child and Teenager, Fifth World and Third World—they were two orphans who wanted to go home.

"What happened to you?" Aaron asked. Laza knew what he meant.

"I didn't always live here in Eldorlorne," he said. "I used to live in an older and larger forest with my parents…" Laza's voice broke. He took a deep breath and continued. "Gertulk attacked. They burned down the forest, they killed my parents, my friends, everyone." He reached into a drawstring pouch around his neck and placed a thumbtack and an ancient toenail on the bed. "This is all I have left to remember them by. I only barely escaped alive. I was on my own for days before Kellaoth found me and brought me here. She saved my life."

"But Kellaoth's wrong," said Aaron. "She made a mistake. I'm not Adinyrom Forahn!"

"I know you're not," said Laza, and Aaron was so surprised, so grateful, he sat up. "But hey, as long as you're here you might as well make the most of it!"

"What do you mean?"

"Ever shot a bow and arrow before?" Laza asked with a slight smile.

Aaron shook his head. Then, in spite of himself, he smiled too.

Aaron raised the bow to shoulder height and drew the string to his ear.

"Just aim down the arrow," Laza said to him. Aaron closed one eye and squinted down the length of the shaft. Once he had the shaft lined up with the center of the tree he was aiming for, Aaron released the string.

The arrow sailed about a foot and dropped lifelessly to the ground.

"No, no, no!" said Laza impatiently. "You is holding it wrong! You is shoulding to..." And he went into a long rant in Elfish that Aaron couldn't understand.

Laza handed each of the boys a stick, rather like a sword, and said "Now!"

Aaron raised his stick and aimed it at Laza's chin. Jack did the same.

Aaron leaned over and muttered to Jack, "Try not to hurt him. I think one blow from these sticks could crush every bone in his body."

Jack nodded and took up a defensive position.

Laza slowly began circling the boys, searching for a weak spot. (Actually, he saw many, but was choosing one that would be most amusing to hit them in.) Like a tiger, Laza pounced on Aaron and knocked him to the ground with a blow to the knees.

Jack turned to face Laza, but was distracted by the sudden cawing of a crow nearby. By the time he had returned his attention to the fight, Laza had already leapt into the air and kicked him on the backside with both feet. Jack staggered, and Laza bopped him on the nose with his stick.

Kellaoth, standing beside Laza's oak tree home, laughed heartily as Aaron picked himself up from the ground, groaning, and Jack rubbed his backside and his nose, both of which were bruised badly.

Laza was leaning on a tree nearby and appeared exasperated. Aaron heard him mutter, "Greatest. All our smiling-ness and they're just a bunch of ninnies. Its gooner be a long afternoony."

"Laza, are you sure this is a good idea?" Jack asked.

"Nope," said Laza. "With your record, you could very easily ride her into a volcano, regardless of the fact that there isn't any volcanos in Eldorlorne. But we need to try it."

Jack looked at the bay horse he was learning to ride and felt a sense of dread. That thing was huge! He had never ridden any more than a pony at the fair. This bay was quite a lot larger than horses looked on television. He took a deep breath and approached the horse. It stared at him for a minute and stamped one hind leg.

"Now pet her," said Laza.

Jack stretched out his hand and stroked the bay. She studied him for a moment and then tossed her head.

"Now," said Laza, "put one footsie into the stirrrrrrup, hold the horn thingymabobber with both hands, and swing your other footsie into the other stirrrrrrup."

Jack did as he was told and soon he was on her back. He felt very awkward, sitting atop the horse like a sack of feed. Laza instructed him how to hold the reigns, and he was ready. Or at least his horse was.

Laza whistled, and another beast came trotting up although this one was a tiny pony. "This is Atom," said Laza.

"Adam?" said Jack.

"No," said Laza, "*Atom*. Because he's so small, geddit? Hee hee."

"Oh," Jack rolled his eyes at Laza's humor.

"Yoursees Pukelu," Laza continued happily, performing an aerial and landing on his pony's back. "Shall we ride?"

"Must we?" asked Jack.

"Yes."

"Drat."

"What?"

"Uh, giddy up, Pukelu!"

They started at a trot, and from there a canter, and then to a gallop.

"This isn't so bad, is it?" Laza asked, looking at Pukelu, but then noticed that Jack was gone. Twisting around in the saddle, he saw Jack lying on the ground a hundred feet back.

Laza groaned.

Aaron collapsed on all fours, gasping for breath as sweat dripped off his nose and a stitch throbbed in his rib like a knife wound.

"Giddyup, Jellylegs!" Laza shouted, poking Aaron in the side with a stick. The Elf danced around next to Aaron, almost beside himself with enthusiasm. "Don't be making me use my important voice!"

Aaron, who had just sprinted from Laza's tree to Buky's and back, merely groaned and rolled over onto his back. Laza continued to mercilessly poke Aaron, chuckling with glee. "Ya don't get nowhere sitting on the ground!"

Aaron felt a sudden urge to seize Laza around the waist and throw him like a basketball into a nearby tree. However, his arms had lost all strength, so he resisted the urge, contenting himself with gasping, "I can't..."

"It's easy," said Laza, sitting down on the grass next to Aaron. "See that patch of grass right there?" He pointed to a spot beneath a tall fern. Aaron nodded. "Just pretend there are several scrumptious females standing right there watching us."

Aaron squinted at the spot for a moment, imagining Ellie and Bonnie standing on it, giggling and pointing at him.

He was never going to see either of them again...

He shook his head, got to his feet, and completed the run once more.

Despite the bruises, sore limbs, and exhaustion, Aaron found he quite enjoyed training with Laza. It was the one thing that could take his mind off the depressing facts of his situation. He hated seeing the other Elves, hated the way they gazed at him in awe. *They expect me to be like the kings of old,* he thought bitterly. *They expect me to lead their armies in a mighty victory against Kane Malvadore. But I can't – I'm not cut out for this! Why me?*

Because you have something that others do not, said a voice in his head. *You don't know it now, but you have power beyond anything else in this World.*

What power? Aaron retorted. *They've got the wrong man!* And he silenced the other voice and returned to his training.

"Nowee," said Laza, "see those three ants crawling up that tree?"

Aaron nodded.

Laza glanced up at Kellaoth. "Could you shed some hocus-pocus on the sityation?"

Kellaoth raised a silvery eyebrow. "Magic is not to be used lightly. You know that, Laza."

"Yeah, but just a wee tiny bit. Please?"

Kellaoth laughed and angled her horn towards the tree. Before Aaron's very astonished eyes, the section of the tree which the ants were on began to grow until the ants were the size of squirrels.

"Nowee," said Laza, "how would you go about shooting down all three ants at once?"

"You mean with one arrow?" asked Aaron. "That's impossible!"

Laza raised his own bow and took aim. One arrow whizzed towards the tree. It struck the topmost ant in the shoulder of its engorged foreleg. The ant screeched and fell, tumbling towards the right due to the weight on its shoulder. It struck the second ant, which had been below and somewhat to the right of the first ant. The first ant knocked the second off the tree to its doom below and rolled to the left. The second ant then hit the third one, which was below and somewhat to the left of the second ant. Aaron look at the ground; three dead ants. One arrow. He looked at Laza. "How did you do that?"

Laza shrugged. "Men-folks sometimes call it Elfin Physics. It's a little thing we Elvesies can do. I dunno why you Men-types cain't. I guess you're all just ninnies. Kellaoth told me that it is possible for you to learn it, so I'll have to teach you to have the instinct of an Elfy.

"Nowee." He pulled a heavy book out of his pocket. "See if you can walk from here to that tree and back, balancing this on your foot."

"Is this Magic?" Aaron asked.

"Eh? No!" said Laza. "'Tis pure skill and instink that we use to do stuff like this!"

Aaron glanced at Kellaoth. She winked and mouthed, *It's Magic.*

"Didntcha ever wonder how Buky carried one drink on her head and another on her foot?" Laza continued, unaware of the exchange.

"I did wonder about that," Aaron confessed, "and also how you slid *up* the ladder to get to Deecal's tree."

"And when you sang that little song about 'Sir Ivan the Young' through your nose so that you could sing and blow bubbles out of your pipe at the same time," said Jack, who was standing nearby.

"Don't forget when Piki sang 'The Song of the Twin Swords of Acklyon' out of her ears," Aaron added.

"Not to mention when Deecal made the teapot twitch by shouting at it," put in Jack.

"And when you tripped in the tunnel to Piki's tree and landed on your head and kept walking."

"And when you burped and made bubbles come out of your mouth—"

"And when Buky swallowed a teaspoon and made it come out her nose—"

"And when Deecal walked with his hands and played his fiddle with his feet—"

"And when—"

"We get the picture," said Laza. "Aaron, put this on yourn footsie."

Aaron lifted his left leg as high as it would go, wobbling on his other foot. Laza placed the book, *A Hundred and One Ways to Be a Complete Loon, by Piki,* on Aaron's foot, and Aaron began hobbling along, bouncing on his right leg and struggling to keep the book on his left.

As Aaron glanced to the side, he saw Laza join him with an even bigger book entitled *A Hundred and Two Ways to Be a Complete Loon, also by Piki.* Laza had the book resting on one leg while sprinting past him on the other leg. As Aaron watched, snailing along, Laza performed a perfect somersault, tossed the book into the air, and caught it with his right foot without missing a beat. That was all Aaron saw before he fell over.

Kellaoth watched as Aaron, Jack, and Laza trooped back inside that evening. "Well," she said. "How was the training?"

Aaron and Jack both groaned, rubbing bruises. Laza, however, burst out laughing. "Those two are the sorriest excuse for combatants I've ever seen!"

9
A Sword for a Boy

Aaron studied the Elf before him, searching for a weak spot. He didn't see any.

Laza saw one in the boy, however, and he dove for Aaron. Aaron saw him coming and swatted with his stick, but Laza changed positions in midair to avoid it.

Laza tackled Aaron, knocking the stick out of his hand, and they both rolled to the ground, wrestling for possession of Laza's stick. Aaron took advantage of his height and strength by picking up Laza around the waist and throwing him. Laza did a couple of aerials before he landed on his feet, twenty yards out.

Jack rode past on Pukelu, his pony, and called to Aaron, "How's the fighting?"

"That thing has more lives than seven healthy cats!" Aaron shouted back as Jack, with Kellaoth galloping along beside him, vanished into the forest.

By this time Laza had returned to the fight, stick raised over his head to strike a blow. Aaron ducked and dove for his own stick. His hand closed around it, and he rolled to the side to avoid another blow from Laza. Aaron came up with a swing of his stick, which hit Laza on the hip. Laza staggered, somersaulted onto one of the lower branches of a tree nearby, and hurled his stick at Aaron. Aaron parried with his own stick and lifted Laza's stick off the ground with his left hand.

Up on the limb, Laza found a sturdy branch, broke it off the tree, and then broke it in half, gripping each half like a sword.

Though Aaron prepared himself for Laza's assault, it still came as a surprise when Laza leapt out of the tree and went on the attack.

The four sticks whistled and clacked as Laza and Aaron began a furious duel. Laza dealt Aaron a blow to the wrist, and Aaron dropped one stick. Then Aaron kicked Laza in the stomach and Laza lost hold of one of his. The fight continued until Kellaoth cried, "Halt!"

Aaron and Laza dropped their sticks, panting for breath as sweat dripped off their foreheads.

"Very good, Adinyrom!" said Kellaoth as she and Jack returned from their ride. "I believe that you are ready for this." She trotted away. Jack dismounted and stared curiously at Aaron. "What's she on about?"

Aaron shrugged.

Laza drew his little sword and pulled a whetstone out of his pocket. Laza's sword was about a foot and three quarters long, which was long for an Elf's sword. It was two-handed, and the blade was slightly curved like a Japanese katana.

Kellaoth returned carrying two long, roughly-wrapped packages bundled up in her wings. "Here." She handed one to Jack and the other to Aaron.

Aaron took his curiously. It was very heavy. He unwrapped the paper and watched as a gleaming sword came into view. No, it wasn't Forvalad. The blade, in its sheath, was silver. It had a long, narrow blade and upturned crossguard with a round pommel. He took it in his hand, flexed it, and swung it through the air. It was Elfish make, he could tell by the feel.

He looked over and saw that Jack had a sword, too, but his was a one-handed broadsword.

"Those are Anvilad, a gift to you, Adinyrom, from Deecal. And Sorving, a gift to you, Jahkon, from Piki.

"That was nice of them," remarked Jack, twirling Sorving through the air.

Aaron said nothing. He still felt a pang of worry every time Kellaoth called him "Adinyrom." The name sounded somewhat foreign to him; he liked "Aaron" much better.

At that moment, there was a crashing sound behind them. All four whirled around to see Buky emerge from a thicket. Her face couldn't have been any whiter if Laza had painted it with shaving cream while she'd been sleeping (which he had done in the past, many times). "Ohmygoshidon'tbelievehelp!you'vegot tadosomethingthey'recomingandi'mscaredasarabbitinafurnace Ah!LazadoesomethingIdon'tthinkwe'regonnamakeitYIKES!ooh ,we'redead,we'reallreallydeadandImeanthatfromthebottomeof my..." She trailed off into gibberish then stared around at them all. "Oh, hi. What was I saying?"

"Something about us all being doomed," said Aaron.

"Us? Doomed?" Buky gave him a blank stare. Then her eyes bugged out. "Oh, yeah! We'realldoomedbecausethey'recoming andwedon'tgottachancethey'llseeusyestheywillandthey'llkillus so—"

Jack could not understand what she was trying to say. Elves talk fast enough under normal circumstances. When they're scared silly and gibbering, even to an Elfish pro, they sound just like a recording in fast forward.

Laza, however, was hanging on every word, his eyes getting larger and larger as Buky talked faster and faster. Then all at once, he started gibbering, too.

"OHMYGOSHareyousure?didyouseethemhowmany werethere?"

Then both Elves started talking extra fast.

"Areyousure?"

"Yes!"

"Positive?"

"Yes!"

"Howmany?"

"Thirty!"

"Anytorches?"

"Yes!"

"Gertulk?"

"One!"

"Men?"

"Twentynine!"

"Armed?"

"Yes!"

"Whyarewestandinghere?"

"Idon'tknow!"

"Maybeweshouldmove!"

"Greatidea!"

"AAAAAHH!"

"AAAAHHHHH!!!!"

"AAAAAAAAAAAAAAAAAAAAAAAAAAAAAHH!"

"SILENCE!"

Laza and Buky stopped gibbering and stood at attention, looking toward Kellaoth.

"Would you two mind letting us non-Elves into your conversation?" Kellaoth asked. Aaron saw that she hadn't understood anything, either.

Laza and Buky answered in a single voice. "A regiment of Men is marching through Eldorlorne. We think they're checking to see if Elves are here! AAAAHHHHH!" They began running around in circles, screaming and yelling. Kellaoth tried in vain to contain the Elves' terror, but when they ran smack into each other and knocked themselves out, she gave up.

She turned away from their unconscious forms, and said to Aaron and Jack, "I never did understand those two. We go through this every time Men scout us. This regiment investigates Eldorlorne every few months, and every time Laza and Buky go into a panic. However, this is serious. If the Gertulk find even the slightest trace of Elves, they will torch the forest to the ground without hesitation. We must stop them if that happens. Come!" She strode away.

Aaron and Jack shared a nervous glance and followed.

10
Attack!

Aaron fitted an arrow to his string and squinted through the thick bushes. The column of men, dressed in tunics of bright red with undershirts of chainmail, continued creeping through the forest, squinting at the trees.

"Halt!" said their captain, a large, lumbering Gertulk with thick tusks on either side of his mouth. "Look at this."

The men gathered around the set of Elf tracks the Gertulk had found, though Aaron noticed that they kept their distance from the lumbering brute.

"There's more o' those tracks we saw back there!"

"Look here!" said one of the men, examining the large oak tree that was actually Laza's home.

"Lemme see 'at," said the Gertulk in his thick accent. He strode forward, knocking the soldier aside with a casual bat of his armored hand. After giving the tree a good sniffing with his snuffling nose, he proclaimed, "There could be Elves in 'ere, but they're hard to smell, they are. But I smell somat else. Smell's like…Man."

The men smirked at each other, and one bright-eyed fellow said, "Well, blow me down! Imagine, you smellin' Men, an' 'ere we are! Men!"

"Be quiet, yeh smart-mouthed cod! I smell Man-children!"

The men looked at each other again and then burst out laughing as the bright-eyed one said, "Children? Ha! Somat must be wrong with your snout, Master Tusks, because there cain't be no chil'ens 'ere, 'ow could they be?"

Aaron and Jack looked at each other, terrified, and gripped their bows tighter.

Tusks wasn't pleased at all. He strode forward, drawing his knife, and drove it through the neck of the man.

Aaron and Jack both recoiled as the dead man fell, but they managed to keep their silence.

One of the men, pleasant looking with a thick beard, whispered something to his friend so quietly that Jack had to lean forward to hear: "What's the bargaining that we won't be next in line?" His friend nodded.

And then the worst thing that could have happened did happen. As Jack leaned forward towards the two men, a hairy leaf tickled his nose, and he gave a sneeze. It wasn't very loud or strong, but it was enough to grab the attention of all the men.

"What was that?" said Tusks. "Hormond, check that out!"

One of the soldiers, who appeared to be the second in command, stepped forward and stuck the butt of his spear into the bush. Aaron and Jack crawled backwards and lay flat as the spear nosed around an inch above them. At last, the man withdrew, saying to his captain, "There ain't nothin' there, Sir."

"Garn!" roared Tusks, striding forward. "You're a sap, Hormond. I heard somethin'!" He drew his ragged scimitar, and with one swipe he cut off the bush at the roots.

As Aaron was revealed crouching behind the one-time bush, he stood, releasing his arrow. Tusks swatted away the arrow with his enormous shield.

Aaron and Jack wasted no time but leapt up and drew their swords, standing back-to-back.

"Aha!" shouted Tusks, flecks of spit flying from his mouth, "I told yer, didn't I? I said Man-children were here, an' here they are! What are your names?"

"That's none of your business," said Aaron, though his voice and his sword were both shaking slightly.

"Ooh, we're all high and mighty today, are we?" sneered Tusks.

"If only you knew."

"Wha'?"

"Nothing."

"Well," jeered Tusks, "I'd 'ate to *force* two chil'ens to do anythin', but—" He lifted his hand, and every man raised a hidden crossbow and pointed it at them. "—I'd *suggest* that you drop those li'l swords there, and stand quietly like good laddies, see. Brotchurd, Hormond, stand guard on our li'l friends."

Aaron and Jack dropped their swords as Hormond and the decent-looking fellow stood over them.

As Tusks returned to examining the tree, the pleasant-looking man, Brotchurd, it seemed, glanced left and right, then crouched down toward Aaron and Jack and whispered, "Who are you?" He did not appear mocking or scornful like the others, but merely curious, concerned.

Aaron said nothing.

"You wear peculiar garments, strangers." Brotchurd persisted. "I have never seen such clothes."

Jack's gaze rolled around casually until he was looking straight up at an Elf perched in the tree. Using a bit of sign language that the Elves used in such circumstances, Jack raised his eyebrows, tapped himself on the hip, and twitched both ears, saying to the Elf, *What do we do now?*

The Elf, Deecal, flicked some hair off his face and then crossed his eyes. *Stall for time.*

Jack raised his eyebrows again, nudged one toe toward Brotchurd, and wiggled his nose. *Can we trust him?*

Deecal studied Brotchurd for a minute, twitched his left ear, and flicked some hair out of his eyes again. *I think so, just don't say anything important.*

Jack twitched an ear. *If you say so.*

Aaron, who was watching, raised his eyebrows and tapped himself and opened his mouth. *What should we say?*

Jack shuffled his feet. *What else? Make it up.*

Brotchurd was staring curiously at them. Then he looked up at the tree, looking for what had their attention. Deecal froze, and Brotchurd failed to spot him. "So where are you from?"

"Well," said Aaron, "We are from, uh—"

Jack scratched his nose. *Somewhere far away.*

"The other side of Acklyon, somewhere over in Parland."

"Then what are doing here?" asked Brotchurd keenly.

In panic, Aaron rolled his eyes five times, tapping his foot with each turn. *Help me, Deecal!* "We were—"

Visiting your sick grandfather, communicated Deecal.

"Visiting my sick grandfather and—"

Again Deecal sent a message. *You were playing and got lost.*

"We were playing, and we got lost and—"

And you were taken in by bandits.

"And we were took in by bandits and—"

"Wait," said Brotchurd. "There are bandits in this forest?"

"Yes!" stammered Aaron.

You just recently ran away from them and are trying to find your way out.

"We just recently ran away and are trying to find our way out."

But you got lost.

"But you got lost."

No, dummy!

"No, dummy!"

"What did you say?" asked Brotchurd.

Deecal pounded the tree with his little boot, swinging his head up and down, while baring his teeth. *You got lost! How hard can that be?*

Sorry! "We got lost!"

"Oh," said Brotchurd skeptically.

"Get off, Brotchurd!" said Hormond, who had a rather unfriendly sneer on his face, "You're supposed to stand guard over 'em, not make friends with 'em!" But he didn't say more for at that moment Blippy, another of the Elves, accidently stepped on a branch atop Laza's tree, making a loud crack.

Tusks stared up into the tree for a moment, then at Aaron and Jack, and gave a cry: "Oi! There's Elves in 'ere, there is! Open up, Elfy!" He began hammering on the bark. Aaron rolled his eyes around seven times to Deecal: *Oh no! They've discovered Blippy!*

Laza, meanwhile, hiding behind the door in his house, was listening to what was going on. When Tusks began hammering, Laza took an arrow from his quiver and drew back his bow but did not open the door.

"Bein' difficult, are yeh, Elfy? Well then, Hormond, bring me that torch!"

Laza raised his foot and kicked open the door. An arrow whizzed off Laza's bowstring, striking Tusks squarely between the eyes. As the Gertulk crumpled, Hormond yelped and dropped the torch he was carrying. The torch landed on the dry leaves, but before the flames could spread, Deecal leapt out of the tree and stamped them out.

Elves poured out of all sorts of odd hiding places—under leaf piles, behind trees. Aaron even saw a few things he'd thought were bushes, but which turned out to be Elves in bush suits.

Jack saw Buky jump up, having been lying on the ground under a green cloak; her friend, Piki, pull off a bush suit and draw her rapier; Deecal fighting three soldiers at once with his sword; and Laza sending arrows thick and fast through the crowd.

Brotchurd, Aaron, and Jack stood motionless on the sidelines, watching the Elves battling the men. The Elves were winning, for they had the all advantages of surprise, skill, woodcraft, numbers, and knowledge of the forest.

Then, Brotchurd and the boys saw a man charging towards them, his sword raised and his eyes on Aaron. An ugly look was stained on his face. Brotchurd, unexpectedly, drew his sword and charged the man, hacking of his head. As the dead man fell, Brotchurd sheathed his sword and said, "It is not safe here!" He seized Aaron and Jack each by the collar and hurried deep into the forest. As Brotchurd dragged Aaron away, Aaron rolled his eyes six times and twitched his foot with each turn towards Laza. *Laza, help!*

Laza winked and wiggled his nose. *It's okay, you can trust him.*

Brotchurd kept running until the trio came to a clearing. There he set the boys down and said, "We will wait here until the battle is over. I fear for your friends, the Elves."

Aaron's head snapped up, "Who said the Elves are our friends?"

Brotchurd laughed. "Come, young master! Even a stone in my shoe could see that!"

"Oh," groaned Aaron. For a moment he sat there, staring at

Brotchurd, trying to see past the thick, scrubby beard.

"What are your names?" asked Brotchurd.

"If you don't mind," said Jack, "we'd rather keep them to ourselves."

Brotchurd smiled. "I am no fiend, sirs. I am merely a peasant from Muln whom Malvadore has forced into service. Unlike others, such as Hormond, I do not wish to kill Elves but Gertulk," he scowled.

For a long time the three waited, Aaron and Jack sitting together and pulling up pieces of grass, and Brotchurd gripping his sword hilt and pacing.

At last, the three heard the sound of footsteps in the leaves. Aaron reached for his sword, then realized that Brochurd had his weapon. But when the figure came into view, Aaron could see it was only Laza, returning from the battle. The Elf's clothes were torn and bloody, and he was polishing his katana with a rag. His eyes were somber, and he looked older than either of them had ever seen him. Brotchurd was standing, frozen, his eyes full of wonder.

"Well," said Laza, pushing up his forester's cap, "we killed all of them except that *pifidoodle*, Hormond, or whatever the doohickey his name was. I fear he'll be back, bringing a squad of Black Warriors with him."

"Black Warriors?" said Aaron.

"Gertulk," explained Laza. "Only they got enlisted into Malvy-door's personal army. They tougher, smarter, and more organized than yourn averaged Gertulk." When Laza lifted his head, he caught a glimpse of Brotchurd and whipped around his sword.

Brotchurd raised his arms to shoulder height. Laza squinted at the man for a moment before saying, "Brotchurd! Is that youee?"

"Laza!" said Brotchurd in perfect Elfish, dropping his arms and looking relieved, "Good to see you, old friend."

Aaron and Jack stared from Man to Elf, dumbfounded. "You two know each other?" Jack said in disbelief.

"Aye," said Brotchurd. "When Laza was a child, his previous home was near my city, Muln."

"Why would they set up camp so close to civilization?" asked Aaron.

"We was able to infiltrate da city walls and make friendly contact with some of the villagers," Laza explained. "Brotchurd and his wife were two of them."

"Indeed," said Brotchurd. "Another was my friend, the former Lord Fortingale. Alas, he was banished from Muln many years ago."

"A shame," sighed Laza. "'Twas a great man, Fortingale."

"So what are the odds that you two would run into each other here?" wondered Jack.

"Not odds," said Brotchurd. "When Malvadore forced me into service, I signed up to the corps whose job it was to investigate for signs of Elves. I was hoping to protect whichever ones I could. Sadly, I was unable to prevent several forests from being burned down."

"Eldorlorne will be among them if we do not act," said Laza very seriously, "Brotchurd, you is welcome to stay and help us if you wishes."

Brotchurd sighed. "Yours is a tempting offer, my friend, but alas I cannot. My wife is still back in Muln. Should the Gertulk uncover my treachery, she would be in serious danger. No, Laza, I shall return to Muln in secret and be reunited with her."

"Very well," said Laza. "In that case—"

Suddenly, twenty or so Elves leapt from the trees and pointed their bows at Brotchurd.

"No! Wait!" Laza waved his arms for them to stop. "He be's a friend!"

"You sure?" asked Deecal, not budging. "Have him swear it!"

Laza nodded at Brotchurd. Brotchurd raised his hand and said, "May I be struck dead if I tell any about you."

The Elves stood for a moment, then cheered, and rushed forward to give Brotchurd hugs.

"I'll take these ninnies back to the tree," said Laza, gesturing at Aaron and Jack. "C'mon!"

As Aaron followed Laza through the trees, he asked the Elf, "Do you really think he'll keep his word?"

"Oh, yes," said Laza, not meeting Aaron's gaze. "I could see it in his eyeses. They say everything, your knowing. All I had to do was watch his eyes with my eyes, to see that his lies were zilch!"

"You can do that, just by looking at him?"

"You saw me sing through my nose, didntcha?"

"Well, yeah, but that's different."

"In what way?"

All three burst out laughing.

Kellaoth met them outside Laza's tree, back where the battle had begun. The Elves had cleared away all the bodies and wiped the blood from the trees and grass.

"Isn't there some way we can track down Hormond?" asked Jack.

Laza chirped a laugh. "Not without revealing ourselveses to everyone from here to Rarzan!"

"What's a Rarzan?" said Aaron.

"That is Malvadore's stronghold and palace," said Kellaoth. "It was once a beautiful city and outpost in Acklyon before the

Darkness came and turned it evil. Malvadore spends his days locked away in its depths, plotting his schemes. It is believed that Rarzan is a direct route to the Sixth World."

For some reason, a cold chill ran down Aaron's spine at the phrase "Sixth World."

"Hormond will have made a straight course for Rarzan," Laza continued.

"Well," said Kellaoth with a brave attempt at merriment, "shall we go inside and—?"

"No," said Laza, pushing himself up to a standing position and looking more serious than most Elves are accustomed to. "I need to meet up with Buky and Deecal and Piki and the others. The Gertulk are coming, and we need to prepare for them."

And with that he strode away.

Hormond galloped wildly in the direction of Rarzan, bobbing up and down in the saddle of the horse he'd stolen in Muln. Thoughts of his regiment swam through his mind and of how the Elves had killed all but him. And now he would report the Elves to King Adinyrom and be rewarded above all others.

At last the dark towers appeared over the hill he was climbing. He rode his horse to the ground before the gates and started hammering on the door. It opened from behind, and two big Gertulk stood in front of him.

"Who goes there?" snarled the first one.

"Hormond, of Tarken's Regiment!" gasped Hormond.

"What business brings you to the Fortress of Rarzan?" asked the other guard.

"I bring news of an Elf colony nearby!"

The guards muttered and then uncrossed their spears. "Enter," said the first guard. "The Kane's office is at the top."

"Thank you!" Hormond panted and hurried into the fortress.

At last, after stumbling up at least a hundred flights of stairs, he reached the highest tower and banged on the door. After a bit, another Gertulk opened it from the inside. "What do you want?" he said sourly.

"I must speak with the king!"

The Gertulk gave him a suspicious glare and was about to deny entrance, when a voice from inside said, "Bring him in, Arguth!"

Arguth shot Hormond a look of mistrust and opened the door all the way.

Hormond scurried inside, where he found King Adinyrom and Kane Malvadore lounging in chairs by the fire. Adinyrom was dressed in a fine, blood-red tunic and cape, but Malvadore, as he always seemed to be, was dressed in spiked cruel black armor. Hormond went straight to Adinyrom and sank to his knees. "My liege!" he gasped. "I bring news of Elves nearby!"

It seemed that Malvadore started to say something, but Adinyrom shot him a halting look. Malvadore nodded slowly and sat back in his chair while Adinyrom turned back to Hormond. "Elves, you say? And nearby? Where?"

"In that big forest northwest of Muln, believed to be haunted, my liege!"

"Eldorlorne…" murmured Adinyrom. "Yes, it makes sense… You're sure, are you?"

"Yes!" said Hormond. "I saw them. I fought them. They killed all of the regiment except me!"

"He is right, Adinyrom," said Malvadore unexpectedly. "He knows… But there is something else, is there not, Hormond?"

"Yes, lord," said Hormond with a frightened glance at

Malvadore. "There were—there were two boys, sir."

Malvadore and Adinyrom stared at each other then started laughing. "Two *boys*, commander?" laughed Malvadore. "Not likely."

"It is true!" said Hormond with the merest trace of annoyance. "As I say, there were two of them. One was taller, fairly broad around the shoulders. He had lightish brown hair that came almost to his shoulders and sea green eyes. The shorter one, he was stockier and stouter than the first. He had eyes that were a strong shade of blue and golden hair!"

Adinyrom and Malvadore were not laughing now. They were on the edge of their seats, both looking slightly worried. Malvadore gave Adinyrom a superior I-told-you-this-would-happen kind of look before saying to Hormond, "You have done your country a great service, Hormond. I think you deserve a promotion. Shall I?" He turned to Adinyrom.

"Go ahead," said Adinyrom. "You are better at it than I."

Malvadore stood up. "Come here, commander."

Hormond walked slowly over to Malvadore. All of a sudden, he wasn't sure he wanted this promotion. Malvadore took both of Hormond's hands in his cold, creepy, long-nailed ones and looked hard into his eyes. Hormond was now very uncomfortable and was heartily wishing he hadn't reported the Elves at all. He felt as though Malvadore's blank red eyes were boring into him, encircling him, surrounding him, killing him, changing him—

11
The Battle of Eldorlorne

For more than a week the Gertulk made no assailment on the forest, giving the Elves time to prepare. Laza, Deecal, and others began digging trenches and deep holes covered with leaves in the outskirts and building walls out of mud, trees, and stones. Kellaoth was walking all over the forest, casting anti-fire spells over the trees, the bushes, and the grass.

Many of the women were packing up their clothes, their food, and their most treasured possessions. Aaron and Jack were training harder than ever. Although most everybody tried to hide it, they were all terrified about the battle to be. Aaron did not like this new Eldorlorne, full of sad faces, defensive walls, traps for the Gertulk, and tension hanging in the air like some unknown, ghastly apparition in their midst, reminding everyone that their lives and their homes could come crashing down at any minute.

"I wish they'd stop this!" said Aaron to Jack one day. "The Gertulk. Why haven't they come?"

"My guess would be that this is part of their strategy," said Jack. "Divide and conquer. Get us so worked up and worried, we start fighting amongst ourselves, and then they can wipe us out."

At that moment, Piki came running up. She was white faced and holding her sword. For a moment she just stood there, gibbering and jumping up and down, but then she managed to gasp, "Gertulk! Here! Torches! Fire! Eek! Help! Shut the gates! Murder! Moo!"

"Where?" asked Aaron, his hand gripping his sword hilt.

"Over there!" squeaked Piki.

"Lead the way," said Jack.

Piki vanished into the underbrush with Aaron and Jack close behind her.

When they got to the edge of the forest, they found their way blocked by a deep moat, enchanted and piranha-filled, circling the forest.

"Look," said Piki.

Across the moat was a camp of Gertulk, several hundreds of them – growling, grumbling, snarling, lumbering, hulking hideous brutes.

At that moment, Laza, Ploppy and Deecal emerged from the trees. Instead of their usual brown and green, they were clad in shirts of mail with their bows and quivers slung across their backs and their swords in their hands. Laza was looking more serious than ever.

"How do we stop them?" asked Piki.

"How else?" said Deecal. "Trickery and blood."

Laza nodded.

Aaron studied them for a minute then turned his gaze to the Gertulk. There were so many…

"Do we even have enough troops to hope to stop them?" asked Jack.

All four Elves shook their heads.

"Nevertheless," said Aaron unexpectedly, "we *will* fight

them. Because—because that's why Jack and I are here."

Laza looked at him in wonder. It was the first time Aaron had acknowledged his right to the Throne.

Laza was giving orders for he had been named the Captain of the Elves. According to Piki, he was the youngest-known captain, being only eighteen. Deecal, his right-hand man, was twenty-two, while Buky was also eighteen.

The Elders had chosen Laza because he had once been part of another forest, one even more prosperous than Eldorlorne. When Laza was young, his father had been the captain of that forest—at least until the Gertulk attacked. The Gertulk had managed to uncover Laza's forest and torched it to the ground. Laza's father had died defending his comrades while his mother had been trapped beneath a fallen tree and burned. Laza was the sole survivor of that terrible battle and had managed to drag himself to Eldorlorne. He had more experience in battle than most others and was a very skilled fighter, as well as a good tactician. He now gave the order for the sharper bowmen among the Elves to accompany him in defending the outer rim of the forest, once the Gertulk found a way around the moat.

Laza had requested that Aaron and Jack remain hidden during the fighting, which the two boys had been relieved to hear, but Kellaoth had disagreed. For some reason that perhaps she alone knew, she had ordered Aaron and Jack on the front lines with Laza and the others. Laza had argued back and forth with her until conceding that she was hundreds of years older than he and thus had seniority. He then indulged himself in training Aaron and Jack harder than ever to the point that they nearly collapsed from exhaustion several times. However, despite his terror at the prospect of being in a battle and his weariness of training, Aaron felt a certain bloodlust about him as his Forahn side began to show through.

His sword was on his waist, his quiver across his back.

He was ready.

Aaron looked around. In or behind every tree he saw an Elf with his or her bow strung and ready for action. Quite a few Elf children—the cutest kids you can imagine—were also in the trees with buckets of water, ready to dump them on fires.

He could see dozens of Elves gathering deeper in the forest, invisible to untrained eyes.

Hidden all around him, he could see Elves: Laza, Buky, Deecal, Piki, and some others—Blippy, Binky, Peeply, the triplets, Wrinky, Dinky, and Stinky; Meemee, Pokee, Jolly, and many more.

Across from him, crouched behind a big cottonwood tree, Aaron saw Jack, in bright mail and holding his sword.

Not far from Aaron's oak-tree hiding place, Aaron could also see Ploppy crouched behind a bush. Ploppy waved at Aaron, not looking particularly concerned by the advancing Gertulk, and Aaron managed to grin back. Laza had allowed Aaron and Jack to join the battle, but only under the condition that he assigned twenty Elves to bodyguard the two. Ploppy was the captain of these.

Aaron returned to staring at the edge of the forest, waiting for the Gertulk to come, his sword shaking in his hand. To say he was scared would be an understatement; he was mortified. The thought of killing repulsed him, and he suddenly felt a hatred for the sword he was carrying.

Ahead, he could see the Gertulk trying to cross the moat by building a bridge of thick wooden planks.

Laza's head slowly rose from a bush. He looked left and right at the other Elves and twitched his ears.

Every sword slid back into its sheath, and every bow tensed.

The Gertulk had finished their bridge and were tramping towards the forest.

Laza raised his left eyebrow, slowly and deliberately.

Quiet as a herd of mice, a hundred and twenty-seven Elves put an arrow to their bowstring and drew it back.

The Gertulk entered Eldorlorne and started lighting their torches.

Laza slammed his eyebrow down—a signal.

With many a *twang* and a *zing*, the air became so full of arrows Aaron could hardly see.

Aaron tried to release his bowstring, but found his hand was locked in place. The mere thought of really killing someone, even a Gertulk, prevented him from action.

But unlike Aaron, the Elves were hardened soldiers and showed no mercy to the Gertulk, shooting so fast their arms were merely spinning blurs attached to their shoulders.

But the Gertulk were also hard, and they fought back well. They raised their wall shields and drew their swords and began creeping towards the spots from which the arrows were flooding. Though many Gertulk fell, the rest, using their keen noses, managed to pick out where the Elves were hiding. When Aaron saw this, he immediately shouldered his bow and drew his new sword, Anvilad. Terror enveloped him.

Perhaps the Gertulk heard Aaron's teeth chattering. Perhaps his shivering sent tremors through the ground, alerting them to his presence. Perhaps he was shaking so hard they could see him. Either way, one of the meaner-looking Gertulk spotted him and charged with a roar, holding out his shield to block oncoming arrows.

As Aaron saw the lumbering brute bearing down on him, something in his mind snapped, and he sprang into action. Using some of the methods Laza had taught him, Aaron lunged, allowing the Gertulk to block, and then sliced the monster across the wrist, and with a sideways swing, knocked the axe from the beast's hand. Aaron stood there for a moment, pointing his sword at the Gertulk's chin. He tried to kill him, but, again, he could not. The Gertulk took advantage of his hesitation, raising an armored fist to strike a killing blow. At that moment, one of his bodyguards leapt out from behind a tree and charged, yelling and trying to get the Gertulk's attention. The Gertulk turned, sneering at this new arrival. The Elf slashed at the Gertulk, but his narrow scimitar merely glanced off the Gertulk's thick armor. The Gertulk responded by slamming his armored fist into the Elf's skull.

Aaron froze, staring in horror as the Elf staggered with a dent in his helmet, then fell to the ground. As Aaron watched, something erupted inside him, and he charged the Gertulk, the blood pounding in his ears.

The Gertulk heard him coming and turned with a snarl—which melted when he saw the ferocious expression on Aaron's face. Before the Gertulk could react, Aaron lopped off the monster's head with a quick blow and dropped down on his knees and crawled towards the dead Elf.

It was Ploppy.

For a long time, Aaron just sat there, too stunned to comprehend the cold facts of the matter—that Ploppy was dead, that he would never have lunch in his cozy holly tree, or chat with him about sword tactics...

Aaron gazed in misery at his friend, now gone where none could follow. *If I'd killed that Gertulk when I had the chance, Ploppy would still be alive,* he realized. Slowly his head came up, and he stared without much interest at the Gertulk and Elves battling.

Then he had an epiphany. He would never enjoy killing, but the more Gertulk he killed, the more innocent and decent people could survive. Ploppy hadn't deserved to die, but he had anyway—and his death was Aaron's fault.

Then a reckless rage hit him. He stood up, grabbed his sword, and turned towards the Gertulk. Without thinking, without planning, he dove into the center of the army, hacking, slashing, cutting, parrying, dodging, stabbing, leaping, swinging, kicking, and dancing around like a demon possessed.

Jack lifted his head. Just moments before, he had made his first kill; a Gertulk had been about to smash Piki into a puddle of jelly when Jack struck the beast from behind. Though the sight of the body in the dirt and the blood on his sword sickened Jack, he knew it was necessary to survive. He glanced into the thicket of Gertulk and was surprised to see Aaron in the middle of them, fighting for his life. *What is the birdbrain doing there?* Jack wondered. *He'll be slaughtered!* Jack was an intelligent boy. He knew full well the dangers of trying to be heroic and that stunts like Aaron's would get him killed in a matter of seconds. The plan was to stay out of sight and hit the Gertulk on the blind side, but there was Aaron, presenting himself as a target. Jack briefly wondered why Ellie and Roger could stand such a jerk.

But then he returned to reality: Aaron was about to die. None of the Elves, busy with their personal struggles, had seen him. Did Jack allow Aaron to pay the price for his foolery or did he charge in and help?

Against his will and not believing his own stupidity, Jack charged into the fray.

Aaron noticed Jack by his side with a rush of surprise and gratefulness. He was about to make a comment when three small Gertulk closed around him. He ducked under their blades, stabbed one through the chest, and caught the second with his shield. Jack dispatched the last one.

As Aaron fought, he felt that now-familiar rush of adrenalin; he was no longer Aaron Tackers of Avondale, he was Adinyrom Forahn, son of Adinyrom I of Fortilly and heir to the Throne. In his mind, he saw that same mighty sword, Forvalad, again.

Yet the boys were not experienced fighters and soon found themselves struggling just to stay alive. Gertulk closed in on all sides, swinging viciously as Aaron and Jack stood back-to-back, fending off attacks. Aaron had just been thrown off his feet, cowering behind his shield as a four-legged Gertulk raised a claw to crush him when Laza, from up in a nearby tree, tossed Aaron a rope. Piki, Deecal, Buky, and Dinky rushed to the boys' aid, forming a circle around them as they dragged themselves up the rope to safety.

"Good work!" Laza said, impressed. "Let's skedaddle."

"Laza," said Aaron painfully. "Laza—Ploppy's dead."

"Of course he is," said Laza distractedly. "But—*what?*"

Aaron nodded. "I saw it happen."

Laza grimaced in shock and said quietly, "I'm sorry to hear it. But it's done now, there's nothing we can do for him. Let's get outta here." Aaron and Jack hopped down from the tree, while Laza stuck out his head and bellowed "IYEEEEE!"

And suddenly, the forest went quiet. The arrows stopped flying. The Elves disappeared. As Aaron and Jack slipped nimbly away, Aaron paused to look back. Elf and Gertulk bodies littered the ground. He could see Ploppy's body, sprawled in the blood-soaked grass, forevermore wearing a slightly surprised expression as though he hadn't expected this to happen. Aaron glanced at the Gertulk and seized Ploppy by the arm, slinging him over his shoulder. He wouldn't let his friend's body be squashed, trampled, and possibly eaten by the Gertulk.

The Gertulk stared around in confusion, searching for their prey, until they heard a noise deep within Eldorlorne. Soon, the murmuring took the shape of words, and then the Elves burst into song as Grampa Ponkerd conducted the choir from his seat on a stump:

I went to a mirror,
And saw a handsome face.
It reminded me of
The Lord of Grace.
And then I saw you,
Uglier than sin,
Stinkier than a cosmic zoo!
And I said to myself,
That face could sink a thousand ships!
And as I looked,
This song came to my lips:
"So nya, nya, go away,
Don't come back some other day,
Because if you do that, we shall have to call you fat,
And Ha! Ha! You are dumb,
You could not beat my old mum,
And she is old, quite old,
Ninety-nine or one hundred

But Hee! Hee! You are slow,
Slow and fat and dumb and mean,
And we are fast and slim,
Smart and nice and you are not,
Just Ho! Ho! Where're your guts?
Go away,
Cause if you don't –
We shall have to kick – your – butts!

As the Gertulk listened, their snarls increased in volume. Their haunting yellow eyes grew wider and more inflamed with each verse. Though most of them couldn't properly understand the language, there was no mistaking the Elves' mocking tone – nor the tomatoes that Wrinky, Dinky, and Stinky chose to throw into the ranks of the Gertulk. For a moment, the Gertulk seemed stunned by the sheer boldness of the Elves, but then the largest in the group let out a bellow like an angry ox. His fellows responded in kind, and the entire horde charged towards the choir, fumbling with torches.

As the Gertulk pounded over the soft grass, the choir scattered, fleeing into the trees. Foolishly, the Gertulk pursued, crashing deeper and deeper into the forest. The choir Elves led them straight to a large clearing where they were met by a cluster of three hundred Elves, carrying spears and round green shields, led by Deecal. Each Elf wore a shirt of mail which shone brightly in the sunlight. The choir Elves joined the ranks, harmonizing with each other while they sang loudly and rudely about how stupid the Gertulk were. Aaron and Jack were with them.

Again, the Gertulk roared their displeasure and charged – so intent on making the Elves pay for their insolence they did not notice yet another company of Elves, all in green and brown, sneaking in behind them.

The group of Elves coming from the rear, led by Laza, efficiently struck the Gertulk forces before the monsters had a chance to strike Deecal. Two hundred Elves scattered the ranks of the Gertulk, sending pandemonium through the battle.

Aaron winced at the bloodshed, but when Deecal sounded the charge, the boy raised his sword, Anvilad, high over his head and fitted a shield onto his arm. With Deecal in the lead, the heavily-armed Elfin warriors leapt into the skirmish, sending even more chaos thundering through what had become a pitched battle.

Aaron and Jack were close behind Deecal, waving their swords and shouting encouragement to the Elves.

The Elves may have had the Gertulk surrounded and ambushed, but years of combat and training made the cunning monsters more than a match for the Elves.

The Gertulk formed a circle, raised their shields, lowered their spears, and charged outward. The clanging of sword on sword, the *twang* of bowstrings, the grunts of the surprised Gertulk, the high-pitched squeals of fallen Elves, and the sickening *crunch* of hammer on helm nearly deafened Aaron, but he held his ground and fought for his side. The Elves' strategy was to keep the Gertulk too preoccupied with their own fights to throw their torches, and so far it was working, though Aaron didn't know how long they could manage this. He himself was having the fight of his life but was making good use of his shield and his feet, Anvilad gleaming and flashing and spewing Gertulk blood.

The Elves might've been able to win, but then, one Gertulk managed to hurl his torch at a tree nearby, which immediately burst into flames.

Aaron froze, watching the tree burn. An Elf child rushed up and dumped a bucket of water on the fire.

The flames didn't go out.

They got bigger and spread to other nearby trees.

Aaron noticed that Laza was at his elbow. "What's up with that fire?" he asked.

"Dragon fire!" squeaked Laza. "It doesn't get extinkwished by water!"

"THEN HOW DO YOU PUT IT OUT?" Aaron bellowed.

"You don't!" squealed Laza. "Though me momma had a recipe she said would put it out. It was a mixture of warm vinegar, maple syrup, and—"

Aaron ignored Laza's rambling, watching in horror as a passing Gertulk swung his curved sword, cutting down the Elf boy who had tried to put out the flames. By now, all the trees in sight nearby were withering and toasting under the flames.

The Gertulk pressed their newfound advantage, and the Elves began to fall beneath their might. Aaron's heart sank as he watched the Elves struggling to hold off the advancing Gertulk.

"Fall back!" shouted Laza. "Fall back deeper into the forest!"

The Elves began backing away slowly, trying to make it past the onslaught.

As Aaron struck down another Gertulk, he glanced up to see yet more Gertulk streaming into the clearing. His heart sank. Weren't there enough already?

His eyes focused on the last one in the new column, a Gertulk taller and slimmer than the rest. He had a mustache of something that looked like seaweed, a sunken and lost expression on his face, his yellow eyes shrouded in evil. Yet even through this ghastly mask, Aaron could still see who it really was, or once was, before being ruined.

Hormond.

12
THE FALL OF ELDORLORNE

Aaron gazed in horror at Hormond, now a Gertulk. Kane Malvadore must have recruited him to his personal army after he gave the news about the Elves.

Hormond saw Aaron, too, and Aaron thought he noticed a trace of recognition in the hollow eyes. Aaron never thought he'd feel sorry for one who'd caused the destruction of Eldorlorne.

But he did.

For a moment, Aaron and what had once been Hormond stared at each other. Aaron's mind was racing—was there anything he could do for Hormond? No. Kellaoth had told him once that there was no known cure for the Sixth Dimension. *Even death must be better than what he's in,* Aaron thought. And then he knew; *even* death *must be better.* Yes, there *was* something he could do for Hormond: kill him.

Anvilad whipped up as Aaron raised the sword. He brought his shield in tighter to his chest and began circling Hormond.

Hormond, upon seeing this, prepared himself to duel. He leaned toward Aaron, his front foot forward, his big wall shield raised in the blocking position, his sword over his head and pointed at Aaron

Aaron studied his opponent carefully, searching for a spot

on the monster's body that neither his sword nor shield was protecting. He didn't find any. Then he remembered one of the combat tips Laza had given him: "If you cain't find no openings on his body, then check his feetsies. Gertulk are naturally clumsy with their feetsies. Try to get 'eem off balance, then attack."

A plan formed in Aaron's mind. An absurd one, but a plan nonetheless. Gertulk were hotheaded creatures, so if he could just get Hormond angry enough, the beast might get reckless at which point Aaron would be at a supreme advantage. A sneer worked its way across Aaron's mouth. "So tell me, monster," he said mockingly, "are all of you that ugly?"

Hormond stiffened angrily and slashed with his sword. Aaron blocked coolly.

"You're a little slow with that move, aren't you?"

Hormond made a downward strike which Aaron blocked again with his shield. Holding Hormond's sword down with his own, Aaron made a gap in Hormond's defense. Aaron couldn't get his sword into the hole, but he was able to get his shield through and took the opportunity to rap Hormond on the head with it. Aaron listened to the clang the shield made on Hormond's helm and remarked, "Dragon bones, it sounds empty in there, doesn't it?"

Hormond snarled and went on the attack. Aaron dodged and weaved away from the sword, then retreated a few steps and said casually, "I don't know why Malvadore wants an army of Gertulk," Hormond growled. "I'd rather have someone a little smarter and quicker on my side, say—" He thought for a moment then added, "inchworms."

At last, Hormond did what Aaron had been coaxing him to do; the beast lunged so hard that when his sword came out, his back foot left the ground and he was off balance.

Aaron parried Hormond's attack, leapt into the air and rolled down Hormond's back. As the new Gertulk turned to face Aaron, Aaron drove his sword through Hormond's heart, so powerfully that the blade passed through his chest and out his back. Hormond staggered, and collapsed. With some effort, Aaron dragged his sword out of Hormond's body, wincing as he felt it scrape past flesh.

Aaron gazed down at Hormond's dead body for a moment. It had been fun tormenting Hormond, but the killing blow had not been fun at all. Perhaps it was because he had known Hormond, however bitterly. He had never had anyone he knew die until this day. Would this same feeling stay his hand when he faced Malvadore, as he knew he would, someday? Was he weak? Was he so sheltered that he couldn't stand even to see an enemy die?

His thoughts were interrupted by a neighing roar. He froze.

The Elves and Gertulk froze.

Even the flames froze.

Then a familiar voice came booming through all of Eldorlorne as though Kellaoth were talking into a megaphone. "Elves! Running or fighting is useless now. If you stay or try to escape, the Gertulk will kill you. You have fought bravely, but now you must give up your forest."

Aaron never thought he'd here the Unicorn say that. He glanced at Laza, who was looking dismayed but also indignant.

Kellaoth seemed to know what Laza was thinking, even though she was hovering a hundred feet above the battle, for she said, "This is no time for chivalry! If you stay and fight, you shall be slain. Quick! I have placed a spell on the Gertulk and the fire, immobilizing both, but it won't last long. Run back to your homes, grab what you can, and hide in the shelter in the tunnels. Go!"

As the Elves fled towards their homes, Aaron found Jack, and they ran with Laza back to Laza's tree.

When they reached it, they discovered that Kellaoth had stopped the flames just in time; the immobile fire was just inches from the old oak tree. Laza pulled the house key out of his pocket, unlocked the door, and the three rushed inside.

"Hurry!" Laza said. "Jacky, you get some clothes and stuff, Aaron, you get some food, and I'll get the horses." He ducked outside, and Aaron and Jack hurried around the tree, scooping up various items and stuffing them into their rucksacks.

When Laza returned with Atom, Pukelu, and Aaron's pony, Coopy, the boys and Laza began throwing items into the closet that doubled as the tunnel's entrance. (Getting the horses down there was not fun, you can imagine.)

Once they themselves were the only thing left worth preserving in the tree, Laza shoved Aaron then Jack into the now-cramped closet then stepped inside himself. Before Laza closed the door, he took one last, long look at his home.

What he saw was Kellaoth's spell breaking and one wall catching fire. Gertulk smashed down another wall and streamed inside.

Laza hastily slammed the door, feeling sick, and pulled the lever which dropped them and their luggage, like an egg yolk falling into a bowl, into the passage.

The boys and Laza did not delay in putting their things into the ponies' saddlebags before they themselves mounted.

They galloped down the tunnel—Aaron on Coopy, Laza on Atom, and Jack on Pukelu—racing towards the shelter the Elves had built.

When Aaron, Jack and Laza made it to the shelter, they found the rest of the Elves already there. Laza steered Atom into the round door, and Aaron was about to tell Jack to hurry up when he saw, with a thrill of horror, that Jack was not on Pukelu's back!

Craning around in his saddle, he saw Jack, now lying unconscious, twenty feet back. Aaron estimated that Pukelu had stumbled over an irregularity in the floor, causing Jack to slip off his back and hit his head on the ground.

An explosion rocked the tunnel, emanating from the hatch in Laza's closet. Perhaps the flames had found a bottle of rum or undetectable-flaming-red-hot-pepper-juice, or perhaps the Gertulk had grown angry and thrust a torch into the closet. The cause didn't matter, what mattered were the crimson flames now spreading rapidly through the tunnel, devouring all in their path.

Even though there was nothing to burn in the tunnel.

For a moment, Aaron sat frozen in his seat, watching Jack draw closer and closer to a fiery death. Memories flashed through his mind in a heartbeat. He remembered all the mean jokes he had pulled on Jack so long ago and all of Jack's retaliations, many of which involved Aaron getting into trouble with teachers. Then he remembered training in Eldorlorne with Jack and fighting side by side with him against a whole army of Gertulk…

Before he could think about it, he leapt off Coopy's back and sprinted towards Jack.

"Aaron, no!" squealed Laza. "Itees waaaay too dangerous!"

But Aaron did not care. He saw nothing except Jack and the crackling fire. Once he reached his downed companion, Aaron hurriedly seized one of Jack's arms and dragged him onto his own back and began tottering back down the corridor. He was not strong enough to carry Jack and run at the same time. It was clear to every Elf in the shelter that, unless Aaron abandoned Jack, they would both meet their ends that day.

Sweat dripped off Aaron's nose as he staggered towards the

hatch, his muscles burning. He glanced back and saw that the flames were rapidly gaining on him. He pushed his exhausted body to the breaking point, forcing it to keep going. The door seemed so far away…

By now the flames were right behind Aaron, and he could feel their heat beginning to scorch his armor. Both he and the Elves knew quite clearly that neither Aaron nor Jack would survive. Inevitably, Aaron's legs gave out on him. He collapsed, helpless to save himself or Jack from the burning heat. He turned and looked at the fire, now less than ten feet away. He closed his eyes, waiting for death to come.

But then, just before he withered beneath the flames, he felt himself being scooped up in a set of talons. Kellaoth turned in midair and flew hard for the shelter, making sure as she did that Aaron had a firm grip on Jack's wrist. She soared into the shelter, and Laza slammed the hatch after her, one step ahead of the flames. Fortunately, the Elves had lined the reinforced hatch with dragon scales, the one thing that was impervious to dragon fire. They were safe for now.

The Elves clapped and cheered for the valor of Kellaoth and Aaron. Aaron felt many hands patting him on the back, but he couldn't muster the energy to care.

A second explosion sounded, reminding the Elves of their plight. Their homes were destroyed, and the Gertulk would surely find them. The tension in the room was tangible; every Elf stood motionless, making naught more than a squeak. They listened and waited, hugging each other for comfort.

Aaron was pacing the floor, gripping his sword's hilt and waiting for the noise aboveground to stop. While he paced, his mind was a blur—Hormond, Brotchurd, Laza's home going down in flames, the fear in the eyes of the Gertulk as he himself struck them down—everything. He felt ashamed of himself for the destruction of the Elves' home. Though part of Aaron knew he couldn't have done anything, something the Elves assured him of, he still felt that as the future king defending the Elves was his responsibility. He also knew that if Hormond hadn't discovered Jack and himself then the beast never would have figured out where the Elves were.

Buky and Kellaoth were tending to Jack, who had not awakened yet. Aaron still didn't know why he'd rescued Jack the way he had, for both boys where still struggling to hang on to their old hatred of each other despite the events that were pushing them closer together. Though Aaron hated to admit it, he supposed that he was growing fond of Jack, no matter their history.

A sudden crash brought him back to the present situation. It seemed as though the dragon fire had burned through the support pillars in the tunnel, causing the ceiling—the ground above—to cave in, everywhere except over their shelter. A voice came from outside. "Oy, look a' this!"

"A tunnel," said a sly, second voice. "That must be where they went. Find them, quick!"

The sound of pounding feet came from just outside. Terrified, the Elves huddled close together. Aaron drew his sword.

But no Gertulk ever saw them, and soon the sly voice—oddly loud—said, "They must've escaped before the tunnel collapsed. Back to the fort, boys!"

Dead silence. Jack drifted awake, and Piki clamped a hand over his mouth.

Aaron waited ten seconds, then half a minute, then ten minutes. An hour crept by, and no one dared to move. Time ticked by painfully slowly. Two and a half hours later, Aaron summoned the courage to go to the door and push. It didn't open. Debris must have covered the hatch. "We're stuck," he said, his voice sounding strangely high and loud after the muffled grumbling of the Gertulk.

"Here." Kellaoth trotted over to the door and placed a clawed foot on it. The door melted.

Jack stood beside Aaron. "Come on." Jack began creeping through the opening, gripping his sword, Sorving, in front of him. Aaron followed, holding Anvilad high and staring around for Gertulk.

Buky had her arms around Laza's neck with her face pressed into his shoulder, but now Laza tapped her on top of the head. When Buky looked up, Laza jerked his face towards the door and stood up. He held his sword in his left hand while his right found Buky's hand and held on. He began leading Buky out the hole. Kellaoth followed, the rest of the Elves in step behind her.

The tension was so thick Aaron felt like he was walking underwater. When the group stepped out of the shelter, they found that, indeed, the roof of the tunnel had caved in. In its place was a peculiar trench winding through the forest. Wordlessly, Aaron picked up Laza and placed the little Elf on the lip of the trench. Also silently, Laza fished a rope from his belt and swung it down for the others.

One by one, painfully slowly, Aaron, Jack, Kellaoth, and the four hundred or so Elves came out of the former tunnel and gazed around at the incinerated forest.

The grass, the trees, the bushes—everything—was scorched, burned, and sometimes still smoking. Not one tree was left standing.

While Laza picked up a charred rabbit skull, shaking his head, Buky sprinted over to a smoking trunk, buried in ash and debris. Aaron knew the forest well enough to know that this had once been Buky's home. Buky began digging through the blackened mess until she found something that appeared to have once been a picture frame. Dimly, through the darkened glass, Aaron thought he saw a male face in the picture.

Buky pressed the picture to her chest, bowed her head, and began to cry.

Aaron was picking through the remains of the forest ground, which was littered with pieces of blackened wood, torched grass, and bodies in varying states of decomposition. He found one Gertulk body whose armor had been melted away, the clothes burned to ash, the skin devoured by flames, and the flesh roasted and boiled until nothing was left but a blackened skeleton. Aaron snatched up the skull and threw it as far as he could with a detached scream of fury and pain.

Jack looked around. They were standing near the border of the forest, and he could see their moat and the bridge the Gertulk had made. It had been right about here that Ploppy had died… He opened his mouth to remark how thorough the damage to the forest was, but an arrow, whizzing past his face, interrupted him. His nerves had been on edge for a week, and at this, he exploded like a stick of dynamite. He whirled, drew his sword, and in one slice, sheared off the head of the Gertulk that was charging him. "A trap!" Jack shouted, meeting another Gertulk head on.

Aaron rushed to Jack's side as Gertulk poured out of various hiding places. Aaron was suddenly reminded of the Elves ambushing the Men.

Screaming with rage, the Elves charged the Gertulk, waving swords and knives, and shooting arrows. The Elves no longer looked even remotely cute. They resembled nothing more than short, angry goblins, dancing around and screaming rude, inappropriate, yet perfectly true things about the Gertulk. Laza shouted at them, trying to restore order, but the other Elves ignored him. Aaron saw that they were becoming reckless in their anger, and soon the Gertulk forced them back.

"Retreat!" Aaron shouted, waving his arms at the Elves. "Fall back! We can't win here!"

The Elves saw the sense in his words. They began backing away, trying to blend with the background before they realized they were wearing lush shades of green and brown, which stands out exceedingly in a blackened and dead forest.

Jack noticed that Kellaoth wasn't fighting but merely standing, staring at one of the less-destroyed trees and muttering. But as she chanted, the blackened wood began to rise, shift, and form a sort of giant cart or sleigh. Once it assembled itself, ropes burst from its front and it harnessed itself to her. "Get in!" she yelled.

Aaron and Jack took the task of shooting down the chasing Gertulk as the Elves loaded into the cart. When all the Elves and their luggage were aboard, the boys scrambled onto Kellaoth's back as they had done before.

With a roar of effort, Kellaoth lifted off and began flying upward, the Elves and boys in tow.

Down below, the Gertulk howled in frustration that their prey was getting away. The Elves began firing arrows back at the monsters to keep them from loading their long, sturdy crossbows. Laza, standing atop three stacked Elves, was dipping the heads of his arrows in oil and launching them down at the Gertulk. Where the arrows struck, fire sprouted.

"THAT'S FOR MOMMY AND DADDY!" he screamed at the top of his lungs, striking a Gertulk in the chest and watching the heat scour his armor. "THAT'S FOR PLOPPY!" he cried again, shooting two arrows at once. "AND THAT'S FOR ELDORLORNE!" He fired and struck the lead Gertulk squarely in the face. The Elves cheered.

Aaron was about to clap with the others, but then he saw with a jolt of horror that Kellaoth was having trouble staying airborne. Even as strong as she was, the weight of two hundred Elf soldiers, two hundred Elf children, and their luggage was too much for her.

She wouldn't make it.

Ahead, Aaron saw a large cave protruding from the side of a small mountain nearby. Kellaoth had seen it, too, and she made straight for it.

Looking down, Aaron watched the Gertulk chasing them on foot, running almost as fast as Kellaoth was flying.

The wheels of the cart struck the ground and rolled as Kellaoth swooped low to enter the cave. Barely in time, too. They hadn't gone twenty feet into the cave when the Unicorn crash-landed in the dust and skidded for another ten feet. Aaron and Jack only barely leaped off her back before Kellaoth struck the ground.

The Elves formed a semi-circle around the Unicorn, prepared to defend her from the Gertulk while Buky, Aaron, and Jack examined her. They discovered (to their great relief) that Kellaoth wasn't dead but that she was exhausted and would need to rest.

The Elves and Gertulk stood for a moment, neither wanting to make the first move, when a shrieking roar erupted from deeper in the cave.

"What now?" asked Aaron, as he and Jack drew their swords and Buky loaded her crossbow.

"Imee not so sure that you want know!" said Buky.

"It can't be *that* bad," said Aaron, reflecting on all the things he'd seen and done that day.

But as it turned out, he wished he hadn't seen what it was after all.

A huge, scaly, horrible thing came swooping out from the back of the cave, flying on bat-like wings. In the light of a fire burst from its mouth, Aaron saw long, curved teeth, a spiked tail, and catlike yellow eyes.

"A DRAGON!" screamed Buky, rolling out of the way of a blast of fire.

Aaron looked at Jack, and they both raised their swords above their heads, prepared to fight to the death with this horrible, gigantic thing.

Buky backflipped out of the way of a second spout of fire, shouting, "Aim for the eyes and mouth!"

Laza had come to their aid, firing arrows at the dragon. Most of Laza's arrows glanced off the dragon's scaly hide, but several struck it in the eyes, causing it to howl with pain. This gave Aaron enough time to leap upwards, grab one of the dragon's horns, and drive his sword down its throat.

"Good shot, Aaron!" said Laza.

But rustling bursts of light and roars from the back of the cave told them that there were many more dragons and perhaps other hideous creatures.

There were.

13
Nimbun

More and more dragons, great black or grey reptiles with snapping, crocodile-like jaws and huge wings, came pouring out of the shadows.

"Of course, the cave we picked *would* be full of dragons," grumbled Jack. "Otherwise, this would be too boring."

"Exactly!" chirped Laza. "And where's the fun in that?"

"Not to rain on your parade or anything, Laza" —Aaron leaped out of the way of a dragon's flailing claws— "but the rest of us aren't exactly having the time of our lives here!"

"Too bad!" squeaked Laza, who had climbed onto a beast's back. The Elf didn't seem at all worried about this new and deadly threat.

The large dragon was roaring and writhing in pain as Laza hacked at its head, trying to break through the tough skin. Finally, the monster staggered and began to fall. Laza somersaulted off the beast and onto the ground, watching with satisfaction as the monster flattened several Gertulk as it reeled in agony.

Buky's eyes popped open, and she whirled on Aaron and Jack. "Quickety," she said hurriedly. "When da Dragowoofio landses on da Gerrytulkety and dey-dey getting orll squashy-squashy-squashified, we'll all scatterdoodle so's whens dey're getting bleckfted dey'll all ching-chingapore wiff da others drabio and we-we can maketing ourn escapedee!"

Aaron and Jack stared at her for a minute, and Aaron said, "What was that?" Her Elfish slang was so strong they couldn't figure out what she was trying to say.

Buky rolled her eyes. "Nevomind," she snapped. "Just get ready to hide."

No sooner had the other Gertulk turned to see who had joined the fight when Buky shouted, "PEEKOPOOF!" to the Elves. (*Peekopoof*, in Elfish, means about the same as "hide, and don't make a peep unless you want to feel my sword.")

The Elves vanished behind various rocks, dirt piles, stalagmites, and mounds of bodies.

The Gertulk whirled and faced the onslaught of dragons. Foam dripped from the dragons' mouths as they threw themselves at the Gertulk, ripping at their armor.

The Gertulk met them with swords, shields, axes and torches. However, even if the Gertulk weren't outnumbered, the dragons had all the advantages. Eventually, the soldiers gave up and fled into the growing night, the entire pack of dragons on their tail.

The silence rolled over the fugitives like ocean waves washing up on the beach. Quiet waves. The abrupt cease in the noises of battling Gertulk, Elves, and monsters was almost deafening. Though Aaron knew the danger was past, he couldn't help twitching towards his sword hilt as several Elves lit some candles and set them up around their camp, the striking of matches unnaturally loud in the dead quiet.

An unexpected whine from the back of the cave made them all jump. Before you could say, "Yikes!" thirty-two Elfin warriors strung, loaded, and bent their bows. But Laza held up his hand, signaling them not to shoot.

"Listen," he said quietly.

They listened.

There it was again! Not the fearsome roar of a dragon, but a high, pitiful moan, seemingly for help.

Without a word, Laza picked up a candle from the ground and headed into the darkness to investigate. Buky scurried along behind him. Aaron glanced at Jack, and they followed, drawing their swords.

Kellaoth looked at Deecal.

"I ain't goin' in there," said Deecal stubbornly.

Kellaoth tapped him on the rear with her horn, causing a tiny electric current to pass into his hindquarters. After yelping, jumping five feet into the air, doing three forward somersaults, and landing hard in a sitting position, Deecal suddenly decided that he should go, too.

* * *

"My lord." The False Adinyrom stepped into the study, where Kane Malvadore was peering down at a map of Acklyon.

"Shh!" his master said sharply before Adinyrom had even closed his mouth. "Do not call me that unless you're sure no one is even close to being within hearing range. Fool!"

Adinyrom dipped his head. "I apologize, my lei—Malvadore."

Malvadore seemed to calm down a bit. "No one heard you?"

"I think not," said Adinyrom, peering out the door.

"Well, what is it?" asked Malvadore, once Adinyrom had closed and locked the door.

Adinyrom was looking nervous. "I have news of the assault on Eldorlorne."

Malvadore smiled. "Ah. So tell me, what happened?" His red

eyes narrowed. "The mission was a success, wasn't it?"

"Partly, my lord," said Adinyrom, looking more nervous than ever. "Our troops destroyed the forest, lord, but half of the Elves still escaped alive. A Unicorn was with them."

"Kellaoth," whispered Malvadore. "She has been sniveling and scheming against me from the start! She and that accursed Wizard, Cygon. And now, she is raising Adinyrom and Jahkon to kill us, both of us! She never did want to get her hooves dirty. Always left the hard work to the lesser people. Well, this will be her last trick, I promise. If it is the last thing I do, I shall kill her!"

He turned to Adinyrom. "Summon your troops, Forahn. Take as many Gertulk as you like! Find them, destroy them, and do not rest until you bring me Adinyrom Forahn and Jahkon Parnor as well as the horn of Kellaoth!"

Malvedore's crooked snarl faltered. "Wait…" Slowly he paced around and back to his desk, that familiar leer working its way across his face. "Wait. They'll be planning a war, no doubt. And for that, they'll need reinforcements. We have weakened them in the battle, so they'll be looking for more Elves to help them… Or, more truthfully, additional Elves for us to kill."

He looked up. "Forahn, take your Gertulk and follow them. If they get suspicious, attack them, but don't eliminate all of them. More than likely, they know where more Elf forests are, and they'll make a straight course for them. Get there before they do, and let them find a forest of charcoal and dead bodies. Ha ha ha!" He gave an evil cackle. So did Adinyrom.

"I will, my lord. It won't be that hard."

"No!" shouted Malvadore, so that Adinyrom jumped. "Enjoy yourself, but don't get overly confident! Elves are made of a stuff that neither Men nor Gertulk nor even Kane can understand! Perhaps it is mere skill, or luck, or favor of their god, but it is strong. These same Elves outsmarted our best soldiers. They can easily do the same again. Against Elves, our military advantage alone may not be enough."

"Of course, my liege." Adinyrom nodded, turned, and swept out of the room.

* * *

Laza studied the creature before him. He couldn't see it very well in the flickering light of the candle, but it seemed to be a very small, green dragon-like figure. In the insubstantial orange light of Laza's candle, the creature looked distinctly creepy and repulsive. As Laza's hand reached out to pet it, the reptilian thing lashed out, and the Elf had to move quickly to dodge the attack. Buky, Aaron, Jack, Deecal, and Kellaoth gathered around, staring down at it.

"What is it?" asked Aaron.

"Not *it*," said Laza indignantly. "*He*. And I 'twould say dat he's a mixed-breed. Mostly dragon, of course. Also some lizard, and maybe a dash falcon…" He stretched out his hand, and this time he did manage to pet it—*him*, as Laza wants us to call him. As Laza's hand ran over the thing's shoulder, he suddenly stiffened and withdrew his hand. It was covered in dark liquid. "Blood…" he whispered. "This baby's bleeding! Hurt bad, I'd say. Quick!"

Aaron didn't move. "Are you actually thinking of helping this…thing?"

Laza stared at him. "Yeppypoof."

Aaron looked down at the creature, back at Laza, and then at Jack. Jack nodded.

While Buky sat on top of the creature sweet-talking him,

Deecal, Aaron and Jack carried the little lizard thing outside and laid him down on the cold ground.

Now that they could see properly again, Aaron noticed that the creature wasn't half as ugly as it had appeared in the cave's poor lighting. Indeed, he was really rather cute! He was about the size of a large dog and covered in green scales. He had drooping, bat-like wings and a vicious slash across his left flank, probably from a larger dragon that had attacked him.

"Getting me some bandages, and some of that—oh, bickeroo, that stuff that heals thingies, thatees so difiticult to remembering? Oh, yes! Savvy! Get me some savvy."

Deecal and Buky went scattering in several different directions all at once, rummaging up several wads of bandages and a jar of white ointment to tend the creature's injury.

Laza and Buky sat down beside the creature and began nursing him. While Laza rubbed some salve over the thing's torn skin and ruptured scales, Buky sat by his head, tickling his chin and baby-talking him. "Hi, there. You're a cuuuuty little fella, aren'tcha? Yes, you are. Yes you are! Hee hee! Are you a little nimbun? Are yooouuuu a little nimbun? I think you ar-re. Hee hee!"

"What's a nimbun?" asked Aaron as he came over.

"Means cuuuuuuty-pie-pie," said Laza as he wrapped bandages around the creature's wound.

"He's a cutie-pie?"

"Heck no!" said Laza, looking up. "A cutie-pie is *nikelpuff*, you ninny! A cuuuuuuty-pie-pie is a *nimbun*. Come to thought about it, he *is* looking like a nimbun! Whatdya think, Nimbun?" he consulted the creature, who seemed to like that name. At any rate, the creature crooned happily and licked Buky on the face. "I tink so!" said Laza. "Yourn new name is—da-da-da-DA!

Nimbun!"

Nimbun licked Buky on the face again.

Laza stared at him. "Nimbun!" he said again.

Nimbun licked Buky on the face again.

"Nimbun?"

He licked Buky again.

"Cool."

As Laza, Buky, and the other Elves treated Nimbun, Aaron wandered off by himself, gazing away to the west, where a plume of smoke rose through the air directly over Eldorlorne. Fleeing from the Gertulk, battling the dragons and watching Nimbun had dulled the pain of the battle and of Ploppy's death, but now it all came back full force. Half the Elves of Eldorlorne had died in the struggle, and now, Aaron didn't know what would happen to the rest of them. He pulled the yoyo out of his pocket and idly began spinning it up and down.

"What now, Aaron?" Jack had come up behind him.

Aaron shrugged. "Who knows?"

"I wish I'd never heard of Malvadore," growled Jack.

"I wish I'd never heard of Acklyon," muttered Aaron.

"You saved my life in the tunnel."

"I couldn't just stand there," said Aaron, avoiding Jack's gaze.

"I'd say most people could," said Jack bluntly.

"It still didn't make much difference," said Aaron. "If Kellaoth hadn't grabbed us, we'd both be barbecue."

"That's not the point."

"Well, what *is* the point?"

"Aaron—" Jack stared off at the winter sky "—I'm tired of being stubborn."

"What's that supposed to mean?" Aaron thought he had a pretty good idea what.

"We've been—or tried to have been—bickering ever since we came here, even though I can't help admiring you—" Jack paused, and Aaron's head came up. This was the first compliment Jack had ever given Aaron. "I'd hoped you'd cave first, but I can see we're both too proud, so here goes: Aaron, I'm sorry for everything I've done to you, and I want to be your friend."

Aaron studied him for a whole minute, then smiled. "Apology accepted, although if you ask me, I should be the one apologizing. Don't forget, I pulled most of the pranks."

"Well, don't forget when I put an egg on your seat in math," Jack said with a half-laugh.

"Yeah, but that was only because I pulled your chair out from under you in the cafeteria," Aaron smiled reminiscently.

"And remember when you put that note in my desk that said, 'Principal Roberts looks like a moose'?" laughed Jack.

"And then he found it and—" Aaron was trying hard to suppress his laughter.

"And his face went purple!" Jack howled with laughter.

For several minutes, the two of them roared with laughter. Aaron could hardly believe how good it felt, laughing *with* Jack instead of laughing *at* him.

To Aaron's surprise, he found that very little changed after Jack made peace. He supposed that they had been growing fond of each other for months and had just been too proud to admit it.

From Eldorlorne, a small explosion sounded. Perhaps one of the fingers of flame had found another jar of Buky's undetectable-flaming-red-hot-pepper-juice. That killed their laughter immediately.

Aaron sighed. "What are we going to do, Jack?"

"I don't know," said Jack wearily.

"*Why* did this burden have to come to *us*?"

"Because it is your destiny."

Both boys turned at the sound of Kellaoth's voice.

"This is who you *are*," she continued. "It is who you were meant to be."

"I just wish I were back home in Avondale," said Aaron for the umpteenth time.

"But you would never truly be happy there," said Kellaoth. "The Forahn spirit is strong in you, Adinyrom. You can no longer hold back the royalty that surges through you."

"Watch me!" Aaron shouted rebelliously.

As Aaron stormed away, Kellaoth turned to Jack. "Even if I now arranged for you to return to the Third World, you would not be satisfied. Your spirit would always be longing to come back."

"Says who?" demanded Jack. "You keep calling me 'Jahkon,' but I'm not him! I'll never be up to the standards you want of me!"

"That is the Oswald in you speaking," said Kellaoth patiently. "I believe you do not understand. I do not expect you to be a hero right now. It will take time, years, for you to be ready to receive the Throne of Parland."

"You know," said Jack, who was sounding very upset, "I don't think I ever will!" And he raced away, too.

Kellaoth stood for a long moment, staring at Aaron, who was pacing in the mouth of the cave, and at Jack, who was sulking off by himself. She had known it would come to this, no matter how brave the boys were.

Presently, she noticed a man standing beside her. He was tall and wrapped in an old brown cloak with the hood up. His age was hard to tell, but judging by his bent stature and wooden staff, you might guess that he was very old. Kellaoth wasn't surprised to see him. She had been expecting him, in fact.

"They are downcast?" he said.

"Obviously," murmured Kellaoth. "Though, admittedly, most boys their age would have broken down long ago."

"They have not truly given up," said the man.

"I know that they have not," said Kellaoth.

"I believe," said the man, "that they will need something more than what you can offer."

Kellaoth turned to face him, suspicion in her eyes. "What are you planning, Cygon?"

Cygon merely chuckled. "I will be back at a later time." And with that, he vanished.

14

Choices

"Here we must make a difficult choice," said Kellaoth, looking down at Aaron, Jack, Laza, Buky, Deecal, and Piki, sitting around a long rock. "Malvadore knows that Elves are on the loose and quite possibly knows about you two as well." She nodded to Aaron and Jack. "He will be sending Gertulk after us to kill the Elves and to bring Aaron and Jack to him. We now must make this decision: do we inhabit another forest and hide, or do we strike back against Malvadore?"

"We have barely an army," said Jack. "And no fortifications, either. Fighting back would be difficult."

"But if we is hidey-holeying," said Piki, "Malvy-dore will just keep looking until he finds us. Ourn numbers were cut in half in the Battle of Eldorlorne, and the same thing could happen again, and again, and again—until he's completely obliterated us."

"But," said Laza, "we doesn't even coming close to having enough Elfies to hope to overrun Rarzan, not even if we enlisted the help of every Elf this side of Castram—"

"Castram!" cried Deecal. "That's it!"

Everyone stared at him, so he explained.

"Idn't it obvious? If we're gonna start a revolution, what better place to set up shop then Castram? 'Tis still the hugest and most fort-ee-fied castle in Acklyon, even if 'tis in ruins. Me votes we point our hineys towards the City of Castram!"

"You're a genius!" said Laza.

"Itees long been Malvadore's worst fear that Castram re-awakes and the kingsees would return to deal him justice," said Piki. "Great idea, Deecal!"

"Me never knew you was that smart!" said Buky, impressed.

"There is only one thing," said Kellaoth. "Acklyon is *huge*. Castram lies in the exact center, and we are near the coast. The trek could last months, and there will be danger along the way. Malvadore will follow us, trying to stop us from reaching the castle. The decision is yours, Adinyrom, Jahkon."

Aaron blinked, alarmed at being brought into this. Why was she asking him? Every Elf present was older and smarter than he was. But then he imagined Castram in all its glory, and the answer came to him.

Aaron didn't even have to consult Jack. He knew what the answer would be. "We want to go to Castram. If Malvadore's after us, than we want to stand and fight."

Kellaoth smiled. "Your father would be proud of you right now, Adinyrom."

* * *

It was announced to the Elves that they would begin their quest for Castram as soon as spring came.

But they had plenty to do while they waited for winter to pass. They built horse drawn carts to carry their supplies and to carry the smaller children. They hunted game and gathered food to take with them, for they had no idea how the hunting would be on their long trek.

Kellaoth had shown Aaron a map of Acklyon, dictating the path they would take to Castram. She also pointed out the Elf-inhabited forests along the way from which they hoped to receive help in their newly beginning rebellion. Aaron was astonished at just how few of these forests there were. Indeed, the only two colonies nearly as large as Eldorlorne were Niybay and Capptiung, two forests not far from Castram. The rest were little more than clusters, no bigger than nine or ten Elves total, dotted around the map.

Laza was training Nimbun to be his steed, pet, and battle associate; it was quite amusing to watch Laza trying to sit on the bucking creature's back. Nimbun was as like an Elf as any creature could be—smart, happy-go-lucky, agile, and playful—so he and Laza made a very good team.

Laza, Buky, Deecal, and Piki made a snow-Malvadore, which they all took turns kicking, mocking, and abusing. Probably the most comical part of this was when Nimbun saw Laza sticking out his tongue at snow-Malvadore, guessed that this was some sort of enemy, and tried to eat it. Watching Nimbun snarl and bowl the snowman over, tearing into him the same way he would eat a deer—then getting a brain freeze—that was worth having to make a completely new snowman.

As Aaron watched this, laughing, he noticed that Kellaoth had come up behind him.

"How are you, Adinyrom?"

"I'm fine," Aaron lied, trying to sound casual.

"You are your father's son, Adinyrom," said Kellaoth, reminiscently. "Only a true Forahn could have adapted to the amount of stress and of change the way you have."

But you're not a true Forahn, a nasty voice in Aaron's head was saying. *You're still more schoolboy than prince, and you always will be.* Aaron shook himself mentally, trying to get rid of these thoughts. "Have you ever been scared?" he asked Kellaoth quietly. He felt foolish, yet at the same time he yearned to speak his mind, to be comforted by a parent.

"Many times," said Kellaoth calmly. "We all have two sides to us, Adinyrom: the side we conceal from everyone, even our friends, and the side we show the world. The challenge is finding which one you truly are. I may not look it now, but I was once young like you. I was foolish, I was immature. I did not listen to my mentors."

"What happened?" Aaron asked.

Kellaoth looked at him, smiling. "I grew up. I changed in ways I had never thought possible. One day, you will too."

"If the change is there, I don't see it," Aaron muttered.

Kellaoth smiled. "We never do, not until we've completed our journey. But I believe if Malvadore met you now, he would not be as confident as he usually is."

"Especially if Nimbun eats him again." Aaron, in spite of himself, gestured at Nimbun, who had continued gobbling the snow-Malvadore.

Kellaoth laughed. "Aye," she murmured.

Spring had come, and they prepared to start their journey. Coopy, Pukelu, Atom, and the few other horses in the group were laden with luggage. Sacks full of provisions were mounted on the carts and the two hundred or so Elf children began settling around them, clutching dolls made of grass or wood.

There was one more rather depressing matter that they had to deal with before they left, though. Aaron had successfully smuggled Ploppy's body out of Eldorlorne, and they had to give him a decent funeral. (They hadn't done it during the winter, because it's an Elfish tradition that funerals during winter are bad luck for the one being commemorated.)

The Elfish customs of funerals are different than those of Men. Instead of burying the deceased in the ground (which Elves also consider bad luck), they send their dead into the sky, via large air balloons. What they do is place the dead Elf (Ploppy, in this case) onto a blanket or stretcher and place flowers on and about the Elf. They don't put the Elf's treasured possessions with him, because that would make it too heavy to fly. Then, they tie fourteen or fifteen large balloons to it and send it off into the sky.

As such a thing soaring up into the air would act as a beacon for the Gertulk to find them, Kellaoth cast a spell rendering the floating monument invisible.

Aaron stared up at the sky, where, cloaked to his eyes, Ploppy's body was drifting higher and higher. Aaron felt his lungs constrict painfully. He would miss Ploppy – he had seemed to understand Aaron's predicament better than any of the other Elves. Still, the boys, Elves, and Kellaoth had work to do. They couldn't afford to waste time grieving. Work recommenced, building more carts and wagons to carry the young Elves in or hunting and gathering food for the journey. Quicker than Aaron expected, Laza told him that they were ready.

"Then we should start loading up our luggage," Aaron said, his heart sinking at the prospect of more journeying and hardships. "We'll leave at first light tomorrow."

15
On the Road

As the sun set, the survivors set off on their long journey to Castram. They had decided to travel during the night, hiding and sleeping during the day, for fear of running into pilgrims. Pilgrims scarcely traveled at night because of wild animals.

As heavily armed as the Elves were, they had little to fear from animal attacks. Indeed, most of them welcomed the idea of running into a wild boar or lion. They needed all the food they could get. Also, traveling at night, away from the sun's glaring heat, would mean they would need less water. Aaron and Jack walked side by side, behind Kellaoth, who was leading the caravan. Behind them was a long line of Elves and tiny ponies, all burdened down with baggage. Aaron and Jack both carried walking sticks, each with a torch mounted on the head. Aaron was surprised at how much he enjoyed the hike. After the horrors of the battle—something he frequently revisited in his nightmares—he was glad to put his energies into such a task as traveling by foot.

"You know we don't have enough provisions to last us the entire way," Aaron said to Kellaoth, "and the game's not good out here. We'll be lucky to find any wildlife to hunt."

"We'll stop in Muln for supplies," Kellaoth explained. "It's about twenty leagues from here and heavily guarded."

"Sounds like a party," said Jack grimly.

"We have a few men on the inside. With any luck, we'll be in and out before they even realize we were ever there."

"But how will we—?"

Kellaoth cut him off, her ear cocked. "Hide, all of you!"

The Elves obeyed without conscious effort, leaping behind bushes and trees and readying their weapons. In a matter of minutes, every last trace of the Elves had vanished.

Kellaoth glanced around slowly, searching for someone coming down the road, but no one was there. "Laza, you and Nimbun scout it out," she whispered.

Laza called to Nimbun, and the dragon-like creature came slithering out from behind a tree, looking scared. Laza patted him on the head and then climbed onto his back, whispering as he did, "Giddyup, boy."

Nimbun made a crooning sound and leaped into the air, flying off under cover of the tall trees.

It seemed hours later, though in truth only a few minutes, that the caravan could see the shape of Nimbun swooping low over the trees and coming their way.

"What didid youee see?" squeaked Buky.

Laza dismounted, leaning against Nimbun's leg and closing his eyes wearily. "Notta whole lot," he said. "Trees, rocks, prints, no Gertulk."

"Did you say you found some prints?" Aaron came over and joined them.

"Yup," said Laza. "Stomped boot prints in the dirt. Twasn't made by us, I'll tell ya theat. Elfies don't wears biggy-boots."

"Something is not right," said Kellaoth, pacing back and forth. "This obviously means that Gertulk are somewhere behind us, but why are they not attacking? They must know we are here, I am sure of it."

No sooner had she finished talking when a black arrow whizzed through the air, impaling a nearby Elf.

"Gertulk!" Deecal screamed.

By the time Deecal had finished, Kellaoth, Aaron, Jack, and the four hundred Elves had vanished. All the Elf children slipped quietly back into the trees that lined the path while the adult Elves took cover, strung their bows, and waited for the Gertulk. Aaron slammed his back against a big oak tree nearby, holding his sword tightly in his hand.

Several dozen Gertulk came blundering onto the path, staring around.

"Don't let 'em take you by surprise," the captain warned his men. "They're hiding, I'll bet!'

"Got dat right!" cried Laza, and suddenly the air became thick with the Elves' arrows. The Gertulk tried to retaliate, but were outnumbered.

The Elves quickly picked the beasts off with their bows and then ran for it—only stopping half a mile up the road.

"Well," panted Piki, "you was right, Kellaoth... They *were* following us."

"I still don't like it," Kellaoth replied. "If Malvadore sent those Gertulk to kill us—why were there so few?"

"Just be glad there weren't more," Aaron said, "or we'd have been vulture bait."

Their worst problem, apart from Gertulk, was that even though the Elves had spent the entire winter hunting and gathering, they still had a pitiful food supply—at least for feeding four hundred very hungry mouths. They had begun to ration their supply of food, and nobody got as much as they'd like. Fortunately, Elves, being so small, can survive long periods of time without much food. Kellaoth, being a Unicorn, could last months without a single bite.

The real problems were Aaron and Jack. Both boys had been hitting rapid growth spurts since coming to Acklyon, which meant they needed more food than usual. Not a happy predicament when you are confined to a small hunk of meat and a loaf of bread a day. They soon became cranky and lost their tempers easily. This was not good either.

Laza had calculated just how far the Elves could make it with the food they had; the answer he had come up with was just a little past Muln, a large city they would pass soon. This news came with some relief, because they could buy or steal some food there for the remainder of the journey. *Let's just hope our spirits last that long,* Aaron thought grimly.

16
Muln

That morning they made camp and prepared a scanty meal.

Aaron, deep in thought, stumbled around camp in the cold morning air with a cloak around his shoulders and a bowl of untasted stew in his hands. According to Laza, they would make it to Muln sometime tomorrow, which meant that this may be their last pitiful breakfast.

It's not fair, Aaron thought grouchily. *I'm starving! I wish I'd never heard of Acklyon. I could be in bed right now, enjoying spring break and sleeping late! But noooo. I'm the future King of Fortilly, and I have to tramp around in this stupid cold with this ridiculous excuse for a breakfast.* He stepped on a large root sticking out of the ground and tripped, almost dropping his stew. Executing a very trick turn, he managed to catch himself, but a bit of the stew slopped over the sides of the bowl.

He growled angrily at the burn on his hand and at the grayish patch on the grass. He looked down into his bowl, noticing in dismay how much soup he had lost. *Darn root,* he thought, kicking it.

He then looked up and noticed a little Elf girl sitting all alone on a hollow log. She couldn't have been more than five or six, and she was crying her eyes out and shivering in the cold, an empty bowl at her feet. Aaron watched her for a minute, and his heart went out to her. *She's easily less than half my age,* he thought sadly, *and she's stuck like this, same as me*. Then he felt ashamed of himself. He had wanted more food to satisfy his snarling stomach, and this little girl was sitting there, all alone.

Aaron went over to her and sat down. He considered asking if she were alright, but as she obviously wasn't—none of them were—he merely sat in silence, placing a hand on her shoulder.

"I'm c-cold and I'm h-h-hungry, and I m-miss M-mommy and D-daddy, and I want to g-g-go home!" the girl burst out.

Aaron removed his cloak and draped it around her quivering shoulders. "Where are Mommy and Daddy?"

"T-they were k-k-killed in the b-battle, and I-I've been all a-alone ever since!" she wailed.

Aaron set down his bowl and put an arm around the girl.

"What's your name?" he asked.

"Auri," she replied in a quivering voice.

"Well, Auri, you just wait," he said encouragingly. "You wait until we reclaim Castram, and there'll be trumpets, and flags, and cobblestone streets, and a big palace, and as much food as you can eat!"

Auri smiled briefly, but then began crying again. "I'm h-hungry."

"Here." With a supreme effort, Aaron picked up his bowl and pressed it into her hands. "You need it more than I do."

Aaron, trying to ignore the gnawing hunger inside him, watched her devour the stew. He looked up and saw Kellaoth watching him. She smiled approvingly, and he smiled back.

In another part of the camp, he could see Buky and Deecal sitting on either side of a little Elf boy, who was also crying. Buky looked up at Aaron and the girl and winked. Aaron winked back.

Then Aaron noticed Laza, who was standing beside the large black pot of stew, which was already half empty. Laza gestured Aaron over to him. Aaron glanced down at Auri, gave her shoulders a little squeeze, and walked over to Laza. "What is it?"

"The food supply," said Laza, looking worried. "We're running out fast. I don't think we can make it to Muln."

Aaron thought for a long time. He tripped over his tongue several times before he forced it to say, "Put us humans on half ration." That hurt. It really hurt him badly. "And the adult Elves, too. But keep the children on full ration," he added. "They're barely surviving as it is."

As Laza scurried away to tell the cooks, Jack approached. "Aaron, I don't think we're going to make it."

Aaron's stomach rumbled. "Just keep praying," he said.

The journey was a hard one; stumbling over rocks and potholes in the old road, barely able to see where they were going. No one spoke to anyone else, too busy listening to the growling of their stomachs and having wistful fantasies of roast boars on silver platters, horns full of fruit, goblets full of rich drink—instead of bitter stream water and various plants, squirrel and snake meat, an occasional fox or wolf if they could catch one. Everyone was yearning to reach Muln, where they could buy some supplies.

At last, they topped a little hill and looked at the city down below.

"Muln…" said Kellaoth.

"Heres's what needs to be happened," said Laza. "We need snacks, and therees noway that Aaron or Jack could buy all of that without attracting suspicions. So you'llee go down theere one by one, and each buy soma da stuff. After a few trips, we should have enough. Me would go, but people might stare, and

Me hates being stared at."

Everybody laughed.

Jack looked at Aaron. "D'you want to go first, or should I?"

Aaron, having ridden on Kellaoth's back part of the way, felt a little more rested, so he volunteered to go first.

Fifteen minutes later Aaron was wearing an old brown tunic and travel-worn cloak, clutching a walking stick.

"Do you remember what you are to do?" asked Kellaoth for the fifth time.

"Yes," said Aaron for the fifth time (speaking in the tongue used by Men in Acklyon). "Find a butchery, buy ten pounds of venison, then head to the market and get three dozen loaves of pie." Pie is a hard, flat cake of meal, similar to hardtack. "I won't talk to any strangers, and I'll come straight back when I'm done."

"Very good," said Kellaoth. "And remember, don't say *anything* in Elfish, or anything even remotely sounding Elfish."

"I'll be fine, Kellaoth," said Aaron, a little irritated. "It can't go too wrong, can it?" Kellaoth was beginning to remind him of his mother.

"Well, don't take any chances," Kellaoth said.

"I won't," said Aaron and started down the hill towards Muln.

The money system in Acklyon is different than anything in the Third World. Instead of using coins or bills or checks, the Acklyonians use gems of varying sizes. Jewels and precious metals such as gold, diamond, and silver are more common in Acklyon then in the Third World, so they are less valuable. There are five different gems used for money in Acklyon. Rubies have the lowest value. A one-inch ruby is worth about one dollar.

Emeralds are worth about twice as much as rubies, and silver is worth three times as much as emeralds. One gold nugget is about the same as two-and-a-half blocks of silver, and diamond, the most valuable, is worth two gold nuggets. With a one-inch ruby, you can buy a piece of candy from the candy store, and with a three-inch diamond, you could buy a horse. The bigger the gem, the greater its value. Most Acklyonians carry a large purse with them, full of varying sizes of jewels.

As Aaron walked down Market Street, he saw that Malvadore's shadow had just about ruined what had clearly once been a happy town. Many stores were boarded up, and very few people were out and about.

As he turned onto the next corner, he found a boy about his own age, standing at the corner selling newspapers.

Wondering what might be in an Acklyonian newspaper, Aaron walked over to the boy, fishing a half-inch ruby out of his pocket as he went. Remembering not to talk to strangers, he silently handed over his ruby, and the boy, equally silent, gave him a paper.

As Aaron walked away, he could feel the boy's eyes on him. He realized how conspicuous he looked, strolling downtown alone. Trying to keep himself from worrying, he looked down at his newspaper, the *Daily Messenger*. His mouth dropped open in horror as he stared down at the front page:

ELVES SIGHTED NEAR MULN!

Aaron swallowed and read the article beneath it.

Last winter, Elves were discovered living in Eldorlorne, the old forest twenty leagues northwest of Muln. The Gertulk assaulted the forest and burned it to the ground, but most of the Elves escaped and are now on the run.

Accompanying the Elves is a Melsob (Unicorn, as Elves call it) with deadly powers. These Elves are highly dangerous, and any persons who encounter them should report to the local Gertulk immediately.

With these Elves are two boys who claim to be the real Adinyrom Forahn and Jahkon Parnor. It is the king's belief that these individuals will attempt to overthrow his rule. This possibly insane group has been sighted near Muln, and all villagers should remain indoors as much as possible. Villagers should be on the watch for suspicious characters, for this group may attack Muln.

Madame Adrian, a local resident, is an eyewitness to an attempted Elf attack. "I saw a smallish man," she said to our reporter, "barely three feet tall lurking over the bank. He carried a sword and was trying to break through the roof. He looked up and saw me. I was about to call for help, and he vanished!"

You are advised to watch closely for any other thefts, but do not take unnecessary risks. If you should gain any information about the whereabouts of this group, you are advised to tell local Black Warriors immediately.

Aaron didn't finish the article. He felt sick. So this was why nobody else was out. Malvadore had clearly taken over the press, and now he was turning everyone against the Elves. He was creating a story that the Elves were bandits or rogues, cut-throats who should be killed on sight. There had been no Elf attack on the bank, and Aaron seriously doubted that Madame Adrian even existed.

Aaron suddenly realized the full danger of his situation as he saw a drawing of himself on the front page of the paper. If he were discovered—he didn't want to think about that. Raising his hood higher over his head, he broke into a run, streaking down Market Street and taking dead aim for the butchery. He had suddenly become aware of every little sound, imagining Gertulk spilling out of doorways, pikes pointed at him. He nearly fell over in fear when a caged parrot next door to the butchery gave a loud squawk.

He stopped once he was close enough for the butcher to see him through the window and slowed his pace to a casual lope. Before entering the shop, he pitched the newspaper into the gutter; the only reason he could think of for a villager to be out shopping alone with Elves running loose was that he hadn't heard the news.

He strolled inside, causing the bell above the door to tinkle. He walked up to the counter and leaned against it, looking around for the butcher. At last, the butcher came from the back room, wiping his hands on his apron. A large, beefy man, he had a fairly unfriendly look about him with coarse black eyebrows, small, beady eyes, a thick beard, and little hair. He cast Aaron a suspicious look, eyeing him up and down. "What brings you out and about at times like this?" he grunted.

"I'm passing through," Aaron recited. "My parents and I are traveling to Colten, where my father is going to join the army."

"Why are you not traveling with a caravan?"

"Well," said Aaron, a little too quickly. "We can't find any that are heading for Colten. Nobody seems to want to travel these days."

"And for a very good reason," growled the butcher.

"What reason?" Aaron asked politely.

"Yeh haven't heard?" The butcher slapped a copy of the *Daily Messenger* onto the counter.

Aaron picked it up, scanned the familiar article, and put on a show of surprise. "*Elves*?" he said. "Elves near here? Oh my gosh, I thought they were extinct!"

"Aye," said the butcher. "There's lots 'oo'd like to believe that they're extinct, but 'ere they are."

"And two imposters, pretending to be the kings?" said Aaron, pretending to peruse the article.

"Scary, in' it?" said the butcher. "You watch yourself, boy. I'd say that the one who's being King Adinyrom, I'd say he's about your height and build, probably around your age, too—"

"Well, I'd better buy my stuff and go tell my parents," said Aaron quickly, wanting to change the subject before the butcher became suspicious. "Let's see…I need ten pounds of venison, please."

The butcher wrapped up the meat, put it in a sack, and shoved it toward Aaron, saying, "That'll be one inch of diamond."

Aaron pulled out his money, sifted through it, and placed three three-inch emeralds and one three-inch silver coin on the counter. The butcher studied the money. "Yer about an inch of silver too much, lad."

Aaron counted the money and saw the butcher was right. He looked through his money again, searching for a two-inch silver coin to replace the three-inch. His hands were shaking as he fumbled with the drawstrings, so much that the purse slipped through his fingers, showering the wood floor with gems and coins. "Bickeroo!" Aaron hissed as he scrambled to collect his money.

The butcher stared at him. "What did you just say?"

Aaron stood up, realizing with horror that he had just sworn in Elfish. "Nothing," he said quickly, but the butcher was still suspicious.

"It sounded like 'bickeroo'? Is that some kind o' new swear word?"

"Sort of," said Aaron, grateful that he had not noticed it was Elfish. "It's kind of a Tackers family joke."

"Tackers family?"

Aaron remembered, too late, that only people of nobility have last names in Acklyon. "Uh, well, Tackers is…is what we call ourselves, it's kind of another inside joke."

"Oh, really?"

"Yes, well, I'd better get going. Bye!" Aaron walked as fast as he could without appearing conspicuous, even though the butcher was already suspicious. As Aaron moved briskly to the door, he stumbled on the edge of his cloak, and his hood fell. He whirled around, his proud green eyes, his straight nose, and his light brown hair exposed.

The butcher stared at him for a good ten seconds, and bellowed like a rhinoceros. The heavy man heaved a massive, Gertulk-style axe from below the counter and rushed Aaron, yelling, "MURDERER! TRAITOR! IMPOSTER!"

He knows! Aaron thought as his hand flew to his sword hilt.

Looking back, Aaron never really remembered what happened from there. He had vague flashes of seeing a grown man that looked like a Gertulk barreling towards him with an axe upraised, a mad struggle with the red-faced butcher, and then standing there, holding a bloody sword in his hand, and a dead butcher, viciously slashed across the chest, at his feet.

Aaron stared down, appalled at what he had done. He had just killed a man!

However, he had little time to brood over it, for he could hear the sound of footsteps growing louder and louder. Immediately, a gear in his mind clicked into place and he began flying around the room, altering the evidence. As he dragged the dead butcher behind the counter, his thoughts were racing. How could he excuse the dead body? His eyes fell on the axe. It was made for a Gertulk, no doubt, and that set his mind working. He seized the weapon, and gritting his teeth, swung it overhead and struck the butcher with it, shuddering as he felt the blade make contact. With any luck, this would make it appear that a Gertulk had killed the man, thus turning the townsfolk against the Black Warriors.

He also snatched up his purse from the floor, raking the money back into it and stuffing the meat within the folds of his cloak. With this done, he sprinted for the back door, hoping against hope that he could make it before the people got there.

Too late.

Just as Aaron's hand closed around the doorknob, the front door burst open. There stood twenty or so peasants, staring around for the source of the commotion. Aaron only barely had time to raise his hood again.

"What's going on?" one elderly man said.

"Orkus!" shouted another.

One man rushed over to the counter and examined the body. "'Ere, look! Those confounded Gertulk killed Orkus! I told you they couldn't be trusted!"

"Shh!" hissed a woman. "Not so loud, Sammel. There's some of them just outside!"

"I don't think they done it," said an old man, examining the body. "This looks like false evidence to me!"

"What makes you say that?"

"See how narrow and fine that cut is? No heavy axe could accomplish that. It was done by a light weapon, a sword, probably. Someone did this to cover up!"

None of the townsfolk had noticed Aaron, who was standing by the door, too stunned to move.

"You don't reckon it was—was them *Elves*, do you, Rallen?"

"More than likely," said Rallen. "Or else—" He noticed

Aaron, who immediately felt a rush of fear. "You! Boy!

"Y-yes sir?" Aaron stammered.

"Did you see who did this?"

"N-no sir. I—I came to buy some meat, but when I got here, the butcher was dead!"

"You sure?"

"Oh, leave him be, Rallen!" said the woman, who came bustling out of the crowd and put an arm around Aaron. "The boy's frightened! Who wouldn't be, in his shoes? Are you all right, boy?"

"Yes ma'am," said Aaron, thanking heaven that she was on his right side, not his left where his sword was hidden. If they found Anvilad, they would know for sure that he'd done it.

"You don't reckon *he* did it, Narra?"

"Think, man, think! He's just a boy! Do you really think he could have done something like this? You were in the war too long, Rallen. But where are your parents, lad?" said the woman, whose name seemed to be Narra.

As Aaron tried to think of a good cover story, he noticed something that made his mouth drop open. A face was in the window, a small red-headed face, which was peering around and studying the shop. Laza stared at Aaron, at Narra, at Rallen, and then at the dead butcher. His eyes rolled up in his head in irritation, and then he raised both eyebrows, pointed his nose at Aaron, and twitched his ears. The message, in Elfish sign language, was, *What did you get yourself into this time?*

Aaron twitched his right ear, darted his eyes right to left, and rolled his eyes five times, tapping his foot with each turn. *It's hard to explain. Help me!*

Laza sighed and signaled, *Tell them that the Gertulk captured your parents under charges for suspicious behavior. And you won't go to the orphanage, so you're trying to live on your own. And quit staring at the window, numbskull! They're noticing!*

Aaron snapped his head around to the crowd and repeated Laza's story, feeling a strong sense of *déjà vu*, remembering Brotchurd's company questioning him in Eldorlorne.

"You're trying to live on your own in these dangerous times?"

"Well—"

"You men do what you can," said Narra. "I'm taking this boy to my house. He looks like he could use a few square meals. Good day." She marched Aaron towards the door.

Aaron twitched his eyebrows once, tapped his own leg, and twitched his ears: *What do I do now?*

Laza replied, *It's okay. Stay with her and don't be afraid.*

What are you, crazy?

Trust me! I know what I'm doing. Just stay calm, don't goof off, and avoid looking like an idiot. Ta ta!

Laza spoke lightly, but, in truth, he really was worried. What would they do now? Aaron was incognito as an orphan boy who was living on his own. He and Laza were trapped in Muln, and Laza's capture would mean his and the other Elves' death.

He merely thanked the Lord for allowing Narra to get Aaron before the Gertulk did.

Though Aaron wasn't aware of it, Laza knew Narra. She and her husband had been helping the Elves survive for a long time, and she had no doubt been keeping an eye out for the first sign of odd movement in Muln. He would have to thank her later.

Even though they were safe for the moment—Narra being a respected member of the town—they needed to get out of Muln, and fast. No matter how he looked at it, they were in a huge mess. He had no way to warn Kellaoth, and the Gertulk were likely to put Muln under curfew due to the murder. This was about as fine a pickle as he had ever seen. If he got caught, he and the others were doomed. If Aaron was uncloaked, then it would mean certain death. If only Laza could contact the others…

"Three rubies a pie! Three rubies a pie!"

Laza jumped three feet into the air, did a back flip, and drew his sword all in one motion, squinting around for who had spoken.

His eyes fell on the parrot in its cage, sitting on the windowsill of a nearby house.

He smiled.

Narra led Aaron outside and down the street with Aaron trying to walk as evenly as he could. He clutched his sword under the cloak, trying to keep it from swinging. His mind was whirling with panic, wondering what he was going to do. He would have to escape from Narra's house, which probably wouldn't be easy. His only feeling of comfort was that Laza had seen the whole thing and could hopefully hatch a plan with the others to save him.

"Guys, we're in a *huuuuuuuuuuge* mess!" Deecal charged into camp, carrying the parrot on his shoulder, his eyes wide with fear.

"What has happened?" cried Kellaoth urgently.

"Aaron and Laza are in double trouble!"

"*What*?" shouted Jack, hurrying.

"Here." Deecal set the parrot on the ground and the bird croaked, "Message from Laza! Message from Laza! Aaron and I are trapped in Muln! Aaron and I are trapped in Muln! Aaron got in a scuffle, killed a butcher, and Narra took him in! You need to save us! You need save us! Fly to the nearest Magical source!"

"The bonehead!" fumed Piki. "I *told* yous, Kellaoth, that you could've found some other pair of nuts that would have done much better! How could Aaron've got himself caught? Well, now what?"

"If we doesn't do something fast, Jack could very well have to be King of Fortilly, as well as Parland! Not to mention we'll need a new Captain of the Elves," said Wrinky.

"Don't panic!" said Jack. "Here's what we need to do. I'll go down to Muln, find out where this Narra lives, go to her house, and get him out of there. Laza can sneak out with us. If they have any sense at all—"

"—which they don't—" Piki added in.

"—they'll play along, and we can leave!"

"I don't know if it will work," said Kellaoth uncertainly, "but it is the best plan we have. Remember, keep your hood up, your head down, and don't talk to strangers."

"And don't be an idiot," Piki put in. "Remember, the fate of Acklyon is in your hands, so no pressure."

But it was only half an hour before Jack returned, and when he did, they could all see that something was wrong. His cloak was torn, his face and clothes were splattered with blood, and he carried Sorving in one hand. The sword, too, was bloodstained. His face was sweaty, he had a wound on his shoulder, and Aaron wasn't with him.

"What happened?" asked Buky.

"Things didn't go quite as I expected. Apparently, as I overheard by the gate, some butcher, Orkus, was murdered, so the Gertulk have shut all the gates and are conducting a full investigation. That'll be the butcher Laza mentioned in his message. No one is allowed in or out of Muln until the authorities catch the culprit. The two of them that were guarding the main gate, they kept asking me funny questions. I guess I looked pretty suspicious, out there all by myself. Well, one of them asked if I'd seen any Elves around, and right then, I understood he knew who I was. I ran, and they followed. I killed one of them, but the other escaped."

"That is not good," said Kellaoth, looking concerned. "You're sure they knew who you were?"

"Definitely," said Jack. "I could see it in their eyes...also in the fact that they drew their swords and starting chasing me."

"Could Aaron and Laza sneak out at night?" suggested Buky.

"Nope," said Jack. "Muln's under curfew. Everyone must be indoors before sunset and can't leave until daybreak."

"So this has to be a day job," said Piki slyly.

Kellaoth whistled and chirped, and the parrot hopped onto her shoulder. "I will take this beast and train it to send a message to Laza. This will not be easy."

"You know, you really don't have to do this."

Narra led Aaron upstairs and showed him a small bedroom. She had rejected his every insistence that he was perfectly willing to make his own life. "This shall be your bedroom, at least for the moment. The less the other townsfolk see you, the better," she said as she straightened the blanket on the bed.

You don't know the half of it, Aaron thought grimly.

"The bathroom is down the hall," said Narra as she left. "Dinner is at seven—you'll want to wash up before then."

"Okay."

Narra left the room, closing the door behind her.

Once she'd left, Aaron automatically looked at his watch—before he remembered that his watch had gone haywire when he came to Acklyon. He looked outside, where the sun was dropping below the horizon. *Drat,* He thought. *Curfew's activated, I can't leave tonight.*

At that moment, he heard a rustling sound outside his window. He turned and saw a freckled face waving at him. Aaron sprinted to the window and opened it, and Laza jumped inside.

"Laza!" whispered Aaron. "How did you get here?"

"I followed youee," said Laza. "So what did you get yournself into this time?"

Aaron explained about the butcher.

"Great," said Laza. "Yourn first mission, and you blow it like a balloon."

"Never mind that," said Aaron. "How are we going to get out?"

Laza shrugged. "I sended a messssage to Kellaoth, so our friendses our working on an escape plan."

Aaron and Laza spent the next two hours discussing how to get out.

"If we can just get the Gertulk away from the gate, maybe we can open it and flee," Aaron pointed out.

"But how are us supposing to do dat?" said Laza.

"I don't know," said Aaron. "Maybe Kellaoth could put a spell on them?"

"Nup," said Laza gloomily. "'Tis part of the Sixical World contract, dey can sense Fifth-Worldy Magic."

"Wait a minute," said Aaron as an idea occurred to him. "Why do we have to sneak our way out? Why can't we get the townsfolk's help?"

"Remember what the last guy who figgered you out did?" said Laza shrewdly.

Aaron shuddered at the memory of killing the butcher.

A knock at the door and Narra's voice interrupted further planning. "Aaron? Dinner is ready!"

Aaron seized Laza by the scruff of his neck, the way he would have done with a cat, and threw him under the bed—and just in time, too. Narra opened the door a second later. Aaron instinctively grabbed his sword under his cloak and released it again.

"Aaron, dinner's on the table," she said.

"Right," said Aaron. He glanced underneath the bed, where he could just see Laza's flickering eyes in the darkness. He briefly puffed up his cheeks with air, telling Laza to wait until he returned. He thought he saw Laza roll his eyes, but whether in irritation or telling him to hurry, he couldn't tell.

After stopping in the bathroom to wash his hands (he kept his face dirty, for fear of recognition), he followed Narra downstairs. "We'll be eating in the cellar," she said.

Aaron raised on eyebrow. "The cellar?" His hand closed around his sword hilt.

"My husband," Narra explained, "is an outlaw. He was once part of Malvadore's army, but Elves attacked his platoon, and he escaped to live with me again."

"And why are you telling me this?" asked Aaron. After all, if he had been anything less than a devoted rebel, her life would have been shortened to the length the time it would take him to contact the Gertulk.

"Because Laza told me who you are."

Aaron jumped. How could she possibly know Laza?

Narra noticed. "Come now," she said patiently. "I know your name."

Aaron's sword was halfway out of his sheath before he figured it out. "You're a rebel," he said in amazement.

Narra nodded. "My husband and I have long worked against

Malvadore. Recently, we've had to give up helping the country, for now that my husband's home, we cannot draw any attention to ourselves lest he be caught."

"And you're telling me," Aaron said slowly, "that you and Laza are in cahoots. And that you know who I am, and where I'm going."

"Yes." She smiled. "You are Adinyrom Forahn II of Fortilly. You and the Elves of Eldorlorne are traveling to Castram to reclaim it and thus begin the Rebellion."

"Describe Laza," he said as a precaution.

"Buoyant," said Narra. "Always cheerful. He's been in charge of Eldorlorne since the last leader died. He's close friends with Kellaoth. He and Buky have a crush on each other. He knows how to sing through his nose."

"That's Laza," said Aaron, then he caught himself. "I'm not saying I trust you."

"I understand," said Narra, smiling. "I think when you see my husband, you'll understand."

They had reached the door.

"If you're really on my side, you won't mind if I pull out my sword before I walk in there," Aaron said cautiously. Narra smiled and nodded. Aaron tugged his sword out of its scabbard. "You go first."

When Narra stepped through and vanished from view, Aaron crept slowly through the door, all his senses on edge.

They passed down the stairs and into the cellar. There was her husband, sitting at the table and eyeing a pot full of delicious stew. Aaron's stomach screamed so forcefully in protest when it saw the stew that Aaron almost made a dash for it.

The man was tall and powerfully built with a scrubby brown beard covering his mouth and cheeks. Aaron had to look twice before he realized that he knew the man. His sword clattered to the ground as his mouth dropped open in shock.

"Brotchurd!"

17
The Return of Brotchurd

Brotchurd stood up. "Hello, sire."

Narra was beaming, looking between the two of them.

"Wha—how—?" Aaron looked at Narra. "Brotchurd is your husband?" he said incredulously, astounded by this coincidence.

Brotchurd nodded. "Laza sent word that we were likely to run into you. As such, Narra volunteered to scout the area, pretending to be shopping."

"It was a good thing, too," Narra added. "If I hadn't, you would likely be in captivity right now."

It all fit into place in Aaron's mind; Brotchurd had been forced to serve the Mulnian Garrison. After the Elves killed Brotchurd's platoon, he returned to Narra. Narra hid him in the cellar.

That also explained why Laza had told Aaron to go with Narra—because he knew Aaron would be safest at their house. It was also the reason that Narra had insisted on bringing him back to her house in the first place, defending him from the accusations of being the murderer. The answers to questions that had been nagging Aaron were now uncovered. Brotchurd had killed one of his own men to save Aaron and Jack because Brotchurd knew who they were. Aaron sank into a chair as mystery after mystery revealed itself through this one bit of knowledge.

Narra walked over to Aaron's sword, still on the ground, picked it up, and examined the bloodstains on it. "You really did kill him?" she asked.

Aaron nodded. "I tripped and my hood slipped. He saw my face and figured out who I was. He attacked me and almost killed me. I had no choice." His throat constricted as he remembered the fight, how the butcher had swung overhead, how Aaron had ducked, rolled, leapt up and slashed across the butcher's chest. How the butcher had staggered, his hands scrabbling at the wound. The lights had left his eyes then as he glared up at Aaron with a snarl…

"Of course you had no choice!" said Narra. "I know Orkus. He loves Malvadore, perhaps more than anyone in Muln. He spent years in the army and is responsible for the deaths of many an Elf."

"Orkus was the one who died?" asked Brotchurd. A shadow crossed over his face, and he kneaded his palm with his fist. "No less than he deserved. If you ask me, being cut down by the Prince of Fortilly was a fitting end for him."

At the phrase *Prince of Fortilly*, something snapped in Aaron's mind. A surge of panic swept through his body at the sound of it.

Without warning, Aaron sprang to his feet, snatched Anvilad from Narra's hands, and sprinted to the staircase. He stood in front of it and pointed his sword's tip at Brotchurd and Narra. "Don't come near me, or I'll stick you!" he shouted feverishly.

Brotchurd smiled. "My liege, you are mistaken. Long have Narra and I yearned for the day that justice would once more rule Acklyon. Laza and his company are not the first Elves we have seen. For a time, we housed an underground sanctuary for renegade Elves—until the Gertulk began to get suspicious, and we had to close down. I was forced to join the army, due to laws set up by the False King—but escaped when your friends conveniently slaughtered the rest of my company."

"It wasn't so convenient for us," said Aaron. "Gertulk burned Eldorlorne to the ground, taking many Elves with it. Look at this!"—he shook back his sleeve to reveal an arm covered in bruises, scars, and burns—"We've been on the move ever since, running from the Gertulk. Supplies are low, we need food. I had to come here to buy supplies, but I was discovered. If Narra hadn't taken me in, I'd be on my way to Rarzan right now."

"Your tale is one of sorrow, my Prince."

"It's the tale I'm stuck with until I meet my maker, which could happen any day now."

"Well," said Brotchurd, "the thing is, how do we get you out of here? Gertulk have barred the gate, and no one is allowed to enter or exit Muln."

"I have a feeling that we won't be alone," said Aaron.

"We've got work to do," said Jack. "We need to find out how to smuggle Aaron and Laza out of Muln without alerting the Gertulk."

"We just need to get the gate open," said Buky. "Then they can sneak out."

"Did you say that when you went to the gate, *both* Gertulk chased you?" said Piki suddenly.

"Yeah," said Jack. "Are you saying—"

"You go to the main gate and get the Gertulk to chase you," Piki explained. "We'll ambush them, steal their keys, open the gate, grab Aaron, and get out!"

"No," said Kellaoth heavily. "We must not kill any Gertulk or open the main gate; that would draw too much attention. No, we must find a back way in."

"Every entrance will be guarded," Buky pointed out.

"Then over a wall," said Jack.

"Gertulk patrol them day and night," said Wrinky.

"So we dig a tunnel!" said Piki. "We can't go over, around, or through the walls, so we go under them!"

"That would take too long," said Dinky. "It could be weeks before we could dig a proper tunnel, and we don't have time."

"Kellaoth could Invisiblize herself and them and fly them out," suggested Piki.

"Gertulk can sense Magic," said Kellaoth. "They would know I was there."

"Then what is we doin'?" asked Buky.

"I don't know," said Jack, "but it needs to be quick. Gertulk will be swarming these hills soon looking for me."

"Methinks we need to get 'em out from the inside," said Deecal. "Lazee can sneak past the guards and steal deir keys without them lookin', and Aaron can slip out when da guards change or somat."

"I will take Nimbun, and we can meet Aaron and Laza outside the wall and fly them back to camp," said Kellaoth. "Once they're out, we'll need to get them out of sight as soon as possible."

18
Escape

Via the parrot, Laza and Kellaoth plotted the details of getting the Elf and Aaron out of Muln unnoticed.

Soon they developed the entire plan and were ready to put it into action. They would do it around four o'clock in the afternoon, just before curfew was activated. Narra and Brotchurd were to help, too. Narra would rush into town, shrieking that she'd seen Elves running to the west (the exact opposite direction the real Elves were heading). This would send most of the Gertulk into a pointless search of the western horizon, emptying the city of all but a few soldiers.

Then, they would find the least guarded, most hidden exit. Laza would slip past the guards, steal their keys, and sneak outside. Then Brotchurd, at a safe distance, would lure the Gertulk away from the door. Laza would then open the door from the outside, and Aaron would slip out. Unfortunately, Aaron only had the ten pounds of venison from the butcher and Narra had loaded his pack with provisions, but it wasn't nearly enough to last them until they reached Castram. They didn't dare steal what they needed from a store nearby because if they were caught, they were dead. Besides, Aaron couldn't afford to be loaded down with food when he escaped. He needed to move quickly.

Minutes before they were to put their plan into action, Aaron went down to the cellar to check that Brotchurd was ready. To Aaron's surprise, he found Brotchurd waiting for him at the foot of the stairs. He had a big, wood-framed pack on his back, and a sword hung at his side.

"You're coming with me?" said Aaron.

"Aye," said Brotchurd. "Narra and I discussed it last night; there's nothing more we can do to help these people. The Gertulk are suspicious of us anyway, and they'll be arresting us any day now. We're going to Castram."

Aaron's heart leaped with joy. It would be wonderful to have some company of his own species, apart from Jack; to have a strong warrior in battle, not these scampering Elves; to have someone to show them that not every Man in Acklyon thought him a murderer and imposter.

Four o'clock came, and they began. Aaron, Laza, Brotchurd, and Narra slipped out of the house in the growing twilight and hid in the alley.

"Go, Narra," whispered Brotchurd.

"Do your stuff," hissed Aaron.

Narra closed her eyes for a minute, opened them, and crept away. She stationed herself underneath one of the towers and glanced back at the others, who all nodded encouragingly. She took a deep breath, filled her lungs, and let out a long, piercing scream.

Immediately, things began to happen. Heads poked out of windows, staring around for the source. The few people outside—children playing in their yards or mothers heading to the grocery store—charged back to the sanctuary of their porches. Listless, half-asleep Gertulk and town guards sprang to life as Narra went flying down Main Street, still screaming at the top of her lungs. "ELVES!" she was crying, "ELVES! MELSOB! MURDER! WE'RE ALL GOING TO DIE!"

"She's good," said Aaron, impressed, watching as she stumbled, fell, and kept running, her eyes wide with terror.

The chief Gertulk rushed up to her. "What's wrong?" he demanded.

"E-Elves!" Narra gasped, clutching a stitch in her side. "I saw them—saw them running to the west—hundreds of them! I-I think they're going to attack the capital. If you hurry, you can probably catch them!"

The Gertulk didn't waste time asking questions. He threw back his head and let out a great, bull-like roar that shook the town. Gertulk, dressed in black armor, and the town guards, dressed in silver chain mail and red tunics, poured out of guardhouses and off of walls. The main gate opened, and they went charging out and to the west.

The moment they were out of eyesight, Narra made her way back to the alley.

"Nice job," said Aaron.

"Thanks," she panted. "Come on, we don't have long."

They sneaked over to the east wall where they found a small door leading to the outside. Only two Gertulk were guarding it.

"Okay, Laza, your turn," Brotchurd whispered.

Silent as death, Laza stood up and began creeping through the shadows.

He walked right in front of the Gertulk and stopped in between them. It was funny to watch; a renegade Elf was standing between these two Gertulk, and they had no idea.

Slowly, Laza crept around behind one of the Gertulk and very quietly slipped a big metal key off of its hook on the beast's belt. The Gertulk never saw it. Laza silently placed the key in the lock and turned it. Fortunately, the door was well oiled, so when Laza opened it, it made not a sound. Unbelievably, Laza slipped out the door and closed it again without the Gertulk even noticing.

"Your turn, Aaron," whispered Brotchurd.

Aaron also got up and tiptoed away. Soon, they heard the sounds of someone moving about and then whispering in a high-pitched voice. The Gertulk stiffened.

"What was that?" one said.

"I dunno," said the other. "I'll check it out." and he stalked away in pursuit of the troublemaker.

Brotchurd picked up a stone off the ground and threw it in the other direction, causing it to clatter in the alley. The last Gertulk paused, glanced back at the door, and muttered, "Oh, what the heck," and crept off towards the sound.

Seconds later, Aaron returned.

"Okay, now!" he said, and the three of them made a dash for the door.

"OY, YOU!"

Aaron's heart stopped dead in his chest. Both Gertulk were pounding down the alley back to the door, each with drawn swords. Aaron and Brotchurd also drew their swords and attacked.

Aaron darted around one of them and stabbed it in the back as Brotchurd hacked off the other's sword arm and ran him through.

But it was too late. Townsfolk were running toward the sounds of the commotion. Aaron caught Brotchurd by the shoulder.

"Find Narra and get back to your house," Aaron said. "Leave this to me."

"No!" said Brotchurd. "We're going with you!"

"Brotchurd, listen to me," Aaron pleaded. "These people will try to arrest us—if they see you with me, you'll be in more trouble than you've ever been in your entire life! I'm already a fugitive, but you still can still go back to being a villager!"

"Alright," said Brotchurd. "Good luck, my Prince."

He grabbed Narra's hand, and the two disappeared into the crowd now pushing around Aaron. The mob would have carried Aaron off, but the boy managed to hold them back with wild swings of his sword.

"Say! You're the one in Orkus's shop, aren't you?" said the elderly man, Rallen. "Oi! This boy is the one 'oo murdered the butcher!"

"I had no choice!" shouted Aaron. "He attacked me!"

"And with good reason," one women jeered. "Imposter!"

"I am NOT an imposter!" cried Aaron. "Malvadore has hoodwinked you! Your King Adinyrom isn't the real one. I am!"

The crowd laughed at that.

"King Adinyrom was your age an 'undred years ago!" one man shouted.

"It's because of a time slip," Aaron tried to explain. "I've been in the Third World for thirteen years while it's been a hundred here!"

No one believed him. No one ever would. The throng had surrounded him. He couldn't reach the door.

"Listen to me, all of you!" he yelled in desperation. "I can help!"

"You're not the true king!" someone said. "You can't help us!"

"Yes I can!" Aaron replied. "I'm on my way to Castram to reclaim it. If I had your trust, we could overthrow Malvadore!"

"Or get pulverized!" another person shouted. "No one can kill a Kane!"

Aaron had begun easing toward the door in hopes that he

could make it out before the Gertulk came back. But the townsfolk, seeing this, pushed harder around him, blocking him from the door.

"Don't let 'eem get away!" shouted one man.

"Someone call the Gertulk!" another shouted.

Aaron gave up all attempts at reasoning. Now, all he could do was get to the door. He raised his sword over his head, unleashed a bloody war cry, and charged. He never intended to harm any of them, and he never did. But his sudden attack was enough to send them scattering, giving him access to the exit. He fumbled with the latch, flung it open, and galloped outside. He flew past Laza, yelling "RUN! RUN! THEY'RE RIGHT BEHIND ME!"

The moment Aaron was outside, Kellaoth swooped out of the sky, snatched him up in her claws, and flew back towards the Elf camp. Out of the corner of his eye, Aaron saw Laza leaping onto Nimbun's back. The Elf sentries saw them fleeing from Muln in the night and hastened to pack up all their belongings. Once the four of them had reached camp, they could see Gertulk rallying and stamping across the lawn like an army of black widow spiders. The Elves fled, shooting into the night, holding hands to keep from getting separated, stumbling over rabbit holes.

Soon, the cries of the Gertulk faded into the distance. Only then did the Elves stop to rest. Aaron wasn't sure if it he were imagining it, but he thought he saw many of them giving him resentful looks.

19

In Desperate Times

The fiasco in Muln led to much unhappiness among the group, most of which was caused by the fact that they had only gotten one package of meat from it.

"You coulda at least nabbed a few more bundles of stuff on your way out," grumbled Stinky one day as they made camp.

"Well, what was I supposed to do?" demanded Aaron hotly. "I never had a chance to get more food! Laza was the one who had run of the town while I was locked up at Narra's! If you want to blame someone, blame *him*!"

"Don't look at me!" said Laza angrily. "I was trying to get us outta there! You were supposed to get da food!"

"Well, in case you hadn't noticed," Aaron retorted, "*you* were the one who was in a position to steal some food while *I* was undercover!"

"None of this would've happen if *you* hadn't got yerself caught!" shouted Laza. "*Again*!"

Aaron was about to reply that it was because of Laza and the other stupid Elves that Aaron and Jack were there—and that they would be perfectly happy to leave—when he glanced at Kellaoth and saw her giving him a silencing look. Aaron scowled, but said no more.

Though outbursts such as these were rare, and though the Elves all did their best to hide it, Aaron could see that they were becoming discontented with putting up with Aaron and Jack. *And with good reason,* he thought miserably. *Face it. We got caught in Eldorlorne, which led to the attack and destruction of Eldorlorne and of them being stuck on low ration out here in the wild. Then I muffed it in Muln, nearly getting myself caught, and failed to get them some food. And what have we done in return? It's just good we're with Elves and not Men... They'd have kicked us out long ago.*

Another painful thought in Aaron's mind was Brotchurd and Narra. He had come that close to having an adult by his side day and night. He wondered what had happened to them. Had they successfully slipped back to their house and hidden themselves again? Had the crowd noticed their packs and arrested them? Or had the Gertulk recognized Brotchurd's face and hauled him to jail? Aaron had no idea, and in the end he decided to simply avoid thinking about it, which was a good idea because he had many other problems to contend with—hunger and loneliness being at the top.

Three days later, the caravan witnessed a herd of tricebu—large, triple-horned cows—grazing in a field. According to Laza, tricebu spend most of their time near the water, so the sight of so many so far from the coast was exceptionally rare.

For a moment, it appeared that these beasts would be the answer to their prayers: there were about fifty, maybe more, showing no inclination to run. The travelers could have shot down a couple dozen and been saved—when it all went wrong. Mopee, a young Elfin archer, became so carried away in his hunger that he rushed forward and fired at one of the younger tricebu. Laza cried out a warning, but it was too late. The calf's mother stepped in between the arrow and her child, allowing the projectile to glance off the armor-like plating on her head. Then she charged like a rhinoceros and gored poor Mopee, flinging him into the air with her horns and smashing his corpse into a tree. She and the other tricebu then formed a semi-circle around the youngster and prepared a defense.

"Don't move," said Laza, and for once there was no humor in his voice whatsoever. "If we run, they will charge."

"So what the heck do we do?" cried Aaron.

"Get behind me!" said Kellaoth. The Elves obeyed, bunching together as tightly as possible behind the Unicorn.

Kellaoth gave a feral snarl, daring the tricebu to attack.

The beast did. She pawed the ground, lowered her head and charged again, roaring. Kellaoth leapt into the air and landed behind the beast. The tricebu paused, confused, and Kellaoth slashed the herbivore's flanks with her talons.

The beast howled, turned, and swung her three horns at Kellaoth.

Kellaoth dodged, and in one motion, turned, kicked the tricebu in the back, flipped over her, and landed on the beast's back.

Though the Unicorn was outmatched in size, strength, and number of horns, she was vastly more intelligent and powerful. She began stabbing repeatedly with her single horn, driving down into the beast's neck. The tricebu howled, moaned, and keeled over. The other tricebu began edging back from this new foe. Kellaoth advanced and neighed menacingly, and the tricebu began to retreat.

"Easy," Laza said quietly to the Elves. "Don't make a move, and we should be good. As long as—"

A black quarrel whizzed past him then as a patrol of Gertulk streamed out of the trees.

"Of all the times!" cried Jack in dismay.

Laza dodged the missile, but saw that it had been aimed at Kellaoth. He started to cry out, but he needn't have. Kellaoth reared back and snatched the quarrel out of the air with her talons and hurled back at the Gertulk who had fired, striking him between the eyes.

The Elves drew their weapons and charged the Gertulk, yelling war cries. The tricebu herd, angered by the loud noises, panicked and stampeded. One of them took advantage of Kellaoth's distraction and rammed her, throwing the Unicorn towards the sky. Kellaoth flapped her wings and managed to stay aloft, then dived like a hawk and attacked the beast.

Meanwhile, the rest of the herd had already joined the fight between the Elves and the Gertulk, bludgeoning both sides.

Aaron then noted that the creatures had left their young unprotected and sprinted over to the collection of calves. However, he underestimated them; the calves may not have been mature, but each one was almost as tall as Aaron.

One of the bigger ones rushed forward and collided with Aaron, knocking the boy backwards several feet. He landed and rolled but was unable to prevent himself from being trampled by the young animal.

Aaron staggered to his feet and looked over at the beast, who was preparing to charge again. He drew his knife and hurled it at the animal but missed. The baby tricebu attacked him again, but this time Aaron was able to draw his sword and cut down the creature before it could do him any more harm. He then went after the other dozen or so calves, but they had scattered—so he turned back to the battle.

His heart stopped when he realized that he had drawn the attention of an adult tricebu. He braced himself, holding his sword in front of him. The bull clawed up some earth and roared. Aaron breathed hard and yelled, "Come on then—get it over with!"

The tricebu had just begun to attack when Laza leapt in between them, slashing the beast on the leg. The tricebu howled angrily, threw Laza into the air, and fled into the trees. Aaron rushed over to Laza, who was picking himself up off the ground.

"Are you alright?" Aaron asked.

"Me thinks so," grunted Laza, clutching his ribs.

Aaron glanced around. The tricebu herd had vanished, taking the Gertulk with them. Aaron's heart sank when he saw how many Elves had been killed in the scuffle.

Though they had gotten two grown tricebu and a baby, they had more than paid in lives. The tricebu meat was wonderful, but it did not last long and soon they were back where they had started.

God, Aaron prayed one day, stretched out on his bedroll, *you know what's happening: food is too low, tempers are too high, and I don't think that our unity will last much longer. It's a long way to Castram, and it's impossible for us to make it all the way without so much as a proper meal for any of us. I've done my best, but it isn't enough. Wild animals are scarce in these parts, so hunting's off. Please. Just anything that'll keep us alive until we reach Castram. Thanks.*

Aaron's stomach ached. When had he last had a decent meal? Months, though it felt like years. Images of pizza parlors, all-you-can-eat buffets, and fast-food restaurants filled Aaron's dreams, often punctuated by strange visions of Forvalad, always followed by feelings of emptiness. Whether these were because his stomach was completely empty, or somehow because of Forvalad, Aaron couldn't tell.

* * *

The next day was even worse. Aaron awoke to see Jack kneeling over him. Jack had whispered that Pooka, one of the elders of the tribe, had died in the night. This news added yet more enmity into the camp. Aaron hadn't known Pooka very well, but he had known that Pooka was a close relative to Buky. Now Buky and her family had turned against Aaron and Jack. That was one of the worst things that could happen—Buky was Laza's girlfriend and had a lot of respect in Eldorlorne. If she turned her back on Aaron, then maybe Laza would, too. And the day Laza decided that Aaron and Jack were no longer worth putting up with, Aaron knew, would be the day Aaron died.

But Laza had remained by Aaron's side. He was one of the stronger and more optimistic Elves, and it took more than low food and a few deaths to crush his spirits. Kellaoth also was still loyal to the boys. She was by far the wisest of them all and knew things that the others did not concerning the future. But those two were at the top of the dwindling list of allies Aaron and Jack had in the tribe, and no one needed to tell them that those two might very well become the only ones.

As per Kellaoth's orders, Wrinky, Dinky, Stinky, Piki, and Deecal formed a sort of guard around Aaron and Jack, in case any of the more rebellious Elves attempted to assault the boys. The five Elves took up this responsibility willingly, following Aaron and Jack wherever they went.

Though there were very few outright acts of insurgence, the Elves showed many subtle signs of discontent. Often, when

Aaron and Jack walked through camp, mutinous grumbling could be heard from the Elves in their tent, to which Piki or Deecal would shout "Itees rude to point! If ya got something you can say to get us out of this mess, then say it!" At which the Elf in question would merely shrink away back into the shadows.

However, all this defense and offense shouldn't have been necessary. Aaron and Jack should have been able to convince the Elves that they were, in fact, the kings. But they could not, for they, in their hearts, did not believe in that destiny. So the feud continued.

Aaron had taken to writing in a journal. A year ago, back in Avondale, he would have said that diaries were for girls. But now, he appreciated the little book. It helped him take his mind off his situation.

May 2,

Slept real bad last night. My stomach kept growling so loud, the noise woke me up. I don't think I can take this much longer. The Elves are turning against me, and there's nothing I can do about it. They should desert me. I mean, what have we done for them? Had them burned, killed and starved, that's what.

Why is all this happening to me? What have I done to deserve this torture? I was happy back in Avondale. No, no, don't think about that. Wishful thinking won't get us out of this.

I heard Laza and Buky had a fight last night. Apparently, Buky had said that she wished she could go back to Eldorlorne and that Jack and I had never come. She really loved her cousin Pooka. Well, Laza said that they were doing this for the greater good and that she would say she was wrong when we're standing in the rubble of Rarzan, declaring victory.

Laza's been a true friend. I don't know what I would have done without him. Sometimes I think he's wiser than all the elders put together. He's close with Kellaoth, you know. I think she tells him things. Anyway, Buky said that that was a longshot and that being killed by Gertulk or starvation was far more likely.

Laza said that no rebellion had ever been easy.

Buky shouted that this one was doomed to failure.

Laza snapped back that we would fail if she took that attitude.

They've been close for so long...I can't believe they're actually fighting. It shows just how depressing our situation is. I'm going to bed. Maybe I can wash away all these pains.

May 3,

Slept horribly. I dreamed that the Elves had tied Jack and me to a stake and they burned us alive. Laza tried to stop them, but they shot him down with their bows and threw his body into the fire. Then Ellie, Gallagher, and Bonnie attacked the Elves, but they were killed, too. Kellaoth struck and killed half the Elves before they sheared off her horn and crushed it. And in my dream, the Gertulk came and wiped them all out. Then I saw something in the distance. It was golden. It was Forvalad, the Sword of the King. It hovered over the battlefield and spoke to me. It said that I was weak. I tried to tell it that I was trying to help the Elves, but it told me that I would never be king. Then the flames took me, and I woke up.

That wasn't the first nightmare I've had recently. They're getting worse.

Today, Laza had one young Elf, Cooty, whipped for yelling in public that I didn't deserve the Throne. Cooty's sort of the leader of all this hatred. I don't think the whipping did much. He got a good ten lashes (which is a lot for an Elf), but that just made him madder. One of these days Laza might have to strip him of his rank. That would be horrible for my position. I've asked Laza to try to avoid punishing the haters. I mean, if they get banned from the tribe just because they disagree with Laza, that would basically say, "Love Aaron and Jack, or we kill you." We're trying to stop a tyrant, not to make a new one. I just hope that Cooty or one of the others doesn't try starting a riot and that this all gets worked out before something terrible happens.

20
Return Home

Day by day, Aaron and Jack had grown steadily more miserable. It was as though their entire lives were crashing down around them, and there was nothing they could do about it.

Aaron really didn't care much about stopping Malvadore anymore; all he cared about was getting home to his mother and father and his friends. The boys had made it this long by clinging to the notion of a magical fairytale land full of wonder and excitement. But now, after witnessing a full-scale and utterly brutal battle, the destruction of the Elves' home, and starvation, the boys saw neither of those elements.

The once grand and interesting world had mutated into a bitter, harsh, and twisted land where only those with enough will survived.

Having also lost some of the loyalty of the Elves, the pair were left with only one thought: getting home. And indeed, one afternoon after the Elves had made camp and gone to sleep, Aaron woke up Jack.

"It's time we did something," he stated.

Jack nodded. "We should have a long time ago…but what *can* we do?"

"Only one thing," said Aaron, gripping his yoyo in one hand.

"Go home."

Jack hesitated. True, the prospect of going home sent tingles of relief through his entire body, but at the same time…

Kellaoth and Laza had based their entire strategy upon getting Aaron and Jack to Castram alive. If they left now, they would be leaving the Elves for dead. That's not a very noble thing to do, said the Parnor side of him.

But I can't rule a country! Jack argued. *I'm just a small town schoolboy!*

So what? You know what's right and wrong, you have your people's best interests at heart, and that makes you a much better king than Malvadore, the voice in his head replied calmly.

It's not that simple.

And tell me, why not?

Because! Jack felt a twinge of annoyance. He shoved the voice out of his mind and looked at Aaron.

"I think we should do it," Jack said finally. "But what about Kellaoth and the Elves?"

Aaron brushed aside the question. "They'll be fine. Really, it won't be much different without us. I mean, we were just a figurehead, that's all. We're their poster boys. They're the ones who actually carry the weight. We just get in the way…" His voice lost a bit of its conviction, and he murmured, "They'll be better off without us."

"Really, the whole debate is moot unless we can actually figure out *how* to get home," Jack pointed out. "I mean, we can't exactly catch the next bus back to the Third World, can we?"

They heard a chuckle behind them. "I believe I can help with that."

By the time the stranger had finished talking, Aaron's sword was out of its sheath and pointing at his neck.

"Who are you?" asked Jack, jumping to his feet.

The stranger was an elderly man wrapped in a patched and dirty traveling cloak. In his hand was a roughly carved wooden staff. His hood was raised, casting his face into shadow. He chuckled again, clearly unconcerned by the blade now pointed at his throat.

"That question rather has some depth to it. You see, I have had many names over the centuries in many tongues. But I suppose you might know me as Lord Cygon."

"Lord Cygon?" said Aaron, so surprised that he lowered his sword. "The Wizard who—"

"Helped Kellaoth rescue you both from the Fall of Acklyon and has watched over you ever since? Yes."

Jack blinked. He had never met anyone like Cygon before.

"Why are you here?" asked Aaron.

"You did say you intended to leave, did you not?"

"Yes," said Aaron.

"And I believe Jahkon said that there was no way you could leave under your own power?"

"Yes," said Aaron. Then he started. "Wait a second! You're not offering to take us home, are you?"

"Indeed I am," said Cygon, smiling.

"But…why?" asked Jack. "I mean, you spent all that work just getting us here and starting up a rebellion, and now you're volunteering to take us home?"

"If you wish to return to the Third World, then you are not the True Kings. Clearly I made a mistake. I must take you home and find the real ones."

For some reason, Aaron didn't like Cygon saying he wasn't really Adinyrom Forahn, even though he had detested that name for a long time.

"Anyway," said Cygon in a more businesslike tone, "we have spent enough time here. Are you ready to go home?"

"Yes," said Aaron before he had really had time to think it over.

"Then let us be off."

Cygon threw off his worn cloak, and Aaron and Jack immediately shielded their eyes from the blinding glow within.

The old man was gone, replaced by a shining, angelic figure. A long sheet of golden hair fell over his back and seemed to fan out, even though there was no wind. He was dressed in golden chainmail over white robes, and a small silvery knife hung on his belt. His skin was pale and smooth, and his deep hazel eyes showed a wisdom and age far beyond what his frame suggested. In his hand was a long, golden staff with a five-pointed head shaped like a star.

As the initial shock subsided, Aaron and Jack saw him running the tip of his staff around in a circle on the ground. When he was done, the circle he had drawn transformed into a pool of water. The same pool that had brought them to Acklyon.

Knowing what to do, Aaron and Jack stepped forward and dove into the pool, landing once again in the River of Time.

Aaron's body was gone, but his mind and Jack's soared freely through the sea of golden light.

Presently, Aaron saw a tiny black dot in the distance, the one dark patch in an otherwise solid golden plain.

As they hurtled forwards, the dot grew bigger and bigger until it was a gaping hole in Time, through which they could see a dark, abandoned playground beside a middle school.

Before long, Aaron and Jack shot like two cannon balls through the portal, landing ungracefully on the pavement.

Aaron blinked and sat up, staring around with wide eyes.

Yes, there was Avondale Middle School, where he had spent a good part of his life studying, learning, and goofing off with Bonnie and Roger. There were the old woods which he had explored many a Saturday afternoon. They were home! They had made it! They were…

Somehow, he didn't feel the way he thought he would. It all felt so wrong to him after spending months in Acklyon. Everything had a flat, two-dimensional and incredibly mundane feel to it.

He got awkwardly to his feet and nearly stumbled—he was shorter and rather stouter than he had been in Acklyon. The toned muscles that had lined his arms, legs, and chest were gone, replaced by a layer of puppy fat. Likewise, the bruises and burns that covered his arms (trophies of the Battle of Eldorlorne) had also vanished, leaving his skin smooth and undamaged.

He felt his head and found that the dirty, overgrown hair he had acquired on his journeys had reduced to its short, neatly parted appearance.

He looked over at Jack, who was also getting to his feet, and saw that he, too, had changed back. The hair which had turned flaxen in Acklyon was back to its curly, strawberry-blonde appearance, and he, too, was shorter and less fit than before.

Aaron wasn't sure he liked being back to his Tackers self… He had taken pride in his abs and arm strength while in Acklyon, and now they were gone again.

He shook his head and shoved these thoughts away, turning instead to Jack and saying simply, "We're home."

"Yeah," said Jack, who was equally subdued.

"We should get back to our houses before the sun rises."

Jack nodded, and the two started off towards their neighborhood. Both were silent the entire way. Indeed, neither made a sound until they reached a stop sign a few blocks from Aaron's house.

"My house is this way," said Jack, gesturing in the opposite direction.

"Right," said Aaron, and they parted company.

As Aaron walked towards his house, his mind was a blur. He tried his best not to think about Kellaoth or the Elves, but he did anyway. They had counted on him, had trusted that he could save them, and they had been wrong. He didn't know what would happen to them. Would they be killed or captured by Gertulk? Would they continue on and make it to Castram, or would they die of starvation? He mentally shook himself. *It's not my problem,* he told himself, but with little conviction.

Soon he saw his house looming up on the right.

In spite of his worries, he smiled. It had been so long since he'd seen it. Funny, he had taken it for granted, seeing it there every time he came home from school…but now he thought the old house was more beautiful than a mansion. His pace quickened, and he ran to it. He went straight to the side of the house and looked up, knowing that his room was right there, one story up. He set to work, nimbly climbing the wall until he reached his window and opened it, crawling through and landing catlike on the floor in his room.

The room was so dark, he could hardly see anything. He took one step, and immediately stumbled over a pile of dirty clothes on the floor. Funny, it had been so long since he had occupied his room that he could no longer navigate through the mounds of clothes, papers, and games that littered the floor. He tipped over a bucket full of Legos and a coffee mug which contained the remains of hot chocolate before he fell into his bed. He pulled himself into it properly and tucked himself under the blankets.

He lay awake for what seemed like hours, staring up at the ceiling and assuring himself he had made the right decision. But no matter how much he tried, he could not shake the images that flooded through his mind—Kellaoth, the Elves left for dead out in the wilderness, on the brink of starvation. They would have no chance to defeat Malvadore… Admittedly, they'd never had a chance, but now the odds would be worse than ever.

It's not my problem, he told himself again, and fell into an uneasy sleep.

21
Life in Avondale

The first thing Aaron heard the next morning was his mother's fretting voice.

"Aaron? Aaron, wake up! You've overslept!"

In response to the loud noise and commotion, Aaron leapt out of his bed, rolled across the floor, caught up a plastic light saber from the floor, and pointed it at the door before realizing it was only his mother. He dropped the light saber and took a deep breath of relief.

"Aaron, get up! The bus will be here any minute!" said his mother, knocking frantically on the door.

"Mom?" he mumbled blearily, blinking the sleep out of his eyes. His dreams had been punctured by visions of the Elves surrounded by Gertulk and of Malvadore burning more forests.

He got shakily to his feet and went to the door. He opened it while his mother was in mid-knock, so that she stumbled forward when her fist did not meet the expected resistance.

She staggered over the threshold, but regained her balance and straightened up.

Just the sight of her sent rockets of joy shooting through Aaron, exploding through his body, so that the only thing he could say was "*Mom!*" and threw his arms around her in a tight hug. He knew she wouldn't understand, but he didn't care. He had missed her more than anything else—her smile, her kind words when he came home from school.

He held her for a long time. He felt as if, if he let go, he would lose her again, so he remained safely in her arms, not wanting to move or do anything else.

At last, he got control of himself and released her, his eyes shining.

She looked bemused but also touched as she led him downstairs to the kitchen.

She had laid out an empty bowl, a jug of milk, a box of cereal, and a spoon on the table for him. When he saw these, his stomach gave a great yell of joy, and he rushed to them and started gulping down large amounts of cereal. He stuffed down everything she put down in front of him. It had been so long since he'd had a proper meal…

"Aaron," laughed his mother as he swallowed his fifth piece of toast, "you act like you haven't eaten in months!"

That's not far off, he thought grimly, but he merely shrugged, helping himself to more cereal.

"Oh my!" said his mother after another ten minutes. "That looks like the bus. You'll have to hurry to catch it!"

Aaron jumped to his feet, swallowed his last bite, and seized his backpack from the counter. "Bye, Mom!" he said hastily, grabbing a handful of granola bars from the pantry and sprinting out the door.

He raced down the driveway and to the curb just as the last few kids were boarding the bus. He put every last ounce of strength into his small frame and slid between the two doors just as it was closing.

He straightened up, panting. He could have run that far with a horse on his back in Acklyon, but with his weaker body, it had taken all his energy to make it. He staggered down the aisle until he found Roger, who had saved him a seat. He sat down next to his best friend, doing all he could to hide the emotions he felt at seeing him again. "Hey," he said, trying to regain his schoolboy swagger.

"Hey," said Roger, who was finishing an essay.

Aaron prayed that he, Aaron, had finished his homework the day before. He looked over at Bonnie and Ellie, who were sitting across from him and Roger.

"Hi," he said to the two of them, again containing the joy he felt rising in him at the sight of them.

"Hey," said Ellie, but Bonnie raised her hand for silence.

"What?" Aaron asked.

"Loser at twelve o'clock," Bonnie muttered, gesturing to a boy sitting a few seats in front of them.

Aaron squinted at the boy. "Oh, it's Jack," he said smiling, realizing too late that his friends still hated Jack.

"*Oh, it's Jack*?" repeated Bonnie in shock.

"Well..." Aaron struggled for something to say. "We see him every day. What should make now anything special?"

"Well, let's see," said Bonnie, her eyes starting to catch fire. "One: he's a dorkbag. Two: he's stupid. Three: He's a wimp—"

"He's not a wimp," said Aaron before he could stop himself. He was thinking about the Battle of Eldorlorne, where Jack had cut down Gertulk after Gertulk for the Elves.

Bonnie looked at Aaron as though he was losing his mind. "Do you feel okay, Aaron?" she asked, "Do you actually *hear* what you're saying?"

"I know what I'm saying," Aaron said impatiently. He had no idea if he were about to lose all his friends, but he had to stop them from making fun of Jack. "Look, he's really not *that* bad... Can you even remember why we hate him so much?"

Bonnie, Ellie, and Roger were all silent, racking their brains for the answer. After several seconds of silence, Aaron continued.

"That's what I thought," he said pointedly. "None of us even remembers anymore, it's been so long... It was probably something stupid anyway," he added.

Ellie seemed to be taking in what Aaron was saying, nodding thoughtfully, but Bonnie and Roger both looked mutinous.

"Look." Aaron was starting to lose patience. "How bad can it be? Can you at least give him the benefit of the doubt? Would that kill you?"

"You said he's actually pretty cool?" said Ellie.

"Yes," said Aaron, glad someone seemed to get it. "He's really a great guy."

Ellie looked over at Jack, who was sitting alone next to a window. "He *does* look lonely," she sighed.

Bonnie didn't seem to have a retort to that.

Aaron nodded. "Yeah, he does...and that's mostly to blame on us."

Roger was still silent, but Bonnie spoke up. "Well, if *you* think we should, Ellie, I guess it can't be *that* bad."

Aaron smiled at her.

When they arrived back at Avondale Middle School, Aaron caught Jack's eye as the many children jostled towards the door. Jack nodded at him and winked. Aaron fought his way through the crowd until he made it to Jack's side. "I've talked to my friends," he said in an undertone. "I think I've convinced them to let you in."

"Thanks," whispered Jack, trying to look pleased, but he was just as subdued as Aaron.

"How was your night?" Aaron asked after an uncomfortable silence.

"Not bad," said Jack a little glumly. "Really weird."

"I know what you mean," said Aaron quietly.

There was silence again until Jack broke it. "Are you sure we did the right thing?" he asked Aaron. "Leaving Acklyon?"

"Course we did, Cygon said it himself." There was little conviction in Aaron's voice.

That day at lunch, Aaron convinced his friends to sit with Jack rather than with the cluster of cool kids at the center of the lunchroom. Though Bonnie was reluctant, Ellie was able to persuade her. Together, Aaron, Ellie, Bonnie, and Roger took their trays and walked over to where Jack sat, as usual, by himself at the end of the table.

"Alright if we sit here?" asked Aaron.

"Oh...sure," said Jack, feigning surprise.

Aaron and Ellie took seats next to Jack. Aaron noticed that Bonnie and Roger seemed to be trying not to get too close to Jack, as though he were contaminated.

Ellie immediately struck up a conversation with Jack. Aaron tried his best to join in, but somehow he seemed to have lost his social skills back in Acklyon. Funny, there hadn't been any need for them there...

This was one of those times that Aaron realized just how amazing Ellie was. While she chatted carelessly with Jack, she subtly involved Bonnie and Roger in the conversation, such as, "Remember when we went to Niagara Falls together, Bonnie? Jack said he went there last year on vacation. Did you go on the Maid of the Mist, Jack? That was fun." Or, "Hey, Roger, Jack said he saw that movie, *Three Days to Live* the other night. Wasn't that the movie you and Aaron were talking about?" And so on, so that by the time lunch period was over, Bonnie and Roger were considerably warmer towards Jack.

"Thanks," Aaron muttered in Ellie's ear as they were leaving the cafeteria. Ellie smiled at him.

As they were walking down the hallway towards their next class, chatting aimlessly, Mo Sawyers, one of the bigger boys and a real bully, rammed Jack in the shoulder as he passed, knocking Jack's books to the floor. Mo chuckled and walked on.

"Pick those up," said Jack. It was not a question.

Mo turned, looking a little surprised. Jack was standing, feet apart and arms crossed where Mo had bumped him, a fierce and stern glare on his face. "Pick those up," he said again. "You bumped me. You should pick them up."

Mo recovered from the shock of Jack Oswald challenging him, and a leer spread over his face. "Who's gonna make me?" he taunted.

"I will, if you don't do what I say."

"Help him, Aaron!" said Ellie.

Aaron grinned inwardly. "He'll be fine," he assured her. After seeing Jack slaughtering Gertulk, Aaron had a suspicion that Mo was about to get a big surprise.

Mo had raised his fists now and was circling Jack, who stood rooted. "You need to be put in your place, Oswald," snarled Mo, "and I'm the guy to do it."

"Try it," Jack said coolly.

Mo swung one fist towards Jack's face. Ellie screamed, but there was no need to worry. Jack, without even looking or showing much effort at all, raised his hand and blocked Mo's fist.

Before Mo could retaliate, Jack closed his fingers around

Mo's wrist, twisted it in the manner Laza had taught him, forcing Mo to turn sideways at an awkward angle. In a single motion, Jack turned and flipped Mo over his shoulder. Mo landed in a crumpled heap on the ground as the onlookers gasped in shock. Mo got shakily to his feet, and upon seeing Jack's upraised fists, hastily dropped down and began gathering Jack's belongings off the floor. He handed them to Jack and sprinted off, looking rather scared.

The circle of children who had been watching the fight now cheered Jack. Aaron smiled, though something tugged at his mind…

Jack learned those fighting skills in Eldorlorne. He never could have beaten Mo before, nor mustered the courage to stand up for himself. And indeed, Aaron's knowledge of combat, both armed and unarmed, far exceeded what most people even thought was possible. He had learned these skills training mercilessly with Laza and the Elves.

And then he understood.

He could never really go back to his old life. He had left Aaron Tackers far behind, abandoned his previous personality. He was Adinyrom Forahn, and there was no hiding it anymore. He had been a fool to convince himself he could go back to Avondale and continue living as though nothing had changed.

We have to get back to Acklyon, he thought. There it was, plain and simple. They were needed back with Kellaoth and the Elves. He and Jack had to go home.

As the bus stopped at the corner and let the children out, Aaron slipped a piece of paper into Jack's hand. "That's my number," he muttered. "Call me tonight. There're things we need to talk about."

Jack nodded and pocketed the piece of paper. The two turned in opposite directions and sprinted towards their respective houses.

Aaron flew down his driveway and burst through the front door. "Hi Mom!" he said hastily, giving her a quick hug before charging upstairs to his room. He was gone before she had even said hello.

Aaron paced back and forth restlessly in his room, his heart pounding. How could they get back to the Fifth World? It didn't seem possible. To distract himself, he switched on the little TV he had bought at a yard sale the previous year. He tried to sit down but was too restless, so he continued pacing as the news report washed over him. He remained deep in thought until a news bulletin drew him out of his thoughts.

"Another murder has taken place this afternoon," said the female announcer. "Alice Fieldsworth, 78, was found dead in her house. Evidence suggests that her home was broken into where she was brutally hacked with a machete. Her house was ransacked, causing police to believe that the killer or killers were looking for something."

Brutally hacked with a machete? Aaron thought in horror. *Killer or killers were looking for something? It can't be!* He raced back downstairs, skidding to a stop in the kitchen where his mother was cooking dinner.

"Aaron?" she asked, concerned. "What's wrong?"

"Never mind," said Aaron breathlessly. "Where's today's paper?"

His mother seemed surprised, but gestured to the counter, where the mail sat. Aaron ripped through the bills and letters until he found the *Avondale Local*. He took it back up to his room where he laid it out on his desk, looking at the headlines:

ALICE FIELDSWORTH MURDERED!

Aaron scanned the article beneath it, looking for clues that would confirm his suspicion. He found little in the article that he didn't already know—except toward the bottom of the page it mentioned several pairs of large, heavy boot prints leading to and from the house...

And there it was.

As to the identity of the murderer, police have only one clue. When inspecting the house, policeman Walter Bryan found a small, black, metal spike broken off at the base. Investigators have confirmed that this spike was broken off of some sort of suit of armor.

Aaron felt as though he couldn't breathe. Scanning the black-and-white picture on the front page, he saw it. Officer Bryan was holding the black shoulder spike in his hand. There could be no question as to the identity of the killer any more: *Gertulk!* The word tore through Aaron's mind, sending chills running down his spine. *They're looking for us!* Aaron thought in terror. *Me and Jack! Malvadore must know we're here. And the longer we stay here, the more people will be killed. We need to leave before they find us! But we have to stop them first. We can't let them kill anyone else.*

His eyes landed on the door. It was unlocked and left open a crack. It occurred to him how careless that had been of him. He sprang over to it, slammed it shut, and locked it. It wouldn't stop Gertulk, he knew, but he felt better with it locked. His thoughts were interrupted by the sound of his cell phone ringing. He dove for it, fumbling as he caught it up and pressing it to his ear. "Hello?"

"It's me," said Jack's voice through the speaker.

"Hey," said Aaron, relieved to be able to tell someone of his fears. "We need to talk. In person. Can you get to the bus stop?"

"Yeah," said Jack.

"Great," said Aaron. "Meet me there, now."

"Okay," said Jack.

"Oh, and go armed," Aaron added. "Whatever you can find to protect yourself. Don't let your parents go outside alone. And lock your doors."

"What's wrong?" asked Jack, sounding surprised.

"I can't say now," said Aaron. "Just be *very* careful." He hung up and looked for something with which to defend himself. He slipped downstairs and into the garage, where he searched for a weapon. He eventually found several pocket knives and a metal baseball bat. He crept outside, careful not to alert his parents to his disappearance. Stealthily, he made his way to the bus stop. He found Jack waiting for him there, clutching a pitchfork in his hands and looking around. He jumped when Aaron approached and turned the pitchfork to face him, only relaxing when he saw it was Aaron.

"What's going on?" he asked.

"We need to get indoors," said Aaron, looking around in the growing darkness. Gertulk could spring on them at any moment.

Jack nodded. "My house is just around the block."

"Let's go," said Aaron, never taking his eyes off his surroundings.

Jack led the way to his house, while Aaron kept his senses tuned to everything around him.

It was night by the time they made it to Jack's house. The two boys climbed the side of the house and crawled through the open window to Jack's room.

Aaron fell onto the floor and immediately looked for signs that Gertulk had been there. But no, just the homey comforts of a thirteen-year-old boy.

"So what's going on?" asked Jack, closing the window.

Aaron told him everything about both his decision to return to Acklyon and the knowledge that Gertulk were after them. Jack was silent as Aaron spoke about returning to Acklyon, staring vacantly at the corner of his desk. However, when Aaron told him of the Gertulk, he gave a cry and leapt to his feet.

"*Gertulk*?" He said, fear entwining his words. "But...but they can't! How could Malvadore know—?"

"He must have ways of tracking us," Aaron said. "That or he's captured..." He couldn't finish his sentence. The thought of Malvadore holding Kellaoth or Laza captive, torturing information out of them was too horrible to think about. Jack seemed to have picked up on Aaron's meaning, for he hastily changed the subject.

"First of all," Jack said, beginning to pace, "we have to stop these Gertulk before they kill anyone else. We can worry about getting back to Acklyon once they're dead."

"But there are only two of us," Aaron pointed out, "and we don't even have any proper weapons! Who knows how many Gertulk Malvadore sent?"

"And we don't know where they are, either," Jack continued, "but they could find us any minute."

"We can't search for them now," said Aaron, "it's too dark. We'd be toast if they found us."

"Get back to your house," said Jack, picking up his pitchfork, "and make sure they don't touch your parents. I'll guard mine."

"I'll stay on the phone with you until I'm safe," said Aaron, taking his baseball bat and heading towards the window.

Jack nodded and punched Aaron's number into his cell phone. Seconds later, Aaron picked up his own phone and pressed it to his ear as he climbed back out the window.

"I'm on the ground," he whispered into it. "I'm leaving your yard..."

He continued to give Jack a run-down on everything he saw as he crept with painstaking slowness toward his house. Despite his terror, as he passed the bus stop and headed towards the cul-de-sac, not a sound echoed in the night except the occasional whoosh of a car passing or a radio playing inside someone's house.

Aaron crept on, the phone in one hand and the bat in the other. "I'm almost at my house," he muttered. "I can see it up ahead—" He broke off, whirling around. He had heard something in a clump of nearby bushes.

"What is it?" Jack's voice came through the phone, sounding terrified.

"I hear something," said Aaron quietly. "It could be a cat, I don't know. I'm gonna check it out."

"Be careful," Jack warned him.

Aaron crept towards the bush, bat at the ready. He paused in front of the bush, listening. Nothing. He gathered up his courage and jabbed the bat into it.

A monster leapt out of the bush and tackled Aaron, hissing. Aaron struggled with it as it clawed his face and arms, finally throwing it off of him while ignoring Jack's cries of concern coming through the phone. Aaron squinted in the darkness to get a look at his foe, at last making out its shape.

It was Baubles, his neighbor's cat.

Aaron sighed with relief, his body shaking. "I'm fine, I'm fine," he said into the phone. "It was just Mrs. Ferguson's cat."

He heard Jack let out a long breath.

Aaron sprinted the rest of the way to his house, scaled the wall as before, and toppled through his bedroom window. He collapsed into his bed and lay there, breathing heavily.

"I'm home," he told Jack.

"Great," said Jack.

"We'll decide what to do at the bus stop tomorrow morning," said Aaron. He was tired and couldn't think straight.

"Alright," said Jack. "I'll see you then."

"Don't lower your guard for a second," Aaron reminded him.

"I won't," said Jack. "And be careful, Aaron."

"I will," said Aaron. "Just stay alive until morning."

"Bye."

"Bye." Aaron hung up the phone and lay back against his pillow. What could they do? What chance did two schoolboys, no matter how skillful, have against Gertulk? They didn't even know how many there were! Malvadore could have sent five or six or an entire army.

A knock at the door sent him into a panic. He scrambled out of bed and grabbed the bat off the floor. He turned, springing into the on-guard position Laza had taught him, his eyes centered on the door. "W-who's there?" he called, his body rigid.

"It's your mother!" said a familiar voice. "Aaron, why is your door locked?"

"N-no reason," said Aaron, relaxing a bit.

"Well, dinner's on the table, come on down."

"Right," said Aaron, though the last thing he wanted to do right now was to eat.

22

Best Friends

Aaron and Jack arrived at the bus stop at almost the same time. Both were armed, Aaron with his bat and Jack with his pitchfork. Upon seeing each other, they immediately went back to back, scanning the streets for Gertulk. Aaron could feel the eyes of the other children on them, half curious and half amused. Aaron and Jack ignored them. The others did not understand, and never would, the serious danger they were all in—heads down, texting their friends, chatting aimlessly with one another, or else peering down the street trying to catch a glimpse of the bus. No, these kids had no idea that Gertulk could come crashing into their midst at any moment, swinging their large swords and throwing spears.

Aaron and Jack merely tried to ensure that they saw the Gertulk before the Gertulk saw them.

As Jack scanned the neat yards, dew clinging to the grass in the early morning hours, his eye caught on something at his feet. "Aaron," he muttered.

Aaron turned.

"What is it?" he asked in an undertone.

Jack pointed at the ground. Both boys crouched down and studied it. Aaron felt his lungs constrict.

Huge, heavy boot prints were stamped into the ground, many sets of them. They were outlined in a dark liquid, which Aaron discovered to be blood. The boys stood up, trying not to be sick.

"They're here," Aaron whispered. "They're in our neighborhood. They've found us!"

Before he could say anything else, the bus pulled up, and Aaron was buffeted through the doors by the crowd of kids. Numbly, Aaron and Jack searched for two empty seats.

"What's with the pitchfork, Oswald?" someone shouted at Jack. Jack ignored him.

Aaron and Jack sat down in an empty row at the back of the bus. Aaron immediately pulled out his cell phone and called his mother.

"Mom? Mom are you okay? Have you seen any strangers in the neighborhood? No reason. Just keep the doors locked, okay? And be careful…I love you. Bye."

He turned to Jack, who had also just finished calling his mom. "They haven't found my house yet," Aaron told him.

"Mine either," said Jack. "But it's only a matter of time before they do. We need to find them, today."

"Yes," Aaron concurred, "but how do we find them? We can't just wait for them to attack us!"

"I don't know," said Jack.

Neither said anything to the other until the bus pulled up in front of Avondale Middle School though they each called their parents twice more in that time.

"This isn't right," Aaron muttered to Jack as the children exited the bus. "We should be at home making sure the Gertulk don't get to our parents! If anything happened to Mom…" He couldn't finish the thought.

"I know," said Jack, "but what can we do? We need to draw

them away from our neighborhood."

"What are you guys talking about?"

Both Aaron and Jack jumped at the unexpected voice behind them, turning their weapons to face the stranger. It was Ellie, looking extremely bewildered at the sight of them clutching a baseball bat and a pitchfork. Aaron lowered the baseball bat.

"What's up with the bat?" asked Bonnie, who had joined them.

"Nothing," said Aaron quickly.

"You know they won't let you bring it inside," Bonnie pointed out.

"Let them try to stop us," grunted Jack. Bonnie gave him a poorly disguised look of contempt.

They passed the bus driver then, and he, unfortunately, heard their conversation.

"Hey," said the pale, skinny man. "She's right, you can't take those inside."

"Then we won't go inside," said Aaron and marched away from the school, followed by Jack, ignoring the spluttering of the shocked driver.

"What the heck is wrong with them?" said Bonnie in surprise, watching them go, "They could get thrown out for that!"

Ellie said nothing, but merely gazed at the two boys. Something was wrong with Aaron. She knew him well enough to see that. He wasn't himself.

"You know what?" said Bonnie, unaware of Ellie's concern. "I bet it's from hanging with Oswald too much. He's gone nutty. Poor guy."

Ellie still said nothing.

Roger approached. "What's up with them?"

"I have no clue," said Bonnie. "Aaron got on the bus, and

he was with Jack again. He was holding a baseball bat like his life depended on it, and they just *left* when the driver said he couldn't take it inside."

Roger raised his eyebrows. "That's odd," he said. "I wonder why." He didn't seem particularly concerned with Aaron's behavior.

Ellie remained quiet.

Once Aaron and Jack were out of sight of the school, they stopped.

"So now what?" said Jack.

"Well," said Aaron, "with any luck, the Gertulk are tracking us directly and not our usual whereabouts. If they're following where we usually are, then they're either looking for our houses or the school. I just hope they're following our scent. It'll lead them here and won't put anyone else in danger."

"I doubt they could track down Aaron Tackers and Jack Oswald," Jack said. "Remember, they don't know about things like phone books and internet searches. They don't even speak this language!"

"Right," said Aaron, "so the only way they could find us is to pillage Avondale and kill everyone in sight until they find us, or else they have means of detecting our presence. Seeing as they haven't killed more than a few people, Malvadore must have a way of knowing our location."

"That makes sense," said Jack. "How else could they know we're in Avondale and the Third World?"

Aaron didn't answer. The only other way the Gertulk could know was if they had captured Kellaoth or Laza and tortured the information out of them. He couldn't bear that thought.

"Mr. Anderson, could I have a hall pass?"

Ellie had spent the entire day worrying about Aaron. It had been hours, and he hadn't returned. She had never known him to do anything this radical. The story had spread all over the school of how Aaron Tackers and Jack Oswald had stormed away from the buses, refusing to enter the school.

Most of the children regarded it as a spectacular feat, but Ellie knew Aaron well enough to know he would never do something like this. Bonnie maintained that it had come from spending too much time with Jack—that it had turned Aaron crazy. But Ellie had had a lengthy conversation with Jack the previous day and had found him to be intelligent, perceptive, and level-headed. Something bad was happening to the two of them and she knew it. And if she considered herself to be Aaron's friend, she had to do something. Halfway through her history class, she made her move. She had gotten the idea from Roger—ten minutes ago he had been caught launching spitballs at the other students, and Mr. Anderson had sent him to the principal's office.

Mr. Anderson looked up from his notes. "Yes, of course, Ms. Birch,"

As Ellie got up, she gave Bonnie a knowing look. With the hall pass clutched in her hand, she made her way to the restrooms. Once she was safely within the ladies' room, she paced back and forth, waiting. She knew Bonnie had understood the look she gave her. And sure enough, five minutes later, Bonnie passed through the door.

"What's up?" she asked, a concerned expression on her face.

"Right," said Ellie. "Let's go, but we have to make sure no one sees us."

"What are we doing?" asked Bonnie in surprise.

"Looking for Aaron, of course," said Ellie. "Come on."

Bonnie nodded and followed.

As they crept down the hallway, Bonnie remembered something. "Roger," she whispered.

Ellie looked over at her. "What about him?"

"He's still in the principal's office. When he gets out, he can come with us."

"Alright," said Ellie. "As long as he doesn't take too long in there."

They doubled back and hid outside the principal's office. Before long, Roger stepped out, looking only slightly ashamed of himself. As he made his way back towards the classroom, Bonnie and Ellie stepped out of hiding.

"What are you guys doing here?" said Roger, startled.

"No time," said Bonnie, grabbing him by the upper arm and dragging him along in their wake.

"We're gonna get in trouble if we don't get back to class," said Roger as they neared the front doors.

"This is more important," said Ellie impatiently.

Roger raised his eyebrows, but said nothing.

"They went that way," said Bonnie, gesturing towards the old woods behind the playground.

"What, Aaron and that Jack?" said Roger in surprise. "Are we seriously going to look for them?"

"Yes!" snapped Ellie.

"Okay, but when we get chucked out of school, don't blame me!" grumbled Roger. Ellie and Bonnie ignored him.

The three of them crashed their way through the thick trees and thorny vines in the outskirts of the woods behind the middle school.

"You do realize we're looking for a needle in a haystack, right?" Roger spoke up, sounding irritated.

Ellie turned on him and opened her mouth to retort, but Bonnie cut her off with a sharp whisper.

"Quiet, both of you! I hear something."

The three became very still, peering through the bushes, for indeed they all heard the rustling of footsteps nearby.

"Aaron?" said Ellie weakly. "Jack?"

The footsteps suddenly ceased, as though whoever had made them was determining whether Ellie's voice was potentially dangerous or not. Ellie, Bonnie, and Roger stood motionless, unsure if they really wanted to know who it was. However, the decision was made for them when a boy stumbled out of the thicket and nearly fell. But it wasn't Aaron. It wasn't Jack either. It was—

"*Gallagher*?" cried Bonnie as Ellie helped him regain his balance. "What are *you* doing here?"

"Looking for Jack!" said Gallagher. His clothes were torn, and he looked distinctly disheveled. "After he ran out like that I knew something was wrong, so I tried to follow him… What are you guys doing here?"

"Same thing as you," said Ellie.

"And what were you thinking, coming out here alone?" demanded Bonnie. "It could be dangerous!"

"You're out here too!" Gallagher retorted.

"Gal, Gal, Gal. I am in eighth grade. I am older, I am more mature, I can wander the woods because I'm not some lame seventh grader like you.

"Last year you told me seventh graders were old and mature and sixth graders were lame…"

"Come on, we'll look together," said Ellie, breaking up the argument.

"Why is it whenever I'm out with my friends I somehow get stuck with my idiot little brother?" Bonnie wondered aloud.

"Why is it whenever I'm trying to save my best friend from psychological stress I get stuck with my idiot big sister?" Gallagher wondered aloud.

Aaron had paced a road through the little clearing, his sweaty hands gripping the handle of his bat. He had no idea what they were waiting for, but he wished it would stop. He felt as though his mind might snap under the pressure soon.

Jack was sitting on the ground, sharpening a twig with his pocket knife. Both boys would freeze on the spot and grab their weapons at the slightest noise, preparing for a Gertulk ambush. But luck was with them, and the Gertulk hadn't found them yet.

Every five minutes, Aaron would call his mother to ensure that the Gertulk hadn't found her. He could tell by her voice that she was getting irritated by his frequent calls, but the urgency in his voice kept her answering him. They were waiting for something—*anything*—to develop. The silence was growing so unbearable that Aaron almost wished the Gertulk would find them already to save him from the terrible anticipation.

"What was that?" Jack's sharp voice cut through the still like a knife. Aaron froze, his hand twitching towards his bat, which was tucked into his belt.

"What?" Aaron said quietly.

"I heard something," said Jack, creeping to his feet. "Over there—" He gestured to a clump of bushes nearby.

Aaron now heard it, too—a rustling, and the whisper of voices from the other side of the thicket. He lifted his nose and sniffed. "Doesn't smell like Gertulk," he whispered.

He crept forward, not daring to make a sound.

The whispering was growing louder, but he couldn't make out any words. He sneaked right up to the bush and peered through the branches. He could not see clearly through to the other end, but he managed to make out one thing through the thick leaves: a human hand, small and soft. Relief flooded him that it was not a Gertulk, but he did not lower his guard.

Slowly he reached his hand into the bush, and like a mousetrap, his fingers snapped shut around the hand and yanked it out of the bushes. Aaron dragged the intruder out of the bush and slammed them on the ground. With one hand, he clamped their neck down, while the other hand raised the bat over his head, prepared to strike.

It was Ellie. Her breathe was quick and terrified, and her eyes had tears in them.

"*Ellie*?" Aaron cried, he quickly got off of her, and hoisted her to her feet. "What are you doing here? Why did you leave school? Do you realize how dangerous it is out here?"

"We came to—" Ellie started to say, but was cut off when Bonnie and Gallagher charged out of the bush and tackled Aaron, screaming incoherently. Jack rushed over, seized Gallagher by the scruff of the neck, and pitched him off of Aaron. Aaron struggled with Bonnie and pinned her to the ground. "If you ever do something that foolish again, you'll pay for it!" Aaron hissed at her, "Don't you realize how dangerous it is out here?"

"Alright, alright, I'm sorry, *Mom*," muttered Bonnie, getting gingerly to her feet, wincing at her bruises. "Why'd you have to go and give us a heart attack?"

"Why are you away from the school?" demanded Aaron. "Don't you realize how much danger you're in at this very *moment*?"

"Of course they don't," Jack said wearily. "They have no *idea* what's going on."

"Way to make us feel included in the conversation!" said

Bonnie sarcastically.

"So what *are* you two doing out here anyway?" Ellie asked Aaron and Jack.

"Nothing," said Aaron, leading her back towards the bushes. "It's not important; just get back to the school as fast as you can—"

"You're in trouble, Aaron," said Ellie firmly, "so it's my problem."

"Ellie, you don't understand—"

"They should know," said Jack suddenly.

Aaron turned to look at him. "What did you say?"

"They have the right to know why we're doing what we're doing," said Jack firmly. "In case we don't..." He couldn't finish the sentence.

Aaron nodded. "Right," he said, turning to Ellie, Bonnie, Gallagher, and Roger. "You're probably going to think we're crazy, but listen."

And he told them everything, starting with the visions they'd seen so long ago, of hearing Kellaoth's voice, finding the Pool of Time, of Eldorlorne and the battle, of their trek towards Castram. He finished by explaining how they had abandoned the Elves and that the Gertulk had come to Avondale. Finally, he told of their plans to return to Acklyon.

His audience never spoke a word through his entire story. After over an hour of talking, Aaron became silent. A long period of shocked silence passed.

Roger laughed sarcastically. "If you don't want to tell us, that's fine."

Aaron smiled grimly. He had known they wouldn't believe him and did not begrudge them for it. After all, who *would* believe that his best friend and worst enemy had been transported to a mystical world where they found out they were long-lost sons of the two dead kings of that place—destined to destroy the evil necromancer who had taken control of that country and oppressed his subjects for over a hundred years? Aaron didn't try to convince them he was telling the truth. He just wanted *someone* to know what had happened if he died at the hands of the Gertulk.

"Simply put, Jack and I are about to take on Lord knows how many of Malvadore's minions. Chances are we're going to our deaths. If that happens...tell my mother what happened." Aaron's voice trailed off as he felt his lungs constrict.

Ellie put her hand on Aaron's arm.

"We'll get through this, Aaron," she said quietly. "We'll stop the Gertulk, and we'll get you both back to Acklyon."

Aaron looked up. "You—you believe me?" he stammered.

Ellie smiled. "Aaron, I *know* you. I know when you're kidding and when you're not, and you're *not* kidding."

Aaron was dumbfounded. He looked at Bonnie and Gallagher, and saw that they, too, were drinking in what he was saying. He smiled and opened his mouth to try to express the gratitude that was rushing through him, but Bonnie cut him off.

"Save the emotional speech," she said. "And for the record, I know you're being serious because I've seen you in the school plays—and you're a terrible actor."

"Hey!" Aaron protested.

"And also, look what Jack's been doing this whole time!" Bonnie continued. All eyes turned to Jack, who had been pacing back and forth, pitchfork in hand, keeping watch for Gertulk.

"You have GOT to be kidding me..." muttered Roger, but the others ignored him.

"So let me get this straight," said Gallagher. "There are who knows how many of these zombies in Avondale?"

"Not zombies, specifically," Aaron corrected him. "Zombies are dead people being controlled by a sorcerer. Gertulk are warriors under Malvadore's control."

"Tom-ai-to, tom-aht-to," said Bonnie. "I say we find these Gertulk and teach them a thing or two!"

"Are you crazy?" Roger snapped at Ellie, Bonnie, and Gallagher. "Elves? Unicorns? An evil warlord trying to take over a mystical land? Please. You know he's pulling your leg."

"You stuck up, obnoxious, conceited little—"

Aaron cut Bonnie off. "It's Roger's choice," he reminded her. "He doesn't have to believe us if he doesn't want to."

"Oh, stop with the whole mature thing," Roger shot at Aaron. "It's not fooling anyone."

"Well actually..." muttered Gallagher.

"You can shut up any time, Roger," said Ellie, glowering at him.

"Come *on*, Ellie," said Roger. "We all know you're only going along with him because you like him—"

"Shut up!" said Ellie, her face going pink.

"Guys, stop," said Aaron stepping in between Ellie and Roger before Ellie could break Roger's nose. "Ellie, he's not obliged to believe everything I say. Neither are you, as a matter of fact. Roger, you can go. Go back to school. You can still live an ordinary life. I'm guessing you won't even remember this conversation a week from now. Just...just stay indoors. Don't go anywhere alone."

Roger rolled his eyes and stormed away, back through the bushes.

Jack rushed over. "What if he runs into the Gertulk?"

"We can only hope he won't," said Aaron, looking off at the

point where Roger had vanished.

"Anyway, now that all morons are removed from our presence—"Bonnie said, glaring at Ellie and Gallagher, as though daring them to follow Roger, "—now all we have to do is to give these Gertulks—"

"Gertulk," Aaron said.

Bonnie looked at him quizzically.

"It's 'Gertulk'," Aaron explained, "not 'Gertulks'. 'Gertulk' is the plural of 'Gertulk', singular. 'Gertulks' is improper grammar."

"Since when do YOU care about grammar?" demanded Bonnie, shocked at Aaron's sudden grammatical skills.

"Since I spent six months in a higher dimension."

"Oh, that," muttered Bonnie. "Gosh, they really did transform you!"

"No kidding," said Aaron. "Anyway, we need to prepare. Go back to your homes, give your mother one last hug. Take anything we might need to combat the Gertulk, but don't go anywhere alone or unarmed. Jack, walk Bonnie and Gallagher home, I'll walk Ellie. We'll meet in the park at five."

In his short life, Aaron Tackers had not done much that required the supreme amount of strength and willpower that he would need for this next task. Not even in Acklyon, training mercilessly with Laza, battling the Gertulk, and trying to help bring the starving Elf colony to safety, had he been forced to harness every bit of determination he possessed as he now did.

He had to say goodbye.

For one glorious day, he had thought that his struggles were over and that he could go back to living an ordinary life. But there was no going back, he discovered. You cannot forget. He had already walked Ellie home and had gathered up whatever supplies he would need, and it was time for one last look.

He gazed up at his mother, who was beaming that beautiful smile of hers down onto him. She had always been there for him, his one friend when he had none, the one happy thought that kept his legs moving, trudging the length of Acklyon, and now…

"Goodbye, Mom," he said quietly and hugged her tightly. She would not understand his unusual behavior, or it might even be erased from her memory along with every other memory of the Forahn side of her son. The next day, her son would be back to his usual, carefree self, and no one would ever know what had happened. He blinked hard as he held her, willing himself not to break down, to give up. It took every ounce of strength in his body to let go of her, to walk out the door for the last time.

Outside, on the front porch, he looked back through the glass door at his mother, looking puzzled but rather flattered.

"I love you, Mom," he murmured, and he turned away from the life he longed to have, but knew he never could.

At the stroke of five, the five children met at the park, grunting under the large packs they wore, all stuffed with items of use. Gallagher was wearing his Boy Scout equipment (pocket knife, a length of rope, compass, survival kit, and so on). Bonnie had brought a backpack stuffed with food. Ellie had her first-aid kit, and a bag full of blankets. Jack came riding on his bicycle, which he had somehow modified, giving it an extra set of wheels in the back, a cushioned seat, and a wagon tied to the back. Riding in the wagon were five walking sticks with a sharpened spike protruding from the head of each. Aaron unzipped a large backpack, dumping three hammers, his father's pickax, and several different-sized knives onto the ground. On his belt was a large hunting knife in a sheath, a tinderbox, a flashlight, and his metal bat.

"Hey, Aaron," said Bonnie, reaching into her backpack. "I found this in the garage the other day… You'd know how to use one of these, right?"

She had brought a compound bow and a sack full of arrows.

Aaron beamed at her. "Perfect," he said as he took them.

"Oh, by the way," said Jack, stopping Aaron, "you dropped this at the school." He was holding Aaron's green yoyo in his hand. Aaron looked at the yoyo, staring at it for a long time. During his time in Acklyon, the yoyo had been his reminder of the Third World, the last part of his old self…

He took the yoyo from Jack and threw it as hard as he could into the woods. "I don't need it anymore," he said simply. "Let's move out."

"Load whatever you don't need with you into the wagon," Jack instructed Ellie, Bonnie, and Gallagher. "We'll take turns pulling it."

"Here," Aaron passed the hammers to Ellie, Bonnie, and Gallagher. "Keep these with you at all times."

Ellie, Bonnie, and Gallagher tucked their hammers into their belts, feeling an odd sense of foreboding. Ellie prayed she would never have to use hers.

The five of them loaded their backpacks, the pickax, and Ellie's first-aid kit into the wagon, and they set off, Jack pulling the wagon via the bicycle.

"So what now?" asked Bonnie, trying for Aaron's sake not to sound doubtful.

"We find the Gertulk," said Aaron, taking out the compound bow, "and we kill them."

Ellie remained silent. She was not sure she liked this new, darker Aaron as opposed to the funny, bigheaded schoolboy he once was.

"They came this way," said Jack, who was standing very still, like a bird dog on point.

"How can you tell?" asked Gallagher.

"For one thing, the smell," said Jack, "and the feel of the air is all wrong. Something evil has been here."

"He's right," said Aaron, now studying the ground. "See, here are their footprints. They lead in…that direction." He pointed toward the woods where Aaron and Jack had first found the Pool.

"Then let's go!" said Gallagher, fingering his hammer.

"Alright, but slowly and keep quiet! We'll need the element of surprise if we want to live through the day. Draw weapons."

The others did as he said, and Aaron led the way as the five of them crept towards the woods. Thoughts raced through Aaron's mind as he aimed his bow at anything that moved. How many Gertulk were there? For all he knew, there could be hundreds or only two or three. Was he leading his friends to their deaths? Did he even have a hope of stopping Malvadore's minions? After all, there was no Kellaoth or Laza here, no one to cover for his mistakes and pull him out of the danger zone. Indeed, he would likely have to be the one to fend for Ellie, Gallagher, and Bonnie. Was it even a good idea to be bringing them this close to the potential showdown?

His mind shifted to Roger. For years, Aaron had regarded Roger as his best friend. They did everything together, slept over at each other's houses, let each other copy their homework. It saddened Aaron to come to the realization that what they had had was superficial. Roger had, like the many lowlife nerds that trailed after Aaron as he walked down halls, merely wanted to leech off of Aaron's popularity.

Then he thought about the three children behind him, quivering with fear but gripping their hammers determinedly nonetheless. He had never dreamed that he had a friend that would follow him to the ends of the earth, literally, but now he had four of them.

"Stop!" Jack hissed at the others, wrenching Aaron from his thoughts.

"What is it?" squeaked Ellie, clutching her hammer to her chest.

"Listen," whispered Jack, taking three cautious steps forward.

Aaron cocked his ear and listened. At first, he only heard the trickle of water and the scurrying of squirrels, but then he heard it; a voice, not the low grunt of a Gertulk, but a high, terrified stutter that Aaron immediately recognized as Roger's.

"No, please! I don't know what you want, I don't. Really, I don't! I don't know anything. Please just let me go! Please!"

And then they heard the unmistakable voice of a Gertulk, speaking in broken English. "Quiet, runt!" it barked, and they heard a sickening crunch. Aaron had a nasty feeling that the Gertulk had just hit Roger's skull against a tree. "What were you doing out in those woods? Talk!"

"Nothing! I swear," they heard Roger reply. "I was with some friends!"

"Where are they?"

"This is barbaric!" whispered Ellie. "We have to save him!"

"You're right," said Aaron. "Ellie, Bonnie, Gallagher, you three hide in that clump of bushes, and *stay there*. Yes, Bonnie, you have to stay hidden! Jack, circle around behind the Gertulk, I'll see if I can take them out with the bow."

The four of them scattered to their positions, and Aaron crept toward the voices. Peeking through the branches of a bush, he saw an awful sight. Roger was huddled on the ground, whimpering, blood oozing down his forehead from beneath his scalp. Standing over him was a large, beefy Gertulk, who was growling at him. Behind them stood three more Gertulk, watching silently.

"You're Gertulk, aren't you?" breathed Roger. "Listen, I know the guy you're after. He's about my size with brown hair and green eyes, he's over there!" Roger pointed off in the direction of the clearing where they had met. "He might still be there! He's with four other kids."

"That traitor!" Aaron muttered under his breath.

"Very well," said the Gertulk. "You'll take us to where they are, and if you're lying, we'll wring your neck and cook you as our dinner. Human makes an excellent stew," he added with a nasty sneer.

Aaron drew back the string on the bow, stood straight as Laza had taught him, and aimed the tip at the Gertulk towering over Roger. Aaron released the bowstring, sending an arrow swiftly and silently at the Gertulk, hitting him between the eyes. As the Gertulk fell, Aaron drew a second arrow, turning the bow around to face the other three monsters, managing to shoot down one of them.

"Over there!" shouted one of the remaining Gertulk, pointing at the bush where Aaron was hiding. Aaron reached into the sheath for a third arrow, but it was too late. The Gertulk were charging toward him, swords raised.

Jack leapt out of hiding, uttering a war cry, and struck one of the Gertulk over the head with the bat. The Gertulk turned, gnashing his teeth, and attacked Jack, but the other ignored both of them and dived at Aaron. Aaron pitched aside the bow and dove out of the bush, drawing the hunting knife from his belt and facing the Gertulk.

"Get out of here, run!" Aaron shouted at Roger. Roger scrambled to his feet and disappeared into the darkness. The Gertulk charged, and Aaron leapt upwards, grabbing a branch protruding from the tree next to him. He swung on the sturdy limb, kicking the Gertulk in the face with both feet. The Gertulk staggered, and Aaron released the branch, executing a midair somersault and landing behind the Gertulk. The Gertulk raised his heavy broadsword and hacked at Aaron. Aaron dodged the blade, raised his knife, and drove it through one of the Gertulk's eyes. The beast stiffened, rolled over, and moved no more.

Jack, meanwhile, was still engaged in a fierce duel with the largest Gertulk. He parried and dodged as the Gertulk swung his sword wildly, weaving in and out of his opponent's reach until he was able to get in a blow smashing the Gertulk's elbow. The Gertulk howled and dropped his sword, and Jack prepared to club him over the head.

"Wait!" said Aaron as Jack raised the bat for a killing blow.

Jack looked up. "What?"

Aaron marched over to the Gertulk on the ground and drove his knife into the beast's shoulder. The Gertulk cried out in pain and anger. Aaron sat down on the monster's breastplate and clamped a firm hand to the Gertulk's throat. "Where is the rest of your crew?" Aaron demanded, tightening his grip on the monster's throat.

"There is no crew," choked the Gertulk. "We were alone!"

Aaron took hold of the hilt of the knife and shoved it upwards, creating a larger wound in the beasts shoulder. The Gertulk cried out in pain.

"Where is the rest of your crew?" Aaron repeated, now twisting the knife brutally.

"On the outskirts of the city!" wailed the Gertulk. "There are ten others!"

"And you're sure?" asked Aaron, and his friends were frightened to see the extreme lack of emotion on his face.

"Yes!" sobbed the Gertulk.

Aaron wrenched the knife out of the Gertulk's shoulder and instead drove it into his kneecap. The Gertulk screamed ever louder and burst out "Alright! Alright! They're not at the outskirts, we were set to meet behind the school at sundown!"

"And how many did you say there are?" Aaron asked politely.

"Twenty-five, now just kill me!"

Aaron stood up. "Thank you," he said to the moaning Gertulk, and swiftly clubbed him over the head with the bat. Aaron turned to Jack, who had been standing behind him. "I guess we now have our heading," he said grimly.

Jack nodded, and Aaron saw his lips form the words "twenty-five..."

Aaron was thinking the same thing. How could the two of them possibly take out twenty-five Gertulk? Just these four had been hard enough. Aaron masked his concerns and turned to his friends. "We need to set a trap. We have the bow, that's our biggest advantage. We'll wait on the roof of the school and pick them off one by one with the bow."

Ellie, Bonnie, and Gallagher simply gaped at Aaron, looking appalled.

"What?" said Aaron.

"You…" breathed Bonnie, "you just tortured that Gertulk!"

"He had information we need, and there wasn't any other way I could make him talk."

"But—but—" stammered Ellie, looking as she was going to be sick. She looked over at the Gertulk's unmoving body and swallowed hard. Aaron sighed, and walked over to her, slipped his arm around her shoulders, and gently turned her away from the scene of the battle.

"This is the part of my life in Acklyon I never wanted you to see," he said quietly to her, "I know it all sounded like a grand adventure, but there was real peril. I showed mercy once, and one of my friends is dead because of it. I can kill Gertulk because I know that they don't deserve this life. But there are many good people who did who died at the hands of the Gertulk. My job is to ensure that the good people survive. In order to do that, I don't have the luxury of a conscience when in battle. I didn't want you to have to see that. I know it frightened you; it frightens me, a lot. I stay awake at nights, wondering what I've turned into. I see the faces of the Gertulk I've killed as I fall asleep. I can remember every last one of them. This is my life, I understand that now. This is why I have to return to Acklyon."

Ellie nodded and hugged Aaron tightly, blinking hard.

"I've seen people get tortured on TV," muttered Gallagher, "but I never thought it would be so...painful."

* * *

As the sun went down, Aaron, Jack, Ellie, Bonnie, and Gallagher could be found sitting on the roof of Avondale Middle School, waiting. Aaron was pacing back and forth, the bow and an arrow in his hands. Presently, Jack got up and joined Aaron's vigil.

"I wonder what will happen to them," Jahkon murmured.

"Who?" asked Adinyrom.

"Aaron Tackers, and Jack Oswald," said Jahkon, "they won't remember any of this, you know."

"No, they won't..." Adinyrom said thoughtfully. "They'll never know they were in a real battle."

"Jack spent his whole life dreaming that something like this would happen," said Jahkon. "He'll never know that it actually did."

"I know what you mean," said Adinyrom. "In a way, I envy Aaron Tackers. He has a good life. He comes from a wealthy family, he has friends at school and parents who love him. I sometimes wish that I could go back to having his life...but I never can. Acklyon needs me, needs both of us."

"Still, I think our presence in their lives will have done them good," said Jahkon. "After all, you introduced Jack into Aaron's group. I think he will have a happier time in school from now on."

"Indeed..." said Adinyrom, his voice trailing off into thought.

The moment was broken by Bonnie, who rushed over to where the two Princes stood. "They're here," she panted. "The Gertulk! They've come!"

Aaron glanced at Jack, who nodded.

The two sprinted over to the edge of the building, where they saw indeed a large group of Gertulk. Aaron did a headcount, and sure enough, there were twenty-five. Aaron swallowed hard. "If any of you want to back out, this is your last opportunity."

"We're staying with you, Aaron," Bonnie stated, eyes on the Gertulk.

"Alright, then," said Aaron, and grimly nocked an arrow. "Jack, sneak around behind them. Take one of the staffs, the bat, and as many knives as you can carry. Flash me a signal when you're in position. Don't be seen."

Jack nodded and slipped away into the shadows.

Aaron turned to the other three, huddled together. "Stay out of the way at all costs. Under no circumstances are you to go near the battle. Got it?"

"Yes sir, Sergeant Grumpy Pants," muttered Bonnie. Even in this moment of tension, Aaron couldn't help but smile. He turned his eyes back to the Gertulk, waiting for Jack's signal. At last he saw it, the gleam of a coin reflecting the glare from one of the big floodlights on the wall.

Every fear, every doubt, every emotion left Aaron's mind. His whole being had become absolute; his vision had narrowed until the only thing he saw was the assembled mass. He stood straight, drew back the bowstring, and released.

23
The Battle of Avondale

For the first time, Aaron fully understood the meaning of "the shot heard 'round the world"—the first shot fired at the Battle of Lexington and Concord during the Revolutionary War. As Aaron released the bowstring, the *twang! whizz!* seemed to him as though it could be heard throughout Avondale, throughout the world. Aaron's aim was true, the arrow striking the captain squarely in the forehead. The massed Gertulk jumped, and immediately began searching for the source of the attack. Aaron took aim again, and a second Gertulk collapsed, dark blood seeping from his chest.

"Twenty-three," Aaron muttered, shooting again. "Twenty-two."

Skilled as they were, the Gertulk, unable to find where the arrows were coming from, were all but helpless. They turned stupidly on the spot, unable to determine which way to point their wall shields.

"Eighteen!" said Aaron as he continued shooting, "Seventeen! Sixteen! Fifteen!"

He had run out of arrows. In the growing dark, he could not see well enough to reload and couldn't risk using the flashlight for fear of the Gertulk discovering his location.Instead, he stood up, one of Jack's carved wooden staffs in one hand and his knife in the other. "Come!" he shouted savagely to the Gertulk. "Come and taste the blood of your kin!"

The Gertulk, upon seeing him, immediately scrambled to climb the walls of the school. Aaron was waiting for them, though. As soon as one made it onto the roof, he struck them with his staff—where they either tumbled to their deaths below or else fell victim to the sharpened spike.

Meanwhile, Jack had taken the fight to the few Gertulk who had not rushed to attack Aaron. His wooden staff lay abandoned on the round, snapped in two by a ferocious swing from a broadsword. Jack now stood against the wall, wielding a saber he had taken from one of the dead Gertulk.

Aaron, for his part, found himself quickly outmatched and outnumbered. No matter how many Gertulk he slew, they could climb onto the roof quicker than he could strike them down. Before long he found himself fending off blows from a steadily increasing cluster of Gertulk. Glancing down at the ground, he saw that Jack was in a similar predicament, with more Gertulk than he could fight off surrounding him. *So this is how I die,* Aaron thought grimly, ducking under a blow from a Gertulk and stabbing him in the gut with his staff. *At my old school, surrounded by Malvadore's minions.*

One Gertulk barreled forward, raising a huge battle axe. Aaron had a sudden image of the butcher in Muln, charging towards him with a similar axe. Aaron raised his staff to parry the Gertulk, but the mighty swing cleaved Aaron's staff in two. Aaron glanced at the now useless broken stick in his hand. *Uh oh.*

"Aaron, get down!" came Bonnie's voice from behind. Aaron turned to see her silhouette in the glare of one of the floodlights, the bow in her hands, a second quiver full of arrows on her back,

Ellie and Gallagher on either side.

Aaron turned and sprinted towards the edge of the roof, all of the Gertulk behind him. Aaron leapt into the air, and with a cry of "SHOOT!" rolled behind an emergency exit. Crouched down in the shadows, he heard the loud *twang!* of the bow again and again as Bonnie sent arrow after arrow into the crowd of Gertulk.

"She's got a bow!" Aaron heard one of the Gertulk shout. "Destroy it!"

Aaron stood up and chucked his knife at the Gertulk, striking him in the neck. The one Gertulk buckled, but the rest persisted: half of them charged at Bonnie while the other half attacked Aaron. Without thinking, Aaron turned and dove off the side of the building, executing several somersaults as he fell. He landed quite painfully in a large shrub. Judging by the searing pain in his ribs, he estimated that at least one of them was broken. A second later, he saw Jack's face above him.

"You okay?" asked Jack, lending a hand to pull Aaron out of the shrub.

"I'll live," grunted Aaron, massaging his ribs.

"Not if we don't stop these Gertulk—and fast," said Jack.

"Where are they?" asked Aaron as he gingerly got to his feet, wincing.

"Right now, they think I'm somewhere on the other side of the building. That's where I lost them. But they'll be here in a few seconds. We need to mobilize."

"I'm no good to you," panted Aaron, sweat dripping down his face. "I think I broke a few ribs. It was a long fall from the roof of the building. Jack, there are at least four Gertulk on the roof, and that's where Ellie and the others are!"

Even in the dim light of the floodlights, Aaron could see

Jack's face grow white.

"What are we going to do?" gasped Aaron, the pain in his ribs growing by the second.

"You hide," said Jack. "I'm going up there to help them out."

Jack disappeared into the darkness, and Aaron staggered back towards the shrubs. He crawled into one of them and stood absolutely still, hoping against hope he wasn't found. Several Gertulk passed right by him. Aaron held his breath and kept still, praying with all his might.

One of the Gertulk stopped, sniffing the air. "I smell something'!" he shouted to his comrades. "One of the 'umans is nearby!"

"Spread out!" said another. "If the bleedin' scamp is here, we'll find 'im!"

The three Gertulk fanned out, probing the air with their noses. Aaron focused hard, as though he could stop himself from smelling like a human through sheer willpower. But it was no good—one of the Gertulk stopped and turned his head to stare straight at the shrub Aaron was hiding in. Slowly, the brute crept forward, sword at the ready.

A sudden rustling came from the left. The three Gertulk turned in the direction of the sounds and immediately stomped over to investigate. No sooner were they out of sight when Aaron felt a hand on his mouth. He turned, horrorstruck, but it was only Gallagher, crouched over him.

"*Gallagher!*" Aaron whispered, removing Gallagher's hand. "*What are you doing here*?"

"Rescuing you, what does it look like?" Gallagher whispered back. "Come on, we need to move before they come back! Can you walk?"

"Barely, you'll have to help me," Aaron grunted. "The fall

broke my ribs."

Gallagher pulled Aaron to his feet and put his arm around him. Aaron leaned on Gallagher, and together they limped away to the right.

"Where are the others? Are they okay?" asked Aaron.

"It's okay. They're alive. We have a plan to get us out of here, and it's going to work."

"How?"

"There were twenty-five Gertulk when we got here. You took out ten of them before you ran out of arrows. Then when you and Jack attacked you took out another eight. Bonnie's already killed three more. That means there are four left. Bonnie's hiding in the trees. Ellie is drawing attention and leading them to Bonnie, and Bonnie picks them off with the bow. They sent me to find you."

"What about Jack? Where is he?"

"We don't know. He could be…"

Aaron turned cold at the very thought. "Where is Bonnie hiding?"

"Over there," said Gallagher, pointing towards the edge of the woods.

"Let's go."

Aaron and Gallagher hobbled towards Bonnie and Ellie's trap. It was near total darkness by now, and they couldn't see what was happening until they were very close. They crept forward stealthily until, at last, in the dim glow of the Gertulk's torches they saw a horrible sight: Ellie, Bonnie, and Jack were kneeling on the ground, bound and gagged. Standing over them were three very angry Gertulk, sneering in celebration at their victory. Behind them lay the fourth Gertulk, dark blood oozing from a wound on his chest.

"I'll give you three credit," one of them gloated. "You and your li'l friends put up a mighty fine fight! Yeh might have even won if we hadn't caught this one—" The Gertulk kicked Jack hard in the stomach "—and threatened to kill him if you didn't surrender. And now all we have to do is wait for your two friends to show up, and we'll be back in Rarzan by sunrise!"

"This is bad!" squeaked Gallagher. "This is really bad! What are we going to do?"

"I have an idea," Aaron grunted, "but we need to fall back. I need to find something."

"What about the others?"

"The Gertulk tied them up. That means they're not aiming to kill us. They should be fine... They want all five of us, which means it's imperative that you and I aren't found. Come on."

They crept away from the light, back towards the school.

"Flashlight," Aaron muttered.

Gallagher pulled a flashlight out of his belt and handed it to Aaron. Aaron switched it on and aimed it at the ground, revealing the gruesome sight of the many Gertulk corpses on the ground. Aaron dropped to the ground and began digging through the bodies.

"What are you doing?" whispered Gallagher.

"Here!" said Aaron, turning over the body of one of the smaller Gertulk. He wasted no time in fumbling with the latches and buckles on the Gertulk's armor. "Help me get his armor off him!"

Gallagher paused, a repulsed look on his face.

"Come on!" Aaron snapped. "We don't have much time!"

Gallagher knelt down and assisted Aaron in stripping the Gertulk of his armor. When they had it all off of the body Aaron turned to Gallagher. "We need to get me into this. Hurry!"

With many cries of pain from Aaron, they finally succeeded

in dressing Aaron in the Gertulk's armor. When they were done, Aaron, looking much like a Gertulk, turned to Gallagher. "Tell me you have some rope with you."

Gallagher pulled a length of rope out of his satchel. Aaron grinned.

"Now let's tie you up," he said. Despite his ribs and the weight of the armor, Aaron managed to bind Gallagher's hands behind his back. "Now let's go," he said grimly.

The two set off again with Aaron dressed as a Gertulk and Gallagher tied up. As they went, Aaron explained his plan to Gallagher. "The important part," he concluded, "is for you to stay out of the way. Get Ellie and Bonnie, and the three of you *hide*. Leave the action to me and Jack."

"But you can barely stand—"

"Trust me," Aaron said through gritted teeth. "Come on. And remember, *stay down*." And with that, Aaron took a deep breath and struck Gallagher in the small of the back, sending him sprawling on the ground in the circle of light.

The three Gertulk turned to face him. Aaron staggered out of the shadows and said in his best imitation of a Gertulk's thick accent, "Caught this one trying to get away! No sign of the last one. He must have escaped."

One of the Gertulk stepped forward, smirking down at Gallagher. "Well, well," he leered. "That makes four. And what happened to you?" he added to Aaron, noticing Aaron doubled over, clutching his ribs.

"Li'l blighter kicked me off the roof," Aaron grunted. "Landed hard, broke some ribs."

The Gertulk nodded and gestured to his two fellows, who stepped forward to help Aaron to his feet. The first Gertulk seized Gallagher and shoved him next to Ellie. "Now we just need to find your last friend!" he said.

The two other Gertulk supported Aaron, one on either side of him.

"Do you suppose we should try sticking a knife in one of you four? Maybe when he hears your screams, he'll come and try to save you!" He advanced on Bonnie, holding a dagger.

"I expect that'll work," said Aaron, just loud enough to draw all their attention. He reached for his belt, pulling out two daggers. Before anyone could do so much as breathe, he stabbed the two Gertulk supporting him.

As they fell, each with a knife in his side, Gallagher leapt to his feet, throwing off the poorly-tied knots.

The last surviving Gertulk was focused on Aaron enough that he never saw Gallagher seize a fallen sword from the ground. The Gertulk had just drawn his sword and advanced toward Aaron when from behind, Gallagher shoved the sword firmly through a gap in the beast's armor. The monster fell, leaving Gallagher standing, with a horrified expression on his face. Aaron crawled over to Jack, Ellie, and Bonnie and untied them.

Upon being freed, Bonnie leapt to her feet and hugged her brother tightly. Both of them had killed that day.

Jack came up behind them and placed one hand each on Gallagher and Bonnie's shoulders. "We owe you three our lives," he said quietly. "Without you, we never could have won."

Bonnie relinquished Gallagher and instead hugged Jack. "Their faces…" she whispered, resting her head on his shoulder. "I killed them."

"It was us or them," Jack said soothingly. "If you hadn't done what you did, all five of us would be dead or captive. You were brave."

"It's not…" Bonnie sniffed. "It's not like in the movies. I saw their faces as I shot them… They never knew what hit them, and then they were dead."

"Well we have kind of been trying to tell you that for a while now," said Jack, but quietly so that she could not hear.

"Guys!" shouted Ellie. The others turned to see her kneeling over Aaron, who lay on the ground, gasping for breath. Jack, Gallagher, and Bonnie rushed over.

"This is bad," said Ellie. She had taken off her jacket and now used it as a pillow for Aaron's head. She had removed Aaron's shirt so as to access the wound better. His rib cage was dented gruesomely on the left side where he had fallen.

"He needs to get to a hospital!" said Ellie. "This looks pretty serious."

"No," gasped Aaron.

"Don't talk," Ellie said quietly to him. "Just try to relax."

"NO!" Aaron choked. "I can't go to a hospital! Hospitals mean lying in bed for days or weeks, not being able to do anything or go anywhere…and it means family and friends, visitors…I can't go through that, not again…I can't say goodbye again."

"He's right," said Jack tersely. "We need to get back to Acklyon, now."

"Are you crazy?" demanded Ellie. "He could die if he doesn't get medical attention!"

"I know," said Jack, "but we don't have a choice. The Elves need us."

"The Elves, the Elves!" cried Ellie hysterically. "Always about the stupid Elves! If we don't get him to a doctor quick, Aaron is going to die! Do you hear me? AARON. WILL. DIE!"

"I know!" snapped Jack. "But we hardly have a choice!"

"Then make a new option!" Ellie screamed, leaping to her feet.

"What do you expect me to do?" Jack shouted, also standing.

"You could start with something that *doesn't* involve killing your best friend!" Ellie shoved Jack hard. Jack had just stepped forward menacingly when Bonnie leapt to her feet and stood in between them. "Guys, STOP!" she shouted, glaring at both of them. "We can't fight amongst ourselves! We need a plan, and fast."

"What can we do?" said Gallagher. "If we put him in a hospital, it could be too late to save the Elves, but if we don't, Aaron could die."

"Right now, I would say Aaron's the main priority," said Ellie. "I'll call an ambulance."

"No!" said Jack. "What do you suppose they'll think when they see the corpses of twenty-five dead Gertulk?"

"Does it really matter?" said Ellie.

"Lord…" Aaron muttered incoherently.

"What did you say?" Gallagher dropped down next to Aaron.

"Lord…" Aaron said again, sweat running down his face in gallons.

"What is he talking about?" said Bonnie, looking scared. "What does 'lord' mean?"

"Cygon…" gasped Aaron, his eyes fixed on a point in the distance. "Lord Cygon…"

"Lord Cygon?" said Gallagher, "Let me think, isn't he—"

"The wizard that helped Kellaoth save Aaron and me from the Fall of Acklyon and who helped us come back to Avondale? Yes," said Jack.

"Lord Cygon!" Aaron repeated with more strength.

"What about Lord Cygon?" asked Bonnie.

Aaron lifted his arm and pointed—in the distance, a golden orb was floating towards them.

"It's him..." breathed Jack. "He's here! Lord Cygon is here!"

"You never told us he could do the Fairy Godmother thing," Bonnie commented as the shining golden ball floated down next to Jack.

"That is a misconception, actually," came Cygon's reproachful voice, echoing slightly. "A more accurate thing to say would be, 'Fairy Godmother can do the Lord Cygon thing.' I was turning myself into a bubble long before she was."

"Oh...sorry," said Bonnie, raising an eyebrow.

"You came just in time, sir," said Jack, smiling at the ball of light. "We were about out of luck."

"Indeed, but you handled yourself remarkably," said Cygon's voice, as light cast the carnage of the battle into greater glory. "My God, did you really defeat all these Gertulk?"

"With a little help," Jack winked at Ellie, Bonnie, and Gallagher.

"That's an understatement!" snapped Bonnie. "Don't listen to him, Lord Cygon. Without us he would be dead already."

"I surmised as much," said Cygon.

"Uh, guys?" called Ellie, who was kneeling next to Aaron. "Can we catch up later? This wound is getting worse and worse."

"Ah, let's see..." Cygon sent a beam of golden mist through the orb. Several tendrils entwined Aaron's chest. Moments later, Aaron sat up, rubbing his newly-healed ribcage.

"Thanks," he panted, getting unsteadily to his feet, leaning on Ellie.

"Cygon," said Jack, "Aaron and I have to get back to Acklyon, now. Can you take us?"

"I thought you were not the Chosen Ones, that you wish to return to having a normal life?" came Cygon's voice, with just a hint of smugness.

"Honestly, I don't know anymore whether I'm Chosen or not," said Aaron, "but we need to get back and help the Elves."

Cygon laughed. "Of course. Welcome back, Prince Adinyrom."

"It's good to be back," Aaron grinned. He then turned to Ellie, Bonnie, and Gallagher. "You three...thank you. There's no way we could have defeated the Gertulk without you. We'll miss you."

"Whoa, whoa, whoa!" cried Bonnie. "Just what do you think you're talking about? We're not going anywhere!"

"She's right," said Ellie. "We're coming with you to Acklyon."

"Absolutely not," said Jack. "You could die!"

"So could you," Gallagher pointed out. "We want to be there."

"Listen," said Aaron impatiently. "I know what you're thinking, but Acklyon isn't some fairytale wonderland! It's a battlefield—you either learn to become a murderer or you're killed or captured."

"You think we don't know that?" demanded Bonnie. "We've seen how much you two changed. We fought and killed Gertulk, for crying out loud! You two would be dead right now if not for us. What's to stop you from dying just as brutally in Acklyon?"

"Besides," said Gallagher, "how could we go back to our normal lives, knowing the truth about you two and where you are?"

"It's out of the question," said Aaron firmly. "I'm not letting you three come with us. It's no place for children."

"Yeah, 'cause you two aren't thirteen at all..." grumbled Bonnie.

"Are you two ready to leave?" Cygon asked Aaron and Jack.

"Yes," said Aaron. "Ellie, Bonnie, Gallagher...thanks. And goodbye."

After briefly hugging each of them, Aaron and Jack turned to the ball of light.

"Take us to Acklyon," said Jack.

Again, the golden mist seeped out of the ball of light, settling on the ground. When it had cleared, they saw again the pool that would take them back to the Fifth World. Aaron and Jack approached the pool, and this time they felt no fear. For a moment, Aaron looked down into the depths and at his reflection, which now wore a whole crown instead of a half. Then he took a deep breath and leaned forward.

"NOW!" yelled Bonnie. She, Ellie, and Gallagher charged forward, flinging their arms around Aaron and Jack. Aaron struggled, but it was already too late. The five of them toppled into the pool, and Aaron felt himself once again streaking away from Avondale and back through the River of Time. As before, Aaron felt as though he had left his body back at the school, sending his spirit swooping through the River of Time. The only difference was Ellie's astral body clinging to his. Also as before, he soon saw a tiny black dot in the distance, which slowly grew larger as he drew nearer and nearer. When he was able to see trees, bushes, and an old dirt road he felt a rush of excitement—*he was going home.*

24
Acklyon Once More

Aaron, Jack, Ellie, Bonnie, and Gallagher shot through the portal all at once, landing unceremoniously on the dewy grass. As soon as Aaron had regained the use of his limbs, he rounded on Ellie, Bonnie, and Gallagher. "*Are you insane?*" he bellowed.

Bonnie got to her feet and turned to face Aaron. "You're taller!" she said in surprise.

"What?" said Aaron, distracted.

"You're taller!" said Bonnie, measuring heights with her hand. "You're supposed to be the short one!"

Aaron looked down at his body. It was true—when he had gone back to Avondale, he had regained the body of Aaron Tackers. Now that he was in Acklyon again, his body had returned to its previous form. Dirty overgrown hair, shrunken stomach, toned muscles, bruises and scars lining his powerful limbs, and as Bonnie had noted, he was at least three inches taller.

"And I'm guessing they don't endorse shampoo in Acklyon," Ellie observed, eyeing Aaron's shaggy, unkempt hair.

"That's not the point!" said Aaron, steering back the topic. "What part of 'don't come with us to Acklyon' didn't you understand?"

"That would be the part where we let our friends go get

themselves killed while we just pretend that a regiment of Gertulk didn't attack Avondale," said Ellie quietly.

Aaron sighed. "Look, it's not that we don't appreciate everything you've done for us, but I don't want to see you three killed."

"So you *won't,*" said Bonnie.

"Yeah, well, when you're on the run from an insane, demonic warlord and his army of hellbeasts, that isn't always an option," said Jack seriously.

"You two have made it this far," said Gallagher.

"Barely," said Aaron, "and that's with the whole 'magical birthright' deal. I'd hate to see what could happen to you three."

"Hey, I've got a compound bow," said Bonnie with a grin, "not to mention three years worth of fencing training. That's way better than any old princehood!"

"This is serious," snapped Aaron, "we have to find a way to get you three back to Avondale!"

"Well, you can forget it 'cause we're not going anywhere!" Bonnie crossed her arms.

Aaron stepped forward, but Jack cut him off.

"Give it a rest, Aaron," he said. "I may not be the leader of this group, but I know a lost cause when I see one."

"See? Listen to the ginger!" said Bonnie.

"Hey, I'm not a ginger!" said Jack indignantly. "It's strawberry blonde! Look, I've had enough experience with Bonnie to know that when she says she's going to roundhouse kick you in the face, she WILL roundhouse kick you in the face. I mean, why do you think my nose is slightly bent to the left?"

Bonnie grinned sheepishly.

"I think they could help us," Jack continued. "As she said, we'd be Gertulk fodder if not for them. Why not give them a chance?"

Aaron looked from Jack, somber and serious, to Bonnie, who still had her arms crossed. "Okay," he said finally, "but you have to do *everything* I tell you to."

"If it involves me making you sandwiches, you're out of luck."

"This is no laughing matter!" snapped Aaron. "This is— "

"Life and death, despair and darkness, apocalypse now," said Bonnie. "*We get it.*"

In spite of himself, Aaron grinned. You never know what a friend is made of until he's tested under severe circumstances, and now Aaron saw that he had three of the best friends a man could dream of having.

25
The Troll Cave

"There they are!"

After several hours' worth of scouting, Aaron, Jack, Ellie, Bonnie, and Gallagher finally located the Elves' encampment.

"Finally!" said Bonnie, standing up. "Let's go!"

"Wait!" said Aaron, grabbing her arm.

"What?" said Bonnie irritably. "You're their predestined leaders, right?"

"Bonnie, Jack and I abandoned them at the first chance we got, left them for dead while we went back to our comfortable lives. I don't exactly think they're going to welcome us back with open arms."

"It's not like we ever even did anything for them," Jack added.

"My point is," Aaron continued, "we need to find a way to win back their trust before we just walk back into camp."

"Any ideas?" asked Bonnie.

"We could kill Malvadore?" suggested Ellie.

"Yeah, just let me know when you find a weapon powerful enough to kill him," Aaron grumbled.

"Aaron, check this out!"

Aaron turned to see Jack kneeling by the path, inspecting the dust. "What is it?" Aaron asked him.

"Look at these tracks," said Jack, gesturing.

Aaron squinted at the prints in the ground. His first impression was that an elephant had been trained to walk on its back legs until he caught the stench—something like several sweating boys combined with moldy cheese.

"A troll!" Aaron murmured, stepping back.

"Aaaaaaand a sled," Jack observed, pointing towards a line of parallel tracks.

"A sled carrying provisions," Aaron continued, picking up a piece of bread which had no doubt fallen from the sled.

"Not too long ago," Jack concluded.

"Um…so?" said Ellie, coming up behind them.

"What did Laza teach us about trolls?" Aaron asked Jack.

"A troll's anatomy is extremely similar to that of a Man's or an Elf's," Jack recited, "meaning, they eat the same types of food that we do, but in much greater supply."

"What are you talking about?" asked Gallagher.

"Trolls always have several tons worth of food near them," Aaron explained. "*Always*."

"You two aren't making any sense."

"On the other side of that hill, there is a starving Elf colony close to death," said Jack, "and somewhere nearby, there's an underground cave that's chock full of meats, cheeses, and bread."

"Are you saying we go kill this troll?" squeaked Gallagher in a high-pitched voice.

"Don't listen to him," said Bonnie. "That's his girl voice."

Gallagher cleared his throat and said in his normal voice, "Are you saying we go kill this troll?"

"Jack, can you trace the tracks?" Aaron asked.

"Give me a second," said Jack, bending down again to examine the prints. "The troll went…that way!" he pointed to the north.

"How did he do that?" Gallagher muttered to Ellie.

"He's a natural at tracking," Aaron explained. "So were a lot of his ancestors. We think there was an Elf somewhere in the Parnor family tree."

"Well that would explain why he's so short," Bonnie said under her breath.

"Hey!" said Jack.

"Anyway, where did you say the troll cave is?" Aaron said to Jack. Jack pointed again.

"Then buckle up, everyone," said Aaron. "We're going troll hunting. And Bonnie, give me that bow, I don't trust you with weapons."

"Oh, please!" said Bonnie. "I've been shooting one of these at my cousin's cabin since I was ten!"

"It was a very traumatic experience," Gallagher commented.

"For her or for you?"

"For me," said Gallagher.

"This way!" said Jack, leading the way. "Aaron, can you help me decipher the tracks?"

Aaron sped up to walk next to Jack.

"I didn't want to say anything in front of the others," Jack said in an undertone, "but do you realize what we're trying to do? Killing a troll? We've both heard the stories about bands of hunters who stumble into their caves looking for shelter and are—"

"Crushed and pummeled, beaten till dead, he ground their bones to make his bread," Aaron finished. "*I know*. Besides, the 'grinding bones to make his bread' part is a misconception. Everyone knows that..."

"Still and yet, a troll is among the most dangerous natural beasts that walk this planet, not counting Gertulk or Dragons or other Sixth World monsters," Jack said. "How are five children, with only makeshift weapons, going to take this thing down?"

"Because you and I are not just two children," said Aaron. "We are Princes."

"Here we go!" said Jack excitedly. "This is it!"

"This," said Bonnie skeptically, "is a patch of dirt."

Indeed, there was absolutely nothing in the vicinity that resembled the entrance to a troll's cave. Aaron, however, began stomping on the patch of dust and cocked his ear as though listening for sounds of hollowness.

"There's a soft spot right...here!" Aaron slammed his foot down on the ground, then again, and again. He then took the baseball bat and began pounding the spot until he finally punched straight through the thin layer of dirt.

"Flashlight!" said Aaron. Gallagher passed him their flashlight. "I can't see much," he said as he shined the ray of light into the hole. "Get me the rope!"

Ellie fished through her pack until she found the length of rope, and two minutes later Aaron was being lowered into the hole, flashlight in hand, the bow strapped across his back.

"Aaron?" Bonnie called from above. "Do you see anything?"

"Not yet," Aaron said as he touched ground. "Jack, come on down!"

Jack slid down the rope, landing gracefully next to Aaron. "What is this place?" he asked.

Aaron put his hand on what seemed to be a cooking stove and a stone countertop. "It's a kitchen," he breathed, "but not nearly big enough for a troll to use... It's hardly big enough for a Man to use."

"The troll must have a slave doing the cooking for him...

probably an Elf, from the size of this stuff."

"Who goes there?" said a high-pitched, frightened voice.

In an instant, the flashlight was off and Aaron and Jack disappeared into the shadows. The stranger stepped further into the kitchen. Judging by the soft footsteps and the voice, it was indeed an Elf, probably female.

"You can't hide from me!" said the Elf. "Come out!"

In a split second, Aaron made his decision. "It's okay!" he said, standing up and turning on the flashlight. "We're here to help you."

The Elf leapt backwards, swinging an iron poker wildly.

"Don't worry," said Jack. "We're not going to hurt you!"

"I'm deadly! I'm dangerous!" jabbered the Elf. "I'll hurt you! I'll kill you!"

"Aaron!" said Jack suddenly. "We're speaking English!"

"Oh, right," said Aaron, smacking his forehead, "wangypang ywiki!wookaweekeAaronoJackiwookaweekewu?"

The Elf paused, staring at them.

"We're not going to hurt you," Aaron said in Elfish.

The Elf slowly lowered the poker then rushed over to Aaron. "You have to get out of here!" she squeaked. "There's a troll, Orgoth, and he *hates* visitors!"

"We're not visiting," said Aaron. "We're conquering."

"You can try," said the Elf. "He's mean."

"So am I," said Aaron, stringing the bow.

A sudden roar issued from the door.

"Oh no, he's coming!" squealed the Elf, running for cover.

"Get ready!" said Aaron drawing back the bowstring. They could both feel the pounding footsteps now, growing nearer.

"Did you actually think about *how* we're going to kill a troll?" Jack said, bat in hand.

"I'm following Laza's most effective strategy," said Aaron grimly.

"You mean making it up as you go along?"

"Pretty much."

"Aaron," said Jack, "all the stories say that only the fiercest warriors can take out a troll!"

"And my high-tech bow and arrow says otherwise," said Aaron.

The huge, wooden door swung open and there stood Orgoth. He towered twelve feet tall, covered in dirty white fur. Teeth that were easily the size of Aaron's dagger filled Orgoth's mouth, and his yellow eyes blinked stupidly at them. "HOKEY!" bellowed the troll. "WHERE'S MY SUPPER?"

"Hokey couldn't make it," said Aaron, taking aim, "but I have your entrée!"

With a loud *twang,* Aaron released an arrow. Orgoth staggered as an arrow struck him in the shoulder, but regained his balance with a roar.

"What does your high-tech bow say now?" Jack said.

Orgoth seized a heavy wooden club from the wall and swung it at Aaron. Aaron managed to dodge the blow, but Orgoth's club struck the bow, sending it spinning into the darkness. Jack sneaked around behind Orgoth and struck him on the back of the knee with the bat. Orgoth buckled with an angry bellow, but turned and kicked Jack in the abdomen. Orgoth turned, and was about to crush Jack when Aaron leapt onto the troll's back. Orgoth spun around and around until he threw Aaron off of him.

"YOU WILL DIE FOR THIS!" Orgoth shouted, raising the club.

A sudden clanking and banging came from several different areas. Orgoth turned, confused, unable to choose which source of noise to attack.

Ellie, Bonnie, and Gallagher stepped out of the shadows, hitting pots and pans against each other and shouting incoherently. Orgoth turned and roared, becoming disoriented from the din.

Aaron groped through the shadows until he found the bow. He stood and began firing arrows at the troll. Though they did little damage, the blades and their sting helped to drive an increasingly angry Orgoth berserk.

Bonnie hurled the pitchfork like a javelin, striking the troll in the shoulder. Orgoth howled as the sharpened steel dug into his flesh and flailed as he tried to remove it.

Ellie and Gallagher threw rocks at his eyes. Orgoth swung his club manically at the nearest target, Bonnie. Bonnie ducked and leapt backwards into the shadows again. As she did, she slipped on a thick tube which clattered like metal. The bat! She seized it and threw it into the air, yelling "*Catch it!*" to Aaron. But as Aaron leapt to catch the falling bat, something that no one could describe happened.

Aaron's vision seemed to pass in slow-motion; he saw the bat spiraling towards him, Orgoth chasing Gallagher, Jack by his side, and then he felt a presence within him. It was his Forahn side, stronger than he had ever felt it. Fire exploded from all corners of the room, yet no one was burned. As Aaron's fingers closed around the leather handle, he saw that it was not a baseball bat he held—it was a sword. Golden, studded with rubies, slanted crossbar...

Forvalad had come to him.

26

Forvalad and Parvelad

All eyes, even those of the troll, turned to Aaron as the fiery light from the magic blade lit the entire kitchen. Aaron himself gaped at the specimen in his hands. Every inch of the weapon was perfect, flawless. The rounded pommel, the diamond in the blade, the cross guard forged in a shape similar to the letter *M*, everything was exactly as Aaron had envisioned it.

But Aaron wasn't the only one—beside him, Jack held the shining silver, equally magnificent Parvelad, the Sword of Parland. The cross guard, shaped like eagle's wings, twinkled benignly at them. As Aaron felt the adrenaline pumping inside him, he turned with a grim smile to Orgoth as the flames emanating from Forvalad crackled with pure power.

Orgoth, who had thirty seconds earlier been quite enjoying this rumpus, was now backing away from the heat and light.

Aaron, who felt rather taller than usual, charged, unleashing a bloody war cry as he attacked the troll. With one sturdy thrust, he drove the enchanted blade through the troll's heart. Jack was right behind him, leaping into the air and cutting off Orgoth's head in mid-jump. Orgoth's decapitated body flailed for a couple seconds before collapsing next to his detached head.

For a minute, the cave was silent as the children marveled at their victory before a high-pitched squeal came from the shadows. It was Hokey, the troll's slave, and she was bouncing up and down like a lunatic while hugging Jack around the waist. "Youy did it! Youy saved me! Me is forever in your debt! Me is—" She froze when she saw the sword Aaron held. Then she sank to her knees, kissing Aaron's ankles with incoherent cries of "Me lord! Me lord! Youy have returned at last!"

"See?" Aaron said to Bonnie. "That's how you treat a conquering dignitary!"

"Conquering dignitary?" scoffed Bonnie. "Please, like I couldn't kill a troll if you handed me a magic sword."

"Well, they gave it to me, and that's kind of the point," said Aaron with a smirk.

"Yeah yeah," said Bonnie. "I'm starting to think you're enjoying this whole 'destined ruler' thing a little too much."

"Actually, it's a real drag," said Aaron with a smile, "but it means I'll always be one-up on you, and that's worth it."

"Hey, Aaron!" said Gallagher as he, Jack, and Ellie returned from scouting the cave. "We found Orgoth's private stores. Turns out, trolls only leave their caves about once every month or so, and when they do leave, they raid the nearest village of pretty much all their provisions."

"And they don't eat humans, which is a major upside," Ellie added.

"Is there enough in his stores to last the Elves till Castram?" Aaron asked.

"I think a better question is, is there enough distance between here and Castram for the Elves to eat it all?" said Jack, grinning widely. "You should see it, Aaron. It's unbelievable!"

"I tell you, this troll had good taste!" said Gallagher. "Steaks, pies, fruit, it's all there!"

"What about hardtack?" asked Aaron. "Cornmeal? Cider? Things that won't rot or go bad on the long journey?"

"There's lots and lots of meal in my supply closets," Hokey chimed in, "and yuckytack a-plenty in my kitchen... Smelly Orgoth made me live off of it while I cooked him luscious feasts. Excuse me while I stuff me face in the dinner I prepared for him before you so kindly cut his head off." And with that she scurried through a doorway.

"Stock up," Aaron said to his friends. "We'll take what we can carry and come back for the rest after we make contact with the Elves. Bonnie, Gallagher, get the wagon."

"I don't take orders from you!" Bonnie protested, but Aaron had already left with Jack to inspect the cupboards.

* * *

Half an hour later, the five children and Hokey stood above ground again, their wagon loaded with as much food as it would hold.

"Now, which way to the Elves?" Aaron asked, in much higher spirits than any of them had seen him lately.

Jack pointed towards the hills.

"In that case, onward!" said Aaron enthusiastically.

"Aaron?" said Bonnie as they started down the path. "I know we're in a fantasy universe deal, but if you say, 'Onward!' again, I *will* smack you."

"Can I say, 'tally-ho'?" Aaron asked.

"No," said Bonnie.

"Can I say, 'forward'?"

"No!"

"Can I say, 'I'm the Crowned Prince of this group so I decide what we do and don't say'?"

"I suppose... Just don't say it too often!" said Bonnie.

"In that case..." said Aaron, "I'm the Crowned Prince of this group, so I decide what we do and don't say. And I say onward!"

Bonnie smacked Aaron.

"Okay then," said Jack. "I say that I'm just as much a Crowned Prince as you are, meaning that I also have authority over what we do and don't say, and I say act your age, you two!"

"She started it," grumbled Aaron.

"Did not!" said Bonnie. "You said 'onward'! I had no choice but to step in!"

"Remind me to sentence you to two days spent in the dungeons when I become king," said Aaron with a smirk.

"Oh I would love to see you try!" Bonnie retorted.

"Is this what we can expect for the rest of our possibly very short lives?" Gallagher asked Ellie.

"With any luck one or both of them will receive a serious injury to their esophagus and no longer be able to speak," Jack said.

"They'd probably just use sign language," Ellie commented.

"Let's just hope neither of them learns a second language," Gallagher added. "That way, they could learn that many more insults to call each other!"

"I speak five languages!" said Aaron indignantly.

"We're doomed," sighed Ellie.

"Wait, where did you learn five languages?" Jack asked Aaron. "Laza and Kellaoth only taught us three: Elfish, Gertulk, and Acklish."

"French class, seventh grade," Aaron replied.

"You learned something in French?" Bonnie said in shock. "Didn't you spend the entire class whispering to Roger and copying off of Ellie's notes?"

"Well yeah," said Aaron, "but I can say '*parlez-vous français*'!"

"Everyone can say '*parlez-vous français*'," said Bonnie. "Gallagher can say '*parlez-vous français*'!"

"Hey!" said Gallagher indignantly.

"*Je peux parler français beaucoup mieux que vous pourrait jamais,*" said Jack in perfect French.

"Where did you learn that?" said Aaron in surprise.

"French class, seventh grade," said Jack, smiling. "See, I actually paid attention."

"Dork," coughed Bonnie.

Jack walloped her on the back. "That's a nasty cough," he said. "If you like, I can get Laza to make you a warm mug of Moki when we find the Elves."

"That sounds kind of yummy. What's Moki?" said Bonnie.

"It's a healing draught," said Aaron from the front of the column, "made from cactus juice, sea salt, and tricebu urine. The concept behind it is that it tastes so bad anyone who drinks it will work tirelessly to never get sick again so they'll never have to drink it again. Or at least, that's what Laza said."

"Well, he also said that if Aaron ran in circles around the big oak tree in the center of Eldorlorne chanting, 'fuzzy floppy floundering finger foods,' the tree would turn orange," Jack reminded him.

"Wait, you believed him?" said Gallagher in surprise.

"No," said Aaron quickly. "Of course not!"

"You fell for it, didn't you?" said Bonnie with a smirk.

"He fell for it," said Jack. "It was pretty funny!"

"Oh look!" said Aaron, blushing furiously. "Torkleaf!" He pointed at a small, shrub-like plant by the side of the path. "Did you know that tea made from its leaves can cure boils?"

"Did you know I really don't care?" said Bonnie savagely.

"Oh, you will when the plague sets in!" said Aaron devilishly.

"Wait! Plague?" said Gallagher. "You never said anything about plague!"

"Oh, don't worry," said Jack. "You probably won't die from the plague. I'm guessing starvation, heatstroke, or the lunar cycle will do it first."

"Did you say the lunar cycle?"said Ellie with a chirp of laughter.

"You laugh now, but you haven't met a werewolf on a full moon!" said Aaron.

"Werewolves don't exist, do they?" said Jack. "Laza never mentioned them."

"I don't know, actually," said Aaron. "You never can tell—Laza looked at me like I was an idiot when I asked if he'd ever seen a mermaid. But then again, a year ago I didn't even think Elves existed, so there you are."

"We will get to the Elves camp before the next full moon, right?" said Ellie in concern.

"Don't get your strings knotted," said Aaron kindly. "Turns out, most fairytale creatures are also myths in Acklyon. Except for Elves. And Unicorns. And Dragons."

"Oh and trolls." added Gallagher. "Don't forget them!"

"Right!" said Jack. "And also phoenixes, vampires, and goblins."

"And we don't know about werewolves," Aaron added.

"Actually, Laza once asked me if I'd ever seen a real life platypus," Jack said. "Turns out, there's an old Acklyonian myth about a creature that's half duck, half beaver."

"Yeah, and hyenas don't exist here either!" said Aaron. "Laza said something about a beast with the body of a cat but the voice of a human who had a really good sense of humor."

"And Kellaoth said that there are other creatures on Earth that we don't know about!" said Jack, "like Bigfoot, the Loch Ness Monster, et cetera, et cetera."

"Oh, and turns out no llamas in Acklyon, either!"

"No llamas?" said Ellie in surprise.

"Nope, they're another mythical creature in Acklyon."

"But these creatures in Acklyon," said Ellie, "they're not all… you know, evil, are they?"

"No more evil than a pack of lions or a bobcat," Aaron reassured her. "Well, with the exception of Gertulk, of course."

"Hey, Aaron!" said Jack, stooping to examine the ground. "Look at this!"

"What is it?" Aaron asked, joining Jack.

"See here," Jack gestured to the dust. "The Elves passed this way not long ago. And here," he pointed to several sets of heavy footprints. "Gertulk. Shortly after."

"Then that means…" Aaron lifted his head and cocked his ear. Dimly, from the other side of the hill, he could hear the faint sounds of swords clashing. "Let's go!" he said, breaking into a run.

"Ellie, Bonnie, Gallagher, stay here with the wagon," said Jack as he followed Aaron.

As soon as Aaron and Jack were out of sight, Bonnie turned to the other two. "Stay here with the wagon," she said and sprinted off after Aaron and Jack.

By the time Aaron and Jack reached the campsite, the Gertulk had captured the Elves and tied them down. Kellaoth was pinned beneath a heavy net lined with steel with a dozen Gertulk holding her down.

Aaron and Jack crouched down atop the hill, looking at this

horrifying sight. "Look!" Aaron whispered, pointing towards three Gertulk who stood holding one of the Elves's head in a bucket of water.

"Come on, rat!" gloated one of the Gertulk. "Keep it up, and maybe you'll be ready to go a round with a Kraken!"

The second Gertulk dragged the Elf's head out of the water. As the poor creature sputtered and gasped for air, Aaron and Jack saw those red curls, the pointed nose—it was Laza.

"Now," said the third Gertulk with a leering smile, "where are Prince Jahkon and Prince Adornierum—Addmenhiro—"

"Adinyrom," coughed Laza, glaring at his captors. "And you know where he is about as much as we do."

"Yeah, but see here, we know he's with you, we saw him with you in Muln!" cackled the beast. "So where are you scumbags hiding them?"

"They isn't with us no more!" said Laza desperately. "They lefted!"

The Gertulk raised his hand to strike Laza, but Kellaoth cut him off. "You needn't bother," she said between breaths. "The Elf speaks the truth. Nigh on three days ago, the Princes were granted passage back to their world. We have not seen them since."

"Shut up, horse!" barked the Gertulk and spat on Kellaoth.

"Big mistake," snarled Aaron, drawing back the bowstring. A loud *twang* echoed through the hills, and the Gertulk who had spat on Kellaoth staggered and fell, an arrow sticking out of his forehead. A moment later, the three Gertulk torturing Laza also crumpled, one after another. The rest of the Gertulk turned, confused, not knowing where this new and deadly threat was coming from.

Twang! Whizz! Twang! Whizz! Two more Gertulk hit the ground.

"See if you can get to Kellaoth and free her," Aaron said to Jack. "I'll keep the Gertulk occupied."

Jack nodded and slithered down the hill towards the campsite. Aaron continued picking off the Gertulk until he ran out of arrows again, at which point he dropped to the ground, scrambling to find more arrows in his pack.

"They're coming from up there!" a Gertulk shouted, pointing at Aaron's location. At last, Aaron found the sharp point of an arrow and loaded it onto the bow. He turned and shot down the Gertulk who had spoken.

"Spread out!" said another. "Don't cluster together. It gives a better target!"

The monster was right—when the Gertulk scattered, they became much harder to sight in the gathering twilight. Aaron fired two more shots, but he missed both times. He was wasting arrows.

The few Gertulk who carried wall shields had now begun creeping towards Aaron's location, ducking beneath their shields. Aaron shot at one of them—no good, the arrow merely glanced off the Gertulk's shield with a *ping* sound. The Gertulk were almost on him now. Aaron stood, throwing aside the bow and reaching to his belt.

With a blaze of golden fire, Aaron pulled Forvalad from the loop in his belt, spreading golden light into every inch of the valley. At the same time, Kellaoth burst free of her bindings, screeching angrily and diving into the midst of the Gertulk. Jack was right behind her, the sword Parvelad in his hands. Aaron ran, stepping up onto a rock and leaping over the heads of three more Gertulk. He landed behind them and rolled, skidding to a stop next to Laza. With a single stroke, he cut Laza's bonds and helped him to his feet.

"Buky?" Laza mumbled, disoriented. He squinted up at Aaron's face. When he recognized Aaron, his eyes widened. "You's came back," he breathed. "You's alive! How—?"

"No time," said Aaron, in the process of drawing a knife from his belt and throwing it at a Gertulk. "Laza, we need to free the other Elves. We have to get out of here!"

"Got it!" said Laza, picking up his fallen sword from the ground. "You get the guards, and I'll cut the ropes!"

"Jack!" Aaron shouted across the battlefield. Jack turned. Aaron gestured at the dozen or so Gertulk guarding the Elf prisoners.

Jack nodded, striking the Gertulk behind him in the breastplate.

Aaron, Jack, Laza, and Kellaoth grouped together, defending the Elf prisoners from their attackers. Aaron noticed that while wielding Forvalad, he seemed to be having an easier time of the fight. He could go on longer without tiring. He could dodge blows from even the quickest Gertulk and hack his way through even the thickest armor. His every sense was perfectly tuned to the battle around. All five senses gave him information on where the Gertulk would strike next. The sword didn't make him a *better* fighter, but he was able to use the abilities he already possessed without flaw.

"You know how every time we've been in a bad situation, we keep getting rescued by some outside force?" Aaron said to Jack as he dodged a gigantic war hammer.

"Yeah, why?" said Jack, parrying thrusts from a javelin.

"We could really use one of those right now!" Aaron said as he ducked beneath a wide swing from the hammer.

"Well we're not getting one. We'll have to do it ourselves!" said Jack.

"Thank you, Captain Obvious," Aaron muttered, as he roundhouse kicked his Gertulk assailant in the chest.

"We can't win here!" shouted Kellaoth. "We need to get the prisoners and retreat!"

"You heard the Unicorn!" Laza said. "Let's get crackin'!"

Aaron and Kellaoth fought back the Gertulk while Jack and Laza ran down the line of prisoners, cutting their bonds.

"It's no good!" Aaron said to Kellaoth. "We can't fight them all off!"

"I have one last card to play," said Kellaoth grimly. "Keep the Gertulk off me!"

Aaron ran in circles around Kellaoth, dragging his sword behind him, drawing a wide perimeter around her.

Where Forvalad's blade passed, fire sprang up from the ground. Aaron paused to admire his handiwork—a wall of fire surrounding Kellaoth—and then threw himself into the task of fighting the Gertulk away from it.

Kellaoth stood within the circle, her single horn glowing like a lantern. She seemed to be sucking the energy from the air around her, preparing to unleash it. Aaron looked up to see Laza, Jack, and the freed Elves bearing down on him.

The Elves had recovered their weapons and were launching an assault on the Gertulk forces. Aaron caught Jack by the shoulder and instructed him to help keep the Gertulk off of Kellaoth.

Jack spread the word to the rest of the Elves, and soon they had a defensive perimeter around Aaron's fire circle.

"Laza!" Kellaoth cried. "Get the Elves to safety. I can't hold it much longer!"

"Go into the hills over there!" Aaron pointed to where he and Jack had come from. "There's a troll cave in there. Jack will show you where it is."

"What about you?" Jack asked.

"I'm staying to help Kellaoth," Aaron said grimly. "Go!"

Laza and Jack led the Elves in a retreat while Aaron turned and leapt through the wall of fire. The flames created by Forvalad could not hurt him.

"Aaron, you have to get out of here!" said Kellaoth.

"My name," said Aaron, wiping a few streaks of blood from Forvalad's blade, "is Adinyrom."

Kellaoth smiled briefly and released her energy. For a split second, Aaron felt the blast tearing at all five senses—searing light blinded his eyes; a great, rumbling roar filled his ears; the smell of smoke, blood, and the putrid stench of Gertulk filled his nostrils. He tasted metal and sweat on his tongue, and felt fire and energy rays washing over his skin. But it ended when he felt himself being scooped up in a set of talons as Kellaoth lifted off the ground and headed towards the hills.

Aaron tried not to watch the gruesome sight of an entire battalion of Gertulk being incinerated by Kellaoth's spell. Kellaoth faltered in the air. They had dropped a couple dozen feet before she managed to catch herself.

Looking up, Aaron saw that her eyes were wide and bloodshot. Flecks of drool streaked past Aaron's ear, dripping from beneath her bared teeth. The spell had weakened her badly, and she could only barely stay level.

"Almost there!" Aaron shouted up to her, pointing ahead. About a hundred meters ahead of them, the Elves had massed together, tending their injured. Squinting, Aaron could see Jack standing next to Bonnie, Gallagher, and Ellie, who were all staring wide eyed at the many Elves.

As she swooped over them, Kellaoth threw Aaron down into the cluster of Elves.

Seven Elves, upon seeing his plummet, immediately threw themselves beneath him in an attempt to catch him. Unfortunately, Aaron weighed more than all seven combined, and they accomplished little more than cushioning his fall.

Kellaoth, after dropping Aaron, sped uncontrollably towards the ground. She flapped her wings as hard as she could, but she was too weak and could do nothing to prevent herself from crash landing nearby. Jack and several Elves rushed to her side.

Aaron was pulled to his feet by Ellie and Gallagher.

"Are you alright?" Ellie asked.

"Dislocated shoulder," Aaron grunted. "Hold still." Gripping Ellie's arm, Aaron squashed his shoulder back in place. Gallagher cringed at the crunching sound.

"Aaron?" said Deecal in surprise. "Is that being you?"

"Yeah," Aaron panted.

"We thinked you was catched by the Gertulk!" said Piki. "Well, we did until them Gertulk showed up asking where you were... Then we didn't know what to think!"

"Isn't it obvious?" said Dinky. "They ran out on us!"

"Shut up, Dink!" Wrinky hissed.

"Is that true?" said Stinky with wide eyes. "Did you abandoned us?"

Aaron paused. He saw no hope—or honor, for that matter—in making up some story about Aaron and Jack searching for reinforcements or provisions to help the Elves. "Yes," he said quietly. "Lord Cygon offered us a chance to go back to our world, and we took it. But we're back, and we're here to stay."

"Oh, great," muttered Jolly. "Now we has not two but five Manfolk mouths to feed...and Manfolk eat lots more than any Elf."

"We've found a solution to that problem, too," said Aaron,

unable to help himself from grinning. "Over there is a tunnel leading down to a deserted troll cave. It has enough food stocked in it to feed one troll for several months, which is about enough to last an Elf colony the same amount of time."

There was a short silence as the Elves digested Aaron's information, then Buky sprinted forward, leapt into Aaron's arms, and started kissing random parts of his face while letting off indistinguishable sounds of joy.

"Alright, alright, let's not put stuff out of proportion," Laza grumbled, dragging Buky off of Aaron and carrying her off in a fireman's lift. "Aaron's just had a tough fight. He doesn't appreciate these types of uncalled for shows of affection. You're not even his type anyway. You're too short. Nobody wants to date someone who comes up to their waist. Now, I, on the other hand, am closer to your height..."

Aaron didn't hear the rest of Laza's telling-to due to the mass of Elves now surrounding him, cheering and hugging whatever parts of him they could reach.

"Check on Kellaoth!" Aaron instructed the flocking Elves. "Make sure she's okay then I'll take you to the troll cave."

A dozen Elves rushed off to Kellaoth's aid, while Aaron joined Ellie, Bonnie, and Gallagher, who were standing in a corner looking awkward.

"So these are Elves?" said Gallagher, admiring the flocks of midgets. "Fascinating! They evolved from primates like humans?"

"Elves are human, technically," said Aaron. "They age at the same rate as Men. They have the same personality traits and weaknesses. They're just smaller and more forest-bound, and they have better reflexes, but not as much strength or stamina."

"And while you two geeks do your little thing," said Bonnie, turning to Jack. "Do they have pizza here? I could go for some pizza."

"This is Acklyon, not Italy," said Jack.

"That's no excuse for not having any pizza..." muttered Bonnie. "We should teach them to make pizza!"

"Alright, just as soon as we have a stove, an oven, a kitchen, some tomato sauce and pepperonis, you can teach Hokey to make pizza."

"And ice cream!" said Gallagher. "No government institution can succeed without proper quantities of chocolate fudge!"

"Remind me why we brought those two clowns?" said Jack, smiling.

* * *

The next few weeks were some of Aaron's best in Acklyon. He had finally earned the Elves' respect. Even more than the presence of Forvalad for the first time in a hundred years, the story of Aaron and Jack's defeat of the Gertulk in Avondale and the slaying of the troll had spread throughout the camp like wildfire, thanks to Bonnie and Gallagher. The resentful mutterings that had followed Aaron and Jack were now gone, replaced by cheery waves, and sometimes bows. Aaron felt, for the first time since coming to Acklyon, that he truly belonged here.

"Cygon only sent us to Avondale because he knew we'd want to come back as soon as we got there," Jack said to Aaron one day as they watched Laza sparring with Bonnie and Gallagher.

"I know," Aaron said, smiling.

The return of Forvalad and Parvelad to the Acklyon was a matter of great joy and excitement. The Twin Swords were passed from hand to hand, admired from every angle. Aaron noticed that whenever he held Forvalad, the blade glowed with a golden light. But when any of the others (except Jack) held it, it seemed to dim. Most of the Elves agreed that it felt just like any other sword, despite its beautiful appearance. Aaron, who had fought with an ordinary sword and could compare the difference, did not understand the glowing until Kellaoth explained the origin of the swords.

"What you hold is no mere sword," she told him as he continued to marvel at it. "Over time, you will learn to master its many abilities."

"What can it do?" Aaron asked, intrigued.

"No one can be sure of the full extent of its powers," Kellaoth told him. "It is different for each of its masters. Its two most notable qualities are its flame and its tendency to transform to suit its bearer. You may have noticed its design and size are almost identical to that of your old sword? Many kings of Acklyon have even been able to make it change its form in mid-fight—in the blink of an eye, Forvalad would switch from being a sword to a spear."

"So theoretically," Aaron said, "I could turn Forvalad into a rifle or a shotgun?"

"In theory," said Kellaoth, "though I don't believe anyone has ever made anything more advanced than a crossbow. Keep in mind that in order to make it into a new weapon, you must know the exact proportions of that weapon."

"How were Forvalad and Parvelad made?" Jack asked.

Kellaoth smiled reminiscently. "They were forged during the construction of the Acklyonian government under the command of the first King of Acklyon. His name was Terriditon. The city of Castram was built in his honor. During Terriditon's time, a single lump of a peculiar metal had forced its way to the surface."

"What was it?" Aaron asked.

"An extremely rare piece of metal, believed to be from the very core of Acklyon. This metal was incredibly valuable for it possessed qualities previously unknown. It could be made to change its color and texture, had a one-way connection with the land, and was nigh indestructible. This gave Terriditon an idea of how to preserve the strength of his new country.

"So it was that King Terriditon called forth three of the oldest Wizards, three of the most powerful Unicorns, three of the quickest Elves, and three of the strongest Men. Together, they forged the lump of ore, which the sorcerers had named Terriditon after their king, into two swords. The Wizards and Unicorns placed strong magic upon the swords, allowing each to bond with a single, living human. This mortal would be the one who could rule his country, and only he. The swords would give their master an understanding of how Acklyon must be run best.

"When King Terriditon died, he gave the swords to his sons, Prince Forvalad and Prince Parvelad. Forvalad and Parvelad, unable to come to an agreement of the rule, parted ways. Forvalad took his sword and kept half the country while Parvelad took the other half. So it was that Fortilly and Parland were formed."

"And now Jack and I have been chosen to follow in the princes' footsteps," said Aaron quietly.

"Yes," said Kellaoth, "but know this. Forvalad is not the power that binds this kingdom. You are. Forvalad's powers can only be unlocked by you, no one else. But not only do you bring out Forvalad's power—it brings out yours."

"What do you mean?" Aaron asked in surprise. "I don't have any powers!"

"But you do," said Kellaoth, smiling, "deep down. You may

have noticed that in combat while using Forvalad you are stronger, quicker, and more honed than normal. This, and other such abilities, can only be accessed while holding Forvalad."

As he sifted through his belongings one day, searching for his hunting knife, Aaron came upon an old brown sack. There was something long and heavy inside it. He undid the strings and reached inside.

It was his old sword, Anvilad. Slowly, Aaron drew the narrow blade from its sheath. He gazed at the sword, thinking. This steel blade had felled many Gertulk. It had been almost like a friend to him across his journeys. With it, Aaron had killed his first Gertulk, won his first duel, fought his first battle. In many ways, it was almost identical to Forvalad—the design, the efficiency, the hand-and-a-half hilt which allowed him to use it with two hands or one, the rounded pommel, all of it was remarkably similar. He supposed that, as Forvalad changed for each master, the sword took the form of Anvilad, suiting Aaron's design. Aaron favored speed over brute strength and preferred a light, small weapon, even when using both hands. Forvalad matched that design perfectly. Anvilad suited it well. Of course, he would use Forvalad in battle from now on, but what to do with Anvilad? He was very fond of the sword, despite its imperfections. Did he give it away? Get rid of it? Keep it on hand, and use it with Forvalad?

He sheathed the sword, put it back in the bag, and slipped it into his pack. He would keep the sword. He would not forget it. Someday, perhaps, he would find a use for it. *Maybe it will go to another young king who needs it,* he thought, smiling to himself.

Aaron swept a wisp of hair out of his eyes as he walked,

Forvalad on one hip, his bow strapped across his back, and a shoulder-slung pouch crammed with food resting on his other hip. He also carried a medical kit, a tinderbox, and various other goods he would need on the road. He was afoot as his pony Coopy was being used as a packhorse. To his left was Jack, in front of him was Kellaoth, loaded down with luggage, and behind him were his friends and a long, straggling line of Elves. Despite Aaron's weariness from his adventures the last few days, he felt better about being on the move than sitting on his hands in Avondale. He was eager to reclaim Castram and thus truly to become who he was supposed to be.

"Kellaoth," called Ellie from behind Aaron. "When do we stop?"

"When the sun comes up!" Kellaoth answered.

Bonnie sped up to walk between Aaron and Jack. "When do I get a weapon?" she asked.

"A *what*?" Both boys asked at the same time, staring incredulously at Bonnie.

"A weapon," said Bonnie. "Hey, Gallagher and I have been training, you know. Laza says that I must have some Elf blood in me. If you two get swords and bows and all that stuff, then I should get something, too!"

"But Bonnie," said Aaron patiently, "maybe you forgot. We're in a medieval-type world! Girls, especially young girls, aren't *supposed* to fight."

"Oh, and Laza's...Laza," added Jack, unable to come up with a more appropriate word for Laza's flamboyant attitude and absurd comments.

"Who says girls can't fight here?" Bonnie jerked her head at Piki, who had a rapier on her belt and a bow across her shoulder.

"Elves are different," said Jack. "With Elves, it's okay for females to fight, but not with Man species! Ask Kellaoth. *Girls don't use weapons here!*"

"You just keep your eyes on me, Charlie, and we'll see who can use a sword!" said Bonnie a little waspishly.

Jack was about to respond when Gallagher nudged him in the ribs.

"Don't even try," he whispered. "I've known her for twelve years. It doesn't pay to try to make her see sense."

Bonnie shot him a killer look. Gallagher raised his hands to shoulder height in surrender.

"I don't think I'd be good at fighting," said Ellie, more to save Gallagher's life than that she thought anyone else would particularly care. "It sounds scary."

"It is," Aaron assured her. As he said this, the others could see that the Battle of Eldorlorne and the Battle of Avondale still brought back painful memories for Aaron.

To cover this awkward moment, Gallagher said, "Do you think we can really beat Malvadore?"

"Kellaoth says that if we pull together and find reinforcements, then we have some hope." Gallagher could tell that Jack wasn't optimistic about their chances of victory.

"I'm still having a hard time believing this is all real," said Ellie.

"I'm still having a hard time believing Gallagher talked me into this," said Bonnie.

"Well, Jack and I appreciate it," said Aaron, "more than you could possibly know."

When they made camp, Laza began training Gallagher and Bonnie in a little clearing nearby.

Laza faced off against both of them. Despite his being

outnumbered, Laza held his own. He circled them, occasionally countering one of them as they tried to spread out. He was trying, Aaron knew, to keep them from splitting up. If he could keep them close together, he could have a better chance at beating them. Side by side, he could duel both at once at which point his natural speed and reflexes would win the duel. It would be harder for him if they were trying to sneak up behind him.

Bonnie and Gallagher charged, raising their sticks. Laza parried and dodged and sent Bonnie flying backwards. The Elf continued to duel Gallagher, quickly gaining the upper hand.

However, Gallagher was quicker than Aaron or Jack had been, having spent several years fencing. Before Laza could properly outmaneuver Gallagher, the Elf felt an arm around his neck. Bonnie had sneaked around behind him and was now holding him down. Gallagher placed his sword on Laza's chest.

"Surrender," the boy panted.

Laza shrugged, but then leapt up and kicked Gallagher in the chest.

Gallagher stumbled, and Laza flipped Bonnie over his shoulder.

Laza reached for his stick, but Bonnie grabbed him by the ankle and yanked him to the ground. She then sat on him, pinning down all four limbs to keep him from jumping up.

Gallagher retrieved his stick and mimed cutting off Laza's head. Then Bonnie crawled off of Laza, and the three stood up, panting and dripping with sweat.

"Very good match!" said Laza as soon as he could speak. "You's using those tips on unity I gived you!"

"Yeah," panted Bonnie. "I never thought fighting *beside* Gallagher instead of beating him up could work so well."

"In that case," said Kellaoth, trotting over to them, "I believe you are ready."

"For what?" asked Gallagher, but Laza and Kellaoth had retreated to Laza's tent.

Bonnie looked at Jack. "What's she talking about?"

"You'll see," said Jack, gripping his sword and grinning.

Kellaoth and Laza returned, clutching three large parcels. Laza handed one to Gallagher and the other two to Bonnie. Puzzled, Gallagher and Bonnie opened the packages.

Aaron and Jack glanced at each other and smiled, remembering when Kellaoth had presented them with their swords. Gallagher gasped as he drew his new sword from the paper. It was a hand-and-a-half with a long, narrow blade and an emerald in the crossguard. He held it up, admiring the design and efficiency.

Bonnie, meanwhile, was swinging her curved sword through the air and battling imaginary enemies. Satisfied, she sheathed the sword and picked up her new bow and quiver. She held the bow at arm's length and admired it. It was a longbow, almost as tall as she herself was. The handle was polished, and a large spike protruded from each end.

Bonnie strung the bow, placed a goose-feather arrow on the string, drew the shaft to her ear, and fired. She enjoyed watching the arrow's steady progress until it struck a tree.

"This is incredible!" she said.

"These weapons were forged by Deecal and Piki, as yours were, Adinyrom, Jahkon." Kellaoth nodded at Aaron and Jack.

Aaron drew Forvalad from its sheath and said, "I think you'll get a lot out of them."

"Yeah, Deecal and Piki are two of the greatest smiths in the tribe," said Jack.

Gallagher sheathed his sword, looking suddenly serious.

"It's a heavy responsibility," Aaron said.

They continued on into the night amidst a thick forest full of tall trees. They trudged on, pushing their way through clumps of brambles. When at last they emerged on the other side and could see the sky again, a voice came from ahead.

"Hey, guys!" It was one of the sentry Elves. "Look up ahead!"

All eyes turned to where the Elf was pointing. About a mile ahead of them were the Mountains of Acklyon.

27
Crossing the Mountains

"Lord, have mercy! Are we supposed to climb those?" Aaron had stopped dead, staring up at the enormous range of mountain before him.

"I'll never say the Rocky Mountains were impressive again," Ellie muttered, also gazing in wonder and horror at their next path.

"Come!" called Kellaoth, who was helping the younger Elves climb the first slope. "Come! The sun rises in less than two hours, and we must find shelter up here before then!"

Aaron walked up to the jagged rocks and cliffs. "I never was much of a rock climber, were you?" he asked Gallagher. Gallagher shook his head

"Come!" shouted Kellaoth.

* * *

After an hour of hard climbing, the travelers finally reached the top of a cliff. From there, Kellaoth found a narrow mountain path, winding through and up the high mountains.

"Keep moving!" cried Kellaoth as Bonnie, Ellie, and Gallagher all plopped down to rest. Kellaoth had always been in something of a hurry since their last encounter with the Gertulk.

They shouldered their packs and began the long hike for another forty-five minutes. Kellaoth allowed them very little time to rest, and only when the sun peaked over the glaciers did Kellaoth call the order to set up camp in a shallow cave near a large rock outcropping.

While the children slept, Laza, Deecal, and a few others lit a fire and cooked supper (or maybe breakfast, since it was that time of day), and posted a guard while Kellaoth went off to scout for Gertulk.

Aaron sat bolt upright, interrupting a nightmare about shooting down Gertulk at his old school. He had heard something, a kind of high-pitched whistling sound. Slowly, he got up and listened hard.

There it was again! A shrill call of some kind—mysterious, but beautiful. He slipped over to Wrinky, on guard detail. The Elf had an arrow on his bowstring, pulled back as far as his strength would allow. Wrinky had heard it, too.

"What is it?" whispered Aaron, drawing his sword.

"Your guess is as smiley as mine," Wrinky hissed back, as his brothers, Dinky and Stinky, snored loudly. "But me'd say dat somefink is living in these mountanins."

"Elves?"

"Nopee, somefin stronger…sonfing…Magical."

"Did it remind you of…" Aaron hesitated, not wanting to be embarrassed. "…of, well, of spring after a long winter? Or—or sweet candy that you've never tasted? Of something wonderful, but—but also foreign, different, strange."

"I'dee say so, just that," said Wrinky.

"I've never really felt that way except when I'm in the company of someone extremely Magical, like Kellaoth or Cygon."

"Me knows what youee means," said Wrinky. "Like…cherry cobbler in a starving time."

"Yeah…" said Aaron slowly.

Suddenly, a voice interrupted their conversation.

"Get down, both of you! Get down!" The voice was not that of Wrinky or of any other Elf, but Kellaoth, who had just soared in from out of nowhere.

Aaron and Wrinky stared at her for a minute, too shocked to move.

"Get down and hide!" Kellaoth struck each of them with a talon, sending them sprawling backwards. They both turned and wiggled back towards the mass of sleeping Elves. Then, Elf and boy hid behind a nearby outcropping of rock, peeking out to see what was happening.

Kellaoth stood in the entrance to the cave, her horn glowing as she placed various wards around them. The same shrill whistle floated towards them on the breeze. Kellaoth closed her eyes, and an odd feeling swept over the land; it was not fear, it was merely a sudden urge to leave. The Magic was so strong, in fact, that Aaron shifted and would have gotten up and walked away if Wrinky hadn't grabbed his arm and pulled him back down.

For a long time Kellaoth stood in the mouth of the cave, sending her Magical signal. One more call echoed, then silence.

When Kellaoth turned to the others, Aaron and Wrinky stood up and came over to her.

"What was it, Kellaoth?" said Aaron immediately.

Kellaoth ignored this question, saying, "Wake the others! We leave now."

They were on the move again, blinking in the daylight.

Ellie, who had repelled all attempts to be awakened, was now slumped across Kellaoth's back, fast asleep. They had no hope of crossing the mountains before daybreak, so they turned around and headed back down via the path they had tramped into the ground on their way up.

Kellaoth ignored Aaron and Wrinky's many questions about the mysterious whistling, so they fell to discussing it among themselves.

"It all comes down to this," said Bonnie. "Either there's some sort of Magical creature inhabiting these mountains, or it was some trick of the Gertulk."

"It didn't seem like anything Gertulk related," said Aaron. "It was too…real."

"Do you suppose there's a Wizard living here?" asked Ellie, remembering Cygon.

"I don't know," said Aaron. "But whatever it was, it was enough to scare Kellaoth pretty badly. I've never seen her so agitated."

"You think she knows what it was?" asked Jack.

"I think she knows just about every secret in the book," said Aaron wearily. "But it's no use. She's not telling."

"Well, whatever it was, it couldn't have been friendly," Gallagher pointed out, "or else we wouldn't be on the run like this."

"It wasn't friendly," Aaron agreed, "but it wasn't evil, either. I'd say it just wanted to be left alone."

"But here's the clincher," Bonnie pointed out. "You only heard one call—but there could be more of them."

Aaron was silent. He looked around at the high peaks on either side of them, thinking… Was there something in these mountains that could prove hostile? Would it attack? And if so, why didn't Kellaoth want them to know what is was? Surely, if an enemy were up here, they should know about it! But if it weren't an enemy, why did Kellaoth drive it away and lead them back down the mountains so quickly?

Aaron decided to put it out of his mind. If it were anything dangerous, surely Kellaoth would tell them. In her secrecy, she seemed to feel that what they had encountered wasn't going to attack, and that comforted him.

So wrapped up in his musings, Aaron never noticed the tip of a wing protruding over the cliff top or the sight of a creature rising into the sky, so quickly it was merely a colored blur. Within seconds, it had risen up thousands of feet over the earth and now appeared to simply be a falcon or eagle, circling around and looking for prey.

But Kellaoth did see it. Her eyes never left the creature as it swooped this way and that before flying off to the east. She felt her energies rushing to the surface, and her horn began to sparkle.

28
Departing the Mountains

"How much further, Kellaoth?" groaned Gallagher.

"Not far!" Kellaoth called back from the head of the group.

"No, not far at all," said a malicious voice behind them.

The whole group turned and saw a man standing on the path they had just crossed. He was wearing an ornate golden crown encrusted with rubies and a bright red tunic over golden chain mail. Long brown hair flowed over his shoulders.

The False Adinyrom Forahn.

"You!" snarled Kellaoth.

"Me," said the False Adinyrom calmly. "You did not actually think I would miss this opportunity to meet my impersonator!"

At Laza's command, a horde of Elves loaded their bows and pointed them at the False King, positioning themselves between him and Aaron. Nimbun growled, preparing to pounce.

"Come no closer!" Laza said seriously, his arrow pointed at a spot between the Imposter's eyes.

The False King merely smiled at them. "Clearly," he said in a voice that could freeze your blood, "you will see fit to strip down my kingdom and to place these two *fakes* on the Throne!" He took a step forward.

The Elves tensed, but Laza did not give the order to fire.

"Go ahead," said the False King calmly, taking another step. "Shoot me. See what happens."

One young Elf in the front row released his bowstring, sending an arrow streaking towards the False King.

Forahn raised one hand lazily, and the arrow stopped just inches from his breastplate. "Nice shot," he said approvingly to the archer before hurling the arrow back towards him. In a flash, Kellaoth sent a bolt of fire from her horn, incinerating the arrow.

"Impressive," said the Imposter, sneering, "but these shows of Magic are not necessary. My quarrel is not with you, Kellaoth, or with these Elves. Give me the imposters, and I shall let you—"

"NOW!" shouted Kellaoth. Laza and the Elves released their arrows, sending a solid wave of missiles toward the False King. As the Imposter raised his hand to block the attack, Kellaoth sent a streak of light at a cluster of rocks over Forahn's head, sending a cascade of boulders down on top of the False King.

The Elves fled, sprinting down the path, the horses galloping along beside them. Looking over his shoulder, Aaron saw the False Adinyrom vanish in a flash of light, only seconds from being smashed by the rocks Kellaoth had let loose.

"STOP THEM!" came the False Adinyrom's voice from high above.

The group ran hard through the gorge until they burst out onto a narrow rope bridge spanning a huge precipice. On the other side, they could see a large wooden door leading into the mountain. The Elves hesitated, but sprinted down the bridge. It was tedious work; one slip and they would be gone. Looking down as they ran across the narrow ledge, Jack saw the mist below come alive with Gertulk following along below them. About a hundred yards ahead was a large door built into the rock. If they could just make it through...

"Oh no!" screamed Ellie.

A battalion of Gertulk had appeared in the gorge they had just passed through. The Gertulk did not seem to want to cross the bridge, so they aimed their crossbows at the line of Elves, several of whom turned around and shot back at them.

Aaron dodged as an arrow flew past his ear and then jerked his head the other way to avoid another. Once he reached the far side of the bridge, Aaron pulled out the compound bow and fired several shots at the Gertulk.

Kellaoth, who was in the lead, reached the door, reared on her back legs, and kicked it down. Once all of the Elves had jumped through, Kellaoth brought down the roof over the open door to keep the Gertulk out.

Deecal sprinted forward, drawing his rapier, and flicked the point across the face of a Gertulk who had appeared.

The group was underground, and the winding path ahead of them was dotted with torches. From what they could see, it led deeper underground, but then came back up. They couldn't see the end.

What they could see were Gertulk gathering to block them.

"Come on!" said Kellaoth, and they charged down the path, dodging fallen bits of rubble. As they neared the Gertulk, every Elf drew his or her sword. Aaron, Jack, Bonnie and Gallagher overtook them and ran alongside Kellaoth—all preparing to crash through the Gertulk.

The Gertulk raised their shields and lowered their spears, awaiting the Elves.

Kellaoth was the first to break the Gertulk defenses, smashing her way through the wall of shields and spears. Aaron and Jack were close behind her, hacking and swinging at the Gertulk. Gallagher, Bonnie, and the Elfin warriors were close behind, and they managed to break through to the other side. The group continued down the path, stopping here and there to hit back at Gertulk.

"Almost there..." muttered Aaron as the exit loomed into view. "Come on...not much further now...nearly...AHHHHH!"

They burst through another wooden door and into the dazzling sunlight.

Kellaoth, who was in the lead, stopped just short of the huge rocky slope which wound down the mountain. She tottered for a moment on her hind legs and then managed to catch herself.

Aaron, blinded by the sun, ran headlong into her, and they both went tumbling down what felt like a long, rock-covered slide.

Behind them, they could hear the screams, squeals, and thuds as the four-hundred Elves, also overbalanced, came rolling down after them.

Aaron and Kellaoth were the first to reach the outcropping of limestone at the bottom of the slope. Others now began dropping around them. Aaron only just got out of the way of Ellie and Bonnie, who were holding each other tight as they were swept down the hill. Jack whooshed past Aaron, clattering painfully to a stop as he ran into a rock. The Elves then came tumbling down, a few at a time, until they were all accounted for. To the astonishment of all, they had made it through without losing any luggage or ponies.

"Hide!" Kellaoth said suddenly. The Elves obeyed without question, hiding behind rocks and leading their horses into nearby caves. Aaron and Jack had only just squashed themselves behind an outcrop when the Gertulk spilled out of the doorway, looking around for their prey. Several of the giants glanced down the slope, but seeing no sign of Elves, they left to find a safer passage down the mountain.

"Well, that was fun," said Bonnie, once the Gertulk were gone.

"Hey guys!" shouted Jack. "Come look at this!"

He was sitting on another ledge overlooking the valley. They could see the ground now with cities and towns dotted here and there. The others rushed over to him.

"What is it?" asked Ellie.

"Can't you see?" said Jack. "There!" He pointed at a huge grey mass on the horizon.

Aaron squinted at it and realized what it was—a ruin. An enormous castle, overgrown with weeds and trees. The castle was partially destroyed, but the group could see the high outer walls that surrounded the ruins and what appeared to have been a town inside the walls. There were many layers of defenses with the town placed in the exact center.

In the middle of the town was clearly the palace. Age and the legendary attack had not quite succeeded in destroying the glory of the place. Though many towers and turrets were knocked over and destroyed, the stronghold retained its overall feeling of power and majesty. It was still in bad shape though; no banners hung on the flagpoles, no shields were displayed on the walls, no guards stood at the gate.

Age-old decayed catapults and ballistae lined the walls of this castle, and it had a pair of monumental double doors at the front, made from wood and metal.

To say the least, this was a sight for sore eyes.

It was Castram.

29
Arrival at Colten

Aaron was speechless. The sight of his father's home was the most wonderful feeling to him. As they had drawn closer to Castram, he had grown more and more at peace with Acklyon, as though he were returning from a vacation and could see his house in the distance.

The Elves set up a cheer, whooping and dancing with joy at the sight of the castle.

"Come," said Kellaoth. "We shall make camp here and set out at sundown."

So they built campfires and laid out their bedrolls. They picketed the horses in a grassy flat on the outer edge of camp where they could graze.

Next, the group began cooking supper for themselves, talking and laughing all the while. Hokey had conjured the delicious venison stew that was her specialty. It was easy to fix, didn't require too many ingredients, tasted good, and filled you up pleasantly.

While Ellie, Bonnie, and Gallagher chatted happily about what they planned to do when they reached Castram, Aaron and Jack remained quiet, drinking in the joy at seeing their destination at last.

Kellaoth and Laza studied a map of the enormous valley they were in, trying to decipher a route that would steer them clear of the towns and cities that dotted the countryside. They would have to leave the road now, for even after dark the traffic was still heavy between the larger cities.

They worked out a trail they could follow. It led through the woods and then wound around to Castram. It was the safest route to take, for it only brought them into contact with one city, Colten, located near the edge of the valley. Colten was the biggest city in the valley. But by extension, it was also one of the most heavily guarded cities in Acklyon as it was in such a dangerous spot should Castram be reawakened. They would have to sneak past the walls in the night and hope no guards heard the whinny of a horse or the snap of a twig.

Once the moon had risen into the night sky, they set out, searching the rocky cliff until they found a path to the ground. They hiked down it, and after many tumbles and stubbed toes, they found themselves in the valley, the towers of Castram visible in the distance.

The sun rose, and they at last had a few hours of well-deserved sleep. When the moon rose again, they were shaken awake much sooner than they would have liked, but they forced down some hot porridge and continued on their way. The trail Laza and Kellaoth had chosen was a difficult one; they traveled through the woods, not the road. Getting the horses and the children through was most strenuous, but they persevered. This path was more dangerous than their previous one—for though they had lost the Gertulk in the mountains, no one was foolish enough to suppose that the creatures had given up their search. But sooner than the group had expected, they were out of the dense trees. Now, all they had to do was slip past Colten, and they'd be on a straight line course for Castram.

Looking ahead as they crept down the road in the dead of night, Aaron could just make out the walls of Colten. This was at least the size of Muln, perhaps bigger. According to Laza, it was the central trading port of the valley.

Laza and Nimbun flew ahead as scouts and reported back, saying that Colten was heavily guarded, as though the town expected King Adinyrom and King Jahkon to come marching through their valley any day.

"Great," said Bonnie wearily. "I wonder what it would be like to be able to walk out in public without getting arrested."

"We need to get through without being seen," said Kellaoth. "If they report to the Gertulk that we're this close to Castram, we are as good as dead. But *how*, is the question."

"Search me," said Aaron.

"We cannot hope to sneak past the walls. They shall see us, even in the night."

"Can't we just give it a wide berth?" suggested Bonnie.

"No," said Kellaoth. "The main road winds on either side of Colten. In the valley, we must not be anywhere near the road. For the people, it is safer here, so they do travel at night. If we run into a caravan or a squad of Gertulk..." She didn't need to say any more.

"I think," said Jack, "that our best hope is to wait for a night when the moon is gone and sneak past. If we remain right along the wall, maybe the soldiers on top won't see us."

"That could work," Kellaoth agreed. "But there is a problem. If it were just a few of us, or even just the adults, we could pull it off. But the horses and children, that is another thing."

"Okeyday, try this," said Buky. "We cause a diversion over

there—" She pointed away from Castram "—and then we put the kiddies on the horsees and make them flee to Castram, at all quickeyneses. They is shoulding to get there by sunrise, with the horses going as fast as they can skedaddle."

"'Tis a good idea," said Deecal. "We're needing to get them to safety, pronto. This could get dirty."

"Ain't quite what you'd call encouraging," said Laza. "But we is shoulding to do it."

Kellaoth agreed, and the process began. First, Jack, Gallagher, Buky, and several other Elves slipped away from camp and sneaked over to the small village of Farlagay on the far-side of Colten. Buky and the Elves began stalking squads of patrolling Gertulk. They would attack, strike the Gertulk and retreat and disappear. Soon, there was a long list of assaults that frustrated the Gertulk and created a general feeling of fear for the population.

Jack and Gallagher were charged with pretending to be townsfolk and telling the soldiers lies about seeing hundreds of Elves on the move further down the valley. The people of Farlagay, as Buky had hoped, sent word to Colten for help. Aticka, the Duke of Colten, sent word to all the cities and villages in the valley to stay on their guard for Elves.

Because of heightened tension and fear of attack, all travelers and caravans stopped at the nearest city and took refuge there until it was safe again. Though the roads were now clear, the travelers knew it wouldn't last long.

The travelers loaded two or three kids onto each pony along with plenty of rations to get them through until the adults returned. It was an unpleasant thing, really, separating the children from their parents and telling them to go to Castram.

As Aaron tied a sack of wheat onto Coopy, he felt a pair of

eyes on him. He turned to see the little Elf girl, Auri, whom he had given his breakfast to on the morning before Muln so long ago. She was staring at him with a slightly puzzled expression.

"Why do we have to leave?" she asked in her squeaky voice.

Aaron finished tying the knot and knelt down next to her. "Because it's not safe for you here. We need to get all the children to safety, now. It's okay, though. We'll meet you at Castram before long. You'll have to show me around once I get there," he added with a smile.

"You're not coming with us?" she asked in surprise.

"No, no, I'm not," said Aaron quietly. "I have to stay."

"Why?"

Aaron smiled grimly. "It's hard to explain… There's something I have to do. I have to help Laza get us past Colten safely."

She nodded thoughtfully. Aaron glanced over his shoulder to see Laza give him a swift nod, which Aaron understood to mean it was time to go. He stood, scooped Auri up into his arms, and placed her on Coopy's saddle. "Take care of the other children for me, will you?"

She nodded again as Aaron led Coopy over to the other horses. "You're a good leader," Auri said.

Aaron smiled again. "I'm not the leader, little one. Captain Laza is, remember?"

"But they listen to you," said Auri. "They do what you tell them to do."

Aaron said nothing.

The goodbyes were, perhaps, overlong, but eventually each pony was spurred, and the Elf children vanished into the night. Watching through his telescope, Laza reported that the children had only just made it to the sanctuary of Castram before roads began to open again.

"Well," said Laza. "Thatees that."

"How long till the moon goes out?" asked Bonnie.

Kellaoth looked up at the sky at a big half moon. "I would say…two weeks."

"Two weeks?" Deecal cried. "We is being *dead* in two weeks!"

"We is sitting ducks," said Buky. "The Gertulk will surely beat us up in that time."

"I think not," said Kellaoth. "They lost enough troops in the mountains that they are not strong enough to take us for now."

"Yeah, but that's all for now," Aaron reminded her. "By the time we're on the move again, a fresh wave will have left Rarzan and be heading this way."

"I know," said Kellaoth, "but what else can we do?"

So they waited. It was both extraordinarily tense and deathly boring. At all times, they expected to see hordes of marauding Gertulk come bounding toward them, uttering war cries and swinging axes. But none came. At every snap of a twig, and every rustle of the leaves, they leapt behind fallen logs and drew their weapons.

For two weeks, this went on. Aaron half wished they hadn't sent the children ahead—their camp felt more like a military force now without the young Elves running to and fro chasing each other and playing games.

At last, after what felt like years, Kellaoth looked up at the starry sky. No moon was visible.

"It is time," she said quietly.

Without a moment's hesitation, the two hundred Elf soldiers gathered up their weapons and gear; they were all ready to leave.

Quiet as shadows, they crept through the darkness until they reached the walls of Colten. There they flattened themselves against the wall and sneaked along, careful not to even make a whisper.

Aaron was agitated. They were crawling along like snails with their bellies scraping against the cold stone.

"What was that?" The voice came from a soldier on guard atop the wall.

Immediately, the Elves stood stock-still, squashing themselves against the wall.

"What is it?" said another soldier on detail.

"I heard something down below," the first solder said.

The second lifted his torch, splaying light across the ground. Fortunately, the edge of railing that wound around the wall jutted out far enough that the Elves remained in shadow.

"Must be nothing," said the soldier.

"Maybe a squirrel or something," said the first. Together, the two soldiers headed off.

Laza let out a deep sigh of relief and signaled the Elves to move forward.

For an hour that felt like an eon, they slipped through the shadows until at last they reached the corner. There, they quietly but quickly crept until they were completely out of view of Colten. Only then did they let out their breath, and walk at a more comfortable pace.

They were on their way to Castram.

30

Castram at Last

"Hurry!" cried Deecal.

It was day. They had chosen to travel in the light today for no one ever came this close to Castram.

And there it was.

Even bigger than it had looked from a distance, the mighty castle loomed over their heads, a mass of towers and turrets. Overcome with joy, they all broke into a run, sprinting across the broad field that stretched before Castram. They never seemed to grow weary from running.

Through the shattered gates, children came running toward their parents. The parents immediately overtook even Aaron and Bonnie. The families collided about halfway across the field amidst cheering and laughing. Aaron and Jack didn't join in, however. They had eyes only for the ancient castle that towered over their heads. They could see that the next few months would be spent in rebuilding and repairing, for there was an almost inconceivable amount of damage, both from age and the legendary Gertulk attack.

Together, with happy children riding in the arms of happy parents, they made their way through the archway, and into Castram.

31
THE GHOST

"So this is Castram?" Ellie stared around at the ruins around them.

"It was abandoned over a hundred years ago," said Aaron, who was gazing around with whole-hearted happiness and contentment. Really, for the first time in Acklyon, he felt at home and in place. Jack felt the magic, too, and he was smiling as well.

All of them were standing in the courtyard, gazing around at the wrecked towers and abandoned houses. "This place gives me the creeps," said Ellie, shivering and staring around.

"Not me," said Jack, "This is… incredible!"

"Hey, guys, come here!" Aaron was running down the front street, and was gazing up at the palace.

The others went over to him, staring up at the gloomy castle. When Bonnie looked at the palace, she saw buckling, rotted doors, mossy walls, crumbling towers, shattered stain-glass windows, skeletons splayed across the foundation, and a feeling of overall spookiness.

When Aaron looked at the palace, he saw (in his mind's eye) spiraling towers, waving flags, guards at the shiny oak doors, music drifting out the open windows, flowers planted around the place, and tapestries everywhere. These were memories of his Acklyonian childhood and how the place had looked in the reign of his father.

"C'mon!" shouted Jack, sprinting up the steps toward the big double doors.

"We can't go in there!" said Ellie, looking aghast. "It looks haunted."

"Haunted?" scoffed Aaron, who was already standing beside Jack. "Please, Ellie. Everyone knows there's no such thing as ghosts!"

Kellaoth and Laza gave each other a long look.

Deecal studied the locked doors, searching for something. Aaron didn't know what it was until Deecal tapped one finger to a certain spot, and the whole door collapsed. "Pressure points are an awesome thing," he muttered.

While the Elves set up camp, Aaron, Jack, Deecal, Kellaoth, Laza, Buky, Ellie, Gallagher, and Bonnie entered the palace cautiously. "What's d'you suppose is down that way?" asked Gallagher, gesturing to an old door at the end of a hallway to the left.

"Oh, that's just the old dungeon chamber," said Aaron matter-of-factly. "I wouldn't suggest going that way. Once you get into those twisting passageways, you'll never find your way out."

"How did you know that?" asked Bonnie. "You've never been here!"

"Yes, I have," Aaron replied. "Long ago."

"I keep forgetting you guys have a second life," growled Bonnie.

Deeper and deeper into Castram the adventurers traveled, peering into darkened rooms, occasionally bumping into a suit of armor or a rotting cabinet. Kellaoth had lit a fireball from her horn, and it now floated over their heads, casting everything in an eerie glow. Ellie, Bonnie, and Gallagher stayed close to Kellaoth—being native to the Third World, they felt none of the wondrous feelings coursing through the others. Aaron and Jack, for their part, strolled confidently through the corridors as though they had just been crowned and Malvadore's empire was smote to the ground. Presently, they reached a choice of ways.

"That way," said Kellaoth, pointing to the left fork, "is the way to the ancient Throne Room. To the left is a staircase which leads down to the kitchens.

"Hey, Aaron," said Jack, "let's go check out the Throne Room!"

"Great idea!" Aaron and Jack sprinted down the left passage.

"Aaron, Jack, you shouldn't go off by your—" Ellie began, but Aaron and Jack had already vanished.

"They will be fine," said Kellaoth. "They know where they are going, and even if they don't, I do."

"You've been here, too?" asked Ellie.

"Of course," said Kellaoth. "I was here when Acklyon fell. I witnessed the death of Aaron's father." A pained look came over her.

"Can we-we check outta the kitchithen?" asked Laza.

"Maybe there'll still be some foood dere!" squeaked Deecal.

"Let's go!" chirped Buky.

Laza, Buky and Deecal went skipping off down another passage, whistling as they did.

"I wish people would stop going off by themselves in this place," said Ellie. "It could be dangerous!"

"Do not worry about the Elves," said Kellaoth. "They are smart, but they can get a little careless when excited. To see Castram again, even in this state, is any Acklyonian's wildest dream." At that moment, she raised her head up and continued, "...And I must wander off myself for a short time. I believe I am needed at the front gate."

Gallagher drew his sword, and Bonnie strung her bow. "What is it, Kellaoth?"

"Nothing that you should worry about," she said reassuringly, and without another word, she flew back down the passage towards the main gate, taking her fireball with her and leaving Bonnie, Gallagher, and Ellie all alone.

Suddenly it seemed very dark.

"C'mon," said Ellie, shivering. "Let's try to find our way out."

So they headed back towards the doors. However, in the darkened hallway the three had become disoriented. Soon it became clear that they were lost.

Aaron cautiously approached the massive double doors behind which he knew the Throne Room lay. He glanced over at Jack, who nodded, and together they pushed through the oak doors.

The room was easily the size of a cathedral, lined with rows upon rows of pews. At the far end was a stage on which two magnificent thrones sat. While the rest of the castle had been battered to pieces by age and the attack, these two chairs had not been affected at all. They gleamed with all the splendor they'd had a hundred years ago.

As Aaron and Jack walked down the aisle dividing the rows of pews, dust rose in clouds around their feet. When Aaron climbed the stairs onto the stage and gazed upon his father's throne, all the excitement and tension left him, leaving only a sense of nobility and reverence.

He approached the red and gold throne on the right-hand

side, close enough to read the plaque at the base—"King Forahn" in shining letters.

Aaron stretched out his hand, but stopped and retracted it. He dared not touch the regal throne. Not yet.

"Hey, Aaron, look at this!" said Jack.

Aaron turned to see him wiping the dust off an embroidered portrait mounted on the wall behind the Throne of Parland. Aaron studied the faces of the three people that came into view—a king, dressed in a suit of silver armor and a blue cape with a scrubby red beard and hair; his queen, a pale woman with golden hair; and their son, a boy of about thirteen who had his mother's fairness. Aaron had to look twice before he realized who it was.

"Jack—it's you!"

"What?"

Aaron took a closer look at the boy. There was no denying it—this was Jack as a Prince of Parland. He had none of Jack's freckles nor Jack's gaunt, starved body, but the resemblance was unmistakable. Jack stared at his own face in the portrait and at the faces of his mother and father.

"It can't be..." he whispered, placing a hand on the canvas.

But a thought had occurred to Aaron. Fumbling in his excitement, he tore across the stage to the wall behind the Throne of Fortilly. Sure enough, there was another portrait on the wall, the dust on it so thick he couldn't make out the faces of the people in it. Nearly hysterical, he used his sleeve to smear away the grime coating the frame... And there they were.

And there he was, a well-fed and healthy version of himself beaming out through the canvas. His toffee-colored hair hung in elegant sheets, framing his angular face. Then his eyes drifted upwards toward the faces of his parents.

His mother was a beautiful woman, her brown hair tied in

a long braid down her back, a wreath of flowers resting on her head. And there was his father…

His father.

Adinyrom Forahn the First, who, until now, had been the Last King of Fortilly. He was a broad, powerfully built man, his beard and hair long and flowing. His eyes were a deep sea green, and upon his belt was the sword of Forvalad.

However, there was a single mar on the beauty of the painting: a bloodstain, splashed across the center of the portrait. Aaron wondered briefly who had died there.

So intent was Aaron on the faces of himself and his mother and father that it took him a moment to realize there was a fourth person in the picture—a little girl, perhaps nine or ten, whom the Aaron in the painting had his arm around. Aaron wondered briefly who she was until it hit him: *I had a sister,* he realized in shock. Laza and Kellaoth had never mentioned her. He searched the base of the frame until he found a square plaque, reading *"King Adinyrom I, Queen Mariana, Prince Adinyrom II and Princess Anora.*

"Princess Anora…" Aaron murmured aloud. He didn't have any sisters in the Third World. He'd had an older brother, but he was in college out-of-state, so they hadn't seen much of each other in Aaron's last years in that life.

For the first time, Aaron found himself wishing he could remember his previous life in Acklyon. He felt cheated out of a better childhood. What friends had he had? He supposed he must have known Jack, though maybe not very well. For a long time he gazed into the eyes of the boy in the painting, wondering if he had had any inkling of the life that was in store for him.

"I don't think we're going the right way," said Ellie after a bit.

"This doesn't seem right."

"I think we should reach the entrance hall soon," said Gallagher nervously.

"I don't like this," said Bonnie, scared. "I don't like it at all!"

"It should be over soon," said Gallagher.

They walked blindly on in what they prayed was the right direction. Eventually, they bumped into a heavy iron door.

"This is no good," said Gallagher. "We didn't pass through an iron door on our way here… Did we?"

"We passed several doors," said Bonnie, "but I can't remember if any of them were iron."

"Let's just hope they were," said Gallagher, bravely opening the door. The three walked down the long passageway.

"Okay, now I *know* this is the wrong way!" said Bonnie, running her hands over the walls. "Feel this. It's all slimy! The walls weren't slimy near the entrance hall."

"You know where I think this is?" said Ellie suddenly. "I think this is that dungeon chamber Aaron mentioned."

"I think you're right," said Bonnie.

"Get out, get out, get out!" shouted Gallagher. The three turned around and sprinted in what they hoped was the way out. But when they did, they found they were lost. It seemed to them as they ran that they were in the middle of a giant maze, constantly finding dead-ends and having to turn around.

Lining the walls were doors. They could feel the doors' criss-crossed metal bars, and they were horribly sure that these were cells, possibly full of skeletons. This knowledge encouraged them to run faster and to scramble to find the way out, but to no avail. They were completely lost without any sign of getting out again.

"Now what?" asked Ellie in a rather choked voice.

"I—I don't know," said Gallagher.

"There's something here," said Bonnie in a frightened tone.

"Impossible," said Gallagher. "Nothing came through the door. We would have heard it. And nothing could have survived down here for this long. I hope," he added.

Ellie was shivering like a leaf in a high wind. "Bonnie's right...but it's not a physical thing... It—it feels like a—" She broke off with a petrified scream.

"What is it?" asked Bonnie urgently.

Ellie's only reply was another scream of terror. She was clutching her own arm.

Gallagher darted forward, pried her hands away from her upper arm, and felt it. He pulled away instantly. "It's hot!" he said in panic. "Her arm is red hot!"

"Now what?" cried Bonnie. Then a familiar voice suddenly cracked through the eeriness of the dungeon.

"Get away from her, monster!"

A figure, barely taller than Bonnie, leapt out of nowhere brandishing a flaming sword. It was Aaron. Ellie fell backwards onto the stone floor as Forvalad passed within inches of her face. Though the children couldn't see anything, they could sense something leaping off of Ellie and lunging toward the flaming sword. Aaron brought up his sword in a wild swing, throwing it backwards.

Forvalad raged with golden flames, spewing light in all directions. Aaron hardly seemed human anymore; he had become one with the sword as he battled whatever it was.

The shadow again made to attack Aaron. Forvalad blazed, blocking the thing's path. For a minute more tense than the bloodiest battle, Aaron struggled with the spirit until they all felt a lift in the air as the thing swooped away.

Aaron stood for a moment, looking strangely tall and stern, but then the light from the sword faded. Aaron staggered and then fell face forward onto the cold ground and lay motionless. Bonnie and Gallagher helped him to sit up.

"What was that?" asked Bonnie.

"And how did you get rid of it?" asked Gallagher.

"And how did you find us?" asked Ellie.

Aaron just shook his head. He had not been himself when he fought the thing. All he could remember was being in the Throne room, thinking about his past, when he'd gotten a sudden feeling that Ellie and Bonnie were in danger. He had sprinted until he came to the dungeon and had plunged inside. Forvalad had lit up, and Aaron had seen a shadowy figure crouching over Ellie. Next thing he knew, he was here, his whole body aching, his limbs like water.

"It was a spirit," said a voice. The four turned to see Kellaoth trotting towards them, light shining from her horn.

"You…you mean like a…a ghost?" panted Aaron.

"Yes," said Kellaoth. "What you just fought was likely a prisoner who died in here when the fortress fell."

Bonnie shivered, looking around. It made her uncomfortable—to know that unseen spirits could be swooping around them at that very moment.

"They haunt the Third World, too," Kellaoth continued.

"But—" said Ellie. "But wouldn't we notice? I mean, I've never even heard of something like that actually happening back home!"

"Not everyone can see spirits," said Kellaoth. "Some have the ability, and some do not."

"Let's get out of here," said Gallagher.

Kellaoth sent energy shooting through her horn, lighting up

the entire dungeon. They all shielded their eyes for a few minutes until they adjusted to the bright light.

Once they could see again without squinting, they looked around. The dungeon was very dank and gloomy. They could now see row after row of cells. Gallagher and Kellaoth were the only ones brave enough to peer into them, but all they saw were manacles hanging from the walls. Fortunately, there were no skeletons. Age had rotted those to dust.

Kellaoth led the way, being the only one who knew the secret to getting out. Many years ago, Aaron and Jack's ancestors had scratched a tiny groove, not even an inch wide, along the wall. All one had to do to get out was to place one's finger on the groove and follow it. The grooved line led all the way back to the surface and to safety.

It took some doing, but Aaron at last found the tiny slot along the wall. He placed his finger in it and began to follow it. After what felt like hours, they at last reached the same heavy iron door they had passed through previously.

"Do you think there are any more spirits?" Aaron asked Kellaoth.

"I do not know for sure, but it is likely," Kellaoth replied.

"Then we should find the other kids—and fast," said Aaron.

They continued on in silence for a moment when Aaron remembered the painting.

"Kellaoth—did I have a sister?" he asked quietly.

Kellaoth's eyes grew somber. "Yes," she said. "Her name was Anora."

"What happened to her?" Aaron asked, dreading the answer.

"Alas, I do not know for sure," said Kellaoth. "We tried to evacuate her, the way we did you and Jahkon, but we were too late. She vanished during the battle and hasn't been seen since."

"So she's dead?" said Aaron quietly.

"Her body was never found, so it is possible she survived the battle. But she couldn't have lived long—Malvadore began hunting down and killing all members of the House of Forahn as soon as he had captured Acklyon. I am sorry, Adinyrom."

Aaron remained silent. He wished more than ever he could remember Anora, but at the same time he was glad he couldn't. Perhaps it was better if he never knew what he had lost.

For several weeks, they continued to clean out and rebuild Castram. It was a long, tedious job.

More than once, Aaron, Jack, or Kellaoth had to fight some disturbed spirit that attacked one of their comrades—although not all the spirits were evil. Many, Kellaoth sensed, were merely confused. How did they get here? What were all these people doing in their place?

Aaron, for his part, was glad that they had finally settled down. They were not going to travel anymore. It felt strange, after so many months of running from Gertulk, to suddenly be here, safe and well.

But as it turned out, their traveling was not over.

Three weeks after they arrived, Kellaoth called the five children from their work.

"What is it?" asked Jack wearily.

"Gertulk," said Kellaoth. "I don't know how many, but they are nearby. I don't know why they don't attack, but they are there. If they should choose to attack, then we shall be almost helpless. We need reinforcements."

"But Muln wouldn't help," said Bonnie. "Why should any of the other cities?"

"Cities no," said Kellaoth. "Elves. There are many, hidden

all over the countryside. Two forests, in particular, are very near here. Niybay, and Cappitung, will surely be willing to help."

"So," said Aaron, "we need to go and get them fighting?"

"Not we," Kellaoth corrected him. "*You.*"

"But—"

"Adinyrom," she said patiently, "you and Jahkon must be there to prove who you are. I must stay here to fight off any spirits. We cannot afford to send Elves out, for if you were caught..."

"Can we at least bring Ellie and Bonnie and Gallagher with us?" Jack asked.

"Yes, I think that would be for the best," said Kellaoth.

"Well then," said Gallagher, jumping to his feet, "what are we waiting for?"

32
On the Road Again

"Why did Kellaoth have us do this alone?" asked Bonnie as the five journeyed down the old road away from Castram.

"Probably to test us," said Jack.

Aaron said nothing. Deep within himself, he felt a strange attachment to Castram, and leaving it while work still needed to be done didn't feel right to him.

"I think Kellaoth feels that if we can persuade these Elves to help us without her, then in the long run, we won't need her to back us up everywhere," said Ellie. "I mean, let's face it. Just about every challenge we've faced in our life here, she and Cygon have been behind us to keep us from getting our noses too dirty. Maybe she thinks that we need to do something by ourselves."

"That makes sense," said Gallagher. "And, at the same time, it doesn't. Suppose Aaron or Jack, or all of us, gets killed? What will happen to Acklyon then?"

"I think that's what we need to prove," said Aaron. "If Kellaoth shielded us from everything, made sure that no harm befell us, we would be lazy, untested, and, overall, awful kings."

"True," said Bonnie. "But I still say she's being a little careless with the fulcrum of our existence."

"I wouldn't say that," said Aaron, looking off down the road they traveled, clutching Forvalad's hilt as it swung on his hip.

It was an odd feeling of déjà vu, traveling once more—though, admittedly, they were much better off than on the journey up. This time, they all rode on ponies rather than walked, and they had a large supply of food. Most noticeably, they could travel during the day again, for without the Elves they wouldn't attract suspicion so long as they kept Forvalad and Parvelad hidden.

Aaron was a little surprised when no Gertulk attacked them. They couldn't stop until they were out of sight from Castram—too risky should they be caught. So once the crumbling towers were well in the distance, they paused to rest and made a fire. They took shifts on guard, switching out every few hours.

Jack strained his ears to hear voices from Castram, but the Elves were doing their work in silence. No one would ever suspect that the old fortress was under construction.

Every now and then, they heard that same, eerie call coming from the mountains—the one that Aaron and Wrinky had heard while on guard so long ago. They kept waiting to hear the sounds of tramping footsteps and hoarse yells indicating that the Gertulk had found them. But none came, and the sun rose without any encounters.

The rest of their journey was not so peaceful.

They had to slip past Colten again, and it seemed as though the soldiers had doubled their night patrol in the weeks since they had been there. Every time the travelers thought they could make it, they saw another platoon on guard peering down into the darkness.

More than once, soldiers shining torches into the darkness forced the group to hide. After what felt like hours of sneaking, crawling, hiding, and sweating, the children made it to the other side of the city and vanished into the forest.

"Is this the right forest?" asked Ellie.

"No," said Jack. "The Elves wouldn't settle so close to civilization."

"Let's keep going," said Aaron. "Cappitung isn't far from here."

So once again, they hiked through the forest. Aaron and Jack could tell that this was not an Elf forest. The trees were thin, too thin for homes to be built. And, too, this forest had none of the natural beauty that Eldorlorne had possessed.

Also, there were too many thorns. No Elf enjoys trying to crawl through prickly bushes any more than a man would. They could no longer ride and had to lead their ponies through the dense underbrush.

Eventually, the five broke out on the other side of the wood and into a broad field. There they mounted their steeds again and rode over the clearing. They found an old, weather-beaten road that looked as if it hadn't been used in years, so they followed it through the valley and then over a hill until they reached another forest. This forest, they could tell, *was* Elf-inhabited; the trees were huge and sturdy, greenery was on all sides, and an overall feel of Elves lay about the place.

However, to an outside observer, all these traits were those of an ordinary forest. Ellie, Bonnie, and Gallagher couldn't see much of a difference in this forest than in the other one, even though they had spent the past months in the company of Elves.

"Be wary," Jack warned them. "These Elves will have had a hard time, living so close to Men. If they find us before we find them, they'll likely kill us without hesitation."

They rode silently down the path, through the thick trees, and into Cappitung.

33
The Elves of Cappitung

Together, the five of them continued on without speaking through the old forest. It was smaller than Eldorlorne but was just as beautiful.

"Be careful," Aaron warned them. "The Elves won't take kindly to strangers in their…" His voice trailed away into nothing, as he found an arrow pointing directly at his nose.

Jack grinned broadly as Elves stepped out of hiding places and pointed their bows at them.

"He who walketh into Cappitung and grins when having bows pointed at his face surely isn't very smart," said a female Elf wearing a feather in her cap. She seemed to be the leader of the group.

Aaron immediately began to speak in Elfish

"We come in peace, She-Elf."

The Elf raised her eyebrows in surprise but responded, "I could have sworn that Man-children do not often speak fluent Elfish."

Ellie noticed that this group of Elves looked somehow less friendly than those of Eldorlorne. There were no cheery grins here, no twinkling eyes or happy moods. These looked more stern and wary. Their eyes were hollow, and they scarcely moved a muscle as they held the children at bow-point.

"You're right," said Bonnie. "Normal kids don't speak Elfish, but we're Elf-friends. And can you point that thing somewhere else? Thanks, I can't talk with an arrow in my ear." The Elf who had his arrow in Bonnie's ear did not withdraw it.

"You? Men?" The Elf captain spat, which rather surprised Aaron and Jack. "No Man is our friend. They come, and they burn what we have built up. They are strong but lack the discipline of Elves. We will never side with Men."

"Years ago, you did," Aaron pointed out.

"True," said the Elf. "But that was a long time ago. This is now. I am Cappy, should you care, and this is Cappitung." She gestured at the forest.

"Well, Cappy," said Aaron, "it may've been a while, but I'm sure you still remember *this*." He slowly pulled Forvalad from its sheath.

At his movement, all the Elves took several steps away from them, tightening their grips on their bows. Cappy did not retreat, but her hand did go to her sword hilt. As her eyes adjusted to the light of the flames from the glowing sword, her mouth dropped open. "That sword has not been seen in a hundred years!" she gasped.

"Well, it's back," said Aaron.

"Then you are a Forahn!" she cried.

Aaron nodded.

"No!" said another of the Elves. "Adinyrom Forahn is long dead."

"Um, no, he's not," said Bonnie, "because he's right there!" she pointed to Aaron.

"If he is Adinyrom," said Cappy, "then how has he not aged a day in the past hundred years?"

Bonnie started to speak and then stopped. She looked quizzically at Aaron asking him what to say. Aaron didn't have an answer, for how do you explain a time shift?

"Lock them up," said Cappy, already striding back into the forest. "When they are ready to speak, bring them out."

The Elves closed around the five. Jack and Gallagher gripped their swords but did not draw them.

Bonnie tensed, but Aaron gestured them to surrender their weapons. They had not come to fight; they came to ask for help. Bonnie and Jack looked like they wanted to defend themselves, but that would have meant instant death. Aaron and Ellie both knew that the Elves would shoot if given half an opportunity.

Aaron dismounted, dropping his sword and raising his arms. An Elf stepped forward and frisked him, removing a hunting knife, three throwing knives, his bow, and Aaron's other gear. Devoid of all other options, Ellie, Bonnie, Gallagher, and Jack did the same. The Elves took all the weapons and gathered them up in a bundle. All except Forvalad and Parvelad. They lay on the ground, untouched. "Bring those along;" said one Elf. "Cappy will know what to do with them."

"I don't think that's a good idea," Aaron warned the Elves.

"Oh yeah?" said one Elf.

"Yep," said Aaron. "You don't know what that sword can do, but I do."

"He's bluffing," said the Elf. "Get the sword."

Another Elf diligently went over and picked up Parvelad. There was a flash of light, and with a yelp, the Elf released the sword. It had glowed red hot and singed his hand. The sword vanished, disappearing as though someone had thrown an invisible blanket over it. The Elf chirped with fright but then attempted to take Forvalad. Again, the sword glowed, burning that poor Elf again, and vanished. There was a long silence.

"I tried to warn you," said Aaron, "but did you listen? No."

"Shut up!" said the Elf. Aaron smirked.

"No use crying over spilled Lime Oola," said the Elf. "Take them to the prison."

"I don't believe this," said Bonnie. The five of them were locked up in a large yew tree with Elf guards just outside. "Kellaoth tells us to go ask these idiots for help, so off we go. We sneak past Men and Gertulk, risk life and limb for these stupid Elves, and as soon as we get here, they throw us in a stinking jail!"

"Shut up!" snapped Aaron who was peering out a small window that had a view into the Elf compound. "What would you do if your enemies came strolling into your forest? We need to prove to them that we're real!" Aaron had spied Cappy entering a nearby tree and he presumed that that must be her house.

"We'll need Forvalad and Parvelad for that," Bonnie said dejectedly. "But those stupid guards already took care of that. Who knows where the swords are now?"

"I say we jailbreak," said Gallagher. "We need to find Cappy and knock some sense into her." He got up and ran his hand over the wooden bars of the cell.

"Wood," chuckled Jack. "These Elves aren't used to holding prisoners larger than an Elf, obviously." With that, he roundhouse kicked one of the bars in half.

"Let's go," said Aaron. "And remember, don't hurt any of them! Disarm them if you have to, but no bruises, broken bones, severed limbs, or deaths. Got it?"

The others nodded.

"Although," said Jack, "I could use my sword back."

He happened to glance back at their cell as he said this.

There was Parvelad, lying on a bench.

"How did that get here?" said Bonnie incredulously.

"Look!" said Ellie, pointing to the far wall. "Forvalad's over there!"

"As Kellaoth told us," Jack calmly said as he sheathed Parvelad, "these are more than sharpened metal."

"Okay."

After he had retrieved Forvalad, Aaron led the way to the door of the jail. The door was locked from the outside but with one stroke from Forvalad, Aaron broke the lock, and the door swung open. The guards immediately turned and pointed spears at the five, but Jack and Bonnie seized the Elves' weapons and threw them into the forest. One of the Elves then tried to sound the alarm by sending just the right number of tremors through the earth via slamming a heavy mallet into the ground, but Gallagher caught the mallet and halted the message.

Aaron then led a charge through Cappitung. Elves came out of hiding and tried to stop them, but the five moved as fast as ever they did, and arrived at Cappy's house.

When Gallagher and Jack shoved down the door, there was Cappy, poring over a map of the forest.

She leapt to her feet and fired an arrow at them. However, the five had expected this and were able to drop to the ground fast enough to avoid it. Then it was a simple matter of tugging the bow out of her hands, and she was caught.

"Listen," said Aaron. "We came here to help you, not fight you. We're starting a war, and we need your help. We need Elves to fight the Gertulk. We have Laza and the population of Eldorlorne, but it's not enough. Will you help us?"

"If not," Jack added, "Bonnie here could always run outside

and scream until the Gertulk find us. She has very powerful lungs, you know."

Bonnie nodded and beamed.

Cappy looked surprised. "You know Laza?"

"Of course we know Laza!" said Jack. "Let's see… He thinks Buky is the cutest Elf in the forest, he carries his mother's favorite thumbtack and his father's favorite toenail in a bag around his neck to remember them by. He's the youngest Elf captain to have come out of Eldorlorne. He used to live in a bigger forest south of Muln until the Gertulk attacked and killed his parents, and he's close friends with Kellaoth the Unicorn."

Cappy's eyes went to the glowing swords in Aaron's and Jack's hands. "Well, why didn't you say so?" she cried. "Laza is not a bad fellow! Maybe a little irresponsible, but quite pleasant to be around. Come! We have planning to do."

Aaron looked at Jack, Jack looked at Bonnie, Bonnie looked at Gallagher, and Gallagher looked at Ellie. None of them knew quite what to say.

The Elves led Aaron, Jack, Bonnie, Ellie, and Gallagher through the forest to their self-fashioned "City Hall," which was actually a huge, aged oak tree in the center of the forest.

Aaron, Jack, and Cappy discussed their situation all the way. From what Cappy said, the Elves of Cappitung had had a hard life. Men and Gertulk were sent almost monthly to search for signs of Elf inhabitance. Fortunately, the beasts had never found anything, but there had been some near misses.

"Malvadore is obsessed with Castram," she explained as they walked. "His deepest and darkest fear is that the two of you will sit on the Thrones of Fortilly and Parland again. Like all tyrants, he's afraid of losing his power."

"How many swords are you?" Aaron asked.

"One hundred and two," Cappy replied.

Aaron's heart sank. That was less than a quarter of the Eldorlorne population.

"Are there any other Elf forests in the area?" Jack now asked Cappy.

"Yes," said Cappy. "Niybay, on the other side of the mountian."

"Do you know of any other Elves in Acklyon?"

"No," said Cappy. "Not unless you're willing to travel all the way across Acklyon. Cappitung and Niybay are just about the last in Central Acklyon, and I guarantee that the Gertulk will find us soon."

"All the more reason to hurry," said Aaron. "Once we establish friendship here, I say we sneak over to Niybay, form an alliance, and then we storm Colten."

"Why?" asked Jack in surprise.

"Because we'll need every soldier we can get our hands on, as well as a good blow to Malvadore," Aaron replied. "If we can defeat the Gertulk of Colten, then maybe we can persuade the leader to help us. Also, I will not sneak past there a third time." He turned to Cappy. "By the way, who is Colten's leader?" he asked.

"The duke's name is Aticka. A ninny if I ever saw one, but a great general nonetheless."

"We'll need his help," said Aaron. "The more Men that help our cause, the better."

"Niybay is not too far from here," said Cappy. "We built our forests close to each other so that we could join forces in an emergency."

"Well, we've got one now," said Jack grimly.

34
Strategizing in Niybay

"The city is weakest by the southern walls," said Cappy.

"So if we can slip a few Elves over that wall," said Aaron, "and get them to open the doors, we stand a better chance against the Gertulk."

"The less they're expecting an attack, the better chance we have of success," said Jack.

It had been a week since they had made contact with the Elves of Cappitung.

In that time, Aaron, Jack, Cappy, and a dozen Elf warriors had traveled to the nearby forest of Niybay. They now sat about a round wooden table in the largest tree in Niybay, discussing their battle strategy with the leader of that forest, an elderly but sturdy Elf named Deepy.

"Lord Aticka will be in his office," Deepy now said. "Which is in the palace. If we can get ourn troopies into there, then we can get him to surrender and join us."

"If Ellie were here," Aaron pointed out, "she would say that there was no hope for a mere two hundred Elves to take a heavily guarded city like Colten."

"And if Bonnie were here," said Jack, grinning, "she would say that just makes it more fun."

Ellie, Bonnie, and Gallagher remained in Cappitung with the Elves. They had objected to this; but as Aaron pointed out, this trip was not one of establishing friendship. It was a War Council.

"I'd say our best hope is to capture Aticka early on and to get him to give the order for his men to attack the Gertulk," said Aaron. "A big trading city like Colten should have a decent garrison."

"We've checked," said Cappy. "Over two hundred swords."

"But the Gertulk got over five hundred," said Deepy. "They don't want to take the chance of losing the city."

"All the more reason that we need it," said Jack determinedly.

"Taking Colten will be difficult," mused Cappy. "It's making our first move against the Gertulk."

"Right now," said Aaron, "with the way our chances are looking, we are going to need every strike we can get."

"Let's go fer it," said Deepy.

They mustered every Elf in Niybay and crept back to Cappitung where they met up with the others and told them the strategy. Departing Cappitung, they all marched back through the forests until they could see the walls of Colten looming up before them.

From there, they continued the plan; a dozen of the smallest and nimblest of the Elves crawled over the walls and sneaked down to the double doors where on the other side the rest of the Elves waited.

Aaron and Jack were part of the second column of Elves with Bonnie and Gallagher nearby.

"If anything happens to me," Aaron muttered through the lump in his throat to Jack, "you'll have to take Fortilly."

"Don't say that," said Jack tersely. "Of course we're going to survive this… Right?"

Aaron attempted to respond, but the lump got bigger, and he couldn't speak. However, speaking wouldn't have done much good for at that moment, the great double doors began to quietly slide open. Every Elf drew back his bow a few inches—until the group saw it was their friends.

The Elves opened the doors enough for all of them to get through and beckoned the amassed Elfin army inside. Once the last Elf was inside, they silently closed the doors again.

When the two hundred Elves were all in position, Cappy looked at Deepy, who had his sword drawn. Deepy nodded. Cappy reached for the bugle slung across her back and blew a long, clear blast.

The invasion had begun.

35
Storming Colten

"Remember!" Cappy shouted as the Elves eagerly charged into the shadows of the town. "Kill only Gertulk! Leave the townsfolk be. We want them as allies and not enemies! And don't break anything!"

Seven Gertulk spilled out of a nearby guardhouse, saw the group that had remained behind. The Gertulk bellowed and charged.

Jack looked back at the fierce Elves, clicking and blowing raspberries at the Gertulk.

"Fire!" shouted Cappy.

Twenty-two Elves drew back twenty-two bowstrings and shot twenty-two arrows at the Gertulk, all of whom immediately staggered and fell, each with multiple arrows in his body.

"Nice one," said Jack.

"Look!" cried Gallagher.

Seventy or eighty Gertulk had gathered deeper in, and they now charged.

At Cappy's command, the Elves once again fired arrows into the crowd, though it was clear that arrows alone would not stop the beasts.

Once the Gertulk were within fifty feet of the Elves, Jack

pointed Parvelad at them and shouted, "CHARGE!"

The Elves hooted with bloodlust and sprinted towards the Gertulk.

A *twang* and *hiss* filled the air once more, and one of the leading Gertulk dropped. Jack looked up to see Aaron and Bonnie crouched on a rampart. Aaron and Bonnie both had bows and rained arrows down on the Gertulk. As the Elves collided with the Gertulk, Aaron and Bonnie dropped down to the ground. Aaron drew his sword, and he and Bonnie fought their way back to the leaders.

"Come," said Cappy. "We have an appointment with the duke."

So Cappy, Deepy, Aaron, and his friends went sprinting down the lane, heading for the Town Hall, occasionally stopping to beat back the Gertulk. Finally, they reached the palace. They charged up the steps and burst through the doors. The Gertulk guards attempted to block them, but Elves leapt out of the shadows and eliminated the hulking beasts.

"The duke will be up there!" said Cappy, pointing towards the main spiraling tower. So they continued on, stopping only to destroy any guards. Once they had climbed seven staircases, they found a heavy wooden door guarded by two Gertulk—Duke Aticka's residence. The Elves surprised the guards and shot them down with their bows.

Aaron charged the door, swinging his sword. With one hack from Forvalad, he sent the door crashing down in flames.

The duke, a sturdy, handsome fellow with long fair hair, leapt to his feet as his Gertulk bodyguards closed around them.

Cappy launched an arrow from her bow, sending one of the Gertulk to the floor. Aaron swung hard at the other, sheering through the Gertulk's breastplate and digging into his chest.

The duke reached for his sword, but Cappy and Bonnie both drew back their bows threateningly, and the nobleman raised his arms.

With a disgusting squelching noise, Aaron pulled his sword out of the Gertulk. "Your servant," he said to the duke, sheathing the golden blade. "Bonnie, quit pointing your arrow at him, we're guests in this man's house."

Bonnie slowly lowered her bow.

"Thanks," said Aaron. He turned to the duke. "Lord Aticka? Aaron Forahn. A pleasure to meet you." He held out his hand, as though they were at a formal meeting.

Lord Aticka stared at him in a bemused sort of way. Clearly, he hadn't often had the true king of Fortilly burst into his study, kill his bodyguards, and then shake his hand.

"What do you want from me?" the duke asked quietly.

"We want your loyalty," said Jack, "and your help in our war."

Aticka studied him closely. "There are few who can hope to oppose the king."

"The False King," Aaron corrected him. "He's merely a pawn; we want Malvadore's blood, not his."

"Kane Malvadore is a foe even greater than King Adinyrom," said Aticka stubbornly.

"All the more reason that we need your help," said Aaron.

"But if you decide not to work with us," said Bonnie, twanging her bow threateningly, "we can oblige."

Aticka became quiet as he weighed the odds, but Aaron knew what his response would be before he gave it. "What do you need me to do?" the duke asked in a determined voice.

"Call the order for your men to attack the Gertulk," said Cappy.

Aticka nodded and went to the open window. Outside they could see Elves and Gertulk wrestling with Men darting around, unsure of which side to help. Aticka called a page over and instructed the boy to fetch his shield and helm. He was already wearing a coat of chain mail with his sword on his belt.

Once the page returned, Aticka slid the shield onto his arm and placed the gold-plated helm on his head. He then vanished out the door, crying for his men to attack the Gertulk.

Aaron, Jack, Bonnie, Gallagher, Cappy, Deepy, and their troop of Elves followed him out.

"Halt, rebels!"

Aaron whirled around. In the doorway through which they had just exited stood a man. He was dressed all in shining gold which had a strange, even cold, look to it. He was clean-shaven, and his eyes behind the crown-like helm were icy blue.

The False Adinyrom Forahn.

To see him standing there matter-of-factly was somewhat unnerving to Aaron. Whenever he'd thought about the imposter, Aaron had always imagined him as a sort of dummy or hand puppet that Malvadore used. To see him there, holding a sword made Aaron shudder. *It's me or him,* he realized.

Aaron stepped boldly out in front, brandishing his sword at the Imposter King. "Get back!" he shouted. Aaron made a swing at the imposter, but the False Forahn parried with ease.

The Elf soldiers began launching arrows at the imposter, who somehow dodged all the shots. Then, as casually as if he were scratching an itch, Forahn unleashed a bolt of chain lightning which struck the entire column of Elves, killing them instantly.

Gallagher swung hard, only to find himself flying backwards at high speed. He fell back down the stairs and slid to the bottom where he lay, motionless. Bonnie yelled in fury, firing an arrow at the False King, and darted down the stairs to check on her brother. Forahn raised his hand, as though bidding the arrow to halt.

It did.

The arrow paused in the air, hovered for a moment, and then turned around and sped towards Jack, who dropped to the ground to avoid it.

Aaron, Jack, Cappy, and Deepy were left to handle Forahn. They spread out and closed around him.

"Give it up," said Deepy. "You're outnumbered."

"Outnumbered," the False King conceded. He raised his arm, sending a burst of red lightning at Deepy. It hit the old Elf, sending him shooting backwards into a window and through it to his doom below. "But not defeated."

Aaron stared in horror. One of the greatest Elfin leaders and warriors alive had just been killed by this madman with one shot! A scream of fury broke from Aaron's lips, and he charged, intending to kill this man. The False King was surprised at this show of daring but defended himself calmly.

After three quick parries, the False Adinyrom went on the attack, barraging Aaron mercilessly. Forahn attacked and Aaron defended, losing ground as he did.

Just before Aaron's limbs went out on him, a voice came from behind: "Hold, Traitor!"

They all turned to see Aticka, one hand raised, with the entire mass of Elves and Men behind him. The battle was won.

The False Adinyrom whirled his sword and prepared a bolt of lightning, but Aticka cut him off.

"Think about it," the duke said. "Can you really pull a bolt of chain lightning big enough to kill all four hundred of us before we shoot you down? See, all I have to do to end your existence is to drop my hand"—he twitched the hand he held aloft in a threatening manner—"and even you won't be able to dodge all the spears and arrows that'll come flying your way."

Though Forahn despised admitting it, Aticka was right. There would be another time to kill, and then all of the insolent fools would die by his own hand. Sneering, Forahn vanished. Aaron was quiet for a long time, despite the cheers of the Men and Elves. Aaron now saw where his destiny lay; he must kill the False Adinyrom. He didn't know how he was supposed to kill such a powerful magician—but there must be a way, and he had to find it. He thought of Deepy, blasted into submission by this fiend who no doubt never thought twice about the horrid deed.

"Aaron?"

Aaron turned at the sound of his name. It was Bonnie.

"Come on," she said. "Everyone is gathering in the Banquet Hall."

Aaron really wanted to be alone, but he nodded and followed her out.

36

Homecoming

Deepy's body had been recovered. He was found, broken and crumpled, at the base of the duke's residence. In the idiosyncratic customs of the Elves, Deepy had been wrapped up in a blanket with several lilies and a note to God asking him to accept Deepy's soul into heaven. This had been tied to eight large balloons and sent off into the atmosphere as Ploppy had been. Due to the loss of Deepy, Cappy took charge of Niybay as well as Cappitung.

"But we'll need to make it invisible like we did with Ploppy," Bonnie pointed out. "And we don't have Kellaoth to do her Magic!"

"We don't need to," said Cappy. "Malvadore knows that the Elves are on the move again. Let this beacon be fair warning to him. The Elves have taken Colten, and soon the rest of Acklyon will follow!

"Gather up your troops and your villagers," Cappy later said to Lord Aticka as the Elves were leaving. "We'll expect you in Castram before the leaves turn red."

"Aye," replied Aticka, saluting Cappy. The Elf returned the salute and faced the children, who were mounted on ponies at the front of the column of Elves. Cappy executed a perfect midair somersault and landed on her own pony.

"To Castram we go!" Cappy cried, looking far happier than Aaron had ever seen her.

The Elves headed out of Colten amidst cheers and waves from the townsfolk. Aaron smiled at the flowers that now littered the street ahead of them. It felt good to have someone applauding him finally.

They began their trek back to Castram, stopping at Niybay to pick up Ellie and the Elfin villagers from Cappitung and Niybay. Then they turned their horses north towards the now-hidden spirals of Castram.

The closer they came to Castram, the more contented Aaron and Jack grew. Bonnie, Ellie, and Gallagher assumed they were simply glad to be able to rest, but it went far deeper than that. Over the millennia, the ancient castle of Castram had become one with the Thrones of Fortilly and Parland to such an extent that Aaron and Jack felt uncomfortable away from it.

They had expected trouble on their trip back to Castram, but to their great surprise, they saw no sign of Gertulk. Though Cappy and Gallagher theorized on this, they could not come up with a good explanation. Why would the Gertulk want more Elves joining the rebellion?

Though the group did not know it, as the Elves from Niybay and Cappitung returned to Castram, they were walking right into the schemes of Kane Malvadore. He had known for years that Elves were still in existence, but had been unable to track them down due to their ingenious hiding skills. He now saw this rebellion as a chance to eliminate all Elves once and for all.

Malvadore had sent his Gertulk to chase, but not to destroy, the Elves of Eldorlorne, knowing they would go to Castram and that they would recruit other Elves to help.

Castram was built into the side of a mountain, a mountain in which Malvadore had stationed legions of Gertulk. Kellaoth and Laza had now walked right into his trap, drawing more Elves to Castram. The rebels had nowhere to run from there, and Malvadore knew it. He would wait a little longer to see whether any more Elves were coming. Then he would launch a massive attack on Castram, and the Elves would become an extinct race.

37
Castram Reawakened

"Wow," said Bonnie again, staring up at the castle.

It had completely changed. When they had left, it had been a forsaken ruin, dingy and more than a little creepy. But in the months they had been gone, the Elves had done much to finish the place.

Most of the crumbled towers were restored, and the rotting double doors had been replaced with two that were solid and shiny. As the five approached, someone sounded a horn and the gates opened.

When the children rode through, they could see that half of the great city within was converted into a luscious jungle. The Elves had already set up houses within many of the trees and had begun the civilization of Castram.

Jack grinned broadly at the Elves working tirelessly to mend the damage done. As the group neared the palace, Aaron noticed another change: hanging on two turrets above the main doors were two new banners. The one on the left was blue with a vine wrapped around a silver chalice stitched on it. The one on the right was bright red with a golden, eight-sided star.

Twin Elf guards stood at the doors to the palace, holding long spears. They saluted as Aaron, Jack, Bonnie, Ellie, Gallagher, and

Cappy dismounted.

"Where is Kellaoth the Unicorn and Laza the Quick-footed?" asked Cappy.

"In da Great Hall," replied one of the guards. "Welcome to Castram, oh Cappy the Courageous!"

Cappy dipped her head, and Aaron led the way to the Great Hall.

"Cappy the Courageous?" said Jack, once they were out of earshot of the guards.

Cappy shrugged. "We Elves have stayed close over the years."

"This way," Aaron said, rapping three times on the oak doors to the Great Hall. More Elves opened it from the inside, and Aaron, Jack, and Cappy stepped in.

Kellaoth and Laza were deep in discussion about the fortifications of Castram, pouring over a huge map of the castle. They both looked up upon seeing visitors. Kellaoth smiled proudly, and Laza leaped out of his chair and rushed over.

"Youee came! Youee came!" He said excitedly, running over to Cappy and giving her a bear hug, lifting her off her feet and spinning her around in circles.

"Laza—get off!" Cappy snapped, struggling to pull away from Laza's embrace, but Laza refused to relent, now kissing her rapidly on either cheek. As she made another effort to free herself, her feet got tangled up in his, and both Elves crashed to the floor. Cappy leapt to her feet at once, straightening her tunic, her face cherry red.

"Kellaoth, I apologize for this display," she said quickly, casting Laza an angry look. "I must insist—"

But Kellaoth was laughing along with the others. "At ease, Captain of Cappitung," the Unicorn said.

Cappy nodded, then walked over and kicked Laza, who was still on the floor. Laza squeaked and stood up. It was very strange with Laza, bouncing up and down and beaming at all of them, and Cappy, stiff, straight, and dignified.

"Our troops have begun settling in the forest," Cappy now said. "I hope there is room for all of us." Aaron could tell by her tone that she was still angry with Laza.

"Aw, no, not a'tall," said Laza boisterously. "We got more room in dere than we is knowing what to do wiff!" He bounded across the room and peered out the window at the two hundred Elf soldiers from Niybay and Cappitung. Their children also moved into the forest and some were already beginning to hollow out trees. Laza's smile dropped. He turned to Cappy with a quizzical look. "So few?" he said seriously.

Cappy gave him an icy glare, a hand on her sword hilt. "We have not been as fortunate as those of Eldorlorne, Laza. You were situated by the coast, well away from Malvadore's peering eye. We were right on the outskirts of Colten and less than twenty miles from Castram. The two hundred you see here are those lucky enough to survive."

"Two hundred?" said Laza incredulously. Clearly disappointed, he looked at Kellaoth. "That's less than half of what we got from Eldorlorne."

A long, uncomfortable silence followed, broken by Bonnie. "The good news," she said, "is that we captured Colten."

Cappy nodded. "Indeed," she said. "Lord Aticka has agreed to fight for us. Right now he is preparing the Men of Colten to migrate here."

"Goody!" said Laza, evidentially forgetting the discouraging number of reinforcements. "Men on our side will do a bunch!"

"That they will," said Kellaoth. "If we can get enough of the towns around here to help us, Malvadore will not take us so lightly."

"It's the good old days again, huh?" Aaron said jokingly to Laza.

"That't is!" said Laza.

With an explosion like that of an erupting volcano, Gallagher's head broke the surface of the pond, gasping and spluttering. A moment later, Ellie's popped out, too, and Jack appeared not long after that. Aaron and Bonnie were still underwater, though, having a furious battle of endurance, trying to see who could stay under longer. Bonnie gave in, eventually, and came up for air. When Aaron saw her come up, he, too, kicked off the stony bottom and a moment later was coughing and choking for air, crying triumphantly, "I am the winner!"

"Fifty-eight and a half seconds!" said Gallagher. "That's got to be a record!"

The five of them, having been given swimming outfits all made of a comfortable yet durable material from the Elves, had decided to enjoy the burning July heat by swimming in the fountain in the courtyard. This magnificent fountain was ideal for swimming (though Aaron and Jack's ancestors would have likely never have used it as a pool). The fountain was at least fifteen feet in diameter and about four and a half feet deep, so they had plenty of room to swim around and to go underwater.

About six feet over their heads sprouted the second pool, smaller than the first. Above that one was the third basin, and above that was the fourth, which was about the size of a large bucket. Laza and Buky were splashing around and laughing in the top bowl, looking absurdly like babies in a washbasin.

"Hey, quit it!" shouted Aaron as a sprinkle of drops fell from the top basin and onto his head. "We came in here for a bath, not a shower!"

"Sorry!" said Laza from the heights.

"Well, we'd better dry ourselves off before dinner," said Ellie heavily, ignoring Laza, who had just dive-bombed out of the fourth bowl and landed in the second, cascading water over the five of them.

The children climbed out of the fountain as Laza leaped artistically back into the top bowl, and began drying themselves off with the towels they had brought.

"Aaron, your hair's completely out of control!" said Ellie, laughing at the ridiculous spikes that Aaron's hair made after he'd dried it with his towel.

"Look at yourself in a mirror!" said Bonnie.

A hand mirror fell out of the sky and landed in Aaron's towel.

"Thanks, Laza!" Aaron shouted up to him.

"No problemo!" Laza shouted from atop the fourth bowl.

"What were you doing with a hand mirror while swimming in a fountain?" demanded Bonnie. Laza shrugged.

Chuckling, Aaron looked into the hand mirror, dimly aware that this was the first proper mirror he'd looked in since Eldorlorne. His mouth dropped open.

His hair looked ludicrous, yes, but there were other aspects of his face that had completely changed. Though it was hard to tell while it was wet, Aaron was sure that his hair was rather lighter, and it reached his shoulders when he smoothed it down. His eyes, which had been a dark, pine green in Avondale, were now sea-green. His nose was somewhat longer and had a more regal look to it. His face was more narrow and thin with a slightly haunted appearance. He had definitely lost some weight. He noticed that every move he made was sharp and sudden, and that his grip on the mirror was hard as steel. It also occurred to him that he had grown quite a lot. There was a noticeable shadow on his upper lip, and his arms and legs had become scraggly with hair. It occurred to him that if this were July, he would be fourteen in a month.

Bonnie was staring over his shoulder. "What's wrong?" she said, peering into the mirror. "Got a zit?"

Aaron stared at her. "Do you see anything different about me?" he demanded.

Bonnie studied his face. "No," she said. "I don't see any zits."

"Not acne!" said Aaron. He gestured to his face. "Have I always looked like this? Back in Avondale?"

Bonnie thought. "Come to think about it...you didn't look quite like this in Avondale. I guess you changed. It was so gradual that we never noticed."

Now that Aaron looked closer, he saw that his friends had all changed in small ways. Gallagher's hair was overgrown, and he had a battle-hardened look about him, punctuated by a scar across his shoulder. Ellie had tanned considerably and moved with much more confidence than he had ever seen in her. Bonnie's eyes had grown sharper, darting over Aaron, up to Laza and Buky, and to Forvalad, which was resting on a blanket nearby.

But Jack... Jack had changed more than any of them. He had the same battle-weary look as the others, but there was more. His eyes had a clear, noble look in them, his reddish-blonde hair had become golden, and he held himself with much more dignity than back home. He had also grown taller. Aaron didn't have to ask what had brought the change, for he knew already as surely as he knew that Laza had just splashed water on him.

He was becoming a Forahn.

38
Kellaoth's Mission

The five children along with Kellaoth, Laza, Buky, and Cappy, ate dinner in the Banquet Hall. Under normal circumstances, this magnificent hall would have been decorated with tapestries, music would be playing, and the lords and ladies would alternate between feasting and dancing while the kings and queens sat at the head of the table.

Under normal circumstances, an evil, maniacal Kane would not be in control of Acklyon.

The nine of them ate at a great round table with a large ham sitting in the center.

Nimbun was curled up on a rug by their feet, rather like a very large dog. He had grown quite a bit and had changed from a starved, scrawny, abused hybrid into a fat, happy, faithful pet. Somehow, Nimbun could understand speech, though could not speak himself. This made him even more of an effective steed for Laza as Laza would not need a rein or have to steer.

"So," said Kellaoth once they were all seated, "we now have two hundred Elves from Eldorlorne, one hundred from Cappitung, one hundred from Niybay, and two hundred Men coming from Colten?"

"That is correct," said Cappy.

"Four hundred Elves is all well and good," said Bonnie, "but we need those Men now!"

"Just be patient," said Kellaoth. "It takes time to move an entire population."

"But how do we know they'll come?" Bonnie persisted. "You realize nothing's stopping them from calling in more Gertulk, don't you?"

"Aticka's on our side," said Aaron. "He's not an evil man. I could tell. My guess is he'll set out once the heat of summer's out. We got back with the Elves in a few days, but a troop of Elves goes much faster than a caravan of Men with their children and goods. I'm thinking they'll be here around December."

"Just as long as he doesn't come with an armed escort of Gertulk," Bonnie muttered.

"Still," said Jack, "six hundred soldiers on our side isn't too bad."

"So now we wait for the Gertulk to come," said Aaron gloomily.

"That's the part I don't understand," said Ellie. "Why doesn't Malvadore wipe us out now? The castle is still under construction, and Colten hasn't arrived yet! He's just letting us get stronger!"

"Who knows?" said Gallagher. "But I say, as long as he's giving us time, use it to finish the fortifications of this castle and to get more troops."

"There might be a few towns nearby that would help," suggested Ellie.

"Nope," said Aaron. "They're all crawling with Gertulk. Malvadore doesn't want any more of his country falling into Enemy hands. Not even if we had all the advantages that we had in Colten could we hope to pull it off."

"I just wish we had the Dwarves," said Cappy.

"What?" said Jack. "Are there Dwarves here?"

"There were," said Kellaoth, "long ago in the days of your ancestors. They formed an alliance with Acklyon, did a great deal to help in the battles ahead. But not even their fierceness and bravery could stop the Shadow falling." Aaron gaped at her. He knew what this "Shadow" was.

"When Malvadore attacked Castram, we appealed to the Dwarves for help, but they refused. Years before, the Dwarves had fought against the Acklyonians in the Gold Wars, and Dwarves have long memories. They fled deep underground, far beneath the surface of Castram. No one has seen them since. Who knows if they're still alive?"

"But if they are," said Aaron, "they could help us!"

"Yes," said Laza. "And then the Centaur would come up from the ground and dance the polka."

"Centaur?" said Bonnie.

"'Tis an old myth," said Cappy, frowning at Laza's joke. "Legend says that the Centaur lies underneath this castle. They say that he will rise from the ground when greatly needed. Although," she gave a hollow laugh, "it looks as if Malvadore disproved that one. He never showed, not when Malvadore attacked, nor now when we need him."

There was another pause, and then Bonnie summed up the story. "Well, that stinks," she said.

"Kellaoth, where are you taking us?" demanded Aaron as Kellaoth led him and Jack deep into the cellars beneath Castram. After dinner that night, Kellaoth had insisted that Aaron and Jack follow her down there.

"You shall see in a minute," Kellaoth replied.

Aaron had never been down this deep. They must be at least a mile below Castram, and there was no sign of the tunnel coming to an end.

At last they reached the bottom. Aaron, who had expected a secret doorway, or some rubies and gems, was disappointed to see nothing but a mural on the wall. On further inspection, the mural turned out to be two of the Kings of Fortilly and Parland. The men were wielding Forvalad and Parvelad, but the swords, instead of being painted, were in the form of an imprint on the stone wall. In fact, Aaron suspected that the real Forvalad and Parvelad would have fit in them. This suspicion was confirmed when Kellaoth stopped and turned to the boys. "Put your swords in the slots," she said.

Aaron and Jack looked at each other, drew their swords, and placed them in the indentures on the mural. There was a pause, and then the Twin Swords lit up like burning embers, one glowing cherry red, the other silvery-blue.

Then, with a great roar and the scraping sound of stone sliding over stone, the mural slid away to reveal a hidden chamber. Without looking at the boys, Kellaoth strode into the room. Aaron and Jack followed, pulling their swords out of the wall as they went.

Kellaoth sent a fireball out of her horn, and it hovered into the middle of the room, throwing light over suits of gold or silver armor, shields, various weapons, spears…

"Behold!" said Kellaoth, smiling. "Your fathers' armory."

Aaron and Jack stared in wonder. One half of the room was blue and silver, the other red and gold. It was perhaps the most glorious room the boys had ever seen. Helmets of all different designs sat on a shelf over there. In this corner was a golden breastplate. On that wall there was a shirt of silver chain mail.

Different-styled greaves, bracers, gauntlets, everything in bright gold or silver. On the back wall were two statues, one gold, and the other silver.

Aaron walked over and stared at them. The statues were of two kings, wielding the Twin Swords of Acklyon. Was it his imagination, or did the gold one look a lot like…him? Across the figures' backs were two magnificent cloaks. These were not carved into the statue, but were real, shimmering fabric. The one on the gold statue was blood red, and the one on the silver was deep blue. They were such beautiful cloaks, Aaron didn't dare touch them. It seemed as though the statues had been made as racks for the cloaks.

Kellaoth and Jack joined him.

"Ah," said Kellaoth, "I thought you'd find these."

"What are they?" asked Jack in awe.

"They are the Cloaks of the Kings. It is said that only the true Kings of Fortilly and Parland may wear them.

"The reason I am showing you this," Kellaoth now said, "is because you will be on your own for a while."

"What?" yelped Aaron.

"Aye," said Kellaoth. "There is a job that must be done, and I am the only one qualified to do it. I must leave. I do not know when I will be back."

"But—"

"You will understand when it is over," Kellaoth said over Jack's protest. "But for now, I cannot say. The time may come, sooner than you think, when you will need this armor. Goodbye, Kings of Acklyon."

"Wait!" said Aaron, but too late. Kellaoth dissolved into nothing, leaving the boys alone.

Jack stared at Aaron. "Why would she need to leave, right

before a battle?"

Aaron shook his head. "I don't know..."

Further conversation was put off by the sound of a horn blowing.

"What is that?" asked Jack. "The people of Colten can't be here already, can they?"

"No," said Aaron grimly, "but I think we may still have some company,"

39

Reinforcements from Muln

Aaron stared in amazement at the column of marching soldiers dressed in red and silver armor. In their hands were long spears and round shields, and on their heads were pointed silver helmets.

Aaron and Jack had raced back up the passageway when they heard the horn, and burst out the double doors to see this troop of Men marching calmly towards Castram. They were not attacking, simply strolling towards the castle as though they belonged there. It wasn't Colten, either. Instead of the blue Raven of Colten, on their banner was the red Bear…of Muln!

"Keep your bows on them," Jack shouted to the Elves. "This may be a trap."

The commander of the soldiers, who wore golden mail, a gold helmet, and a long red cape, stepped up to Aaron and bowed low. "Hail, Sire!" he cried in a grim voice.

"Who are you?" asked Aaron, trying not to sound rude while keeping his sword in front of him.

The man lifted his helmet, revealing long, graying hair, a hard set of eyes, and a rugged beard. "I am Lord Fortingale, Captain of the Garrison of Muln."

"Why do you come?"

"To aid you in the battles ahead," said Fortingale.

"You didn't seem so willing to help us when we were in Muln," said Aaron coldly. Being driven out by an angry mob was still a sore spot in his memory.

"That was under different circumstances. The Gertulk were in charge, and we had not the men to fight them," said Fortingale.

"But they're not in charge anymore?"

"Nay," said Fortingale.

"When did that happen?" asked Bonnie.

"I believe I can explain." The voice wasn't Fortingale's but rather from one soldier near the head of the column who stepped up beside his captain. The man removed his helmet, and Aaron could see the now familiar thick, scrubby beard, wiry hair, and twinkling blue eyes.

"Brotchurd!" he cried.

Brotchurd smiled. "Shortly after you left, my liege, I tracked down Lord Fortingale. At my urging, the garrison in a bold move launched a rebellion against the Gertulk. Though badly outnumbered, we caught the beasts by surprise and drove them out of Muln, temporarily. But they did not stay defeated for long. Soon, we heard news that yet more Gertulk were marching towards Muln, conquest on their minds."

"Yeah," said Aaron. "We had the same problem in Eldorlorne."

"We set up a council and voted to evacuate Muln, for we had neither the weapons nor the men to hold off the Gertulk for long. You said, my lord, that you and these remarkable Elves—" Buky primped at her hair and Laza flicked a speck of dust off his tunic "—were heading for Castram to reclaim it, so we agreed to make haste and come to aid you."

Aaron looked deeply into Brotchurd's eyes. They were the eyes of a friend.

"But," said Bonnie, "why haven't you come sooner? We've been here for a month already!"

"Because a band of rogue Elves moves much quicker than a caravan of Men," said Brotchurd, smiling.

Jack prowled down the line of men, who stood completely motionless before him. "They're highly disciplined," he said to Aaron as he returned, "and we could use more soldiers."

"The Gertulk are not far behind us, sire," said Fortingale. "They will be upon us soon."

Aaron flicked a bit of hair out of his eyes and said, "How many are you?"

"Two hundred strong, my lord," said Fortingale.

"Very well. Your help is much appreciated. We will begin the civilization of the other half of Castram."

The Men from Muln did a great deal to uplift the standards of Castram. It felt much more like a city with buildings, streets, markets, and houses, instead of half forest, half ruin. The Elves and Men got on fairly well. They soon devised a system to coexist peacefully: the basic structure was that of an average town although the dwellings lining the streets were only partly comprised of houses. Half of the homes were actually trees, only with doors, windows, and the occasional chimney or picket fence.

In truth, a real Elf village isn't all that much different from a Man village. Aaron was so used to Elves concealing their houses and making their whereabouts completely hidden, he found it odd to see outdoor campfires, Elf women hanging clothes on clotheslines, welcome mats, and even a few porches.

Construction of the new town began immediately. The Elves had nearly completed repairing the palace and the outer walls, so they were glad to chip in and help. Aaron was glad to have some more work to do to keep his mind off of the ever-growing fear of the Gertulk's arrival. He knew they were coming. It was now a question of *when*.

When Laza and Buky explored the courtyard, they stumbled upon a huge garden surrounded by high stone walls. It looked more like a forest than a garden, and that's exactly what they made it into. They set to work raking up the dirt, pulling all the weeds, and planting seeds. As the work steadily continued over a number of weeks, they watched the forest grow and blossom. Soon, the trees towered twenty feet over their heads. As they dug ponds and planted flowers, the result was so reminiscent of the Eldorlorne that they fondly named it "Eldorlorne II" in memory of the old forest.

Months passed. Steadily, one by one, houses were finished. Due to the vast amount of work that needed to be done, each man was assigned to build a house for himself and his family and then to help his neighbors. It was difficult, especially without the help of Kellaoth, but they labored on until homes had been built and businesses were started.

Summer passed, and fall came. Aaron had now been in Acklyon a full year. Life was easier now that they had stopped their dreadful journey, but the rigorous training, combat, and traveling had taken its toll on his fourteen-year-old body. It was cruel to observe his young body with scars running across his arms, his chest, and his face, accompanied by a pair of hard eyes showing a type of maturity that no boy deserves to bear. The burden of his title weighed him down like a sack of feed slung across his shoulders.

He missed Kellaoth, her warm smile, her encouragement, her protection. *She'll be back soon,* he told himself over and over again. *She'll be back soon to help you...* She had been gone many months now. Aaron couldn't stop wondering where she had gone in such a rush. Was she flying over Acklyon, attempting to talk people into joining? Was she searching for Elf inhabitance? Whatever she was doing, he hoped she'd finish soon.

While exploring the palace, Aaron and Jack had stumbled upon a small flat, comprised of several bedrooms attached to a circular common room.

After clearing out the cobwebs and dust, they and Ellie, Bonnie, and Gallagher had made it their home. It felt nice, having an actual room again, a private sanctuary where Aaron could be alone with his thoughts. He always slept with Forvalad clutched in his fist, partly as a precaution, but partly because he was so attached to his sword.

Jack and Gallagher slept in the room adjacent to Aaron's, and Ellie and Bonnie shared the room on his other side.

Fortingale's room was nearest one of the alarm bells. As commanding officer, he needed to be the first to get the news of Gertulk attack. Brotchurd and Narra lived near the ground, for though a high-ranking officer in the army, Brotchurd was, at heart, a worker, and ran a lumberyard at the foot of the castle.

Two months passed, and the weather began to get chilly again. Lord Aticka and the citizens of Colten arrived, bringing with them the first snow of the season. Work recommenced on building homes for the people of Colten. With the combined help of Muln and the Elves, the work was finished quickly. By the time December arrived, they had built a decent town. Everyone had a proper house to come home to when work was done.

But their hardships were not over yet; game was scarce, and thus food was running low again and winter was upon them. By mid-January, hunger was a constant problem. Some chose to kill and eat their horses or pets, just to make it through to spring.

But February came, bringing a fresh surge of hope and all thought that if they could just hold on a month longer then they would make it.

On the morning of February the fifteenth, a team of hunters returned from a trip deep into the forest. There they had found a rather large herd of deer and had hunted down and killed the lot. They marched triumphantly through the gates, dragging their prey. Though the town could only make a very small meal out of the venison, it was nice to at last have some proper food to eat.

At last, March arrived. The snow melted, crops began to grow, and the hunters were daily bringing back large amounts of deer, rabbits, and many other delicious meats. Soon, the newly-started town was in good shape.

Aaron, standing on a balcony by his room and breathing in the smell of lumber, looked down at it all: Elves hanging laundry out to dry, horse or ox drawn carts rattling down Main Street, loaded with hay or feed. He could hear the steady *tap tap tap* of hammers on nails as the last of the work was consumed. Rows of soldiers lined the outer walls, overlooking the vast fields that stretched for miles away from Castram. He listened to the continuing cries of salesmen.

"Fresh produce here! Get your fresh produce here! Come on now, folks, no use letting it go to waste. Only three rubies a tomato!"

"Extra! Extra! Read all about it!" and so forth.

Castram had awakened once more. This happy time lasted until June. On the twelfth, Jack celebrated his fifteenth birthday. This celebration was particularly enjoyable compared to their last two Christmases and Aaron's birthday. Admittedly, two years ago Aaron would have said it was lame, but just now it felt worthy of a king. They had a small cake with two candles placed on it. Laza and Buky crafted a banner to hang over the entrance to the Great Hall, reading "Happy 15TH Prince Jack!"

Bonnie and Gallagher helped Hokey cook the feast, teaching her to make some Third World dishes.

"So," said Hokey for the thirtieth time, "let me get this straight…" She gestured to the dough on the counter, molded into a large, thin circle. "Youee take the tomato sauce and pour it onto the crust."

"And then sprinkle parmesan cheese on top of the sauce," Gallagher explained.

"And you can add pepperonis or sausages or whatever you want on top of the cheese," Bonnie added.

Hokey stared at her. "Can I add mustard?"

"Ah, no," said Bonnie. "Bad idea."

"So after it's done," Hokey summed up, "youee put it in the oven for twenty minutes, right?"

Gallagher nodded.

"And you call this a…peetsa, right?"

"A *pizza,*" Bonnie corrected.

"That's weird," said Hokey.

"Just wait till you try it," Gallagher assured her. "It's great stuff!"

After they put the pizza in the oven, Bonnie said, "So now let's check on that ice cream."

"First," said Hokey, "tell me about these French fries you're so fond of."

Laza, Buky, Deecal, Piki, and some of the other Elves put on a performance about a cowardly knight attempting to fight a dragon to free a lady, only to discover that the lady had, in fact, fallen in love with the dragon and they now had seven children. Even Cappy cracked a reluctant smile. Afterwards, they sat down for a Birthday dinner.

Jack laughed out loud when he saw the meal—two large pizzas, a basket of French fries, a small cake, and a freezer of chocolate ice cream.

"Hokey, you should have started a fast food restaurant," said Aaron as he dug into a slice of pizza. Hokey blushed.

"This is weird!" said Buky, holding up a French fry for inspection. "Was this seriously once a potato?"

Bonnie nodded.

"Well, I'm lovin' this 'ketchup' stuff," said Laza, munching on a French fry dipped in the ketchup Bonnie and Gallagher had made.

"How do you suppose it would taste on pizza?" asked Deecal, then seized the bowl of ketchup and spooned some onto his pizza. He tasted it and cried, "Exceptional!"

"You just wait till you try a cheeseburger," said Aaron, grinning.

"Cheeseburger…cheeseburger…" said Laza, searching his memory. "Oh yes! Wasn't he da dude who flew over the Atlantic?"

"No," said Aaron.

"That's right, that was Hamburger."

"No," said Jack.

"Hamlet?"

"No!" said Bonnie.

"Omelet?"

"His name is Limburger!" cried Gallagher. "A cheeseburger

is a sandwich."

"Lindbergh! Not limburger," Bonnie said in exasperation.

"What about Hamlet?" inquired Laza.

"He's a Shakespearian character," explained Ellie.

"Well then who's Omelet?" demanded Laza.

"That's a way to prepare an egg!" said Aaron.

"And what is this 'Shakespearian' garbage anyway?" asked Deecal.

"Isn't that da thing where you take some o' this magnificent ice cream and add some milk and blend it all together?" said Laza.

Aaron stared at him. "That is a milkshake!"

"I could have sworn you said it was a Shakespeare," grumbled Laza.

"Shakespeare was an English playwright!" said Jack.

"He wrote plays?"

"Right."

"Were they about a knight and a princess and a dragon?"

"I don't think so," said Bonnie. "He wrote comedies and tragedies."

"This is crazy!" said Buky. "Your world must be a confusing place!"

"But as long as it got pizza, I ain't complaining," said Deecal, his mouth full.

When they were done eating, Laza raised his goblet of punch. "A toast," he said, "to the Prince of Parland on his birthday!"

The Elves cheered, and Aaron added, "Just hope that you little goody two shoes are ready for what's coming!" Ellie, Bonnie, Gallagher, and Jack all laughed, but Laza looked confused.

"Wha?" he asked indignantly. "The Geeertulk?"

"No, you bonehead," said Aaron. "You see, when boys are in

puberty… Oh, never mind."

Laza shrugged, and then downed his entire goblet in one before burping loudly.

Buky, sitting next to Laza, kicked him under the table with a hiss of "Lazee!"

"What?" demanded Laza. "Burping is fun!"

"You ought to be ashamed of yourself!" snapped Buky. "That was weak!" With that, she seized her own goblet and drained it. She paused a moment, then let out a five-second-long burp that rattled the windows.

"Pathetic!" said Deecal, burping so loud that he shattered a delicate glass goblet

Piki then belched so loud she shattered a whole tray of glasses.

Dinky drew in a deep breath as though he had intentions of shattering one of the stained glass windows, when Ellie cut him off.

"Listen!" she said. They did, and what they heard sent shivers down their spines.

The alarm bell sounded, sending a series of high-pitched clanks through the castle of Castram from atop the bell's perch on the highest tower. When the alarm bell sounded, it meant that Gertulk or something worse was on its way.

The party died. Glasses slid from trays and shattered on the floor. Nimbun screeched, leapt into the air, and landed in the punch bowl. Hokey, carrying the birthday cake dropped it on the floor with a smack. Deecal fell down, knocking over a lantern which landed on the carpet. The flames from the lantern lit on the rug, burning it to ashes before Laza and Aaron could stamp it out.

All over Castram, they could hear the sounds of Men and Elves rushing to their weapons, hurling themselves into their chain mail, and rushing onto the walls.

Aaron glanced at Jack, and Jack glanced at Laza. All three were thinking the same thing: *What can we do without Kellaoth?*

40

Attack!

Aaron, Jack, Bonnie, Ellie, Gallagher, Laza, and Buky raced up the stairs and flew onto the wall over the gate, Jack still wearing a paper birthday crown. In the distance, they saw a swirling sandstorm heading towards the castle. No, not a sandstorm—an army! Their metal-shod feet had upset the dust, causing it to rise into a cloud.

Gertulk.

Aaron had never seen so many of them. Thousands of them. More than ten times the size of their army. More Gertulk than any of them had ever thought existed now began setting up camp about a mile from the castle. Behind the Gertulk, the heroes of Acklyon could see trolls, siege towers, and catapults.

Aaron groaned. "How are we going to survive this time?"

"*Why* did Kellaoth have to leave right now?" demanded Gallagher. "We're doomed!"

"We're backed against a corner," said Jack. "There's nowhere else we can escape!"

"Now what?" said Bonnie desperately.

"We should—" Jack froze.

Over the never-ending mass of Gertulk, they saw a red

dragon rise up about eye level with them. A gold-clad figure rode on its back.

The False Adinyrom.

Aaron sprinted up a flight of stairs, and then across a landing and through the door into his room. After retching violently into the chamber pot, he flung himself onto his four-poster and stared up at the canvas top. They were sunk. They were doomed. There was no possible way to survive this fight. He had failed in Eldorlorne, failed in Muln, failed everywhere. Now was the time that he would pay for his mistakes with his life and with the lives of all the Men and Elves in Castram.

If they surrendered, Malvadore was certain to kill them all after he wrung all knowledge of the whereabouts of Elf colonies nearby. Surrender was not a good idea. But if they fought back, they would all die anyway. They could not run because their only escape route, back through the mountains, was completely sealed, and the mountains were Gertulk infested anyway. It was a die-die situation, thought Aaron. Stand and fight and get crushed by the Gertulk, or surrender and be tortured to death by Kane Malvadore.

A knock sounded at the door "Aaron?" came Ellie's voice, sounding concerned. Aaron didn't bother to answer. He thought he would vomit again if he did. The door opened, and Ellie came in. She looked pale, but her eyes were set.

"Are you alright?" she asked quietly. Aaron did not respond.

Slowly, she sank onto the bed next to him. "This is it," she said.

"Yes," said Aaron, his voice strange and croaky. "This is the time when all our planning, our skills, our cause, all of it ends."

"No," said Ellie, "no, it's not. This is the time when we show

Malvadore that it takes more than a sorcerer and a horde of Gertulk to win Acklyon."

Aaron stared at her.

"But it's hopeless," he said. "You know that, right? This is not a fairy tale. No army will unexpectedly charge out of nowhere and save us all. There're no reinforcements to be had. It's lost."

"It's not lost until the end," Ellie said stubbornly. "It's not lost until you and Jack are dead, until every Elf alive is fed to the dragons, until Bonnie, Gallagher, and I are thrown into the deepest well in the universe, until Kellaoth and Cygon are ground into dust, until Brotchurd, and Fortingale, and Aticka, and all the Men of Muln and Colten, and all the other cities in Acklyon are tried and executed. It won't be over until Castram has been blown into a thousand pieces and the pieces scattered to the four winds. Only then will it be truly lost."

Aaron stared at her. "You haven't given up hope yet, have you?"

"No, I haven't," she said. "Malvadore killed your parents, Aaron. He may not have killed you yet, but if you give up hope, you're dead."

A sudden vision of Malvadore loomed into Aaron's mind: Malvadore, leering and cackling as he watched Ellie and Bonnie and Gallagher and Jack and Laza and all the others being burned and tortured in Rarzan. Malvadore had once before overrun Castram and killed its leaders, among them Aaron's parents and Jack's too—leading to the unbelievably complex situation Aaron and Jack were now thrust into. As hot anger filled him, Aaron wrung his blanket so hard that he tore it. Malvadore would *not* get the satisfaction of watching them suffer. They would fight. They would show Malvadore that you didn't need to be a superhero to face a tyrant.

He stood up, looking hard at Ellie.

The battle was coming, and they were going to fight.

41
The Siege of Castram

The plans were complete, and soldiers were assigned to their positions. Aaron, Jack, Ellie, Bonnie, and Gallagher were to stay in the cellars below the castle with the women and children. Aaron had objected, but only half-heartedly for deep down, he did not want to be in a battle.

Before the battle, Aaron, Jack, Ellie, Bonnie, and Gallagher said goodbye to Laza, Buky, Brotchurd, and all their other friends. Each of them tried not to think about the fact that it may be the last time they would ever see them again. As all the Elves headed for the wall overlooking the main gate, the five children put on very light armor and brought their weapons in case the Gertulk found them.

Watching the children head for the cellars, Brotchurd felt a rush of sympathy for Aaron and Jack. The two boys had been thrust into one of the most difficult situations imaginable. They had been ridiculed, and much anger was directed towards them because they could not lead the armies of Acklyon. The boys had been accused as if this were their fault. But Brotchurd knew that Aaron and Jack were not to blame; they had been through things no child deserves to see and had shown a kind of bravery Brotchurd had never before witnessed.

But he had no time to worry about the boys because his fear of the battle ahead was sinking down on him. How could the Acklyonians win this battle? Freeing his people in Muln had been bad enough, but thousands of Gertulk had gathered here. Opposing them were two hundred Elves from Eldorlorne, one hundred from Cappitung, one hundred from Niybay as well as two hundred Men each from Muln and Colten. Eight hundred Acklyonians against nine thousand Gertulk was, in Brotchurd's opinion, pretty grim.

Laza positioned most of the Elves and about one hundred Muln archers in several long lines across the walls. He had ordered a battalion of men from Colten to safeguard the palace, Brotchurd and the cavalry of Muln to hold the courtyard, and the rest of the Men to guard the castle. Laza and his company guarded the wall directly over the main gate, which Gertulk would surely target.

As Laza surveyed the sea of Gertulk before him, nearly nine thousand strong, they seemed to be a simple mass of black and grey from up on the wall.

He turned and looked behind him at the rows and rows of Elves and Men. Each one of them was hardened to the core, survivors of many dangers and difficulties. They now stood behind Laza, awaiting his orders. He was only eighteen years old and had never led anything this big.

Laza looked up to the tower to his left where he knew General Fortingale was standing, although the height of the tower made him almost invisible to Laza. The Elf then looked back at the Gertulk, lumbering brutes of much strength and hatred. He gazed at his girlfriend Buky standing beside him. She wore a corset of chain mail and carried her crossbow. "'Tis it," Laza said quietly. "This is the big one."

"And now is the time to…do something or other," Buky replied, looking very pale under her steel cap.

Cappy joined them. "Remember," she said seriously, "we fire as soon as they are in range. We can't afford to be forgiving."

"And what if they're willing to parley?" asked Buky. "What do we do then?"

"Ignore them," Cappy said sternly. "Anything they try will be a trick to get under our defenses."

Laza looked over at his troops, a long line of Elves wearing light armor. He studied the various Elves, most of whom were the survivors from Eldorlorne. He had fought alongside every one of them and couldn't have been prouder of them if they had been his own children.

Fortingale left his tower and came down to Laza.

"Are you alright, Laza?" said Fortingale quietly. Laza nodded sharply. Fortingale clapped him on the shoulders and continued down the line. A tense and fearful knot formed in Laza's stomach as he anticipated the battle to come. Now that he thought about it, he had only fought in one true battle in his life. That suddenly seemed pretty meager.

A horn blasted, and Laza saw, once again, the False Adinyrom on his great dragon flying up over the horde of Gertulk. "I request permission to speak with your kings," he shouted.

"You shall speak to me," said Fortingale. "You shall not go near Adinyrom and Jahkon!"

"Very well," the False Adinyrom called back.

Laza lifted his squeaky voice. "Come on and land, but you is shoulding to leave that faky Forvalad behind, squid-butt!" Fortingale rolled his eyes, and Cappy glared at Laza.

"What kind of general are you?" she hissed. "I just said not to bother with a parley!"

"Cappy, Cappy," said Laza calmly. "You know nothing about strategy. If we can talk to him under peaceful terms, we can learn more about him. Besides, he cain't do nothing to us so we can make fun of him!"

Cappy began to retort, but stopped when the huge red dragon swooped past, dropping False Adinyrom in front of them. The Traitor King raised his arms and said warmly, "O brave and exalted lords of Acklyon, may you—"

"Skip the flattery and bandying of empty words, traitor, and tell us why you have come!" snapped Fortingale so viciously that the false clone's smile faltered.

"I have come with a simple question: why, with such brave hearts as yours, have you decided to throw away your lives in this rebellion? Even these Elves—" His eyes wandered over the line of Elves, all of which, at Laza's command, stuck out their tongues and crossed their eyes, "—must see that this is hopeless. Come. In my house, I shall give you—"

"Now you just look at this," said Laza roughly. "We both of the knowingness that yousees a fraud, a faky, a imposter, a pawn of Malvee-dunce, so get to the point." Most of the authority in Laza's voice was a bluff. Yet he knew that Forahn would not attack them bearing no sword. Also, Forahn knew full well that if he so much as laid a finger on one of the Elves, he would have seventy-eight arrows in his chest.

The False Adinyrom gave Laza an icy glare (to which Laza stuck out his tongue).

When Forahn spoke, all the warmth had left his voice. "Have it your way, Kane, ahhh 'Malvee-dunce'—" Laza curled his lip "—is perfectly willing to join sides with you, all you have to do is agree, and you can have the all the luxury you can imagine."

For a long time, Fortingale simply stared at the False Adinyrom, grappling with the temptation to hand over Aaron and Jack and to live in peace. Then he spoke, his voice cold and humorless. "Well, villain, tell your master that 'the brave and exalted lords of Acklyon'"—Laza sniggered—"told you to boil your head in troll manure!"

The Elves cheered and every inch of smugness about the False Adinyrom vanished, replaced by a crooked snarl and flaming eyes. "Curse you, Fortingale!" he shouted. "Curse you till the Moon drops from the sky! Curse you and your pigheaded ways!"

"Archers to the ready!" bellowed Laza (or at least he tried to bellow, no Elf can master that kind of yelling) as the False Adinyrom leapt onto his dragon and flew back over the Gertulk.

Simultaneously, each Elf raised their left arms, which held their bows, while their right arms found the quiver on their backs. Each drew an arrow and fitted it to the bowstring

Laza watched as the Gertulk charged the wall, a lump forming in his throat.

"Aim!"

The Elves tensed their strings.

"FIRE!"

Arrows rained down on the Gertulk, successfully flattening the first wave. But the second was not far behind.

"Fire at will!" screamed Laza as the second wave began mounting ladders.

"What if we don't want to fire?" inquired Deecal.

"Then make it up as yah go along!" Laza cried back.

"Works for me!" said Deecal and started launching arrows over the wall.

A Gertulk arrow whizzed past Laza's ear, striking one of the archers in the shoulder. The Elf staggered and fell as Laza and Buky rushed to his side.

"He's still alive," said Buky after examining the soldier, "but not for long unless we get him some medical help!" Buky gestured at three Elves nearby. "You, you, and you! Get this boy to the tower pronto!"

"No!" shouted Cappy.

Laza glared at her. "What's the matter with you?"

Buky curled her fist and muttered, "I'm gonna make something the matter with her—"

"We don't have time to waste!" snapped Cappy. "We can't afford to sacrifice three soldiers so that another one can live to fight another day when all of us won't last the night. If this Elf dies now, it'll only save him pain."

Buky narrowed her eyes. Cappy spoke these words with no hint of emotion, giving no sign that she regretted that she had just said she didn't care if Elves died. What kind of Elf was she?

Laza gave Cappy a long, cold glare then said to the three Elves, "Well? What is you waiting for? Get him up to the medical tower!"

"But Cappy said—"

"NOW!"

"You'll do no such thing!" Cappy screamed. "Leave him where he is!"

"But Laza said—"

"Don't argue!"

"Take him to the tower!" said Laza, almost beside himself.

"Leave him where he is!" screeched Cappy.

A flaming boulder whistled over their heads, launched from a Gertulk catapult. It struck a nearby wall, shattering it like glass and spreading fire over anything flammable.

"Never mind!" said Laza against his will. "Leave him! Put out that fire!"

The Elves scurried away, glad to get away from the argument, and Laza turned on Cappy. "Why did you do that?"

"I did what had to be done," Cappy retorted. "You can't be so naïve, Laza. This is war!"

"This is insubordination, this is!"

"Now is not the time to discuss it," Cappy said coldly.

Laza turned back to the tide of Gertulk sweeping over the walls and launched himself into the middle of them, pretending each one had a picture of Cappy's face on him.

As arrows fell all around them, the Gertulk archers began shooting back as others managed to raise the ladders.

"Get ready!" Deecal drew his sword and waited like a jungle tiger about to pounce on his prey as the first Gertulk climbed up to the wall. When Deecal saw the grinning face appear over the edge of the wall, he yelled and gouged the Gertulk in the eye with his rapier.

So 'tis beginned, thought Laza as he fired arrows into the Gertulk. How it would end, he didn't like to think.

Aaron listened in the quiet of the cellars to the muted clanging and booming of the battle overhead. Forvalad lay bare across his lap. He was clutching the sword tightly.

Jack, sitting next to him, was looking sick. "It's because of us, you know," he said after a while.

"Huh?" said Aaron, staring at him.

"It's because of us all this is happening," Jack explained. "The Gertulk are attacking because they want *us*. They don't care about Brotchurd or Fortingale. They don't even care about the

Elves as much as they care about us. It's our fault."

A rush of guilt surged through Aaron as he realized that Jack was right. He leaned back against the cold, wet wall, and let out a deep breath. "This isn't what I thought it would be," he said slowly. "The movies always made out a lot more glory, a lot less dead fear."

"This isn't right, Aaron," said Jack in a voice of suffering.

"I know," said Aaron in a defeated tone. "The king should be out there, fighting and dying with his men, not crouching in the cellars with the women and children; we're not who we're supposed to be, Jack."

"That's not entirely true," said Bonnie, across from Aaron. Aaron turned to her.

"That sword"—Bonnie gestured to Forvalad—"came to you for a reason, Aaron. And it wasn't because of your military ability or skill with a blade. You may not have noticed it, but there's a lot more about you than one would first guess."

"What do you mean?" asked Aaron.

"You're a lot more than you give yourself credit for, Aaron. You sit here, thinking about your men, and everyone else in our rebellion but not of yourself. You think you should be out there fighting, even though you really don't want to because you feel you owe it to your men.

"I think someone like Roger wouldn't have cared about anyone else. He would be scrunching himself into a corner and putting everyone else in front of him to shield himself. You ordered the cooks to put you on the lowest ration when you were on the road even though you were faint with hunger. You gave that little girl your stew because she needed it. Most boys your age would have wanted the most food for themselves. They might have even tried to steal some extra! You never wanted the

Throne, but you accepted your fate when you saw how much everyone needed you, sacrificing your own personal comfort. You're an admirable person, Aaron."

"That makes me sound better than I am," said Aaron shamefully. "I was just doing what my conscience said."

"Exactly!" said Bonnie, "You listen to your conscience, and do what it says; that's the best way to live an honorable life."

"But what will it lead to?" asked Aaron hopelessly. "I mean, even if I am all that you said, so what? We're all going to die anyway, so it won't make any difference."

"I wouldn't say that," replied Bonnie. "Malvadore is used to walking all over people. He does it every day, and no one can stand up to him because everyone's afraid! We're not, though. We're standing up to him, and if we can do that, then that means others can, too."

"Since when did you become so wise?" asked Jack. Bonnie smiled, but couldn't answer because just then, they heard the sounds of the battle overhead stop.

Ellie gave Aaron a quizzical look. "It can't be over already?" she said incredulously.

Aaron listened. "I don't hear the Gertulk celebrating," he said slowly, "so I don't think they've won already."

"Then what could it be?" asked Gallagher.

"Wait!" said Jack suddenly. They paused and listened: footsteps coming towards them and then grunts of effort as whoever it was began lifting the barricades from the door.

Aaron, Jack, Bonnie, and Gallagher each drew their weapons and readied themselves.

"But they don't sound guttural enough to be Gertulk," one women said.

Whoever it was finally cleared the entrance and opened the

door. Fortingale, Laza, and Brotchurd tumbled in.

"What happened?" said Narra, immediately rushing over to embrace her husband.

Fortingale was looking tired and rather ill. "Well," he said, wiping blood from his sword, "they want Aaron and Jack more than I thought. The False Adinyrom offered to make a treaty with us if we handed you two over."

"In a pig's eye," muttered Laza.

"We're not going to give you up to them. We're going to fight," Fortingale continued.

"But you're not fighting now," Aaron pointed out.

Fortingale nodded. "The Gertulk attacked, and it was all we could do to hold them off. They had just about gotten us when the False Adinyrom commanded his forces to pull back to give us time to reconsider."

"But we don't need time," said Brotchurd. "We already know—if they want Aaron and Jack, they'll have to kill us first."

"Actually," Laza added, "they didded us a favor, givin' us time to make a stratagem."

Aaron could hardly sit there and listen to them say this. Jack was right—it was completely their fault that this was happening. "Maybe you *should* hand us over," he muttered.

"Don't be absurdulous," said Laza. "Dat's about da stupidest thing Me ever heared!"

"Well, we're not being a whole lot of help," said Jack. "All we're doing is hiding in here—we can't even *fight* with you!"

"We can't give youee up!" said Laza, "dat would defeat da hole purpose o' our war thingymabobber!"

"Forvalad and Parvelad are the only things that Malvadore fears, and to fight him without them would be folly," said Fortingale.

"Ya might as well accept it, Aaron," said Laza. "We's fighitn' for ya."

This did nothing to ease Aaron's conscience.

In fact it made him feel worse.

42
Battle Tactics

Cappy walked down a hallway searching for Laza and Buky. The two of them had disappeared shortly after the battle, and no one knew where they'd gone. To Cappy, this showed that Laza was incompetent as a leader. He had no discipline and rarely took any threat seriously. He never thought about his public appearance, always leaning against a wall at briefings or putting his feet on the table during meetings. She spotted a closet nearby and what sounded like Elf voices in it. She walked over and opened the door.

There were Laza and Buky. She wasn't exactly sure what they'd been doing, but they'd been standing very close together, and jumped apart, looking embarrassed when she opened the door.

"We're due at the strategy conference," she said to Laza.

"Oh yeah, me fergot about dat," he said cheerfully.

Buky giggled. Cappy didn't.

"Laza," she said sharply, "may I speak to you?"

"Sure," said Laza. "Be right back," he added to Buky, giving her a light kiss on the nose.

Buky watched them go, Cappy holding Laza firmly by the upper arm. She could guess what Cappy wanted to talk about:

Laza not showing the proper discipline. Buky frowned. She had never really liked Cappy much. Cappy was far too serious. It seemed as if no one were allowed to have fun on her watch. Elves were supposed to be cheery and chipper, but Cappy was just the opposite.

Cappy led Laza out of earshot of Buky and turned to face the Elf leader. "Laza," she said coldly, "you need to straighten up."

Laza, who had been leaning against the wall, stood up straight. "This better?" he asked.

Cappy didn't smile. "You are a leader of Elves, Laza, and should behave accordingly. It gives a bad impression of Eldorlorne to see you acting like you're at a…a child's birthday party!"

Laza shrugged. "On the contrary, my friend. I've often found that a little humor makes everyone's day. You could use a bit of it yourself," he added, strolling off toward the meeting.

"It's hopeless," said Fortingale wearily as he and the other leaders of Acklyon planned their next assault. "If they attack again, we're doomed. If Forahn didn't want to parley so much, we'd be dead right now."

"That leaves us only one option," said Brotchurd quietly.

"Surrender," said Fortingale hopelessly.

"No," said Brotchurd, "I will not now, and never will, surrender to Malvadore. He killed King Adinyrom I and King Rorard of Parland, he wrecked Muln, and he very nearly destroyed Acklyon as we know it! I will never give in, even if it costs me my life. No, I have a better solution than surrendering."

"Then quit the chitter-chatter and be saying what you're meaning," said Laza.

"We've been on defense all this time. We can't win like that, as we found out, so we change our strategy."

"You mean try to beat 'em up?" said Buky incredulously. "Go out ching-ching wiff 'em? We'd get flattedinadoodled!!"

"True," said Brotchurd. "We can't beat them through strength of arms. But we may have a chance if we use cunning."

"How?" asked General Aticka, leader of Colten.

"We take advantage of our resources." Brotchurd explained. "We have a stronghold that we can fall back to. We have the element of unpredictability."

"And?" said Fortingale.

"The False Adinyrom will expect us to do anything we can to stay alive," Brotchurd continued. "He would never expect us to do something rash or reckless."

"Like launch a full-scale attack?" said General Aticka. "I thought we agreed that would be foolhardy?"

"Not full scale," said Brotchurd. "Here's what we do." He cleared the desk, placed a map of the battlefield on it and set up chess pieces to represent soldiers. "We divide our forces into three parts—the cavalry, the archers, and the foot-soldiers." He split the knights, the rooks, and the pawns into separate groups. "If Fortingale and I take the cavalry and attack"—he positioned the cavalry—"and fall back to the castle when they can't hold out much longer"—he slid the cavalry back towards the large circle that represented the castle—"and recuperate, Aticka can take the foot-soldiers and launch a second attack. The archers can stay on the wall and hold off the Gertulk while we advance and retreat—"

"And continue that cycle," finished Fortingale. "We can eventually wear out the Gertulk by continuing to send in fresh troops!"

"And when they can't hold out," said Brotchurd, "we combine forces and launch a full-scale attack and drive them out."

"It could very easily go wrong," said Fortingale uncertainly, "but it's our only chance to survive."

"But what's the point?" asked Aticka. All eyes turned to him. "What is the point of resisting? What difference will it make either way? We'll be slaughtered no matter what."

"What's the point?" repeated Brotchurd. "What difference will it make to resist the most fearsome entity of all time for our cause? All the difference in the world."

"Let's go fer it," said Laza.

43
Contemplation

Aaron sat, once again, in the cellars with his friends.

"What do you suppose is happening?" asked Gallagher.

"I don't really want to think about it," muttered Ellie.

Aaron got up and began pacing, Forvalad in hand.

"I can't believe this is happening," said Bonnie, sounding close to tears.

"But it is," said Aaron, finally speaking, "and we need to accept it. If the Gertulk find us, it'll be our job to keep them off the women and children. That's why we're here."

"You really are more Forahn than you give yourself credit for," said Ellie, smiling for the first time that week.

Aaron blushed.

The defenders of Castram followed their prearranged battle plan by repeating the cycle. First, the cavalry attacked, hitting the Gertulk and inflicting their damage and then falling back to the relative safety of the castle. As the calvary retreated the foot soldiers attacked striking the front but before becoming fully engaged they fell back and the cavalry charged again. All the while the archers relentlessly rained arrows down on the constantly shifting lines of the Gertulk. The fight was hard, teetering on the edge of impossible, but Elves and Men fought with everything they had. Even so, for every Gertulk they downed, ten more took its place.

But the heroes of Acklyon did not know their enemy's plan.

How the False Adinyrom had conjured his army so fast was simple: Malvadore had stationed garrisons of Gertulk in each village or city in Acklyon. By simply drawing on the resources of the nearest cities, the False Adinyrom could have a monumental army everywhere he went.

Having become increasingly bored of the struggle, Malvadore sent out a necro, a huge, black bird that was the symbol of the gathering for the Gertulk. The Gertulk from all of the towns and villages within many miles immediately went on the march, filling the valley with black-clad soldiers.

As Malvadore and his soldiers launched yet another attack, Lord Aticka thought that they might just have a chance to survive until he saw the reinforcements arrive. His heart sank as he realized the brutal simplicity of Malvadore's plan—to crush them under wave after wave of soldiers. It was working, too. Desperately, Aticka fumbled with the horn at his side and blew one long, clear blast.

The great oak double doors of the castle were thrown open, and the cavalry charged out—swelling the ranks of the Acklyonians, but not by enough to stop this black tide that was their doom.

"Nice night for it!" shouted Laza, back flipping out of the way of a Gertulk while shooting his bow.

"A little cloudy," added Buky, "but not bad conditions."

The two were cornered by Gertulk, and despite their conversation, were fighting for their lives.

Laza dodged a heavy battle axe and struck its owner with his sword. Buky leaped behind a stack of rubble and fired her crossbow at the Gertulk.

Though he didn't show it, Laza was worried. There was no way the two of them could defeat all these Gertulk.

But before the Gertulk could claim superiority, a third Elf appeared in their midst—ducking, hacking, and leaping. Before the Gertulk knew what had hit them, and before they could fight back, Cappy had effectively driven them off.

"Thanks for the save," Laza panted.

"Well," shrugged Cappy, "I thought a song about this battle wouldn't sound too good if it involved Laza the Quick-Footed and Buky the Gorgeous getting smashed by a measly twenty Gertulk."

"Did you just make a joke?" demanded Laza, but Cappy had already disappeared into the battle.

I can't believe this is happening.

Aaron hugged his arms, trying to keep warm in the dank cellars, his heart pounding, he imagined what was happening up above. Auri was curled into a ball next to him, looking rather like a small kitten surrounded by several large dogs.

With nothing better to do, Aaron listened to the raging argument in his head; it was reminiscent of an angel on one shoulder, a demon on the other. *You've lived your entire life hoping to start your own chain of pizza parlors, and here you are, about to die in a cellar!* said Aaron Tackers.

Do not take that attitude, Adinyrom Forahn replied. *If that is how you feel then that is how it will happen. We need to stay strong. Whatever you do, do not give up!*

What's the point, though? moaned Aaron. *Whether we fight to the death or let them kill us, it'll end the same way: the last hope for Acklyon dead, and Malvadore in control as he always has been.*

I do not believe you! snapped Adinyrom. *You fought in the battle of Eldorlorne, helped give hope to Elf children and led them here, actually fought the False Adinyrom, and now you are giving up!*

But here's the thing, said Aaron. *How do you know you really* are *the true king? Face it – who looks, acts, talks, and thinks like a real king? Malvadore commanding his forces to keep the peace in his country, or you, not even able to fight alongside your people?*

Adinyrom paused, and the deepest fear he had came rushing to the surface. For in fact, part of him really thought that Malvadore's Adinyrom was far more real than the true Adinyrom. Then he remembered the coldness in the False Adinyrom's eyes, and how he had mercilessly killed Deepy and so many others.

Slowly, Adinyrom began to speak, his voice becoming stronger. *Malvadore's Adinyrom is a monster. He burns crops, taxes unreasonably, enslaves everyone. He takes nearly all the food that the farmers and hunters bring back, so everyone else is starving. He does all that – and* enjoys *it! Even if he* is *the real Adinyrom, you shall still take the Throne from him. What would you do on the Throne? You would do whatever you could to make sure that your people were happy. You would work to make this a place of joy and of music and to rid it of evil. That is what the true Adinyrom should do, and you know what needs to be done, so do it! Even if he is the real Adinyrom, you are a better king, so do not doubt.*

And to this, Aaron Tackers had no reply. Aaron felt a rush of courage, and at long last, he accepted who he was and what he was out to do. He looked down at the sword lying across his knees and slowly picked it up. The blade shone with a pure and holy light, the light of Castram, and crimson flames curled along the diamond edges.

A sudden *boom* shook the entire castle, the unmistakable sound of trolls with a battering ram on the gate.

"It's hopeless," said one woman amidst the screams and gasps. "We're doomed! The Gertulk will have us all."

"Why did we ever leave Muln?" wailed another. "Why couldn't we have stayed there?"

"Because," Narra shot back, "our cause is one worth fighting for! We are the only ones that can stop Malvadore, so we have to try. Acklyon was once a place of beauty. You have heard the tales as much as I! The only way to end this reign of evil is through those two boys—" She shot a finger at Aaron and Jack. "As long as we keep them away from Malvadore, we have a chance."

"Why?" demanded one of the other women, "why must we fight for these two boys who cannot even fight for themselves?"

Aaron felt himself stiffen with anger. He *could* fight, after all, but it was Fortingale's orders that he stay hidden.

The woman continued, her voice bitter. "Why must they sit upon the Throne? Why couldn't we have Fortingale as our king? He is an able leader, why not him?"

"Because Fortingale cannot kill Malvadore." Aaron had not intended to speak, but the words left him of their own accord. A silence fell over everyone and all eyes were locked on Aaron, so he continued. "Malvadore stole my father's rule through conquest. That is the only way to gain control of Acklyon without Forvalad and Parvelad. The person who kills Malvadore can win the Throne from him. Forvalad answers to me alone, and with it I will one day kill him, have no doubt about that. I swear to you that no matter how long it takes, and no matter how much I must give, I will kill him or die trying. Fortingale could not control the power of this sword. But, even with magical destiny, the only way Jack and I can truly become the Kings of Fortilly and

Parland is if we have the people's loyalty. We need you every bit as much as we need us to win this war. I promise you that if the Gertulk get in here, I will die before I see them harm you. What we are fighting for is, indeed, hopeless, which only means we must fight all the harder. I need your help if I am to restore justice to Acklyon, so please. Have faith in me, and have faith in our cause."

Quite a long silence followed his speech, but then Narra began to clap. Auri followed her lead, and soon, the entire congregation was cheering and applauding him. Then came a great chorus of voices, all crying the same words: "Long live the kings! Long live the kings!" A warm glow was in Aaron's heart as he was surrounded by the throng.

He had done it.

44
The Battle of Castram

Laza studied the battle before him. Fifty feet below, he could see Buky and the archers battling all the Gertulk nimble enough to climb the walls. Two-hundred feet below, Fortingale and Aticka's companies were battling the main force of the Gertulk.

Laza's keen eyes found Buky herself, who was backed into a corner, battling three Gertulk at once. Nimbun saw it, too, and went into a power dive, flipping upside down as he went. Laza was dangling, holding the saddle horn with one hand and his sword in the other. Buky saw them coming and ducked. The Gertulk looked up to see what Buky had seen, but were immediately killed by claws and sword.

"Thanks for that!" shouted Buky as Nimbun swooped past.

"No problemoooooooooooooooooo!" Laza called as Nimbun carried him away. He looked up then and saw an armada of Dragons with Gertulk riders soaring towards Castram. Laza looked down at Nimbun, who had a hungry expression on his face. "Can we take 'em?" asked Laza.

Nimbun hooted and shot towards the dragons.

One dragon was heading for the medical tower, so Laza targeted it.

"Hey, you!" he shouted as the dragon neared the tower. The dragon turned its head. "Yeah, you with the stupid expression!" shouted Laza. "Head's up!" Nimbun flew through the air like a cannonball and struck the dragon dead-on, gnawing on its gums, while Laza somersaulted over the dragon's head and stabbed the Gertulk who rode it in the face.

As Laza dropped back onto Nimbun's saddle, he muttered, "Nice work, buckaroo!" Nimbun crooned.

A dragon roared up behind them quite suddenly, and before Laza and Nimbum could retaliate, it took a vicious snap and very nearly took off Laza's head. Nimbun screeched.

"That does it!" said Laza angrily. "No—more—Mister—Nice—Elf!" He stomped hard on the dragon's head, karate-chopped its Gertulk rider in the face, snapped the dragon's neck bone, kicked the Gertulk in the face, broke the dragon's tail in three different places, kicked the Gertulk in the rear, bit the dragon on the nose, spit scales in the Gertulk's face, tore off one of the dragon's wings, and twisted the Gertulk's nose—all in the space of three seconds.

As the battered and bruised dragon and rider fell, Laza flicked a drop of Gertulk blood off his mail and sighed.

"Gertulk just don't Gert like dey used to," he said. Nimbun chirped in agreement.

Laza looked up. A solid wall of dragons was bearing down on them, each one with a Gertulk on its back. "Can we take 'em?" Laza asked his pet again.

Nimbun squeaked and shook his head.

"I though not," said Laza lightly. "Tally ho!" The two shot towards the dragons.

Nimbun met the lead dragon head-on, the two creatures wrestling, clawing, and snapping. Laza shot down several Gertulk with his bow until one struck him in the face with its shield.

Stunned, Laza fell off Nimbun's back. Nimbun screeched, grabbed Laza with one foreleg, and sped away towards the medical tower. An arrow caught the animal in the flank, and he spiraled out of control, smashing into a tower.

"Lazee!" squealed Buky from atop the wall, watching Nimbun fall to the ground. She sprinted over to the two bodies and put her ear to Laza's chest. Yes, there was a heartbeat. Laza had somehow survived, but barely. She needed to get him to the medical tower. She attempted to drag him up to the tower, but he was much larger than she.

"Need a hand?"

Buky turned. Cappy was standing beside her.

"What are yous doing here?" she said quizzically, staring at Cappy.

"What do you think?" asked Cappy. "We're saving Laza."

She put two fingers to her lips and whistled. Instantly, Deecal, Piki, Wrinky, Dinky, Stinky, and Hokey were there beside her.

At Cappy's command, Deecal and Stinky grabbed Laza, and Piki, Dinky, and Wrinky helped Buky in carrying Nimbun. Meanwhile, Cappy and Hokey circled the group, fending off any Gertulk. Together, the seven Elves carried their fallen comrades across the wall, to the tower, up the flight of stairs, and into the medical wing, where several nurses took them.

Buky turned to Cappy. "Thanks," she said, "but I thought you said not to try to save the wounded?"

Cappy shrugged. "Who could leave your fellow Elf leader to his fate?"

And before the very startled eyes of Deecal and the others, Buky and Cappy ran towards each other and hugged, crying into each other's shoulders.

"We're going to lose the castle!" shouted Brotchurd.

He had been knocked off his horse and was now fighting on foot. The smell of blood filled the air. All around him, Brotchurd saw piles of bodies: Men, Elves, and Gertulk—but mostly Men and Elves.

The Acklyonians had been unable to drive the Gertulk back, so they formed a ring around Castram in a last-ditch attempt to keep it safe, though they had no hope of victory.

Twice Fortingale had considered surrendering, but both times he had rejected it. Better to die fighting than to be captured and taken for a coward.

But all around him, Men were dying under the suffocating weight of the Gertulk.

"Very well," said Fortingale finally to Brotchurd. "Pull back our forces into the castle. We'll make our last stand there."

Brotchurd nodded and hurried off to carry out this order.

Shortly, all around them, the Men and Elves could hear horn blasts, signaling the retreat. Brotchurd raised his sword in the air, sunlight reflecting off of it to act as a beacon, and sprinted for the gate into which men were already fleeing. Brotchurd met up with Aticka, and together they led a small force to hold off the Gertulk while the men fled.

"So," said the False Adinyrom, an evil smile curling on his mouth, "they wish to die rather than live." He turned to his assembled band of elite Gertulk. "Let us ease their passing!"

The assembled Gertulk hooted, roared, grunted, and pounded

their breastplates with gauntlets.

The False Adinyrom mounted his dragon, rose into the air, and led the charge into battle.

"Rallen!" said Brotchurd to one of the soldiers nearby, having just dragged his sword out of one of the Gertulk. "Send word to close the gate!"

"But sir, not everyone has made it inside!" said the old veteran.

"I know that!" snapped Brotchurd. "But we've got no choice. We can't keep them out much longer!"

The soldier saluted and hurried through the gate to carry out the order.

"Where is Fortingale?" demanded Brotchurd to Aticka. "I haven't seen him in a while."

"He must have gotten through the gate already," Aticka replied.

"He better have," said Brotchurd, "because we can't keep it open any longer without Gertulk getting in and us getting killed! Retreat! Fall back into the city!" He swung his sword at one Gertulk who had attempted to attack him, catching him in the breastplate.

Their men began to back towards the gate, which was already swinging closed.

Brotchurd and Aticka were the last to go through the gate, and they barely made it through.

"That was *too* close," panted Brotchurd.

"Wait a minute," said Aticka. "What's that sound?"

Brotchurd listened and heard a strange, pulsing horn blast, a loud *boom,* and a chorus of deep voices bellowing, followed by Gertulk screeching with surprise. "It sounds like people..."

Brotchurd said slowly.

"But it can't be," said Aticka.

The two generals hurried up a flight of steps and onto the wall, where the fighting had come to a halt as the Elves and Gertulk stared, open-mouth, at what was happening.

A huge hole had been blown into the ground directly in the center of the Gertulk. Pouring from this hole were hundreds and hundreds of smallish people, but Brotchurd and Atick couldn't identify them.

"What are they?" asked Aticka.

"I think I know..." said Brotchurd quietly. "It looks like...but it can't be—not *Dwarves?*"

45
Kellaoth's Return

But it was. Hundreds of miniature men, four feet tall at the most, were sprinting into the Gertulk, screaming war cries. Most wore beards—some short and scrubby, others so long that the tips had to be tucked into their belts.

The Dwarf in the lead was taller than the others, and he wore a long purple cloak and golden helmet. In his hands was a magnificent iron battleaxe, which he swung with surprising speed. Among the Dwarves were too very large beings, which the generals could not see very well as the beings were moving so fast. One was brown, the other white and gold. Brotchurd squinted and realized that the white and gold one was actually the Unicorn Kellaoth with Lord Cygon on her back. The lord had once again shed his old cloak, and his golden mail and hair were almost painful to look at. Kellaoth had a fearsome snarl on her lips, and her horn was dripping with blood.

"Do you see what the brown one is?" said Aticka in awe.

Brotchurd studied it for a long time before he saw what it was—the Centaur. He was as big as Kellaoth, maybe bigger. His horse body was that of a brown palomino, and his man skin was so dark, it was close to the same color. His arms and chest rippled with muscles, and his wild black hair flew in all directions.

In one hand, he carried a gigantic broadsword and in the other, a double-bladed battle axe. He must have been strong, for he wielded both with dazzling speed. Across his back lay a huge longbow and a quiver full of five foot-long arrows.

"I thought the Centaur was just a myth!" said Aticka.

"Well, you should askes him," said Deecal. "He's the one who's existing."

Aticka stared at him, and Deecal continued. "Just be smiling he *does* exist, or we'd probably lose da battle."

"Look!" said Brotchurd.

The Dwarves, even with their advantage of surprise, could not overwhelm the Gertulk, and were being forced back.

"They can't win!" said Aticka.

Aticka looked at Brotchurd, his mind racing. What now?

"Come on!" said Brotchurd, striding back towards the staircase. "Buky, tell the archers to come, too. Our job isn't done yet!"

A wall-shaking, earsplitting *boom* echoed through the cavernous cellars as the barricaded door wobbled. The Gertulk were at the gate.

"Now what?" someone moaned.

"Get back!" shouted Aaron, leaping to his feet. "Get away from the door!"

He, Jack, Gallagher, Bonnie, and Ellie stood shoulder to shoulder, weapons drawn, waiting for the attack. Outside in the corridor, they could hear the sounds of their guard battling a group of Gertulk. They couldn't tell how many, but there were enough that they could fight the guard and strike the door at the same time. But soon, the sound of clanging swords was replaced by the cheers of the Gertulk and heavier pounds on the door. The garrison had fallen, and those hidden were defenseless.

The Gertulk were coming.

"Fall back! Fall back!" bellowed the chorus of Dwarves as the stampeding Gertulk, jeering and waving their weapons, forced the Dwarves backward. "Get back underground!" shouted Kellaoth. "We have a better chance of winning down there!"

"What's that sound?" said Cygon suddenly, for a strange kind of rumbling was coming from the castle.

The monumental oak double doors of the main gate were thrown open, and hundreds of Elves and Men were charging through the middle of the Gertulk, screaming battle cries and encouragement. Brotchurd, Aticka, and Deecal were at the lead.

"FIGHT!" Brotchurd could be heard bellowing, even over this din. "Fight for our freedom!"

"Drive these monsters from our grounds!" roared the Centaur. The Acklyonians attacked the Gertulk from the front, cleaving a path through their ranks. The Gertulk had only barely engaged them when the Dwarves struck from behind.

The Acklyonians came from one direction, the Dwarves from the other. Together, they fought their way into the center of the Gertulk. When the two forces met, they formed a huge circle and exploded outward, forcing the Gertulk to break ranks. While the Men, Elves, and Dwarves battled the Gertulk, Cygon and Kellaoth combined their powers and created a Phoenix.

A Phoenix is a magical bird, a phantom of hope that, in the days of the king, was used as a symbol of gathering. No one had seen one since Adinyrom I created one to call for help when Malvadore attacked. Cygon sent the Phoenix, set ablaze, over the countryside calling the people of Acklyon to war.

Long had all of the farmers and civilians owned suits of

armor and weapons in the hopes that one day the kings would return. When they saw the Phoenix, hope swelled inside them. All of the Gertulk inhabiting central Acklyon were now fighting at Castram, so the people were free to join the fray. They put on armor and grabbed their swords and spears and sent messages to the nearby towns to do the same. Together they marched to war, at least eight thousand strong.

Aaron gripped Forvalad in both hands, trying to keep them from shaking. He looked over at Jack, who was very pale, but who nodded grimly. The heavy iron door, boarded up with several pegs propped firmly against it, was beginning to give way to the pounding of a heavy war hammer on the other side.

"If we don't make it out of here alive," Aaron said quietly, "I love you all so much. You're the best friends a man could have. I'm just sorry you got drawn into—"

"Would you just shut up? We're not dying today!" Bonnie had her bow drawn all the way back with an arrow on the string, waiting for a big enough hole to be built.

Ellie had taken the crossbow that she had been given and was also waiting to fire. Narra and the other women and children were huddled in the shadows, waiting to see what would come. Aaron watched with mounting dread as the last of the support beams gave way and the Gertulk began chopping down the door.

At last, the remnants of the door collapsed, revealing the rather depressing sight of twenty-five dead soldiers, scattered across the floor. Lucky for Aaron and his company, the guard had managed to severely weaken the Gertulk before being killed, and only three Gertulk survived the fight. Bonnie and Ellie each shot one Gertulk, and Aaron and Jack took care of the other.

"That was lucky," said Gallagher.

"*Too* lucky," Aaron corrected him. "If any more had come, we'd be dead meat. We need to strategize."

He and Jack walked through the wrecked door and peered down the corridor. No Gertulk were in sight. It seemed that this platoon of Gertulk had slipped into the castle, but had been alone.

"We need to barricade the door again," said Jack, "so the Gertulk can't get back in."

"How?" said Bonnie. "I mean, if the garrison falls, the Gertulk will have all the time in the world to chop down any number of planks and iron bars!"

"So we need it to be impenetrable." Jack looked down at Parvelad. The sword was unbreakable, very sharp, and just might be the key. "Everyone stand back," he said. "Aaron, help me with this."

The two boys raised their swords and drove them into the stone of the walls. With many grunts of effort, hacks at the wall, and bursts of flame from their swords, they at last managed to cut away a large slab of rock that would almost entirely block the door.

"Come on, people," said Aaron. "Help me with this thing."

The townsfolk converged on the stone and began heaving it towards the door. The going was smooth until they reached the door. They set it down and stepped inside the cellars. Here was the tricky part. To pull it over the door, they would need someone outside to push it.

"It's no use!" one of the women cried. "We can't budge it!"

Aaron darted around the rock and began pushing with all his might. "Come on, everyone!" he shouted. "Don't give up!"

Jack, Bonnie, Ellie, and Gallagher joined him on the other side of the slab, and they continued to push it towards the door.

Several boys from Colten found ropes in the back and tied them to the rock, using the rope to pull the massive stone.

At last, with a giant heave and a scream of effort, the stone slid into place, resting roughly against the door. However, there was more to be done. The rock was placed against the door, but it could easily be rolled aside. They needed to make it impenetrable.

Aaron studied Forvalad. Oftentimes, it would light up with flame in battle or send fire at his enemies when he swung it. He had never been able to control its flame, but he felt sure he could do it this time. He placed the tip on the groove between the door frame and the stone and sent all his willpower into the sword.

"Wait a minute!" said Bonnie sharply, "don't we need to get inside first? If you seal it shut, how will we get back in?"

"We won't," said Aaron. "Or at least, Jack and I won't. We're going to fight for our kingdom as we should've done from the start. You three are free to leave, though. Go back inside before we weld it shut."

Bonnie looked at Gallagher. Gallagher looked at Ellie. Ellie looked at Bonnie. Bonnie turned to Aaron. "We'll be there. If you two go out into that battle, we will, too."

Aaron and Jack looked at each other, and smiled. "Okay then," said Aaron. "Let's get to work."

He placed his sword on the rock again and continued the flow of heat.

It worked. The blade came alive with fire, almost too bright to look at. Aaron slowly moved the blade upwards. Where it slid between the wall and rock, both glowed orange with heat and began to melt, the metal and stone mixing together. Then it would cool, successfully welding the slab to the frame. However, all this was costing Aaron, and he wasn't even close to finishing before he felt his strength slipping. He saw darkness gathering at the corners of his vision. He was about to faint from the effort when he felt another pair of hands on the sword.

"It's okay, Aaron," said a soft voice in his ear. "You're not alone."

It was Jack.

Together, Aaron and Jack continued to weld the stone over the doorway until at last they were done. Aaron and Jack both dropped the sword and leaned against the wall, panting heavily while wiping their sweaty brows. Once Aaron felt the strength returning to his limbs, he stood up straight and picked up his sword.

"Come on, you all," he said determinedly. "There are some Gertulk outside who are waiting for their lives to end."

As the five of them sprinted for the doors, Jack suddenly stopped and grabbed Aaron's arm. "Wait!" he cried.

"What?" said Aaron, stopping, too.

"The armor!" said Jack.

"Yes!" said Aaron.

"What?" inquired Bonnie.

"Come on," said Aaron, leading the way back down the corridor.

"Aren't we going the wrong way?" Gallagher asked. "The entrance hall is over that way!"

"We're not going to the entrance hall," said Aaron.

"And the armory's over that way," said Bonnie, gesturing down another hall.

"We're not going there either," Jack responded.

"Then where?" asked Ellie.

"You'll see," said Aaron.

The five hurtled down staircases, through corridors, and

back down into the cellars. They flew past the sealed shelter and continued into the tunnel Kellaoth had shown them. They ran on for what felt like miles until they reached the Mural of the Kings. At this point, Aaron turned to Ellie, Bonnie, and Gallagher.

"Right," he said. "This place is entirely secret. Only Kellaoth and we know about it. You must not tell anyone. Promise?"

They promised. Aaron and Jack placed Forvalad and Parvelad in the gaps as they had before and watched as the stone slid away, revealing the Armory of their fathers. The five stepped inside, gazing in awe at all the glistening armor, helmets, belts, and knives.

Aaron stood in the center of the floor, stripped off his old armor, raised both arms and said, "Suit us up!"

The five worked on figuring out how all the various clips, hooks, harnesses, buckles, and straps worked, and suited Aaron.

He wore a shirt of gold chain mail that fell to his knees. He buckled Forvalad's sword belt over it and hung several different-sized knives from the belt. He also had golden greaves on his lower legs and bracers on his forearms. Both were studded artistically with rubies. He then put on tough, red leather gloves. His boots were not armored, as he would need to be swift on his feet. He took a triangular shield off its mount on the wall and strapped it to his left arm. Its crest was an eight-sided star surrounded by a circle of flames. He finished by putting on a gold cap he found. The cap had a long sheet of chainmail rippling down from it, almost like golden hair. Someone had decorated it to look like a crown.

Next, they furnished Jack with much of the same except that the color scheme of his armor was based around blue and silver rather than red and gold.

The two of them stood there, in gleaming silver and polished gold, as princely as anyone alive. As they were about to turn, Aaron spotted the twin statues wearing the Cloaks of the Kings. He walked over and stared at them. He hesitated, then unclasped the red cloak and flung it around his own shoulders.

"Come," said Aaron as he slung the strap on his compound bow across his back, and when he spoke, they noted a different tone in his voice—one more regal and commanding than before. "The battle awaits."

Chaos ruled.

The Acklyonians were a knot in the center of the battlefield when all of the farmers, townsmen, and soldiers within miles came spilling over the hills, screaming war cries and throwing themselves on the Gertulk. With numbers that matched those of the Gertulk, and with their sudden appearance to give them an edge, the Acklyonians managed to successfully scatter the Gertulk to the four points of the compass. Many Gertulk fled into the mountains. A good part of them fled northwest, back towards Rarzan. Most simply ran without paying attention to which way they were going. With encouragement from Cygon, the townsfolk gave chase to the Gertulk, the Phoenix soaring overhead, his call spreading over the land.

And over Acklyon, a very strange phenomenon occurred; as the Gertulk ran further and further from Castram, they passed more cities, villages, and farms where yet more villagers joined the chase. In this fashion, the Gertulk ran until they could not run anymore, fought until they could not fight anymore, and were taken prisoner.

But the heroes of Acklyon knew little of this as at the moment, they and Kellaoth were busy battling the Gertulk that had stayed to fight.

Brotchurd had never seen such frenzied tactics. It was all attack, defend, kill, duck, block parry, dodge, hack, stab, and try to stay alive. But even through all this madness, he could tell that they were winning. The Gertulk had lost their advantage, and were dotted all over the place instead of in a solid formation. Brotchurd had never seen such a sight; not in a story, not in reality.

Dwarves were charging everywhere, swinging their double-bladed axes, spiked war hammers, and short, broad, swords at the Gertulk. Elves were leaping about with crazy joy as they fired their bows and swung their little swords. Men towered over the other Acklyonians and stabbed with long swords and spears. Brotchurd himself was dancing around with wild swings of his sword, struggling to overcome the Gertulk. However, he knew they could win. Elf archers lined the walls of the courtyard, where Brotchurd and his company were currently hammering the Gertulk. How they never hit a single Man was beyond Brotchurd, as Men have little understanding of the minds of Elves, just as Elves have little understanding of the minds of men.

Far away, deep in the depths of Rarzan, Kane Malvadore was plotting his next move. His Adinyrom was currently out destroying Castram. He knew the odds were tremendously on his side, but he also knew that the rebels had Kellaoth fighting for them.

The accursed Unicorn seemed to be everywhere at once, always stopping the spread of his reign. She would die, of course. Sooner or later his minions would track her down and kill her. But until then, she was, and always had been, a thorn in his side. Needless to say, Malvadore did not at all like the thought of losing his grip on part of his country, even such a small part as two cities and a band of outlaw Elves. Still, no one had ever gone as far as reclaiming Castram or setting up a base there. Many had tried, of course, but none had ever succeeded in coming this close to victory. Indeed, the last full-scale battle that had occurred in Acklyon was the one in which Malvadore conquered Castram once and for all. To any of his officers or the Gertulk in his army, this raid of Castram might seem like just another revolt—granted a somewhat bigger one than those in the past. But Malvadore was wiser and far more learned.

He knew that the Acklyonians had a secret weapon, one which not even his power could contend with. One that they, perhaps, might not even be aware of, one that might not take effect for years, and the source of this advantage was in the most unlikely source—Aaron and Jack. To any else, themselves included, there was nothing particularly special about them. They may be descendants of the old line of kings, but on the surface, they were mere schoolboys. Young, innocent, bumbling, far too stupid to be of any assistance, yes, but they had something that no one could take away from them; they were a Forahn and a Parnor, and that was far more than just a surname. It was a title, a sign that great things were to come of these two urchins. That someday, they would be great kings who would lead the charge into battle and end all days of darkness.

For this reason, it would be crucial (to any lesser warlord) that the two be slaughtered as quickly as could be managed. However, Malvadore was no pompous Duke or scheming weasel of a lord. He was a Kane, and he knew what must be done: his conquer of Acklyon had dipped the balance of that place; it was fracturing, unhappy, and unproductive. Soon, the Magic of the continent would break, and who knew how destructive that would be? Malvadore did, and he couldn't let that happen.

Actually, it would have happened long ago except that Malvadore had found a tiny loophole in the ancient Magic. His mother had been the sister of Adinyrom I, and in his life as a mortal, he had been named the Stewart of Castram.

While the king was away, the stewart would take over the throne. However twisted and demented Malvadore may have been, he still had that power, and he had used it to perfection. He had killed every member of the royal family and had tried to destroy Forvalad and Parvelad.

Without the Forahns and Parnors, it became Malvedore's duty to assume control of Castram, a task he willingly performed. His duty was to keep Acklyon running smoothly until Adinyrom and Jahkon took control of the Throne, and he had done that. Acklyon was now one of the most powerful continents in the world. They had the largest army of any country and were the most well defended. The citizens had to obey his every command by right of law. Because of that little quirk in the ancient Magic, Malvadore had retained his icy grip on Acklyon.

And yet he was not in complete control. His subjects did not refer to him as "King Malvadore." He was merely a lord, a stand-in for the actual king.

Now that the rightful kings had returned, the law commanded him to step down, but he had not. He had sent forces to kill or capture these two, an act worthy of execution. He was now no longer the rightful leader, and he had betrayed the ancient laws. Slowly, Malvadore's hand was slipping;

the Elves were active once more, and they had liberated two major cities! No. It was time to settle this, once and for all. He had given the False Adinyrom specific instructions: throw down the Acklyonian defenses, kill every last man, women, and child, but leave those two boys alive. Bring Adinyrom and Jahkon back to him, alive, unspoiled, and well treated well.

"Contain them with all the Magic you possess," Malvadore had said. "It will be a delicate procedure—one wrong move and Forvalad and Parvelad will vanish into the abyss as they did so many years ago. I must have those two boys with the swords!" His reason for this was that he knew that with a high level of Black Magic, he could bend the power of those two swords to his will, strip the boys of their identity, and absorb the names "Forahn" and "Parnor" into himself. Then, he would truly become the rightful King of Acklyon. Adinyrom and Jahkon would be Aaron and Jack again, nothing more than two little brats. They would not die, no, not yet. They would live, for what is being the ruler of such a fine continent without slaves?

One of his soldiers interrupted his musings.

"Excuse me, sir," the Gertulk said, trembling. "I bring word of the battle of Castram."

Malvadore's sharp eyes locked on him. Somehow, he knew that it had gone wrong. "What has happened?"

"Sir—" stammered the guard. "The king requires help. He is being—being defeated."

Malvadore cursed such a horrible curse that even the Gertulk flinched. "That demented fool!" he raged. "The idiotic, bumbling, overconfident, weakling dog! Of course he would find some way to bungle it! Very well..." He seized a knife and threw it, narrowly missing the guard. "Send word back to Forahn," he said in a dangerous hiss. "Tell him that help will come... Tell him Kane Malvadore comes!"

46

Fallen Mentor

Aaron, Jack, Bonnie, Ellie, and Gallagher burst through the oak doors of the palace, tripped, and rolled painfully down the red-carpeted stairs and into the courtyard.

"Oh, my rotten blueberries..." whispered Bonnie.

Mayhem was the word. Trouble was the situation. Gertulk, Men, Elves, and these weird little mini-men with long beards and big axes were running to and fro, clashing fiercely. No one really seemed to have much in the way of order, and indeed their only tactics seemed to be run around and kill the opposing side. All through the courtyard, all through the city, upon the walls, and across the landscape around Castram, duelers clashed, archers on both sides picked off passing soldiers, crouched behind walls or on rooftops, and horses tramped around as their riders hacked viciously at other riders. Aaron had never seen such a massacre. This was nothing like Eldorlorne... At least there, both sides had had an actual strategy... A huge, troll-like Gertulk blundered out of the fray and charged at the children. It swung its heavy sword at Aaron, who only barely managed to leap out of the way.

Jack came around behind it and killed it.

"We need to get a better position!" he cried.

"Is that a Centaur?" Ellie exclaimed, pointing as a gigantic, half-man half-horse dueled seven Gertulk at once. "What is going on?"

They watched as the Centaur, standing on a wall, leaped high in the air and slashed at a dragon that had swooped past. With a cut in its belly, the dragon spiraled out of control.

"We should get back inside!" said Gallagher. But any further arguments were eliminated when the dragon whooshed over their heads, flapping its wings wildly. It crashed into the doorway back to the castle, sending chunks of masonry flying, and blocking the way back.

"Now what?" screamed Bonnie.

"We stay and fight," said Aaron.

Two more Gertulk rushed at them. Gallagher and Bonnie took out one, Aaron and Jack took the other. By now, the battle had swallowed them. Gertulk, Elves, Dwarves and Men ran around them, clashing furiously. A tall man, dressed in golden armor suddenly slammed into Aaron, sending him to the ground.

"Now, little king," whispered the False Adinyrom, his white face mere inches from Aaron's, "you shall die. You and your petty rebellion shall not take my master's country!"

A huge white animal flew out of the sky and landed beside them. The False Adinyrom leaped to his feet, swinging his sword. Kellaoth parried with one talon then struck him with the other. The False Adinyrom staggered with blood dripping down his face. He fled through the archway and over the battlefield. Kellaoth snarled after him then turned to Aaron. Aaron expected her to scold him, to tell him to return to the castle, or that it was foolish of him to come. Instead, she beamed with pride.

"Are you alright?" she asked.

"Yes," Aaron panted. Further discussion was canceled when

several Gertulk attacked them.

"Remember, Aaron," said Kellaoth as she back flipped out of the way of one of them, "keep on defense, and don't attack unless you know you can hit!"

Aaron whirled his sword and with a tongue of flame pierced one of the Gertulk, but the others closed in. Aaron and Kellaoth fought hard, but they could not win. Aaron wasn't sure where the others had gone, probably scattered through the battle. He hoped they were okay…

A man in red and silver armor broke their ranks, scattering them.

"Brotchurd!" Aaron shouted.

"Hello, sire!" he cried.

"Keep with Brotchurd, Adinyrom," said Kellaoth. "I am needed elsewhere." She flew up into the air and out of sight. Aaron and Brotchurd together began to counter the advancing Gertulk. Aaron swung hard with Forvalad and locked blades with a smaller Gertulk. The impact rattled his sword, sending vibrations through it. Aaron dropped it and desperately used his shield to block the Gertulk. Brotchurd, seeing the danger, swiftly moved in behind the creature and killed it.

"It's getting more dangerous!" said Brotchurd after several more minutes of hard fighting. "Adinyrom! Get your friends and get out of here!"

"The way back is blocked!" said Aaron.

"Then I'll see you in heaven," Brotchurd said grimly. Suddenly, a huge troll blundered out of the crowd and took aim for Brotchurd. Brotchurd leapt to the side to avoid its giant mace and yelled to Aaron, "Go! Find the others and go!"

Aaron nodded and sprinted away. He fought his way through the fierce duelers until he found Jack. "Brotchurd says to get out of here!" he said.

Jack nodded. "Where are the others?"

Aaron scanned the battle until he spotted Bonnie and Gallagher in a corner, fighting off several Gertulk.

"C'mon," Aaron said, and they charged for them.

"I can't...can't do it anymore," panted Bonnie, dragging her sword out of one of the Gertulk

"We can't give up!" shouted Gallagher, his eyes red with dust and tiredness.

"There's...too many of them," gasped Bonnie.

"Only...ten," said Gallagher.

"Nine," said a voice as the tip of a golden blade suddenly popped out a Gertulk's chest.

"Aaron!" cried Bonnie in relief.

"Eight," said Jack, swiping off the head of one.

Together, the four of them managed to eliminate the remainder. Once they were done, Aaron leaned on his sword and asked, "Where's Ellie?"

"Not sure," said Gallagher, panting, "I saw her shooting at some Gertulk with a crossbow a while ago, but I haven't seen her since."

Jack scanned the battle with his eyes. "There!" he shouted. "She's over there!"

The others turned to see where he was pointing and saw Ellie sitting atop a one-story shack, clutching a scavenged crossbow in her hands with a quiver slung across her back. Several Gertulk were milling around her while she fired arrows into their ranks.

For a moment, the four of them simply stared at Ellie in disbelief. None of them had ever seen her kill even a spider before. They watched in amazement as a four-legged Gertulk began scaling the wall. Once he made it to the roof and was about to strike, she swung her crossbow hard, whacking him across the face. The Gertulk fell back to earth, but the crossbow snapped on his helmet. She threw aside the useless tool, pulled two arrows from her quiver, and braced herself for the next attack.

"Come on!" said Aaron, leading the four over to the scene. They leapt into the crowd of Gertulk, hacking and dodging, while Ellie threw knives and rocks at the Gertulk. Once they were defeated, Ellie hopped down from the roof.

"Nice work," Aaron said. "I never knew you had it in you."

"Well, you'll find this life is full of surprises," Ellie said, picking up the sword of a fallen Elf.

"This whole thing is pandemonium," said Jack, studying the battle. "There's no way either group can win."

Gallagher was also studying the battle. "I agree. Gertulk keep pouring in through the gateway, but without much of a strategy. The defenders can take them out, but more keep coming."

"So we guard the gate," Aaron decided. "Come on! To the wall!"

The five charged for the main gate, taking out Gertulk that they passed. They made it, spread out in a line, and began fighting off the Gertulk that tried to make it through. *Let's hope for a miracle,* Aaron thought. *And who knows, maybe we'll survive this.*

Kellaoth pulled her horn out of a Gertulk's chest. At this point, the battle could go in either direction. All they needed to do to stay alive was to keep the Gertulk from massing until they surrendered or retreated. Kellaoth's eyes landed on the main gate back into the castle. Aaron and his friends had positioned themselves directly beneath it, fighting the Gertulk out of the castle. She smiled. That might just be the key to winning. If she could only get word to Fortingale and send them reinforcements…

A sudden, loud *crack* pulled Kellaoth's attention. One of the crossbeams holding up the gate had just snapped.

Her eyes swung around to the west. The False Adinyrom was standing on a rock, safe from the battle. He held his sword in both hands, pointing it at the archway. Sweat ran down his cheeks as he whispered incantations. He was trying to bring down the arch, and it would not be long before he broke through the enchantments on it. Aaron had seen none of this, busy with the horde of Gertulk. Kellaoth understood. Malvadore did not care about Fortingale or the Elves. What he wanted was Aaron and Jack. Why? She would have to study that later. But for now, she had to get Adinyrom and Jahkon to safety…

She stood too long. As she was observing the False King's plan, three Gertulk pounced on her. One attempted to behead her with his sword. The blade broke on contact with her magical hide, but it had done considerable damage. The second swung his spiked hammer at her mouth, breaking most of her teeth and filling her mouth with blood, which prevented her from shouting. The third hacked at her rump with his axe. Once again, he failed to do any fatal damage, but did draw much blood. A blast of energy emitted from her body, incinerating all three.

She staggered as pain consumed her. She had felt very little pain in her life. Her strong skin had protected her from most assaults. For a moment, her vision went red as she buckled from sheer agony, but then she pulled herself together. She had enough strength left to make it to the medical tower in order to save her own life. But if she did, Aaron and Jack would die. She was the only one who had seen what was happening. The False Adinyrom was too far away to reach, and anyway she was no match for him in her weakened state. She could make it to the gate to save the boys, she thought, but she would certainly die from pain and exhaustion. Did she save the kings or herself? Did she run to the gate or to the medical tower?

The decision was plain to her. There was nothing else she could do.

She ran for the gate.

Aaron ducked and drove his sword to the hilt into his Gertulk opponent.

Two things happened fast: first, a piece of stone from the archway above him broke loose and landed inches from him. Second, a huge white blur slammed into him and his friends, knocking them backwards away from the gate.

For a moment Aaron lay there, stunned, and then he struggled to his feet. He froze with terror at what he saw. Kellaoth had fallen beneath the archway of the gate, too weak to get up. The False Adinyrom's spell was causing the archway to collapse, directly on top of her.

"Kellaoth!"

Kellaoth turned to look at him. Blood dripped down between her perfectly round eyes as a strange smile spread over her face.

The feeling returned to Aaron's legs, and he began to sprint towards her, intent upon dragging her back out before she was buried beneath the wall, but she gasped, "Stay where you are, Adinyrom!"

Aaron stopped, his muscles seeming to freeze at her command and watched helplessly as chunks of masonry began to fall all around her.

"NO!"

Kellaoth had a smile the likes of which Aaron had never seen before: excited for what was to come, pitying for Aaron, and understanding beyond all else. He struggled and thrashed against the spell she had put on him, willing his legs to carry him over to her to save her from what was about to happen—

Then a huge rock hit her on the head.

Aaron's knees buckled as he watched her head fall, eyes rolling madly. For a fraction of a millisecond, Aaron saw his last ever glimpse of her—limp-bodied, eyes staring sightlessly, covered with blood.

And the archway crumbled and fell over the entrance, completely burying Aaron's mentor.

Rocks and debris exploded in all directions from the fall, blasting Aaron and his comrades off their feet again.

Aaron dragged himself back up and sprinted for the ruin of the archway, though he knew he was too late.

Jack, Gallagher, Bonnie, and Ellie had gotten up, too, and staggered over to him, rubbing bruises.

"Aaron?"

"No…" Aaron whispered in shock. "No…it's not possible… NO!" He ran to the wreckage, scrabbling at the rocks in a desperate attempt to move them.

"Aaron, it's no good!" said Bonnie through tears. "She's—"

"She's not dead!" Aaron bellowed. "She can't be dead! Kellaoth!" He continued to throw himself on the boulders despite the sense of numb shock that was spreading through his body for Kellaoth—Kellaoth who had taught him to be a king, Kellaoth who had saved his life so many times, Kellaoth, the closest thing he had to a mother here—was dead and there was nothing he could do to help her. Aaron threw his body onto the debris one last time, and he was succumbed by sobs of grief.

Jack dropped down beside Aaron and placed a hand on his friend's shoulder.

Bonnie walked over to Ellie and hugged her, and Ellie pressed her face against Bonnie's chest.

Gallagher placed a hand over his face and then looked away as tears filled his own eyes.

"Kellaoth…"

Aaron's mind was spinning, reeling, it could not be true. It *mustn't be*!

But it was.

The cold hard facts were that Kellaoth was dead, really dead, and nothing Aaron said or did could change that. Aaron and Jack were alone in the struggle now. Kellaoth could help them no more. Malvadore would win—there was no way around it now.

Dimly, as the through someone else's eyes, he saw the Elves, Men, and Dwarves battling away at the Gertulk. Memories flashed through Aaron's mind. The Pool. Forvalad. Training with Laza in Eldorlorne. Kneeling over Ploppy's dead body. Fighting in the Battle of Eldorlorne. Talking with Kellaoth. Traveling cross-country. Fighting Gertulk. Looking into the face of certain death, but managing to fight his way out through luck and determination. Crossing blades with the False Adinyrom. The Battle of Castram… It all came back to him, then, staring at Kellaoth's tomb. What did it all mean? What had he really learned?

More memories came to him. He and the Elves cornered by Gertulk, trapped in that old cave with no chance of victory, when dragons had appeared and chased away the Gertulk. Starving, without the food to last even a few weeks. Giving most of his meals to those sick from lack of proper nutrition, and stumbling onto a troll hole stuffed with food and an Elfin cook ready to fix them kingly meals. Chased all the way across Acklyon by Gertulk. Making their last stand at Castram, and receiving help from mythical beings. In Muln, no one had believed in Aaron's royalty, and now they fought alongside him, aiding him in fulfilling his destiny. Malvadore had killed his father and claimed Acklyon for himself, eliminating all hope of freedom for the people, and yet here Aaron was, defying Malvadore and on the road to victory.

It means, he realized, *that even in the most hopeless of situations, help will be given to those in need, even from the most unlikely sources, and that we should never give up, no matter what happens to us.*

He started out of his trancelike state at a strange gurgling sound. The rocks before him were shifting and rolling, and out came a cone-like object. Aaron caught it. It was about a foot long, silver, and spiraling.

Kellaoth's horn.

For a long time Aaron stared at it, then he grabbed it and slid it into his pocket. He stood up, and ran his eyes over the battle.

Jack thought that, at the moment, Aaron looked more like a prince of Fortilly than anyone who had ever lived.

47
True or False?

"Aaron, we need to get out of here!" said Ellie fearfully, tears still glittering on her face.

"Hold that thought," said Aaron, a dangerous light in his eyes. He had seen a figure to the right, a tall, powerful man in golden armor.

The False Adinyrom Forahn.

And like a wound opening, a great rush of adrenaline surged through Aaron's body in an emotion he had never felt before; it was not the boyish and immature annoyance he had felt whenever his nemesis, Jack, had pulled a prank on him. It was not the sharp irritation he had felt whenever Laza slapped the boy's fingers in a duel. It wasn't the bitter thoughts towards Malvadore that had plagued him in the past year or even the righteous anger he felt when he saw an Elf slaughtered in battle.

It was white-hot, pain-mingled, revenge-seeking hatred. He wanted to claw the False King's cold eyes out of their sockets, to turn that awful sneer into a scream of pain. He wanted to see Gertulk die heartless and cowardly deaths. He wanted to see Rarzan burn in the fires of his grief for Kellaoth. He wanted every evil thing in Acklyon to suffer for what had been taken from him.

Since coming to Acklyon, he had never held much stock in revenge. He had learned to forgive mistakes and to take out his anger in duels or in battle. But now…he wanted repercussions. He could feel an evil power surge working its way through his fingers, and he did nothing to suppress it. He was on his feet now. Forvalad was in his hand.

Ellie, sensing danger, tried to stop him, but he shook off her hand and ignored her words. He had eyes for one man alone, and that man was going to die the hard way.

Malvadore's minion saw the young prince slouching forwards like a mummy and a leer slithered across the False Adinyrom's mouth.

Aaron drew the old compound bow, raining arrows on the Imposter King. Forahn blocked each shot with apparent ease. Aaron continued to walk forwards, stopping only to draw more arrows. He continued to fire until his quiver was empty. Then he uttered a bloody war cry and swung the bow like a club at the False King. Forahn swung his sword, cleaving the bow in two. Aaron threw aside the now useless weapon, drew Forvalad from its sheath, and leapt at the Imposter, aiming the sword at his enemy's neck. Forvalad burned with a raging red fire, mirroring Aaron's own pain and anger.

Forahn parried Aaron's blow with the tip of his sword, circled his wrist taking Forvalad with him, and gave a casual flick which caused Aaron's sword to fly out of his hand. As Forvalad struck the ground, point-first and quivering, Forahn said, "You are weak, boy," and lunged.

"I—am—not—WEAK!" Aaron dropped and rolled to avoid the False Adinyrom's sword, drew a golden dagger from his belt, and drove it into the Imposter King's foot with such force that the blade burst out on the other side and sank into the ground, successfully pinning Forahn. As Forahn howled with pain, Aaron leapt to his feet, sprinted over to Forvalad, wrenched it out of the ground, and was just in time to block a blow from the False Adinyrom, who had wrenched the dagger out of his foot.

With their golden blades locked, man and boy glared at each other.

"You shall soon be reunited with your dear Kellaoth," hissed the Traitor.

"Oh, I don't think so," retorted Aaron.

"How does it feel to lose someone you love?" said the False Adinyrom, an insane smile spreading over his face. "I would not know. I do not love, thus I am impenetrable to mental assault, whereas *you* are vulnerable!"

Aaron was struck, not as much by the jibe about his love for Kellaoth, but by the very thought that this – this *monster* – was widely believed to be a Forahn and a noble king....to be Aaron. "You have no feeling, vermin," Aaron whispered.

"Aye," said the False Adinyrom proudly.

"You have no love, no devotion. All you care about is seeing people suffer. You disgust me."

The False Adinyrom's proud demeanor faltered.

Ellie, Bonnie, and Gallagher watch in horror as Aaron and the False Adinyrom struggled.

Bonnie rushed forward to help, but Gallagher caught her by the arm.

"No," he said. "This is his battle. There's nothing you or I can do to help him."

Bonnie did not like what she was hearing, but she knew Gallagher was right. So, instead, they watched.

Aaron was slowly gaining control. "You have no cause, no purpose, and thus, no deeper power."

The False Adinyrom disengaged himself from Aaron, then leapt back into the fray in a clash of golden swords.

Forvalad once again soared out of Aaron's hand and landed elsewhere.

"And now," panted Forahn, his hair unkempt, "you will die. Oh, yes, I know 'Kane' Malvadore wants me to bring you to him so that he can finish you off himself, but I have grown stronger than he. I shall say that you were killed by a rogue troll. And when Malvadore turns away, he shall have my sword in his back." He cackled like a lunatic. "He created me as a ruse to turn the citizens of Acklyon away from you. But now, I have grown stronger than he can imagine. I shall rule this puny continent and many others too come!"

"You despicable piece of—"

All thoughts of his sword forgotten, Aaron charged forward and punched Forahn squarely in the face. Forahn staggered, blood dripping from his nose and mouth. Before he could react, Aaron had him on the ground and was clawing, biting, punching, and kicking every inch of the traitor that he could reach. However, Forahn was a much older, stronger, and a more experienced combatant, and soon threw Aaron off of him. This time, the False Adinyrom did not waste words but simply grabbed Aaron by the throat and pinned him to the wall—his feet dangling from the ground—and began squeezing the life out of him.

"Say goodbye," Forahn whispered venomously.

Aaron's face was turning purple. He was dying, and surely there was nothing he could do to save himself. The False Adinyrom had won.

"Maybe you'd like to take back what you said," sneered Forahn. Aaron couldn't respond. He had maybe ten seconds to live.

And then Jack leapt out of nowhere and swung his sword at Forahn.

The Traitor Forahn turned and parried Jack's attack, his sneer expanding on his face. "So," he said mockingly, "you have come to join your friend in death, have you?"

Jack did not respond, merely attacked again.

As Aaron finally got his first breath, Forahn flipped Jack over his shoulder, sending him crashing into Aaron. Before either of the boys could retaliate, the Imposter had lifted both of them off the ground and slammed them into the wall by the throat again.

"I wonder," he said, holding Jack with one hand and Aaron with the other, "which of you will last longer. Oh, Malvadore wants you alive," he cackled insanely, "but after all, he is not here to hear you scream!"

As Aaron felt the air being squeezed out of his lungs again, he knew this was the end. No Elves or Men were near enough to save them, and none had noticed the duel, anyway. *Wait!* he thought to himself. *This can't be how it ends! Never give up, no matter what! There must be some way to get out of this...* A plan formulated in his mind. He looked over at his friend. He aimed his nose at Jack, darted his eyes left and right once, tapped himself, and clenched one fist. The message, in that wonderful Elfin sign language, was, *you distract him; I'll kill him.* Jack nodded briefly, and drew back his leg and kicked Forahn hard in the stomach.

At the same time, Aaron desperately fumbled at his side, but he had no sword! He had lost his knife, too. (It now lay on the ground, soaked with the Traitor's strangely dark blood). He had nothing to attack with. Then his hand, feeling desperately within his armor, found a long, cone-like object. Of course! In one rapid motion, Aaron drew Kellaoth's horn from his pocket, and drove it through the False Adinyrom's heart.

The False King staggered backwards, blood staining the front of his hauberk, the horn still embedded in his chest. He gave Aaron and Jack a look of deepest shock, and his body exploded. Kellaoth's horn fell with a clatter. Aaron and Jack dropped to the ground, rubbing their throats.

For a long time, neither spoke, staring around in surprise and shock.

"Did—did we just k-kill him?" Jack finally said shakily.

"I th-think so," said Aaron quietly.

Before they could say any more, they both felt the wind being knocked out of them yet again as Ellie and Bonnie ran up and threw their arms around them, screaming, "You did it! YOU DID IT!"

Then Gallagher was there, screaming incoherently.

For a long time they remained in a kind of five-way hug, yelling and laughing.

"We showed him!" said Aaron, whopping Jack on the back.

"Now the Gertulk won't be so..." Gallagher's voice trailed off. He was staring at the sealed gate. The others turned, and saw what he had seen: the wall of rubble was beginning to tremble and shake, as the something was trying to dig through...

A wall-shattering roar, an explosion of flame, the rubble-sealed gate bursting inward, and a huge black shape flying straight for them. Ellie screamed. Bonnie fitted an arrow on her string and fired, only to see it bounce off the thick hide.

As Aaron's heart leapt with terror, he saw a flash of golden light and suddenly felt Forvalad materialize in his hand. Aaron and Jack acted together. Jack shoved first Ellie then Bonnie, sending both stumbling backwards. Aaron saw a giant claw reaching towards him, and lashed out. The gigantic dragon screeched and flew back up towards the sky as blood dripped from its forearm.

Aaron and Jack planted themselves firmly between Ellie and Bonnie and the dragon, swords in their hands and braced for the attack. This time it was Jack that struck the monster. As the long tail hit Aaron and knocked him off his feet, Jack swung hard at the dragon's other claw, shearing off one of its toes. The dragon roared again and flew away, but not before a figure had leapt off its back and onto the ground. The figure was unnaturally tall, but still landed nimbly. Spiked black armor covered his muscular form.

The man straightened up and strode towards Aaron and Jack, the black cloak on his back swirling in the wake of his step. As he drew closer, Aaron saw a strange, pulsing red glow coming from under the helmet.

The boys felt the air stiffen. The shadows seemed to grow broader, as if the sun was being forced away. The wind died. All life forms stopped; wounded soldiers gasped, and rolled over, dead. Vultures screeched and flew upwards into the darkening sky. Moles scampered back underground. When the man was not more than ten feet from them, Aaron saw what had caused the red glow: his eyes were crimson and had no pupils or irises, simply orbs that glowed scarlet. He made no move to draw the sword at his side, simply stared at Aaron and Jack, a leering smile spreading over his mouth. Aaron knew who this must be, and the knowledge sent ice flooding through his body.

Kane Malvadore had joined the fray.

48
Kane Malvadore

Malvadore did not attack, but merely stared and smiled. Despite his terrifying eyes and fangs, he had a certain gracefulness about him. Every move he made was sharp and coordinated, and his features remained impassionate. He was evil and yet beautiful at the same time. He was no monster—he was something more; something far more dangerous and powerful.

He was a Kane.

It was the only word Aaron could think of to describe him—for how do you describe a creature who casts icy fear into the depths of your soul, but at the same time leaves you awestruck? He was not a man, not an earthly creature. He was something else in the form of a man. As he neared them, he removed his black helmet and shook back his long, coarse black hair. As he did so, they could see a single blight in his terrifyingly beautiful features: a long, nasty-looking scar stretching from his temple to his cheek.

At last, Kane Malvadore spoke, and when he did, the children could see a mouth full of teeth as sharp and jagged as knives. His voice was deep and had a malevolent chill in it. "Adinyrom, Jahkon." he said quietly, "It has been a long time. You have managed to turn back my forces and even kill the king, I see. I must say, I am impressed." One side of his lips curled in a sneer. "Your parents would have been proud."

Aaron went rigid.

"They were great people," said Malvadore conversationally, clearly enjoying the appalled looks on the children's faces, "I would have liked to let them live, but they were in my way. As were you two, of course. I would have killed you then if it hadn't been for the meddling of that accursed Wizard, Cygon.

"Last time we met was in this very castle. I remember, even if you perhaps do not, when I had you cornered. I had just killed your parents and was about to kill you, too. As I recall, you actually attacked me, Adinyrom."

"Good for me," growled Aaron.

Malvadore laughed. "You have your father's flare, boy. Mm," he added, as though as an afterthought, staring around at the courtyard, "This reminds of the first time I faced you…but I shall succeed this time. Shall we begin?"

"Are you going to kill us?" said Aaron. There was no fear in his voice but only contempt and disgust. "Your sword is right there. Go on, run me through with it—" his lip curled. "—I *dare* you."

Malvadore smiled. "So much of your father's pride in you, Adinyrom…but pride in the face of death is ultimately worthless, remember that. But I digress; I did not come to exchange banter."

And before either of the boys quite knew what was happening, Malvadore drew a small, slanted knife from his belt and hurled it at Aaron with astonishing speed. Aaron threw himself to the to the side, just barely avoiding the blade. Disoriented, he fell to the ground.

As Jack prepared to attack Malvadore raised his hand and,

without even looking, sent a bolt of energy that hit Jack squarely in the chest. The force of the blow lifted Jack off his feet and threw him to the ground, stunned. Malvadore still had his eyes locked on Aaron. The gloating sneer was gone from his face now, replaced by an emotionless focus. He placed one booted foot on Aaron's throat and prepared to crush it when—

"NO!"

A golden figure had leapt out of nowhere, swinging a mighty golden staff at Malvadore. Malvadore only just had time to whip out his sword and block the blow. It was Lord Cygon, his fair face contorted with concentration, his lips drawn back and baring his teeth, his forehead a maze of wrinkles.

"YOU!" Malvadore screeched, a reptilian look of anger on his face—and yet there was fear there, too.

"Me," growled Cygon.

"You have sided with these disturbers of the peace, these barbarians?"

Cygon barked a laugh. "How dare you call another a barbarian? I was there, at the Fall of Acklyon! I know what you did, what you are!"

Malvadore snarled and struck again.

Cygon blocked and jabbed the butt end of his staff at Malvadore's abdomen. Malvadore parried with the pommel of his sword. Aaron crawled over to where Jack lay, dazed. Malvadore's attack had not been lethal—Jack had only had the wind knocked out of him. As he helped Jack to his feet, Aaron felt something hot and wet running down his cheek and realized that Malvadore's knife had left a narrow cut down the side of his head.

Malvadore flicked his wrist, as if throwing a dagger and a shadow streaked out of his finger tips towards Cygon. Cygon aimed the head of his staff at the speeding shadow and incinerated it with a beam of light. Malvadore didn't waste a second, now conjuring great orbs of jet-black fire and throwing them at Cygon, who dodged them all with amazing agility. He then retaliated with more beams of golden light from his staff, one of which hit Malvadore in the chest. The force of the blast threw Malvadore backwards into the air, limbs flailing like a spider. He recovered, landing on his feet and raising his sword. Cygon charged, staff held over his head. The two weapons collided in between them with a mighty *clang!* of metal on metal. The two powerhouses traded a fury of blows until Malvadore's sword flew out of his hand. Malvadore advanced, raising his gauntleted hand to strike a blow, but Cygon upended him with his staff.

As Malvadore hit the ground, Cygon rushed forward and plunged the tip spike of his staff straight into Malvadore's chest. Malvadore howled with agony, and Cygon raised his staff for another blow. The great black dragon swooped down then and lashed out at Cygon.

Cygon managed to defend himself, but was knocked over in the process. The dragon scooped up Malvadore in its claws and flew off towards the northeast.

Aaron, Jack, and Cygon got to their feet slowly.

"Did—" stammered Aaron. "Did you just kill him?"

Cygon paused, as though he wasn't sure what to say. "No," he said finally. "I missed. I got him in the shoulder, not the heart."

"It looked pretty square to me," said Jack uncertainly.

"It was a miss," said Cygon shortly.

Aaron looked at Cygon. "Malvadore will come back, won't he?"

"He will," said Cygon heavily. "'Tis a mark of the Kane; they never stay defeated for long. They always slither away before you can cut off their heads, and return later at full power.

"Come," he added. "Let us see what has become of the battle."

Aaron followed him out of the blasted gate and onto the battlefield. The battle still raged fiercely, but it was clear that Castram was winning. The Gertulk were scattered, dotted here and there like chess pieces.

"Shall we join?" said Cygon.

Aaron raised his sword and nodded.

49
Victory!

The battle was won.

Gertulk were fleeing in all directions, scattering as the Elves, Dwarves, and Men united under the banner of the crossed swords. Brotchurd, the Centaur, and Lord Cygon led the three armies in the crusade, killing all Gertulk who fought back and capturing all who surrendered.

Aaron's heart was glowing like the sun that had now reached the middle of the sky. They had won! Malvadore had launched a full-scale attack, and the Acklyonians had driven his forces into bedlam. Aaron had killed the False Adinyrom, he had even faced Kane Malvadore himself and survived, and he felt more like a Forahn than he ever did.

As the last of the Gertulk were rounded up, Aaron met up with Jack and Cygon.

"Well done, both of you!" cried Cygon, his golden hair rippling.

"We did it, Aaron!" shouted Jack, hugging his friend. "We finally did it!"

"And we killed the False Adinyrom, too!" shouted Aaron.

"Come," said Cygon. "You must meet King Grimathine."

"King Grimathine?"

"The Dwarves king," explained Cygon, giving the boys a shove towards an elderly Dwarf with a heavy, three-bladed axe and crown-like helm.

As Aaron and Jack walked over to the Dwarf, Jack whispered, "Do we bow to him, or does he bow to us?"

Aaron thought. "I think we should bow to him. He did save our lives."

They approached the elderly Dwarf and each boy knelt on one knee. "Hail, King Grimathine!" cried Aaron.

The Dwarf nodded, unsmiling.

Aaron glanced at Jack, slightly unnerved by Grimathine's silence, then pressed on. "We thank you for your help in the battle. Without you and your men, we could not have won."

Grimathine nodded again.

Aaron looked at Jack again, still rattled. To spare them more of this, another Dwarf, slightly more slender than the others, came up to his king and said, "Er muor vichalz."

"Er meralvis," replied the King Grimathine.

"I think they're speaking in Dwarvish," Jack whispered to Aaron.

"Who do you suppose that is?" Aaron muttered to Jack. Grimathine, who seemed to have heard, grunted, "M'daughter, Merline."

"You mean that's a g—" Aaron stepped on Jack's foot to make him shut up.

"Yes, 'tis a woman," said Grimathine, almost smiling.

"Nice beard," said Jack.

Bonnie came up just then, saying to Aaron, "We've gotten all the bodies out of the castle. The women and children are okay, just a little shook up." Then, turning to the dwarves with a bright smile, "Oh, hi! Thanks for your help in the battle."

"This is, uh, Lady Veronica, um, a close friend of ours," said Aaron, making up the title on the spot. Bonnie's eyes flashed at the sound of her real name.

"Is that a *girl*?" said Merline in surprise and in a thick, dwarfish accent.

Bonnie looked highly affronted. "Of course, I'm a girl!" she said indignantly. "Just because I wear armor and go into battle doesn't mean—"

"Bonnie." Aaron took her by the arm and dragged her off a way. "Bonnie, *that's a girl you've been talking to*."

Bonnie's mouth dropped open. "A *what*?"

"Shh!" whispered Aaron. "She can't believe you're so incredibly fragile, probably."

"I am NOT fragile!" snarled Bonnie.

"Do you wear a *beard*?" said Aaron impatiently. "These are *dwarves*. They're different. Just smile and nod."

They returned to the conversation. "So," said Aaron uncomfortably, rocking back and forth on the balls of his feet "Soooo..." He cast around for something to say until he spied King Grimathine's axe. He hadn't noticed from a distance, but the edges of its three blades were made of diamond. "Your axe!" he said before he could stop himself. "It's—"

"Aye, this is Broknarsh, the weapon of the king," said Grimathine, admiring his axe. "It is made of Tactilite, the same metal that made your sword, though I am told your people call it 'Terriditon.'"

"We do, yes," said Aaron, fascinated, "but I was told the only known source of Terriditon—I mean, uh, Tactilite, was in Forvalad and Parvelad."

He knew as soon as he had closed his mouth that he had said the wrong thing.

"There is much that your kind does not know about the secrets of Acklyon," said Grimathine coldly.

Aaron thought it best to change the subject quickly. "So…you gave your allegiance to us rather than Malvadore?"

"I give nothing," said Grimathine harshly, "Malvadore has defiled this land, both above and below the ground. I wish to see him removed from this land, and the only way of doing that is to work alongside you. So I and my kinsmen have come above ground for the first time in centuries, here to rid Acklyon of his filth."

"Where we come from, we have a saying;" said Jack, "*the enemy of my enemy is my friend*. I suppose that applies to us now."

"I suppose it does," conceded Grimathine.

"Your tongue is wise, master youth," said a strong, deep voice, almost like the voice of a bull, behind them. They turned to see the Centaur trotting towards them, and now the children fully appreciated how very huge he was. From the waist up, he was probably bigger even than Cygon or Malvadore. His four horse legs were each as tall as Aaron, and the wide, sharp hooves were as big as pies. Up close he was quite alarming.

"I am Oriean, Centaur of Acklyon," said the Centaur, saluting Aaron. Aaron didn't reply as he was frozen with shock at his mammoth size.

"Hi," said Bonnie in Aaron's absence. "Thanks for your help."

"It is well received," Oriean replied.

"What did he say?" Bonnie whispered to Jack, who shrugged.

"If I might ask," said Aaron, finding his tongue at last, "according to Acklyonian myth, you live underneath Castram and only emerge in times of dire need. If so, where were you a hundred years ago, when Malvadore first took power?" he tried very hard not to sound accusatory.

Oriean stared at Aaron, who did his best not to shrink away from his piercing gaze. The mighty Centaur threw his head back and laughed, sounding like a line of train cars on steel tracks. "Is that what the top dwellers say of me? Humans. Always convinced that the planets center around them."

Aaron, Jack, and Bonnie silently agreed not to take offense.

"My purpose, young one, has nothing to do with you or your city. The reason I am here is because Cygon and Kellaoth urged me to." Oriean sighed, looking off towards the wrecked gate under which Kellaoth had met her doom. "I liked Kellaoth," he said. "She was very independent."

Aaron choked. Concentrating his efforts on the battle and speaking with Grimathine had managed to keep his thoughts off of Kellaoth, for maybe if he avoided thinking about her dying, it would become untrue. "She was," he said, finally finding his voice.

Despite their victory, when Aaron returned to the palace and headed for his room, his heart was heavy with grief.

Kellaoth was dead.

It didn't matter how many times he repeated it in his head, it simply didn't make sense. Kellaoth was dead, Kellaoth was dead, Kellaoth was dead. Nothing. It wasn't true, he knew that. He knew that she survived the crash, that any second now she would come soaring out of the sky and ask for her horn back in that beautiful voice of hers. She would smile at him, the way she did when she was proud of him. Then he would climb onto her back and she would fly around Castram and tell him stories about the old days, the days of his ancestors. So where was she? Why hadn't she come to let him know she was alright? She must've known he was worried about her, (it had been an awful lot of rock that landed on top of her) so where was she? Where was she?

"WHERE ARE YOU?"Aaron shouted into the night. He hadn't intended to say it out loud, but the words slipped from between his lips before he could process them. Two young Elves making their way back to their home after the battle stopped at the sound of his yell and looked at him. He ignored them.

"COME BACK!" he screamed, seizing a flowerpot off of somebody's front porch and hurling it into the air. When it shattered on the ground, the two Elves jumped and hurried off into the city. "YOU CAN'T LEAVE ME!" A sob now mingled with Aaron's yell."YOU CAN'T LEAVE ME ALONE LIKE THIS!"

Nobody answered. Nobody would.

"Please don't leave me…" Aaron dropped to his knees. She really was gone. She wasn't coming back. She had abandoned him. Aaron curled into a ball on the ground and cried for all that he had lost, for Kellaoth wasn't the only casualty of the day; picking through the corpses of the battlefield earlier, Aaron had found Fortingale's body, pale and blood stained, buried beneath a pile of Gertulk. A war hammer's strike, catching him from behind, had ended his life. This was also a staggering blow, as Fortingale was one of the last and greatest leaders of Acklyon. Laza was next in command, and after him, Brotchurd, and after him, Aticka with Cappy last on the chain of command. They had no other leaders. Their list was running short.

That means that soon I will be taking up the mantle, he realized. Yes, very soon indeed he would find himself thrust into the leadership role he had never wanted. Being student body president in school was one thing—ruling a country was another.

It's okay, he reassured himself. *It won't be your turn for years. First you need to graduate, then come of age. Laza's in charge until then.* He let out a deep sigh. He felt exhausted, his hands covered in blisters, his mind wrought like a sponge. The army the False Adinyrom had conjured was destroyed, and Aaron knew it would be some time before Malvadore could regain that type of strength. This would give the Acklyonians time to repair the damage and strengthen their forces. Perhaps someday they might win back Acklyon. The Dwarves would be fearsome allies, and Oriean did a great deal to recreate the feeling of Acklyon as it should be. For now, all they could do was hope.

50

Kellaoth's Gift

As Aaron opened the door to his chamber, he found that Jack, Ellie, Gallagher and Bonnie were already there waiting for him. He could see by their solemn expressions and tearful eyes that they, too, were thinking of Kellaoth.

When Aaron came in, Ellie rushed over and hugged him. He returned the pressure, glad to have someone to hold. When they broke apart, Ellie led him over to an armchair and seated him. He collapsed into the soft embrace of the cushions and let out a deep breath.

"Well," said Jack after a long silence, "we won the battle, but we lost—"

"But we lost *her*," Bonnie finished, staring at the floor.

Silence ensued in which each child, laid down with burdens that no child should have to bear, grappled with their thoughts.

"It's all my fault," said Aaron quietly.

"It wasn't," said Bonnie sharply. "She—she made her choice."

"But she made that choice to save me!" cried Aaron. "I wasn't quick enough to save myself, so she had to take my place. If I stayed away from that archway or not even joined the battle as I was told, she'd still be here right now." As he understood these disturbing truths, a horrible guilt overcame him.

He leapt to his feet, seized a dagger off the table and hurled it at the wall with a detached yell of mingled fury and sorrow.

"What'll happen to us now?" whimpered Ellie.

"We keep fighting, of course," said Jack sternly. "We turned back the invasion, killed the False Adinyrom, and reclaimed Castram. I can guarantee that Malvadore won't take us lightly anymore. The Battle for Acklyon is about to begin."

"So *that's* why they always say that in video games," remarked Gallagher.

"But how can there *be* a battle when we have a couple hundred soldiers at most and Malvadore probably has millions!" cried Bonnie.

"We have Lord Cygon, and the Centaur, Oriean. Malvadore won't be glad we have those," Gallagher pointed out.

"True," said Jack, drawing his sword, "but even more important, we have *these*." Parvelad gleamed and shined, dazzling their eyes. "If there's one thing Malvadore fears, it's the Twin Swords."

"As long as we never give up," Aaron added, looking stronger, "Malvadore will not win."

They all jumped at a loud rattling sound.

"It's coming from your pocket, Aaron!" said Gallagher.

Aaron pulled out Kellaoth's horn. It was rattling and shaking like an egg that is about to hatch.

"What's it doing?" whispered Ellie as Aaron set it on the table.

The horn was now rolling back and forth as though something was trying to get out of it.

Something was.

With an odd noise like a stopper being pulled out, the horn split down the middle, and out tumbled two strange little beings.

They resembled minuscule horses, one silver-white, the exact same color as Kellaoth, and the other a rich gold. Aaron watched as the horn resealed itself, and he said quietly, "Amazing. Baby Unicorns."

"Did they just—just *hatch*?" asked Ellie.

"They did," said Cygon. No one had noticed him standing in the doorway.

All heads turned to him, even those of the Unicorns, who had been crawling around on the table. "You see," Cygon continued, stepping properly into the room, "Unicorns do not reproduce as humans do. They do not mate, though they will sometimes grow attached to another of opposite gender. When Destiny calls for a Unicorn to die, she will know. When she dies, her body is demolished, leaving only her horn behind. That horn will then give a baby Unicorn. Sometimes, as you see here, it shall produce twins. Kellaoth confessed to me, as we were tunneling underneath the battlefield, that she felt the foals moving about inside her horn. She knew her death was coming, and she faced it with the height of bravery."

"But—" said Aaron, "if she knew she was about to die, why did she go into battle? Why didn't she hide or wait to emerge when the battle was over?"

"Because that would be cowardice," said Cygon. "Who are we to oppose Destiny? If the lord called for her to leave this life, then she was ready and willing to obey."

"So there wasn't anything she could do to save herself?" asked Ellie.

"She could have run away. She could have not joined the battle, waited until she was safe to emerge. She could have chosen not save your lives. If she had, then yes, she would still be alive, but at a cost. The babies would have died. Her horn, having fulfilled its purpose, would rot and fall away. She would be considered, among other Unicorns, a failure and would turn back into a common horse."

"And she'd rather die than to be a coward, wouldn't she?" said Aaron.

"Yes, she would," said Cygon, "but before we entered the battle, she asked me to pass on a message to the five of you." Cygon placed his staff in the center of the table. Immediately, the ruby in the center lit up, filling the room with red light. From a silvery cloud hovering directly over the staff, there issued once again the mystical voice of Kellaoth.

"Adinyrom, Jahkon, Bonnie, Ellie, and Gallagher," her voice echoed, *"as I speak, we are preparing to engage in the battle ahead. By the time you hear this, our armies will have conquered and I shall be dead. How, I don't know, but there is no mistake – Destiny is calling me to ascend to a higher level. But perhaps I can be of some use to you before we say goodbye. In my last hours of life, I have seen much of the future. I wish I could tell you everything that will happen to you in your lives, but it is forbidden for any mortal to know of events that have yet to come. But I can give you each a piece of advice, advice that may prove vital in the upcoming battles.*

"To Gallagher, wise Gallagher. Your intelligence and logic surpasses that of much older and more experienced Men. Your clearheadedness and wisdom may one day save our continent. Trust your instincts, they will never lead you astray."

Gallagher absorbed her message silently, nodding when she had finished.

"To Ellie," Kellaoth continued. *"You have strength, more so than you could ever imagine. The relationship you have with the four sitting around you is your greatest blessing, value it."*

Ellie looked around, a little confused by this message.

"Bonnie, your courage and willpower will one day turn the tide of the battle, but be wary. Do not judge on what you see on the outside. You must look within to find the one you truly love. He will be waiting for you. "

Bonnie furrowed her brow, trying to decipher what this meant.

"Jahkon, you are the most kindred soul I have ever met. Your love and devotion to your friends will become the backbone of our resistance, but loyalty will not be enough. You will be called upon, not to follow, but to lead. And when the time comes...you will be ready. You will do what must be done."

Jack swallowed, feeling a little nervous about that prospect. Kellaoth continued.

"And Adinyrom. Oh, Adinyrom, there is so much I wish I could tell you. You have come so far, yet I fear the worst is yet to come. But remember this, to you and to Jahkon. You two must remain strong in your friendship. It is a powerful weapon and may prove to be Malvadore's undoing. But know this – though your path is the same, your destinies are separate. One of you will eventually have to follow his own path while the other must go down a different road. And know that the road you take may not be the road you expect to travel, but one that you know you must take. You may even now have some inkling of what is to come, of what you must do. Adinyrom, there are many dark secrets you will learn before the end comes, but each one will bring you closer to the sacrifice you will make, for your love. That is all I can tell you. One day, you will understand. I am leaving in your care my twin sons, Domiel and Braxon. Treat them well, teach them in the ways of fighting, and let them know why their mother died.

"Goodbye, Princes of Acklyon, and long live the kings!"

The light and mist cleared. Jack looked over at Aaron and saw silent tears running down his cheeks.

Silence overtook them as they watched little Domiel and Braxon get up slowly and begin staggering around on their spindly legs.

"What did all of that mean?" asked Ellie.

"Separate destinies?" said Jack, equally confused.

"We will understand one day," said Aaron quietly.

"Well," said Bonnie finally, "at least it's over for now."

"I am afraid that this is only the beginning," said Cygon heavily.

"Yes," Aaron agreed, "Malvadore will be on us soon."

"Oh no," said Cygon, "not just Malvadore. If you are to become the kings you were meant to be, you must begin your studies."

"You mean *school*?" said Bonnie.

Cygon smiled. "Yes, I do mean school. Arithmetic and English, I believe you have in the Third World, but there are other subjects, too."

"Like what?" asked Jack.

"Posture, Writing, Literature, Combat, Politics, Judgment, Elfin Physics, Public Speaking—"

"That makes my head spin just thinking about all that!" Bonnie interrupted.

Cygon shrugged. "It is not an easy life at all, that of a Prince. I believe you all shall begin studying as soon as the Week of Mourning is over."

"What's the Week of Mourning?" asked Ellie.

"It is a traditional part of the funeral. Everyone who attends the funeral must wear black and eat nothing but bread and water for a week after the funeral."

The door burst open and Laza and Buky spilled in. "What happened?" demanded Laza, whose head was heavily bandaged.

"I told you, Hunnyboo," said Buky soothingly, stroking Laza's curly hair. "We did it. It's over. We won!" She looked up, noticing their somber expressions. "We won, right?" she asked, fear creeping into her voice.

"Kellaoth," said Aaron with great effort. "Dead."

Laza's mouth opened in horror, and he took a step back. "That's impossible!"

Buky gasped and clutched Laza's arm and cried, "I don't believe it!"

"We saw it," said Jack. "All five of us."

"But she can't be dead!" said Laza his voice rising. "She can't!"

"How—what—oh!" Buky collapsed in tears.

Aaron got up and seized Laza by the shoulders. "Yes, Laza, she's dead!" he yelled, unable to control his voice. "She died because I was too stupid to notice I was in danger! Okay?"

"You're wrong!" screamed Laza. "She's not dead! She can't be!"

"We saw it!" said Aaron.

"It was horrible," said Ellie in a choked voice. "The False Adinyrom Magicked the archway over the main gate to collapse—right on top of her." She gave a hearty sniff.

Laza was now looking around the room as though begging someone to contradict Ellie. His eyes landed on Kellaoth's horn sitting on the table. "No..." he whispered, sprinting forward so fast they could barely see him move and snatching the horn off the table. He gazed at it for ten seconds before he dropped his head onto the table, shaking with sobs. Buky crawled forward and threw her arms around him, crying uncontrollably.

The others watched the two Elves, wanting to cry themselves at the sight of these two pathetic little creatures.

"I never thought it was possible," said Bonnie quietly. "I guess I actually thought, deep down, that even if a sword went through her heart, it would just bounce off or something. I never thought that she could actually—"

"Don't!" squealed Buky.

"It's going to be a tougher from now on," said Aaron, "but we can do it."

At that moment, Kellaoth's horn suddenly rattled, and unleashed a spray of greenish light and a tremor that passed all throughout Acklyon. And all over the countryside, Elves everywhere dropped to their knees and mourned the passing of a Unicorn.

51
The Funeral

Rest in Peace, Kellaoth; a true friend and fierce protector.
Your friends in Acklyon will love and miss you.
May you find bliss and happiness in God's palace.

The golden plaque, placed over the purple robe with a piece of Kellaoth's claw, said it all. One claw was all they could find of her even after clearing out all the rubble. Seven white balloons were tied to the robe.

Aaron was sitting in the front row of the audience, dressed in a long black cloak as everyone in the crowd was. Next to him, he could hear Ellie crying silently into a handkerchief. He himself had a mist in his eyes that made it difficult to see. He looked around at the multitude of people. He could see Brotchurd and Narra, Buky, Deecal, Piki, Wrinky, Dinky, and Stinky. King Grimathine, Princess Merline, and the other Dwarves were off to the side. Oriean stood stock-still at the back of the crowd, and Laza sat on Nimbun's back. Both looked rather tired and ill, and Aaron could see tear tracks on Laza's face. Laza had been very close to Kellaoth, and had known her perhaps better than any other Elf. He saw Domiel and Braxon resting in a big birdcage in Buky's arms, Cappy sitting in the front row, Hokey, wearing a black apron and chef's hat, and Men and Dwarves in the distance, fixing the shattered gate.

The funeral seemed to complete the overall sensation that he would never see Kellaoth again, would never look into those perfectly round eyes. He would not hear the mystically sweet voice telling him of the days of his father's reign or explaining to him what was right and what was wrong.

He remembered the first time he had ever heard that voice calling him to Acklyon from the Third World, and he remembered his first sight of her, fighting two Gertulk off of him and Jack. If he had known then that his time with her would be cut short so soon… He felt a hot tear rolling down his cheek. Cygon was talking, but Aaron could not hear what he was saying. It didn't matter. None of it mattered anymore. He didn't want to be sitting here, alive and well, when it was to save him that Kellaoth had died. His hatred of Malvadore had deepened even more since her death. Cygon finished his speech, and the white balloons were released.

Aaron watched the purple robe rising higher and higher, a pang in his heart.

According to Laza, Kellaoth was the first ever non-Elf to be memorialized in Elfin fashion.

The Week of Mourning was easily the saddest week of Aaron's life. He remembered other sad occasions in his past. He had once come home from school to have his mother inform him that his baby guinea pig had died, and once he had searched his locker, only to find that his wallet had been stolen. His father had once accidentally run over his tricycle when he was four, smashing it to pieces.

During each of those instances, he had wished that he could

be anywhere else in the world. Right now, he would have gladly had all of them happen to him at once if he could only have Kellaoth back.

Nobody spoke much during the Week but instead walked around like ghosts in long black robes. The only thing that made Kellaoth's death more bearable was Domiel and Braxon. If Aaron were to lose Kellaoth, perhaps one of the best compensations would be two baby Unicorns. They hadn't grown at all since they had hatched, but Aaron wasn't surprised. As Unicorns lived for thousands of years, you could not expect them to grow very fast. Aaron and Jack had agreed that Braxon would be Jack's responsibility, and Domiel would be Aaron's.

Of everyone, the Elves of Eldorlorne seemed to be taking Kellaoth's loss hardest, having known her longest. Aaron hadn't seen a single Elf smile since her death, and it was unnerving. When you find a whole tribe of Elves and they aren't grinning and bouncing off the walls, you know something's wrong.

Out of everyone, Laza seemed the most distraught. The only time anyone had heard him speak since the funeral was on the morning after when he dropped down on one knee and proposed to Buky, telling her he could not live without her. He had hardly left his quarters at all, and when he did emerge he was pale, blurry-eyed, and depressed, carrying a strong smell of spirits with him. The only living soul he would make contact with was Buky. She told Aaron in a hushed tone that he spent most of his time sleeping and the rest drinking.

"He's..." She searched for words. "I've never seen him like this, not ever. He's barely said a word, even to me... He's in a bad place right now, and he needs me."

Yet Aaron felt distinctly better after the Week of Mourning. A good part of the shock and misery had ebbed, and the reality had begun to sink in; Kellaoth was gone, and Aaron would have to continue in her footsteps—to help repair the damage and grow up to be the king he was destined to become.

Perhaps the thing that gave him the most strength was his friends: Ellie, Bonnie, Gallagher, and Jack supported him everywhere he went, and he was grateful. Cygon had stayed with the children since the battle, and according to Buky, this was unusual.

Apparently, the gold Wizard only appeared when he was needed and would leave again as soon his task was over. Aaron figured that as Castram was badly damaged and two of their greatest leaders were slain, Cygon felt he could do more good here than anywhere else.

However, despite their recent tragedy, hope was beginning to rise once again. With Fortingale's death, Laza had been named General in Command of the soldiers as well as Stewart of Acklyon. This meant that he was now the temporary ruler of all parts of Acklyon they had conquered. A statue had been sculpted of Kellaoth with Fortingale standing next to her. Kellaoth's mane, wings, hooves, and tail had been carved from silver as had Fortingale's sword and belt. Fortingale's armor and helm were of gold, and Kellaoth's body was of marble with two emeralds for eyes. The Dwarves had crafted it, and it was truly beautiful.

Epilogue
The Silver Tree

Aaron walked slowly along through Eldorlorne II, admiring the tall trees, golden sunlight filtering through the canopy, the lush grass, and the pretty flowers, baby Domiel in his arms. He was glad to be alone for a bit, to think about his life and his adventures and to discern what they meant.

In his heart were mixed emotions; on the one hand, he had finally won, they had driven back the Gertulk and killed the False Adinyrom, establishing to all of Acklyon that he and Jack were, indeed, the future kings. He knew that the road ahead would be difficult—his studies, the war, and his future crowning—but he was ready.

But victory had come with a cost: his armies had been damaged, General Fortingale had been killed, and worst of all, Kellaoth had been slain. Hot tears filled Aaron's eyes at her memory. He felt in his pocket and found her horn and gave it a squeeze. This made him feel a bit better, as though Kellaoth's spirit was reaching out to him through the horn.

At last, he reached his destination, a clearing in the center of the forest. Slowly, deftly, as though following instructions, he bent down, pulled the horn from his pocket, and planted it in the ground point-up, the way he would have if it were a seed.

When he was done, he stepped back and studied it. Already, he could see it growing slightly.

Though he didn't know it at the time, in the years to come, the horn would grow into a great silvery spike, ten feet tall growing out of the ground. This tree-like pinnacle seemed to have a mind of its own for it was imbibed with Kellaoth's spirit. Many times in his later life, Aaron came to the "the Silver Tree," as it was named, seeking counsel and reassurance, and always it provided warmth and comfort to the future king.

Slowly, like snow melting away, the sadness, bitterness, and fear of what was to come passed from Aaron, leaving a shining joy in his heart. He tenderly placed little Domiel on the ground next to the foot-long spike, saying, "There you are, little fellow, there's your mother."

Domiel studied the horn for a long time with his big green eyes, identical to those of his mother, and then gave a little croaking sound that would one day become a fearsome neighing roar that all Gertulk, trolls, Kanes, Vampires, Werewolves, Goblins, and all other evil creatures would learn to fear.

As he watched Domiel hobble around the Silver Tree on his spindly little legs, Aaron noticed that Ellie had joined him. Spring flowers were in her long hair, and a radiant smile was on her lips. Aaron's eyes shone like two beacons as he grinned at her.

For a long time they watched Domiel romping and playing around the horn as unspoken words passed between Ellie and Aaron. They could hear Men and Elves cheering and letting off fireworks in celebration. Then as she smiled up at him, Ellie's hand closed around Aaron's, and silently, she led him back towards the castle. Aaron took a deep breath and let it out slowly, gazing around in perfect contentment.

War was near at hand, and Malvadore would very soon be hunting him, but Aaron was not scared. *Let them come,* he thought. *Let them test the Power of Castram because when they do, we'll be ready for them.* And, together, they strode back, back into the world of pain, and of war, and of sacrifice. They did not once stumble, or waver, they did not feel fear for what they could not help.

* * *

A long, claw-like hand slowly reached out to clutch the hilt of a sword. The mane of coarse dirty black hair blocked the face from sight. Battered black armor with several of the spikes broken off scraped along the ground as the figure dragged himself into a standing position. The great black dragon studied the figure and growled.

The unnaturally tall man stared around, leaning on the sword. Blood, as black as his heart, soaked his armor, pouring from a wound on his chest. It was not fatal to him, though it would have been for a lesser being. He took one staggering step and nearly fell.

He regained balance, and slowly, a smile spread over his face as the gash in his chest began to heal. Muscles knitted themselves back together, blood seeped back into the wound, and the dull red eyes regained their previous fire.

Slowly, ever slowly, the man straightened himself to his full height as strength returned to his limbs. He picked up a fair-sized pebble from the ground and crushed it into powder with his powerful hand. He spread his arms, and a blanket of darkness seemed to drop over the land. Critters scurried for cover, and those who did not dropped dead like stones.

The man picked up his fallen helmet from the ground and placed it on his head.

Soon, the only light on that rocky cliff edge came from his pulsating red eyes. A terrible laugh came bubbling from his mouth like lava. A rugged wind whipped the countryside, bending trees and cracking rock. The man stood in the center of this whirlwind, his arms still raised and his eyes still red.

By now, the dragon and he were the only living things for miles. The man sent a rush of power through the stones of the cliff, and slowly, figures began to rise from them. Hulking, lumbering, undead brutes with catlike yellow eyes. The Gertulk gathered around their master, bowing before him.

Kane Malvadore had risen again.

Elfish Sign Language

The Elves of Eldorlorne use a very complex sign language made up of seemingly insignificant gestures such as winks, taps, and twitches. No non-Elf (even Kellaoth) knows the full extent of this language. Elves can really have full and in-depth conversations using this, and it is not uncommon for young male Elves to ask the girls out in sign language so as not to have to talk directly. Aaron and Jack have a primitive, but useful, vocabulary of this language. Even I don't know all that they know of this strange but efficient dialogue, but here are some of the various signals and there meanings:

Bearing teeth shows aggression or that you're angry

Moving head back and forth means lost or missing

Rolling eyes shows alarm or distress. The more times you roll the eyes, the more serious the situation is. (For example, if you cut yourself with a knife and need a bandage, you would do a half-roll. Whereas if you were cornered by Gertulk, you might roll them five or six times.)

Tapping foot is a call for assistance. It is often combined with rolling eyes to indicate that you're in trouble.

Twitching both ears means *do*. It is used to show action.

Twitching left ear means *yes*.

Twitching right ear means *no*. (*Yes* and *no* are often confused. That is why it is important to be fluent in this sign language before you use it.)

Raising both eyebrows indicates a question. It always comes first when you ask a question (E.g., *may I go?* Would be to raise eyebrows, tap self, and point nose at destination.)

Raising left eyebrow shows *be ready*. It is also Laza's signal for the Elves to get ready to shoot in the Battle of Eldorlorne.

Raising right eyebrow means the same as *give up* or *retreat*. As you can imagine, it is not a signal Elves enjoy using in battle.

Wiggle nose shows *trust*.

Tapping yourself is used to show that you're talking about yourself. You tap yourself, preferably on the hip or leg, as your signal. If you can pull it off without being noticed, you can also tap objects near you to indicate them.

Nose pointing is used to indicate something that you cannot tap without being conspicuous.

Opening mouth means *speak aloud*. (It is not used to tell to signal.)

Clenched fist means *attack* or *kill*.

Darting eyes is very common. Darting from left to right once means *distract* or *diversion*. Darting up and down once means *look*. Darting eyes right to left means *show* or *explain*.

Winking is a sign of reassurance. It means *don't worry* or *it's alright*.

Puffing cheeks says *stay* or *wait*.

Hair flicking means *be careful*.

Crossing eyes means *time*. Combining it with rolling eyes means *you're running out of time*, a means of telling a person to hurry up. Whereas if you wink then cross your eyes, it means *you have plenty of time,* telling the person to take it slow. To flick your hair and then cross your eyes means *stall for time.*

Shuffling feet means *lie.*

Nose scratching means *far,* or *far away.*

Eye contact is very important; do not signal someone unless you have clear eye contact.

Glossary

Bracers Straps made of leather or stone or other material that protect an archer's lower arm while shooting.

Breastplate Armor covering the chest.

Broadsword A sword used to cut rather than to stab and with two cutting edges.

Chain mail Armor made with small metal rings linked together in a pattern to form a mesh. Same as mail.

Crossguard A metal bar at right angles to a sword's blade between the blade and the hilt. Its purpose was to protect the carrier's hand.

Crossbow A bow with a horizontal limb mounted on a stock that shoots projectiles called bolts **or** quarrels.

Gauntlets Pieces of armor worn like long gloves on the hands and lower arms. Gauntlets were especially important because hands and arms were so vulnerable in hand-to-hand combat.

Greaves Armor designed to protects the legs.

Hauberk A shirt of mail, usually reaching at least to mid-thigh and including sleeves.

Helm A helmet that completely protects the head and is supported by the shoulders.

Hilt The handle of a weapon or tool, especially a sword, dagger, or knife.

Katana A Japanese sword with a curved, slender, single-edged blade, a circular or squared guard, and a long grip to accommodate two hands.

Longbow A powerful and tall bow, often six or seven feet long, used in warfare.

Mail Armor made with small metal rings linked together in a pattern to form a mesh.

Nock A small groove on the end of an arrow used to hold it to the bowstring.

Pommel A rounded knob on the end of the handle of a sword or dagger.

Quarrel The ammunition used in a crossbow.

Quiver A container usually made of leather and made to hold arrows.

Rapier A slender, sharply pointed sword for thrusting attacks.

Scabbard A sheath for the blade of a sword or dagger, typically made of leather or metal.

Scimitar A sword with a curved blade.

Tinderbox A small container containing flint and tinder (something dry that will light quickly) used to start a fire.

Wall shield A shield which can be held next to another shield to create a wall.

About *the* Author

It is no exaggeration to say that Adam Lapallo was almost born creating stories and characters. He began dictating stories at the age of two and a half, and by three and a half was creating complete stories, including the characters and story that would (with much growth) become The Kingdom of Dreams and Shadows.

At age nine, Lapallo began writing The Kingdom of Dreams and Shadows. Three years later, his novel had become a 2008 Book Arts Bash national finalist.

He completed the novel at fourteen, at which point an agent showed interest and asked for a book proposal. Lapallo, however, wanted to do a rewrite first. He accomplished this two years later and has already begun writing the second novel in the trilogy.

Lapallo has written, directed, and produced church plays as well as Lego stop-motion videos, one of which has attracted over 110,000 hits on YouTube. He is also a nationally ranked fencer and competed in the 2013 Junior Olympics.